BANDIT'S HOPE

BANDIT'S HOPE

BACKWOODS BRIDES

BOOK TWO

MARCIA GRUVER

BARBOUR
PUBLISHING

For more information about Marcia Gruver, please access the author's website at the following Internet address: www.marciagruver.com

Cover design: Kirk DouPonce, DogEared Design

Published by Barbour Publishing, Inc., P.O. Box 719, Uhrichsville, OH 44683, www.barbourbooks.com

Our mission is to publish and distribute inspirational products offering exceptional value and biblical encouragement to the masses.

 Member of the
Evangelical Christian
Publishers Association

Printed in the United States of America.

DEDICATION/ACKNOWLEDGMENTS

I dedicate this book with love to George Edward Breshears Sr.
I miss you, Daddy.

MY HEARTFELT THANKS TO

My husband, Lee, for your desire to see me soar.

*For what shall it profit a man,
if he shall gain the whole world, and lose his own soul?*
MARK 8:36

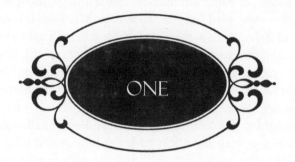

ONE

Pearl River, on the Natchez Trace, June 1, 1882

Mariah Bell reached the bottom landing, stumbling under the weight of the most precious cross she'd ever had to bear. Balancing her father's lifeless body as best she could, she reeled across the kitchen to the door she'd propped wide with her boots, a yawning gateway to the backyard and the early morning darkness.

A breeze laden with the smell of magnolias met her at the stoop. The fragrant gust wrapped around her face, and her labored breaths sucked in the scent of the blooms. Mixed with the odor of Father's pipe tobacco and the vile stench of his illness, the cloying wind threatened to turn her stomach.

Searching blindly with her toes, she found the top step then allowed the drag of her load to shift her forward and over the threshold. Heart pounding, her panting gasps a roar in her ears, Mariah tottered briefly at the edge of the second step.

Exhausted, she surrendered to the pull of the earth, and her trembling legs staggered wildly to the ground. When her bare feet touched the cold, wet grass, she glanced over her shoulder at the shaded windows of Bell's Inn and whispered a grateful prayer.

If one curious lodger peered out and caught her struggling along the hallway, knees bent beneath her unlikely burden, she'd be undone. With her clumsy gait and heavy tread, not to mention the squeaky step at the bottom of the stairs, it amazed her they hadn't.

"Just a little farther," Mariah whispered, a catch in her throat. "Almost there."

If she could get Father's remains secreted away without Mrs. Viola Ashmore, the most meddlesome woman in Mississippi, pressing her nose to an upstairs window, the unthinkable scheme might work.

Last night, the widow Ashmore—Miss Vee, as she liked to be called—had returned from her sister's down in Natchez. Her arrival threatened to ruin everything, and Mariah regretted the hasty decision to summon her home.

She trudged to the waiting wagon bed and eased Father down, her muscles straining from the effort to lower him gently. Clutching his nightshirt with determined fists, she lifted him aside to raise the tailgate.

Three months ago, toting him ten feet would've been impossible to imagine, despite her work-honed arms and sturdy Choctaw ancestry. Squinting in the moonlight at the dear face of the man who gave her life, his once burly frame reduced to a frail skeleton by the wasting disease, she bit off a cry of pain.

Not now, she ordered herself, choking on scalding tears. There'd be ample time for mourning once she hid the body. Covering up his disappearance would be another matter entirely.

From the time she'd leaned over Father's sickbed the night before to find him still and cold, she'd known exactly what to do. She sat at his bedside until the parlor clock struck three times, long past the hour when even the restless Miss Vee had doused her lamp.

Slipping inside the barn, she'd hitched Sheki to the wagon and loaded a shovel before pulling around to the door. The hard part, the dreaded part, had been carrying Father through the house. It took all the strength she could muster, of both body and soul, but somehow she'd managed.

Mariah reached over the tailgate and smoothed his hair. "Forgive me, *Aki*," she whispered. "It's the only way." Straightening, she wiped her eyes and steeled her trembling chin. She'd come this far, and she'd see it through.

Stealthy as a cat, she eased the back door shut, leaning inside at the last minute to snag her boots. Struggling, almost tripping, she pulled them on then crept to the rig.

The side springs moaned when Mariah climbed aboard. Wincing, she settled carefully onto the seat and lifted the reins, clucking her tongue at her little paint pony. Sheki eased forward, any noise from his hooves or the creaking wheels muffled by thick green tufts of damp summer grass.

Fearing a chance meeting with an approaching rider, Mariah avoided the road and crossed the backyard. She held her breath until the horse cleared the lawn and reached the bank of the river.

Sheki picked his way in the meager light, trudging down the yellow, sandy slope alongside the Pearl and into the welcoming shadows of a woody trail. Before the indigo brush and towering birch swallowed them whole, Mariah cast one last glance over her shoulder at the murky outline of the inn.

Just one more storm to brave. Searching the starlit sky with streaming eyes, she pleaded with God not to leave her to face it alone.

Mariah let the horse's nose guide them until they'd gone a fair piece upriver. Unable to bear the darkness another second, especially with her unsettling cargo, she lit the lantern and hung it from a post beside the foot brake.

Soon a swarm of flitting bugs joined the somber procession, dancing wildly around the swaying light. In a strange way, she welcomed their company.

They reached the high bluff overlooking the bend in the river before she allowed Sheki to slow his gait. Pulling up to the broad trunk of an oak, she tugged on the reins and brought her makeshift funeral bier to a halt next to her mother's grave.

In the scanty glow of the lamp, she squinted to read the inscription, though she knew every word by heart: ONNAT MINTI BELL, WIFE OF JOHN, MOTHER OF MARIAH. "The morning light" was a fitting name for her mother. Daylight had gone from Mariah's life the day she died.

Lifting the shovel from the wagon, she glanced at the sky. Dawn would wait for no man, not even the beloved proprietor of Bell's Inn. Drawing a shaky breath, she set to work digging a deep hole beside Mother's humble resting place.

Once she laid him in the ground, swaddled in a soft quilt and facing east as he'd requested, Mariah had a moment's hesitation. It felt wrong to be the only mourner for a man like John Coffee Bell. He deserved better.

Biting her lip so hard she tasted blood, she snatched the shovel. Careful to look away while the dirt rained down on her father, she quickly covered him before she changed her mind.

Hiding the site as best she could, she scattered rocks and dead leaves over the patchwork of grass she'd carefully pieced together over the busted clods. Her efforts might fool the casual eye, but it would take a heavy rain to settle the earth and root the grass again. Many days could pass before her secret was safe.

Unable to walk away and leave the spot unmarked, she hefted a sun-bleached stone and carried it to the grave. Sinking to her knees with an anguished cry, she bowed and placed a tender kiss on the strand of painted beads around her neck, a precious treasure placed there by her mother.

"I'll keep the promise, Mama. I swear on my life." What Father hadn't managed, for all his good intentions, Mariah was destined to finish. Pulling off the wooden beads, she gave them one last squeeze before tucking them beneath his unlikely tombstone.

Against the night sky, the oak tree stretched welcoming arms around her parents' graves. Ancient mourning songs crowded Mariah's throat as she draped her shawl around her head with trembling fingers. Clutching her stomach, she doubled over and wailed her lonesome grief in time with the oak's moaning boughs.

Reddick "Tiller" McRae stiffened and leaned forward in the saddle. Plodding hooves and the steady creak of wagon wheels echoed through the pine and hardwood forest, stirring his heartbeat. From his perch high above the Natchez Trace, his darting gaze watched to see who rounded the bend.

As the rig pulled into view, Tiller rolled the kinks from his neck and dried his palms on the legs of his britches. Some things never got easier.

Ducking beneath a sagging branch, he spurred his horse and rode downslope to the muddy, sunken road. Gritting his teeth, he forced a twinkle to his eyes and a winsome smile to his lips, two tricks he'd gotten plenty good at.

The white-haired old coot, slumped in the seat of the cargo wagon, shot upright and went for his gun faster than a greased thunderbolt, training it at Tiller's pounding heart. "Hold up there, stranger," he growled through shriveled gums. "State your business, and make it quick."

Both hands to the sky, Tiller widened his grin. "Relax, old-timer. I'm as harmless as a snaggletooth viper. Unarmed to boot." Both statements true enough on the surface.

The man's tongue flicked out to swipe his bottom lip, and his jaw shifted to the side. "You take me for a fool, don't you, boy? Nobody rides the Devil's Backbone unarmed." His eyes narrowed, and his gaze tracked up the rise to the shadowy brush. "Or alone."

Tiller chuckled. "It's been many years since this rutted trail was known as the Devil's Backbone, sir. Not since Robinson Road pulled the starch right out of her spine." He winked. "More to the point, you're riding alone."

One gnarled finger tapped the pearl handle of the six-barreled Remington revolver. "Your eyesight's failing you, son. My little friend here don't talk much, but he's pretty fair company in a pinch." His flashing stare demanded answers. "If you like Robinson Road so much, what are you doing out here?"

Slapping his thigh, Tiller laughed with delight in his most charming and persuasive manner—and if anyone could be charming and persuasive, it was Tiller McRae. "You've got me there, mister." He nodded toward the rising band of orange sky on the horizon. "I guess a fellow has to get up earlier than daybreak to pull one on you."

A smug grin lifted the wrinkled cheeks. "You got that right. Now, commence to telling me what you're up to a'fore I dot your eye with this pistol."

Paying careful attention to the man's surprisingly steady hand, Tiller raised the brim of his hat and scratched his head. "Truth be told, sir, I'm a little embarrassed to say."

His new friend sat forward on the seat, his rheumy eyes bulging. "You'll be a sight more embarrassed with air holes in that Stetson and a part in your taffy-colored hair."

Bright smile waning, Tiller swallowed hard, resisting the urge to glance over his shoulder at the empty trail. What was taking them so almighty long? "All right, mister. Keep your suspenders fastened and

I'll explain." Grimacing, Tiller shifted in the saddle while his mind scrambled for a likely account. Quirking one brow at his edgy audience, he released a shaky laugh. "The sad truth is I got hitched a couple of days ago. Up Carthage way, where I'm from." He cocked his head and beamed a sweet smile. "Married the girl of my dreams."

"Married?" The saggy eyelids fluttered. "You don't say."

Tiller drooped his shoulders and sighed. "Our bliss was short-lived, I'm afraid. We'd barely doused the lights in our bedchamber when her brothers knocked down the door. They dragged her from my loving arms, kicking and screaming, and carted her out." He stared off in the distance and shook his head. "Still in her dressing gown."

The gun barrel dropped a quarter inch. The old man gulped and leaned closer, curiosity burning in his eyes. "What'd they go and do that for?"

Tiller cut his gaze to the ground. "Her pa in Jackson ain't so fond of me. He didn't approve of our union, so we ran off together. The scoundrel sent his ill-mannered sons to fetch her."

A long, slow whistle followed. "That ain't hardly right, young fella'... not with you hitched to the gal. Why didn't you stop 'em?"

"I tried my best, sir, but her three brothers are as stout as oaks. I was no match for the burly brutes. They loaded up Lucinda and whisked her away before I could catch my breath."

"Lucinda, huh? That's a real nice name."

Tiller waved his hand across the sky, as if painting a picture he saw in his mind. "I can still see her delicate arms reaching for me...tears shining in those big, doe eyes."

The old man lowered the revolver to his lap. "Now that's a dirty shame. The poor little thing. What do you plan on doing about it, son?"

Sitting tall in the saddle, Tiller squared his shoulders. "I'm bound to bring her home, if I have to waltz clear to Jackson and dance right up to her daddy's door."

"That's tellin' him, boy!"

Tiller nudged back his hat. "So you see...that's why I'm fool enough to brave the Trace alone. I'm on a quest to rescue my darlin' bride. I figured on shaving some time by cutting through on this old stretch of road. Might even catch them before they make it home."

Softness eased the lines of the traveler's face as he holstered the

Remington. "I was engaged once myself. To the sweetest little thing this side of the Mississippi Delta." He worked his jaw, trying to contain his grin. "But her pa was a horse's rear end." Giving in to mirth, he beamed and lifted his chin. "Tell you what, boy. I'm headed to Jackson, myself. Why don't we ride on down together?"

Tiller angled his head. "You mean it, mister?"

"Well, sure I do." His toothless smile seemed childlike. "The good Lord makes fine company on a long trip, but it's nice talking to a fella' wearing skin for a change." He motioned to the rear of the wagon. "Tie that animal to the back and sit up here with me. Two brains ciphering your problem may hit on a plan to bring your little wife home." He leaned closer and lowered his voice. "You ain't mentioned if you're a religious man, but if you'd like, I'll ask God to help you out." He winked. "Him and me are fairly close friends, you see."

Shame—Tiller's constant companion of late—surged in the pit of his stomach. He stole a quick look at the line of brush and young magnolias on the opposite side of the gulch. Except for a few leaves caught in a sudden breeze, the trees were still. "Listen, old-timer"— Tiller nodded at the furrowed road winding in the distance—"maybe you'd best get on without me. It's not safe to lollygag for too long in these parts."

The stranger scooted over and patted the seat. "All the more reason for you to join me. Why, together we could fend off—" He swallowed the rest as his head jerked to the side.

A flurry of masked riders swept over the steep slope, bearing down on him like all wrath.

His mouth gaped in shock, and his palsied hand groped for his holster. Caught off guard, the old man's draw wasn't fast enough.

"Don't try it, grandpa," the lead rider's voice growled. "Twitch a finger, and you'll lose it."

Digging in his heels and yanking his reins to the side, Tiller bolted, the sound of gunfire and the old man's pleas ringing in his ears. At the top of the rise, a bullet slammed into his Stetson, spinning it into the air.

He wove through the woods alongside the road until he no longer heard the shouting voices of the ambushing men. Ducking into a clearing, he dismounted and secured the horse to a branch then plopped down on a fallen pine log.

With his arms hugging his head, he didn't hear a rider approaching, didn't realize he wasn't alone until someone tapped his shoulder.

Fire surged through his limbs. Fists clenched, his chin came up.

His oldest friend in the world, Nathan Carter, stood over him holding his hat. "I reckon this belongs to you," he said, passing Tiller the Stetson.

Tiller snatched his favorite hat, turning it over in his hands and poking his fingers through the bullet holes. "What were you thinking, Nathan? You cut it a little close that time, don't you think?"

Nathan's booming laughter flushed a covey of bobwhite quail. They scattered to the sky in a rush of brown speckled wings. "Don't you believe it, son. That bullet found its mark." He hitched up his pants. "We have to make it look good, don't we?"

Tiller tossed the hat at Nathan's feet. "You owe me thirty dollars."

Nathan grinned, his brown eyes dancing. "That shouldn't be a problem, once we split the take. The old buzzard was sitting on his life savings. Under his seat there was a fortune in—"

Tiller's hand shot up. "Spare the details."

Pushing long strands of his black hair behind his ears, Nathan smirked. "Ignorance makes you innocent, is that it? You don't seem to mind when you're sitting around patting a full belly."

With a devilish grin, he drew back and kicked. The Stetson sailed in the air, landing upside down in the cold, gray ashes of the campfire. "Tiller boy, the cost of new headgear seems a small price to pay for a lily-white conscience."

Tiller tensed. "Nate, that's enough."

Nathan slapped his shoulder. "After ten years, you're still not cut out for this game." He leaned close to Tiller's face. "Don't think I didn't see what you tried to do back there."

Warmth crawled up Tiller's neck. "I don't know what you're talking about."

"Oh, I think you do."

Noticing his hands wringing like a washerwoman's, Tiller clenched them and slid them along his trouser legs. "They didn't hurt that old man, did they? I mean. . .he was all right when you left?"

Nathan gave a harsh laugh. "He'll have a sizable knot on his head, but I expect he'll live."

Tiller scowled at the rugged face he knew so well. "They hit him? Why'd they go and do that?"

Nathan shrugged. "Reckon he asked for it. Or else Hade got one of his urges to hurt something. I didn't hang around to see." He jerked his thumb at Tiller. "I lit out after you."

Propping his sizable foot on the log, he leaned to study Tiller's face. "While it's just you and me, there's something I've been meaning to ask."

Less than eager to hear, Tiller cocked his head. "Well, go on. Get it out of your system."

Nathan's brows rose. "I'm wondering how that mind of yours works, is all. How you can twist the truth around to suit you." His smile turned cold. "Don't you get it, pardner? You may not wear a bandanna or wave a gun, but your part in this operation still makes you a thief." He paused to spit, his mocking gaze pinned to Tiller's face. "The way I see it, owning up to what you are is better than what you looked like just then."

Tiller scowled. "And what's that?"

"Instead of the raider who robbed an old man on the Trace, you're the coward who rode off and left him."

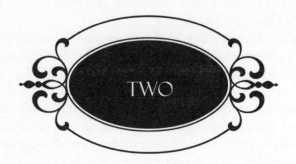

TWO

Mariah beat the sunrise to the house, but just barely. The surrounding forest blocked her view of the horizon for most of the way home, but the glowing sky over the treetops meant the first bright sliver of the sun would soon appear.

Casting a nervous glance at the inn, she wheeled the rig into the barn and leaped to the hay-scattered floor. Grunting from the effort, she wrestled Sheki free from his harness, a worrisome task with the stubborn beast straining his neck for the feed bucket.

Mother did well to name him the Choctaw word for buzzard. The greedy animal nuzzled for every morsel in his trough and never missed a chance to scavenge for a bite of grass.

Sheki pawed the ground and nickered softly. Mariah patted his freckled back and smoothed his white mane. "You're ready to eat, aren't you, friend?"

Urgency surged in her limbs at the reminder of food. For the cost of a night's stay at one of the last working stands left on the Natchez Trace, her father promised his lodgers a fine, hearty breakfast. She'd inherited the promise, if not the inn, and had less than an hour to fulfill her end of the bargain.

Mariah left the horse eagerly chewing a mouthful of oats. Sidling up to the barn door, she made a quick check of the house before stepping outside and heading up the path.

God was with her. Early morning gloom still cloaked the first floor, despite the glimmer of a lamp burning in a back room upstairs. Up front, Miss Vee's tasseled shade was blessedly dark.

She had to rush. Before long, Dicey Turner would trudge out of the woods beside the house, dragging her apron as well as her behind, dreading the workday before it started. Rainy Boswell would come, once the dew dried, to cut the grass.

Crossing the yard, the nagging dread returned to tug at Mariah's spirit. With Father's death, she could lose all claim to Bell's Inn—what should be her rightful inheritance and the only home she'd ever known. It would take a miracle for a Choctaw man in Mississippi to hold on to such valuable property. A miracle wouldn't help a lone, half-breed woman.

In the desperate early hours at Father's bedside, the answer had come. Despite the body she'd rolled into a hidden grave, her father could not be dead.

Whatever it took, Mariah would keep the proprietor of Bell's Inn alive in the world's reckoning until she found a suitable man to marry. What an English father could not do for her, even in death, a pale-faced husband could.

She had plenty of would-be suitors among the sons of her tribesmen, those who stayed behind after the Treaty of Dancing Rabbit Creek and the exodus of her people. Handsome young braves who vied for her attention.

There were even some who'd caught her eye, such as Christopher and Justin Jones, the sons of the tribal physician. Either brother would make Mariah a fine husband. Each had made his interests known, but they couldn't change the biggest mark against them. Indian blood coursed through their veins.

As she mounted the rickety steps, a loose board moaned beneath her feet and paint chips from the rail came off in her hand. The two-story house was a far cry from its humble beginnings, a lean-to run by her grandfather, strewn with bearskins for the lodgers to sleep on. Still, it needed some upkeep.

Minding the inn kept Mariah too busy for outside chores, and most of the jobs were too much for her to tackle. Another reason to find someone to marry as soon as possible.

She'd find a husband with a strong back and feeble mind, an item in ready supply in her opinion. With such a man in tow, no one would question her claim to Bell's Inn, and she could go on running things the way she had since Mother died.

Mariah knew just the man.

Gabriel Tabor had made his interest known by less than subtle glances. One crook of her finger, and he'd be down on one knee pleading for her hand.

Unfortunately, Gabe was coarse and dimwitted. Distasteful traits at best, but he was the only eligible man around for miles.

Tiptoeing across the wobbly porch, she eased through the door, cringing when the hinges squealed. A little oil was in order, a matter she'd make time for after breakfast.

She eased off her boots and started for the stove, but her fleeting image in the speckled mirror stopped her cold. Backing up, she peered into the wavering glass. In the hours since finding her father's body, grief had aged her, stress etching lines in her youthful face. Shock and sorrow had washed the woman in the glass as white as her English ancestors.

Mariah gazed at her high cheekbones and the bump at the bridge of her nose. Odd how a nice dress and upswept hair disguised the truth. Barefoot, dressed in riding britches and a cotton shirt, there was no denying her Indian roots.

"You're a chameleon," she whispered, fingering her long black braid. "One day the lady of the manor, the next an Indian princess. Can't you decide who you want to be?" Thanks to her parents, Mariah was both, stuck in between two vastly different worlds—the Pearl River clan of the Choctaw Indian and her blue-eyed British relations.

The ugly name "half-breed" pressed at her lips. She'd had it whispered in her direction all her life and loathed the sound of it.

"Mariah?"

She whirled, clutching her chest.

By the dim glow of the lantern gripped in Miss Vee's dimpled hand, her tall red curls seemed to hover on the stairs. Turning sideways to maneuver the narrow passage, she took the last two steps to the kitchen and held up the light. "Did I startle you? I'm not surprised, with all this creeping about before dawn." Frowning, she tugged her dressing gown tighter. "What have you been up to?"

"I—"

"Where's your father?" Miss Vee interrupted, leaning to peer past Mariah. "Did you leave him in the barn?"

Jolted, Mariah nearly choked. "Y–you saw me take him?"

Miss Vee's ginger head came up. "I saw an empty room when I stepped inside to check on him, and the wagon just pulled into the yard. I can add two and two all by myself."

Weak with relief, Mariah hurried to change the subject. "I'm pleased you're finally home, Miss Vee. We've missed you something terrible."

"John, too?" She beamed. "Oh, I'm glad. I've sorely missed you both. I came as soon as I could."

"I heard you come in last night."

Her thinning brows peaked. "Impossibly late, I'm afraid. I hope I didn't disturb your poor father."

Mariah hid her twisting hands behind her back. "No, ma'am. You didn't disturb him." That much was achingly true. "How are things in Natchez?"

Miss Vee waved her hand. "Natchez never changes."

"And your sister?"

"Still weak, but on the mend. When I got your wire saying your father had taken ill, I left at once." She stretched her chubby neck to see over Mariah's shoulder. "Where is John, honey? He needs me."

Pity surged in Mariah's heart. The chance to nurse Father, to hover at his bedside, would've meant so much to Miss Vee. She'd loved him for years, a fact that everyone knew but Father.

When Mother died two years ago, the feisty widow turned up on the steps of Bell's Inn, suitcase in hand, to offer him comfort and consolation. Blind to her motives, he hired her on the spot as a chambermaid. She patiently made beds and scrubbed floors, waiting for his mourning to end. Father never seemed to notice her yearning glances across the breakfast table. Now he never would.

Mariah's breath caught on a strangled sob, and she cleared her throat to mask the sound.

Distracted, Miss Vee shuffled to the window to search the yard. "I don't see him. Shouldn't he be in bed?" The concern shining from her faded green eyes made the secret even harder to bear.

"Father's not out there, Miss Vee. He's gone." Pain squeezed her chest. Would she survive such heartrending deception?

"Gone?" Miss Vee pushed away from the window. "I don't understand." Luckily, she was too upset to notice Mariah's brimming tears.

Mariah blinked them away and cleared her throat. "Yes, ma'am. To. . .a place where he'll be well again. Healed once and for all."

Miss Vee's shoulders sagged and her face soured. "But I rushed home to nurse him back to health." Her brows drew together. "What sort of *place?*"

"Umm. . .well, the reverend told us about it. He assured us Father will be much better off there."

Red splotches tinged Miss Vee's cheeks. "Better off than in my care?" She sniffed and shook her head. "I assure you, Mariah, no one else will afford John Coffee Bell more tenderhearted compassion."

Mariah couldn't help but smile. *You're mistaken, dear lady. There's One other, and my father rests in His hands.* So far, she hadn't told a lie, but it was time to change the subject. "Run up and put on some clothes while I start breakfast. We have guests this morning. You don't want to meet them on the stairs in your dressing gown."

Miss Vee absently clutched her bodice. "No, I—Mariah, are you certain John is all right?"

"Gracious, don't fret so," Mariah called on the way to light the stove. "Father will be just fine. I. . .saw him off to his destination myself."

"I see." She touched her plump bottom lip. "He took the train then. Did he say when he might return?"

Mariah shooed her with an apron. "Go along now, and don't worry." She turned away and made a wry face. "It won't do Father a speck of good to worry yourself sick."

Heavy footfalls overhead stifled the persistent woman's next question and sent her scurrying to the foot of the stairs. She paused on the squeaky bottom step and turned. "Mariah, how did John look when last you saw him?"

Mariah cracked another egg into the bowl, stirring briskly with her fork. There'd be no turning back, with the eggs or the scheme. Both were too far along to unscramble. She smiled brightly over her shoulder.

"I've never seen him more at peace."

The roiling fear cooled in Miss Vee's green eyes, and her fuzzy chin rose on a sigh. "Good." She nodded firmly. "That's good to hear." As she lumbered out of sight, her final words tumbled down the stairwell behind her. "Still, it's a crying shame. No one on earth could tend that man better than me."

Tiller's body went as stiff as the pine log where he sat, and a rush of hot air fired through his nostrils. He slapped the fallen tree so hard the notched bark stung his palm. "I know you didn't call me a coward, old friend, since that would make you a careless fool."

He struggled to his feet and pressed his heaving chest close to Nathan, his breath coming in labored gasps. "Take it back fast, and I won't bust your mouth."

Before Nathan could react—or Tiller make good on his threat—the gang rode into the clearing like a raiding muster of crows, their spirited shouts and cackling laughter echoing off the trunks of the loblolly pine.

Hade Betts, the rowdy band's leader, slid off his saddle and gathered his reins. "McRae," he announced with a grin on his face, "you're one talented liar, son. You had that old badger so fixed on your yarn we were cuddled in his lap before he saw us coming."

Tiller shot Nathan one last challenge with hooded eyes and stepped away. "I'd thank you for the compliment, Hade, but I'm not sure lying is an admirable skill."

Hade's jowly face crinkled with glee. "Dodge the praise all you like, but I call it a gift. Your tales get taller each time I hear one. Especially when there's a woman involved."

The men chuckled with Hade. Climbing down from the stolen rig, a beat-up satchel under his arm, young Sonny Thompson slapped his skinny leg. "Ain't it the truth? And this time he gave the gal"—he tipped his hat at Tiller—"excuse me, his *wife* a name."

"Lucinda McRae, with her loving arms stretched wide and her big doe eyes filled with tears." Laughing, Hade wrapped one arm around Tiller's shoulders and shook him. "Where *do* you get your wild imagination, boy?"

In a flicker, Tiller was seated at Uncle Silas's feet in a misty Scuffletown swamp, listening to stories about a ten-foot giant who picked his teeth with railroad ties and fed Carolina lawmen to gators. He shrugged away the painful memory. "Can't say where I get my stories. I reckon they just come to me on the spot."

Sobering, Hade wiped his eyes on his sleeve. "For a second there, you had me believing. Poor fellow, left all alone on your wedding night. I was starting to feel sorry for you." With a loud snort, he bent over howling again.

Tiller gave in to a grin. "That's all right, Hade. Sometimes, I believe it myself. I get to feeling a little sad when I remember I'm telling a yarn."

Overcome by Tiller's remark, Hade eased his broad behind onto a nearby stump, his potbelly shaking.

Nathan sauntered over, a knowing smile on his face. "Tiller boy, I'm wondering if all your talk of marriage lately might be wishful thinking. Maybe you have it in mind to find some pretty little gal, get hitched, and settle down to a respectable life."

A scowl erased Tiller's grin. He shot Nathan a glare, wondering what had come over him. "What are you saying, Nate?"

Nathan shrugged. "You're not planning to split trails with us, are you?"

Sonny squatted in front of Hade and laid open the satchel at his feet, delight on his rawboned face. "Don't worry. Tiller ain't going nowhere. Not while we're pulling in this kind of loot."

Grinning, Hade leaned over to pull out a double handful of bills, the bundles tied up with string. "It's been slim pickings lately, boys, but cast your eyes on the fruit of our patience. Belly up and get your share."

The bright-eyed gang gathered around, their faces lit with anxious greed.

Licking his fingers, Hade counted out equal piles, the thrill in his voice building to a pitch as the stacks got taller.

"Wooeee!" Sonny cried. "Would you look at that?" He glanced over his shoulder. "Tiller, you struck a wide vein this time."

The blissful men jostled closer with outstretched hands to get their share while Hade divided the spoils. Reaching deep into the bottom of the bag, he brought up a leather-bound book, its pages crimped and worn. Opening the cover, he smiled and cleared his throat. "'This Holy Book is the property of Otis Gooch of Tallahatchie County,

Mississippi.'" Beaming, he tossed it into the doused campfire where it landed in a smoky cloud of white ash. "Much obliged, Mr. Gooch. We'll spend your money wisely." He cocked his head. "Well, quick anyways."

The camp erupted in riotous laughter.

Chuckling, Hade lifted his chin at Tiller. "Come get your money. I gave you the extra five dollars."

Hade's wide smile blurred into the traveler's toothless grin.

Cursing, Tiller whirled for his horse.

"Hey, where you going?" Hade spun on the stump. "Come take your split. You earned every cent."

Ignoring him, Tiller swung into the saddle. "What I've earned is some time off. I'm going away for a few days."

Nathan smirked from the ground. "What about your cut?" He snatched the wad of cash from Hade and held it up to Tiller. "A man on a spree could have a high time with this kind of dough."

Tiller plucked Nathan's slouch hat from his head and put it on. "I'll take this to even our score for now. You keep the money. Share it with the boys." He nudged the horse with his heel. "Lay it on those ashes and use it for kindling. I don't rightly care."

Sonny pushed to his feet and came to stare up at Tiller as he passed. "Where you going, Tiller? When will you be back?"

"I can't answer those questions, Sonny. I don't know myself."

"Kin I come?" He waved a wad of cash in both hands. "We could have us a high old time down in Natchez."

"Not this time."

"When will we see you again?"

With a halfhearted salute at the circle of gaping men, Tiller rode out of the clearing. Out of earshot, he drew up his shoulders and jutted his chin. "Tell you what. . .look for me when you see me."

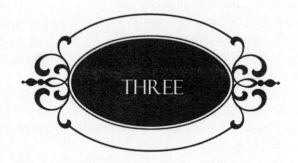

THREE

Choctaw Nation, Oklahoma Country, Indian Territory

Joseph Nukowa Brashears stilled in his tracks. With the ruins of Fort Towson at his back, he gazed northward along the old military road toward Gates Creek, as sure as spit that a fat buck rabbit had just scurried past. The taste of Myrtle's stew teasing the back of his tongue, he held his breath and trained his gun on the brush.

"He's gone, Joe."

The barrel leaped toward the sky, along with his surging heart. Spinning, he gaped at his woman.

Myrtle stood a few paces behind, her fingers toying with the plaited black hair over one shoulder. Her skirt moved as she swayed, the turned-in toes of her moccasins peeking from under the hem. She looked like a naughty child instead of his wife of many moons. She shrugged. "I saw him go. Don't waste your lead."

"You saw nothing." Joe sniffed and turned up the wide brim of his hat. "And you just loud-mouthed yourself out of a fine supper."

She gave an answering snort. "I know what a cottontail's behind looks like, old man. Something's gone off with your vision, and I suppose it's old age. Once you were a lively young brave, one who wouldn't let a meal slip through his fingers." With a strangled laugh, she tugged on his sleeve and pointed. "Hop through in this case."

In the distance, the long-eared critter bolted past a pawpaw tree, bounded thirty yards, and ducked into a knot of flowering staggerbush—stopping once along the way to nibble a dandelion.

"Forty years is not old, wife. My eyesight's keen. There's a pressing weight on my shoulders today, is all."

Myrtle made a sunshade with her hand and gazed at the horizon. "It's early to be wound so tight, Joe. The day has hardly begun."

"Never mind." He yanked his arm free and shouldered the gun. "His furry behind will be mine yet. Wait and see."

Tilting her face, she peeked at him. "I'd ask what's hung in your craw, but I fear you'll tell me."

He stared into the sunrise and pursed his lips. "You'll find out soon enough—when I ride off after breakfast tomorrow."

She shot him a wobbly grin. "So you're leaving me here to pull corn by myself? How long will I be shed of you this time?"

If a stranger happened along to hear the teasing in Myrtle's voice, see the carefree set of her mouth, he'd swear Joe's wife didn't mind his going away.

Joe knew better.

He wound her arm through his and patted her hand. "I'll be gone for a good while, I'm afraid." Urging her forward until her shuffling feet caught up, he started her down the road toward what was left of the fort and their humble cabin beyond. "Don't worry about bringing in the corn. Our neighbors will help."

She trudged alongside him in silence before slipping her hand free and fisting it at her side. If he bothered to look, he'd find the other hand clenched, too, the knuckles of all ten fingers a matching shade of white.

Joe steeled his spine and prepared for battle. "I don't want you to fret, Myrtle. I'll be home before the days grow short. You can count on it."

"Where you thinking to go?" The angry glint in her downcast eyes said she knew the answer before she asked.

Squirming under the scorn in her voice, he glanced to the side of the road. "Thought I'd ride east for a spell."

"Joe." His name hung in the air between them, splitting their hearts like an ax on kindling. "There's nothing left for you in Mississippi."

His brows bunched. "I'm duty-bound to my sister's memory."

Myrtle pinched her lips and blew a long breath through her nose.

"You'll do as much good as you did before. John Coffee won't change his mind."

Joe winced at the sound of his enemy's name. Why had his sister married an ignorant *nahullo* then up and died? And not just any white man. The most stubborn paleface in Mississippi.

To drive the thorn deeper in Joe's side, his sister's husband was named for Colonel John Coffee, a United States representative at the Treaty of Dancing Rabbit Creek, the day that marked the end of the Mississippi Choctaw Nation.

Because of John Coffee Bell, Joe had taken the name Nukowa, or "fiercely angry," in the white man's tongue.

Myrtle prattled on, as if he hadn't growled and set his jaw. "John doesn't hold with the ways of our people. He will never accept that Mariah became your charge the day she was born."

She lifted one shoulder. "Besides, if your niece cared to live with us, she'd be walking this trail with us now. The girl has made her wishes known."

"I can't help what she wishes."

"Mariah's not a child, Joe. She's well past marrying age."

"All the more reason to bring her among her people. John will see her wed to a nahullo, one as stubborn as he is. Then Mariah and her children will abandon our traditions forever." Joe gripped the stock of his gun until his fingers ached. "Every day she becomes more of John and less of her mother. My sister's spirit wails to me in my sleep."

Blinking away stinging tears, he gazed over his shoulder at Fort Towson, abandoned by the military at the close of the Civil War. Once a thriving garrison, the broken-down row of buildings was little more than a burned-out shell.

Joe took Myrtle's arm and led her down the path that branched away from the stark reminder of the past. There'd been enough wars fought in the nation to suit him, yet he found himself crossing swords with his dead sister's man.

With a mind shut tighter than a gulf clam, John ignored Joe's pleas where it came to Mariah's welfare. Joe had swallowed his bitter anger and allowed John to force the white man's way over Onnat, but his heart had stirred at her death.

The time had come to bring Mariah Bell to live where she belonged, under the watchful eyes of Joe and the other men of the tribe. John Coffee's pride would not stand against generations of Choctaw wisdom.

Distant voices brought Joe's head up.

Three boys loped toward them on the lane, their sun-washed faces the color of acorn tops. The oldest balanced a shotgun over his shoulder. The beaming lads flanking him carried bobbing cane poles and a can likely filled with fat worms. They nodded as they passed, no doubt headed for Gates Creek to jerk fish for the family table.

Their laughter and happy chatter pulled at Joe. He longed to swivel on the ball of his foot and fall in beside them. He'd missed so much by never having a son.

"Did you hear me, Joe? You can't force Mariah to come."

He grunted. "I heard."

"But you won't change your mind." Her defeated sigh pricked his heart.

Digging in his heels, Joe gripped her arm and pulled her around. "I've chosen Mariah's husband, Myrtle. A nephew of the tribal chief. It's what my sister would want for her daughter." He blew a frustrated breath. "The girl's future is here now."

Myrtle shook her head. "Your sister embraced John's way of life, especially where Mariah was concerned. How do you know that Onnat—" Her gazed dropped, shame bright in her eyes. "I mean. . .how can you know it's what she wanted?"

He shot her a warning scowl. "You utter aloud my dead sister's name? In your eagerness to keep me here, you abandoned our ways, too?"

She bit her bottom lip. "I'm sorry," she whispered. "I didn't mean—"

A blast rang out, the echo sounding through the nearby trees.

Joe's head whipped around, a sudden thought tensing his jaw. "The boys. They've bagged something."

Sullen, Myrtle nodded. "Sounds that way."

"You don't suppose they crossed paths with my cottontail?"

The hint of a smile teased the corners of her mouth. "I'd say it's more than likely."

Biting back a grin, he tugged on her arm and started down the trail. "In that case, let's go home so you can cook me something tasty. Those three will have my rabbit stew for supper tonight, and it's your fault."

She sniffed. "Since you're bound to leave, I'll cook you something better than stew, a meal to fill your stomach and see you off right."

He nudged her with his elbow. "Not too much for you, huh? Your belly looks full enough these days, and your behind's getting broad in old age."

She ducked her head, pressing the palm of her hand to her middle. "I've grown heavier, I admit. But I'm barely forty, Joe Brashears, and I can still best you in a footrace."

He cocked back his head and laughed, then grabbed her and hugged her close. "You're forty-one years, Myrtle Brashears, but don't fret. You're a fetching woman still. Besides, I don't mind a little extra to hold on to. You were always too scrawny for my taste."

Myrtle's soft chuckle lifted his spirits. She didn't want him to leave, but she'd see him off with a kiss and a smile. A knapsack filled with corn cakes, if he was lucky.

Joe drew a deep, cleansing breath. It was enough.

Mariah slid a plate piled high with steaming flapjacks to the center of the table.

Greedy, grasping hands emptied the Stanley platter before it came to a stop, clear down to the bright bluebirds perched in the center. The four men seated around the kitchen had already cleared a large bowl of scrambled eggs and most of a slab of bacon.

Dicey bustled behind them with a jug of cold milk in one hand, a chilled pitcher of water in the other. She'd arrived to work a half hour late, dragging onto the porch with a frown, her black curlicues braided in haste by the look of her crooked rows. Sighing, she'd fumbled into her apron and set to work mixing the batter. For reasons unknown to Mariah, the girl despised her job.

The steady *whir* of spinning blades drifted under the windowsill. Between the slats of the blinds, Rainy crisscrossed the yard, cutting a swath in the tall grass with the push mower. His bare, skinny wings stuck out behind him, glistening with sweat despite the early hour.

"Any more of them eggs, miss?"

She turned with a smile. "Coming right up."

The patrons of Bell's Inn were a few faithful regulars and those who found their way by word of mouth. Occasionally, daring souls who still braved the overgrown Trace stopped in, but the stretch that passed in front of the inn saw far less traffic these days. For the most part, the men who wound up on her doorstep were of a kindly sort, friendly wayfarers on their way to unknown destinations.

At times, tight-lipped, shifty-eyed strangers arrived, rough and tumble men who looked like trouble. To keep the peace, Father allowed them rooms if he had any free, but Mariah always fed them fast and sent them on their way. It wouldn't do for those types of men to find out she and Miss Vee were running the inn alone.

Thankfully, the group that hunkered over the table, elbows working, seemed as harmless as nursing pups.

Back at the stove, Mariah poured six more beaten eggs into a pan with sizzling butter. Eagerness to see the men fed and out the door sped her hands. Their crude chorus of smacking lips and belching set her teeth on edge.

"These are mighty-fine vittles, ma'am. Most especially these here biscuits."

She craned her neck to nod at the skinny young man smiling up at her with blackened teeth. "Why, thank you. Make sure you get enough, now, you hear?"

The scruffy companion perched beside him nudged his side. "She ain't no ma'am, Jack. That there's *Miss* Mariah Bell. Her daddy owns the place."

At the mention of Mariah's father, tears blinded her. Biting her lip, she blinked them away.

She caught the glint of admiration in both men's eyes and fought a shudder, cautioning herself to be nice. With the scarcity of business, she needed these poor, bedraggled souls and others like them. Resting her spoon, she turned with a weak smile.

The prim gentleman seated across the table smoothed his vest and straightened his cuffs. "This girl's no ma'am or miss, you half-wits." He sniffed as if he'd caught a whiff of the chamber pot. "She's an Injun squaw."

Pain jolted Mariah's heart, and her head reeled as if he'd struck her with his deerskin gloves. Dicey's huge eyes flickered to Mariah's before she slanted her heated gaze to the floor.

The two dullards' interest turned to mischief as they snickered and sparred with their elbows.

A fourth guest, the big man traveling with the prissy boor, bent over his plate with glassy eyes, shoveling eggs in his mouth. He showed no interest in the antics swirling around him, and Mariah suspected the sour smell of stale liquor came from him.

"If you lot are done stuffing your guts, it's time you were on your way."

Heads spun toward the irate voice on the stairs.

Miss Vee always did like to make an entrance. She stood on the bottom step, her cheeks softly rouged, her lashes darkened, and mounds of hennaed curls pinned beneath a small white cap. A crinoline petticoat, out of fashion for years, puffed the skirt of her crisp black dress, and a starched white apron stretched fit-to-split over her ample bosom. With a warning scowl and clenched fists on her hips, she made a daunting figure.

Glaring at the fancy man, she sauntered to the table. "For your information, this lovely girl is the mistress of our establishment, and I'll ask you to treat her accordingly"—she pointed behind her—"or you can hit the road out front, finished with breakfast or not."

The large fellow, who had minded his business so far, gaped up at Miss Vee. Abandoning his eggs and skillet cakes, he spun on the chair and wrapped his arms about her waist. "Look what I got me, Herman. This big heifer's my kind of woman."

Miss Vee gasped and slapped his hands away. Making a run for the counter, she whirled with a war cry and a rolling pin.

Dicey screamed and pressed her back to the wall, both hands clutching her face.

Mariah slid between the vengeful redhead and her drunken suitor just in time to prevent a battered skull. Easing the flour-dusted weapon from Miss Vee's hand, she smiled to calm her rage. "Steady, now. I'll take it from here." Steeling her spine, Mariah faced the disrespectful dandy. "I'll appreciate the removal of your overzealous friend. Even squaws recognize beastly behavior toward a lady."

Avoiding her eyes, he stood wiping his mouth and laid his napkin beside his plate. "Of course." He caught the swaying brute by his collar and hauled him down the hall with Mariah, Miss Vee, and Dicey close on their heels. In the parlor, he collected their waiting bags and escorted his companion onto the front porch. With a tip of his hat and a slight bow, he shoved him past the gaping yard boy to a wagon at the end of the walk.

Rainy nudged his hat toward one ear and scratched his head. "Everything all right, Missy Bell?"

Mariah flicked a sweat-dampened curl from her forehead. "It is now."

Miss Vee shook her head. "Not quite." Spinning on her heel, she led them back the way they came and waltzed up to the table, her crinoline petticoat swaying. With a meaningful glance at her rolling pin, she gave the two remaining guests a pointed look. "I believe you gents were about to take your leave as well?"

Her question ignited a frantic struggle to shove back their chairs and stand. Black Tooth snatched his hat from the hook on the wall and shoved it onto his head. "Yes ma'am. I can see it's about that time."

Still chewing a bite of food, his partner's head bobbed. "We'd like to thank you ladies for a most pleasant stay."

Miss Vee narrowed her eyes. "I'd invite you back, but you won't be coming within ten miles of here ever again." She smiled sweetly. "Ain't that right?"

"No, ma'am," said one man.

"Yes'm," croaked the other.

Swatting with their hats and stumbling over their feet, they battered each other soundly while racing for the back door, clattering off the porch in a sprint.

One glance at Miss Vee's face, red blotches standing out against her rouge, and Mariah doubled over laughing.

Dicey yanked her apron over her mouth, but a giggle escaped.

Miss Vee sputtered a bit then joined in, howling until she gripped her sides.

Eyes shining, they dropped into the empty chairs and stared across the messy table, still grinning.

Mariah sobered first. Leaning her head to stare at the ceiling, she sighed. "Oh, Miss Vee. . .there go four paying customers who won't be coming back. With travel along the Trace so scarce these days, perhaps we should've handled things differently."

"Oh, piddle," Miss Vee said. "There are still plenty of men who'll cross over from Robinson Road just to have one of your breakfasts." She patted Mariah's hand. "Don't fret, honey. We'll be just fine without the likes of those vermin."

She slapped the table, rattling the sugar bowl. "If your father was here, it never would've happened. John Coffee commands respect." Tilting her head, she smiled. "Folks like him on sight. It's a gift."

A leaden weight settled in Mariah's stomach. "You're right, Miss Vee. If only my father was here..."

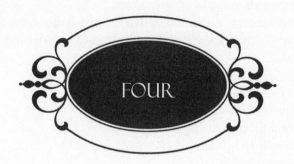

FOUR

The cheerful morning had disappeared. Storm clouds roiling in from the gulf met the afternoon sun overhead, sweeping across it like a giant snuffer dousing the light.

Tiller raised his collar against the sudden gusty wind, glanced up, and winced when the first chilly raindrops began to fall.

A little farther south and the Trace angled close to the Pearl. A few miles past the river bend, the road grew nearly impassable. He had decided to bypass that point, ride cross-country to Canton, and hide out for a few days, but then the squall blew in. With thunder rattling the treetops and lightning lifting the hairs on his arms, finding shelter was the only thing left on his mind.

Faint whistling pricked his ears. He flicked his collar away from his face, tilting his head to listen. Scared to blink, he watched the road ahead, his stomach hot, hands clammy.

He'd never waited in the shadows for an approaching stranger without the comforting presence of his men lurking nearby. It occurred to him that fate may have turned the tables—the bait used to lure unsuspecting prey would find itself ensnared. A part of him knew it'd be justice served.

Tiller reined his horse behind a cluster of oaks and watched, grateful for the cover of the darkening sky.

A gangly boy in a floppy straw hat ducked from the woody canopy, all dusky arms and skinny legs. Humming now, he picked his way down the slope into the misty ravine and ambled toward Tiller with a burlap sack slung over his shoulder.

In the manner of a soul who believes himself alone, he closed his eyes and sang with all his grit, so loud he flushed a chattering squirrel.

"Dat gospel train's a comin',
I hear it jus' at hand,
I hear the car wheels movin',
And rumblin' thru the land.
Get on board, childr'n,
Get on board, childr'n,
Get on board, childr'n,
They be room for many a mo'."

Taking his first easy breath, Tiller nudged his horse onto the road. The boy's head jerked up, and he spun for the opposite rise.

"Hold up there," Tiller called. "I mean you no harm."

Chest heaving, the lad stilled with one foot braced on the grassy incline, watching over his shoulder.

Tiller rode closer. "Did you hear what I said? Don't be afraid. I'm not going to hurt you."

A nod. His scrawny throat worked furiously, as if he found it hard to swallow. By the size of the budding Adam's apple, he couldn't be more than twelve, but his small stature made it hard to tell.

Inching closer, Tiller flashed his brightest smile. "How are you faring on this dismal afternoon?" He ducked his head at the empty sack on the boy's bony shoulder. "About to pick a mess of berries, I see."

The boy twisted around to face Tiller, both thumbs shoved in the waistband of his tattered trousers. "Nawsuh." He stared at Tiller with darting eyes. "Cain't pick nothin', now. We 'bout to get us a drenchin'."

Tiller grinned. "I reckon we are at that." He softened his voice. "Where you bound for, young man? You have someplace to go to get in out of the rain?"

Despite the protection of Nathan's hat, Tiller's wet shirt stuck to his back. Rivulets of water ran along his spine beneath his braces, soaking him down to the skin. It would take a mighty hot fire to dry him out and ease the chill from his bones. He shivered, waiting for an answer.

Say the right thing, boy. Tell me you live close by, somewhere warm and dry with plenty of room by the fire.

The little fellow stammered and slid one foot behind him. "Well, suh. . .you see, we. . .that is, we ain't—"

Together, they spun toward the rustle of footsteps. A taller, meatier version of Tiller's new friend rounded the bend, halting fast when he saw Tiller. The boy's brother. No doubt about it. Gathered brows and a quick flick of his head summoned the smaller one to his side. "What you doing consortin' with strangers? Pa gon' take a switch to yo' behind."

"I ain't consortin', Rainy. I jus' run up on him, same as you."

Like a puppy, the older boy hadn't quite grown into his oversized paws. Lifting wary eyes to Tiller, he spread long fingers over his little brother's chest and urged the child behind him. "Hush up, and come on with me. We going home."

"Wait." Tiller's upraised hand stopped them cold. "I'm hankering to get out of this weather. You know of a place close by where I could hole up for a spell?"

Two sets of eyes studied Tiller, as dark and brooding as the angry clouds rolling in behind them. Jagged shards of lightning scattered overhead followed by violent thunder.

At last, the elder brother nodded. "Yessuh, Bell's Inn." His arm shot out to point behind him. "A short piece that way. Mastah John and his Injun daughter run the finest stand on the Natchez Trace."

Tiller nodded. "I know just the one you mean, but I thought the new road shut down all the stands on the Trace."

"Bell's Inn shut?" The boy wagged his head. "Nawsuh, it ain't no such."

Tiller's gaze flicked up the hill. "Am I close?"

The boy nodded, steadily easing his brother up the slope. "A good gallop will get you there in a tick. Watch for a split rail fence and a whole mess of magnolias out back." At the top of the rise, he flashed a toothy grin. "You cain't miss it. Jus' look for the best tended grounds in Madison County."

Sighing with relief, Tiller lifted his soggy hat. "Much obliged."

But they were gone. Nothing left where they'd been standing but the wind-whipped branches of a young hawthorn tree.

Grinning, he spun his horse into a trot up the Trace, his heart set on a soft bed and the warmth of a roaring fire.

Mariah gripped her forehead and fought to see the swirling digits scrawled across the ledger. She'd come close to crying over the dismal numbers in the past, but today the persistent threat of tears had little to do with the state of her accounts.

Laying aside her dusting cloth, Miss Vee swiped her palms on her apron. "Are you all right, Mariah?" She leaned to look out the window, drawing away again as thunder shook the pane. "You're about as gloomy as this awful weather, and you didn't touch your lunch."

Mariah summoned the will to answer. "I'm fine, thank you."

Miss Vee crossed to the desk and pressed the back of her hand to Mariah's forehead. "You feel a bit warm, child. You don't have a temperature, do you?"

Across the room, Dicey rounded her eyes and slid along the wall to the parlor door, ducking out of sight around the corner.

The yellow fever epidemic of 1878 had ravaged the state of Mississippi, creating ghost towns and wiping out whole families. Four years later, folks still got jumpy around any threat of sickness.

Mariah supposed suffering would resemble the Yellow Jack if no one knew a body was grieving. It would be difficult to hide the bitter ache in her heart, but she'd have to try harder. She drew a shaky breath and glanced up. "I'm a little tired, is all. Got up too early, I guess."

Pulling the accounting book from Mariah's hands, Miss Vee closed the dusty cover. "This mess will keep, honey." Bending, she tossed it into the small safe beneath Mariah's desk and closed it with her foot. "Go upstairs and have yourself a lie-down. There are still a few hours before suppertime."

"I really should—"

"No arguments." Miss Vee, who no one would describe as delicate, had surprising strength in her determined hands. She curled her fingers around Mariah's wrist and pulled. "Come along, now. Don't make me try to tote you up the stairs. We'd both wind up regretting it."

Smiling, Mariah allowed her spunky friend to tug her toward the landing. As they neared the bottom step, a knock came at the door. Miss Vee jumped then stumbled, nearly yanking Mariah's arm from the socket. Her frantic grab for the newel post was all that saved them from falling. Wobbly, they clung together, breathing hard.

Dicey raced into the front hall and stood gaping at the door. "Who you s'pose that gon' be?"

Miss Vee's throat rose and fell. "You don't think it's those same fools?" Her hoarse voice cracked. "Returning to get revenge?"

Glancing toward Miss Vee, Dicey shuddered. "Who be addled enough to go out on a day like this. . .'less they up to no good?"

Thunder rattled the house, and the three of them shrieked.

Feeling ridiculous, Mariah pulled free of Miss Vee's clutches. "For pity's sake, we're behaving like schoolgirls, scaring ourselves silly with ghost stories. Those men are halfway to Jackson." She brushed wayward strands of hair from her eyes. "I'm sure it's just some poor soul hoping to get out of the rain."

The rapping came again, louder this time.

Mariah fought to still her pounding heart. Why did ordinary things suddenly feel so scary? Knowing Father was gone had knocked the braces from under her. Resenting the fact, she balled her fists. Onnat Bell's daughter wouldn't give in to fear. "Answer the door, Dicey."

The girl whined and wrung her hands. "Me, Miss Mariah? Oh, no. Let Miss Vee."

"Go on, now," Mariah said. "We're right behind you."

Dicey inched forward. Pausing, her trembling fingers stretched toward the knob, she pleaded over her shoulder with her eyes.

Mariah urged her on with a nod.

Swallowing hard, the girl eased the door open a crack and peered through. "Um, y–yessuh?"

"Afternoon." The booming voice dripped with sass as thick as country gravy. "I've come to see about a room."

Tension melting from Mariah's shoulders, she released her breath. "Ask him in, Dicey."

Dicey stepped primly aside. "She say come on in."

Framed by the doorposts—his beaming face out of place against a backdrop of driving rain—stood the most curiously handsome man Mariah had ever seen.

Drenched from head to heels, his hair clung to his face in soggy strands, a light orangey red, even darkened by rainwater. Along with soaked-through britches and a damp cotton shirt, he wore a practiced grin and the forced cheerfulness of a man used to having his way.

He ducked inside but kept to the rug, his anxious gaze on his muddy feet. Spotting Mariah, he whipped off his hat. "Good day, miss." Mischief flared in his roguish green eyes like sparks in a hearth.

Smoothing her skirt, she approached the door, glad she'd donned a dress and swept up her hair. For reasons she had no time to ponder, she wanted this man to see the lady of the manor and not the Indian princess. "May we help you, sir?"

He pointed his hat at Dicey. "I was telling your gal here that I need a room for the night. Nothing fancy, mind you. I'd curl up in the pantry to get out of that rain."

Mariah smiled. "I'm certain we can do better than that. As a matter of fact, you're in luck. We happen to have a vacancy." No sense admitting he could have his pick of the empty rooms.

Relief washed over his face. "Well, I'm much obliged." He offered his hand. "The name's McRae. Tiller McRae."

"Mariah Bell, at your service. I own—" Her breath caught at what she'd nearly uttered. "That is, my father is the proprietor of Bell's Inn." She dipped her head at Miss Vee. "This is Mrs. Ashmore. She helps us run the place."

Miss Vee colored like a blushing girl. "Call me Viola. Or better yet, Miss Vee."

He all but bowed. "Honored to meet you both." Handsome or not, a grin that forced couldn't be trusted.

"Your accommodations are down the hall, the first door on the left. We serve an informal breakfast in the kitchen, promptly at six. If you're not seated around the table by then, you stand a fair chance of going without."

He cleared his throat. "Promptly at six. I'll be there."

Mariah touched Dicey's arm. "Bring a towel for Mr. McRae then mop up this mess."

His smile waned, and the merry eyes dimmed. "Sorry, ma'am. If you ladies will excuse my sock feet, I'll shuck these boots and leave them outside the door."

She studied his boyish face, even more striking up close. In the space of a minute, he'd gone from calling her miss to ma'am. He must think her a cranky old matron. Contrite, she relaxed her crinkled forehead and softened her mouth. "Don't you want to settle your horse first?"

He arched his brows. "I hope you don't mind. I left him in the barn sharing oats with your paint."

Irritated afresh at his cocky assurance, Mariah spun on her heels and headed for the stairs. "We require full payment up front, Mr. McRae. For the care of your horse, as well. Miss Viola will take your money."

"Yes, ma'am."

Unwilling to scare off another guest with gold in his purse, she paused halfway up the steps and forced her gritted teeth into a halfhearted smile. "I do hope you'll enjoy your stay, Mister. . .McRae, was it?"

The smile tugging the corners of his mouth seemed genuine, but the insufferable twinkle had returned to his eyes. "Miss Bell, I get the feeling I'll enjoy my stay very much."

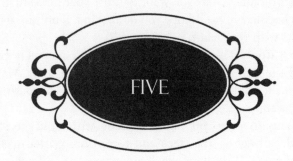

FIVE

Grinning at the thought of Mariah Bell blushing fiery red and flouncing up the stairs, Tiller flopped on the mattress so hard he bounced. After too many days on the road, it felt good to be in the company of a pretty woman—a feisty one, at that—and blasted good to be in a real bed again.

He bunched the quilt beneath him with both hands and sighed. A bed with sheets so clean, the scent of lilac water and sunshine rose in a pleasurable cloud. Turning his nose to the feather pillow, he drew in deep, fairly sure Miss Bell would smell just as sweet.

The trusting, toothless smile of the kindhearted traveler merged in his head with Miss Bell's fetching face—not a pleasing picture to be sure. He shook his head to clear it, the motion sending the pretty parts to the rafters in a wisp, leaving him to stare vacantly at the scraggly, white-haired man named Otis Gooch. Without a doubt, the poor coot wouldn't sleep in a clean bed that night—if the gang had left him alive to care.

In all of Tiller's years in Nathan's company, he'd watched the ambush of many a hapless prey, putting them out of his mind as fast as he rode away. So why did the thought of this old gentleman, slumped in a heap at the side of the road, tear at his heart like a pickax?

What Nathan said was true. Tiller couldn't go on ignoring the fate of the folks he charmed into trusting him. He dangled the carrots that lured the poor rabbits into Hade Betts's perilous snare, so whatever happened next was his fault as much as the men who wielded the guns and struck the blows. Maybe more so.

Along with the realization came the aching truth that he'd never be worthy of a fine, decent woman like Miss Bell. Rolling to his side, Tiller clenched his fists, the admission a searing pain in his gut.

The harsh life of a raiding thief wasn't the adventure he'd expected as a boy, wasn't the path he wanted as a man. He'd grown more discontent with each passing year but didn't know how to escape.

Nathan's vaunted tales of a bandit's life along the Trace had once tickled Tiller's grimy young ears. Somewhere along the way, the dismal truth wore the shine off Nathan's stories.

After a few months of dodged bullets and empty bellies, Tiller was ready to go home.

Nathan, who took to the drifter's life like a tick to a hound, dug in his heels and stayed put. In the early days, two things kept Tiller at his side: the misplaced loyalty of youth and the fear of striking out on his own. Lately, he wasn't sure what held him.

Staring into the past, he sighed, and a stray goose feather shot to the sky. As always, the swirling mists of Scuffletown's swamps lured him. Memories of his brief stay there throbbed in his heart like a sore tooth. Never sure if Aunt Odie's cooking was as fine as he recalled or Uncle Silas's stories as grand, he only knew his longing to return was the closest thing to homesick he'd ever felt.

Tiller jumped at the light knock on the door.

"Mr. McRae?"

He bolted upright, swiping at the tears wetting the hair at his temples. Jogging to the door, he swung it wide, his smile firmly in place. "Yes, ma'am, Miss Viola. What can I do for you, lovely lady?" Gazing at her delighted face, he cringed inside. Remorseful or not, it hadn't taken him long to return to his practiced charm.

Fanning briskly to cool her cheeks, Mrs. Ashmore blushed to her graying roots.

Tiller's gaze wandered to her curls, wondering what she used to turn them the bright shade of copper. The reason she might do so confused him even more. If he could find a concoction to turn his hair a less garish color, he'd shell out the money for a crate.

"Mr. McRae, how you do flatter." She winked and shifted a stack of clean linens to her hip. "Your smooth talk could make a girl forget sagging jowls and wrinkled cheeks." Her tinted lashes fluttered down. "Until she passes that blasted looking glass in the hall."

Compassion nudged his heart. "No mirror reflects a woman's true beauty, Mrs. Ashmore."

Beaming, she touched his arm. "Now, I told you to call me Miss Vee."

"You sure did." He patted her hand. "I won't forget again."

She tilted her head toward the end of the hall. "I came to say I'd be happy to run out to the kitchen and fix you something to eat, seeing you arrived too late for the noon meal."

Tiller's growling stomach answered before he had the chance.

She smiled and nodded. "I'll go put these things away then bring you something light. Don't want to spoil your supper."

He held up his hand. "You'd be hard pressed to spoil my supper, ma'am. When they handed out appetites, I stood in the line twice."

A tender smile softened her face. "John's the same. Can't seem to get the man fed."

"John?"

With a quick breath, she returned from her distant thoughts. "John Coffee, Mariah's father. Such a lovely family, the Bells." Her sagging eyes widened. "Mariah in particular. Wouldn't you agree?"

Tiller's cheeks warmed. "Miss Vee, a man would be blind not to."

Watching him closely, her head slowly bobbed. "I see." A glimmer of something birthed in her eyes, like a scheme beginning to hatch. "How long are you planning to stay with us, Mr. McRae?"

Amused, he lifted his chin and met her calculating stare. "I can't say exactly, but I'm in no hurry to leave." A fact he wasn't aware of until he'd said it. "I suppose you'll have to put up with me until I can't peel off any more greenbacks."

She brightened. "I hope you're well off then. We need a strong young man around this place." She nodded firmly. "One we can trust." With a backhanded wave and a promise to return with some grub, Miss Vee rounded the corner, humming a merry tune.

Tiller closed the door, white-hot needles of guilt piercing his sides.

A trustworthy man? He hardly qualified.

As for his money running out— Wincing, he patted the scrawny drawstring purse at his side. In precious little time, he'd be busted.

His thoughts jumped to the safe in the parlor where Miss Vee stashed the money he'd paid for a night's stay. By the meager few dollars he spotted before she closed the door, they needed his cash to hold out for as long as possible.

Odd how he hadn't remembered the safe until now. Glancing at his reddening face in the mirror, Tiller smiled. For the first time in many years, a pretty woman tempted him more than an easy take.

Mariah slipped down the back stairwell, yearning for a cup of hot tea and a few stolen moments of blessed quiet. Halfway to the kitchen, Miss Vee's tuneless song drifted up to meet her, which meant time alone to grieve wasn't to be. Feeling guilty, she paused at the turn in the stairs to ease her frown and pray for pleasing manners.

Miss Vee often lapsed into singing as she went about her chores. Unfortunately, she sang badly and fractured her lyrics, combining two or three songs at once. Today she croaked out a medley of "Bonnie Blue Flag" and "Dixie," doing justice to neither piece.

The squeaky board at the bottom announced Mariah's arrival.

Miss Vee spun. The corners of her mouth turned down, but her eyes were smiling. "That wasn't much of a nap, young lady."

"I couldn't sleep." A kettle steamed on the stove, and Mariah's tin of favorite tea leaves perched on the counter. She quirked her brow and nodded. "How did you know?"

"That rotted old landing isn't the only board in this house that squeals. I tracked you crossing your room and halfway down the hall."

Mariah's heart sank at the reminder. The inn was falling apart around them. "I'm going to have to lay aside enough money to pay a carpenter. Only the Lord knows how much it will cost this time, and that just for urgent repairs."

Miss Vee returned to her task on the counter. "You know what the Bible says. 'No man putteth a piece of new cloth unto an old garment.'" She shook her head. "I fear you'll find no end to patching this old place.

You need to tear it to the ground and start fresh."

Mariah lifted the lid of the kettle and sprinkled tea over the simmering water. "Well, I don't have that choice, do I? It's far too costly." She settled the pot off the fire. "I can't sit idly by while the walls collapse on our heads."

Miss Vee stepped closer to pat her back. "Of course you can't, but that won't happen, will it? Your father won't allow it." Pulling a knife from the tray under the counter, she slathered butter onto fresh-cut slices of bread. "You bear far too much on your shoulders, honey. Repairs and the like are a man's concerns. I'm certain your father has a plan in mind, and he'll tend to this inn the minute he comes home." She beamed over her shoulder. "After all, he'll be returning right as rain. Healed once and for all, just like you said."

Her cheery words were a blow. Swallowing her pain, Mariah poured the steaming tea while her mind struggled for something to say. "Y–yes. Right as rain."

Miss Vee laid down the knife. "Gracious, what's wrong? You've gone pasty."

The hedge around Mariah's heart began to slip. She lowered her head and let the tears fall. "I miss him so much."

The comforting arms she expected surrounded her. Miss Vee held her, crooning in her ear. "Go on and cry, honey. I've shed many a tear since he's been gone."

Briefly, Mariah pretended Miss Vee knew the truth. She allowed her heart to grieve her father's death with another soul who loved him. Only for a moment, and then she got hold of herself.

She pushed Miss Vee to arm's length and wiped her eyes on a napkin. "Forgive me. I'm acting childish. Go on with what you're doing. I'm all right now." Her gaze slid to the cold meat sandwich Miss Vee had sliced and arranged on a plate. "Oh my, are you hungry?" She leaned to peer at the hall clock. "Have I rested longer than I thought? Where's Dicey? She should be peeling potatoes."

Miss Vee smiled sweetly. "This isn't for me, dear. I fixed it for that nice Mr. McRae. The poor man's so hungry, his insides begged to be fed."

Pursing her lips, Mariah drizzled honey in her cup and stirred. "I'd be careful of 'nice Mr. McRae' if I were you." She tapped the edge of her spoon on the cup so hard the porcelain rang like a gong. "I'm not sure he's the innocent he seems."

Miss Vee's brow puckered. "Mariah! If you can't tell the difference between Tiller McRae and the pack of wild dogs we rousted earlier, then I've lost all hope for you." Grinning, she set a glass of lemonade beside the toppling sandwich and hefted the tray. "And if you can't admit he's the handsomest catch to cross your path in years, well then, you're blind, to boot."

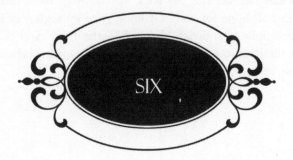

SIX

The sandwich Miss Viola brought had tamed the gnawing in Tiller's stomach, but the smells drifting from the kitchen, oozing under his door like a beckoning finger, watered his mouth like a drooling pup's.

Miss Bell's instructions about breakfast were clear, but no one said a word about supper. Tiller strained his ears for the sound of a gong or a call to the table, but nothing came.

Lured to the hallway by the scent of roasted beef mingled with onions and potatoes, he decided to mosey on down and scout out the kitchen. Just in case they forgot him.

Outside his door, he glanced to the right toward the dim parlor and across the way into what must be another guest room judging by a glimpse of a vanity and a bed made up with a blue and green quilt. No one in sight.

Creeping on the toes of his boots, he moved stealthily toward the kitchen. Halfway there, he sniffed the air and smiled. The first item on his list to explore would be the bread basket. The way he had it figured, hot rolls were the source of the warm, golden-crust aroma filling the house.

Tiller peered around the arched doorway into the dining room, empty except for a long table covered in an eyelet cloth and a place setting for one in silverware and white china. He frowned and tilted his head. If only one guest would be eating, he hoped he was the one.

Crossing the hall to the kitchen, he knocked on the wall before entering. "Miss Viola, are you in there?" A few more steps brought him next to the pantry door. "Hello? Miss Vee?"

The object of his raid beckoned from the sideboard, a metal basket lined with a red-checkered cloth. Tiller lifted away the folds, releasing the steamy baked bread smell into the air. Leaning over the heaped-up rolls, he drew a deep breath through his nose.

Ah! Pure pleasure.

His fingers closed around one of the light brown tops, so soft it gave at his touch. Closing his eyes, he brought the roll to his lips, savoring the moment briefly before he shoved it in whole.

Warm, yeasty flavor melted to the roof of his mouth.

Butter. He needed butter.

Rummaging inside the cold box, he brought out a full bowl, creamy and fresh-churned, then reached back in for a jar of strawberry jam. Placing them on the counter beside the rolls, he scurried across the room to search the cabinets for a plate. "Now where do you suppose they—"

A scream ripped the air.

Whirling with an iron skillet, Tiller backed against the sink.

The young woman cowering in the doorway bellowed louder. "Come quick! Miss Vee! Miss Mariah! He a thief."

Taking a step toward her, Tiller held up his hands, skillet and all, in protest. "Now, wait a minute—"

She let go another ear-piercing screech. "Lord, he'p me! He gon' bash in my head."

Over the girl's shoulder, Miss Bell lurched into sight with Miss Vee on her heels. Sliding to a halt, Miss Bell drew the trembling girl behind her skirts. "Mr. McRae?" Her sultry brown eyes opened wider than Tiller thought possible. "What are you doing in here?"

Frantic, he took in their suspicious glares. "I'm sorry. I was"—he squinted at the food spread over the sideboard—"hungry?"

Miss Bell's silent stare raked him with doubt.

The high-strung girl turned up her nose like something foul had crawled inside. "I s'pose you about to eat the frying pan?" She pursed her lips. "Don't believe him, Miss Mariah. He after the good silver."

Now that the girl's mouth wasn't cocked wide and screaming, Tiller recognized her as the one they called Dicey, who answered the door when he came. Even then, she'd been hesitant to let him in the house. Poor thing must be the nervous sort.

Tiller glanced at Miss Vee, watching him with brooding eyes. "Ma'am, I'm no thief. Just impatient, I reckon. The house is full of the scent of good cooking, and my appetite got the best of me." He shuffled his feet. "It's not the first time, I'll say that much, but this lapse of good sense isn't my fault. Judging by the smell, someone in this house has an inspiring talent for shaking a skillet." For emphasis, he shook the one in his hand.

Dicey ducked and clutched her bodice with both hands, pressing her back against the wall.

A smile edged the corners of Miss Vee's mouth then melted into rowdy laughter. She patted Dicey's shoulder. "Stop it, now. You're wasting a good conniption. He's not going to hurt you."

Dicey moaned. "How you know?"

Miss Bell glanced over her shoulder. "Good question, Dicey. I'm wondering the same."

Slipping one arm around Miss Bell's dainty waist, Miss Vee hugged her close. "Honey, this boy's harmless, as long as we keep him fed."

She jutted her chin at Tiller. "Go into the dining room and tuck in your napkin. We'll be right in to serve you."

Tiller glanced toward the rolls.

Grinning, Miss Vee handed him the basket. "Take it along with you. Dicey will fetch the butter and jam."

He started for the hall with Miss Vee barking orders behind him.

"I've seen men like this before, Mariah. Pile a platter high with beef and ladle ample gravy in the bowl. If we don't get his belly full, he'll be back in the kitchen by nightfall."

Dicey followed Tiller into the dining room with mincing steps. She slid him the butter and jam from across the table, and then lit two tapered candles and poured water from a frosty pitcher. By the time she finished her duties and backed out the way she came, he had finished half the basket of rolls.

"If you eat many more of those, you'll pay the piper. Yeast breads bloat the stomach."

He beamed up at Miss Vee crossing the room with a serving dish.

"I'll take the risk. Who makes these? They're the best I've ever tasted."

She nodded over her shoulder at Miss Bell. "This little thing, that's who. Mariah's the finest cook in Mississippi state."

"Don't believe her, Mr. McRae. My dear departed mother held that honor." Blushing a pretty shade of pink, Miss Bell placed a steaming bowl of corn within Tiller's reach. "I place a distant second to her."

Smiling, Tiller held up one of the rolls. "Not in my opinion." He sobered and cleared his throat. "Though I mean no disrespect to your mama."

Miss Bell seemed pleased. "Of course you don't. I thank you for the compliment. Now eat up, Mr. McRae, before your food gets cold."

"Tiller."

She raised one brow. "Sorry?"

He shot her a winsome grin. "Call me Tiller, if you don't mind."

Mariah stiffened. *You'd like that, wouldn't you?* The man was entirely too forward. Each time she softened the slightest bit toward him, he made a reckless blunder that pulled her guard up again.

Most likely, Dicey had him rightly pegged. Hungry or not, no man was foolish enough to go plundering about where he had no right. Was he?

Flustered, she got busy carving the roast, lowering her lashes to shield herself from his toothy smile.

"Tiller it is," Miss Vee crowed, evidently forgetting herself.

Irritation laced through Mariah. The woman became a simpering girl around this man.

Another roll in one hand, a forkful of roast in the other, Tiller stilled. "Wait a minute. Why am I eating alone? Aren't you gals hungry?"

Miss Vee giggled. "Don't worry about us. We'll have a bite when you're done."

He stood and pulled out a nearby chair. "No time like the present, I say." He made a sweeping gesture. "Please join me."

She blinked at him then raised her brows at Mariah. "Well, I guess it couldn't hurt."

Narrowing her eyes at Miss Vee, Mariah slapped a second hunk of beef in front of him. "Thank you, but we don't take meals with our guests."

Miss Vee propped her fist on her hip. "We certainly do."

Mariah cleared her throat. "An occasional breakfast, but never lunch or supper."

Tiller frowned. "Well, you should, if you don't mind my saying. It's a pitiful waste of this nice, long table."

She opened her mouth to firmly decline, but he held up his hand.

"Miss Bell, I insist." The sugarloaf smile again. "It ain't fittin' for a man to eat alone."

Miss Vee snatched two china plates from the mahogany hutch and plopped one on each side of Tiller McRae. "He's right, Mariah. It's bad for his digestion." Seating herself, she reached for the basket of rolls. "You wouldn't want to be responsible for this poor boy's discomfort, would you?"

Outmatched, Mariah wiped her hands on her apron then tugged on the strings and pulled it off. Handing it to Dicey with a grimace, she walked around the table and perched at the edge of a chair. "This is highly unusual, but I suppose a quick bite won't hurt." She turned her brightest smile on her cunning boarder and shook out her napkin. "Now the stomachache you're certain to have can rightly be blamed on all those rolls."

He raised one in the air, drenched in butter. "Like I said before. . . some things are worth it." He dragged the bread through his gravy, leaving streaks of strawberry jam behind.

Mariah cringed.

Miss Vee beamed at her from across the table, nodding and winking as if his words held special meaning. "You're not the first man willing to take the risk. Men around these parts make utter fools of themselves for a taste of Mariah's cooking."

Playing along with her silly game, he leaned toward Miss Vee and lowered his voice. "Are you're certain it's the food they're after? Miss Bell's a mighty handsome woman."

Her cheeks warming, Mariah hurriedly changed the subject. "Where are you from, Mr. McRae?"

A touch of sadness flickered on his face, gone so fast Mariah wondered if she'd imagined it. "Who me?" He toyed with a kernel of corn on his plate with the tines of his fork, taking his time to answer. "I suppose you could call me a drifter. I try not to stay in one place for too long. The minute roots start to sprout from my toes, I hit the road again." He stabbed the kernel and popped it in his mouth. "Can't have anything pinning me down."

Mariah's glass paused in midair. "That's a dreadful way to live. . .if you don't mind my saying," she added, borrowing his earlier phrase.

"Mariah Bell!" Miss Vee shamed her with a glance. "Mind your manners." Bristling, she ladled him another serving of potatoes. "The very idea."

"Well, I'm sorry, it's true." She took the bowl Miss Vee passed to her, tilting her head at Mr. McRae. "Don't you miss having land or family? I thought such things were important to men."

He rolled his shoulders as if casting off a weight. "Too confining. When I get ready to light out, I don't want anything riding my coattail."

His lowered lids were hiding something. When trouble plagued Mariah, she'd saddle Sheki and race along the bank of the Pearl, drawing strength from the rushing water. Tiller McRae seemed more like a man swimming upstream.

Another glance at his forced brightness pierced the shell of his posturing. The handsome young man's swagger covered a deep well of discontent. Mariah's heart stirred with unexpected pity.

Tittering, Miss Vee raised her goblet of water. "Here's to living free."

Strident knocking on the front door startled Miss Vee so violently she jumped. The glass slipped from her hand, hit the table, and tipped over, landing in front of Mariah on its side. A ring of moisture spread in a wide circle from the mouth, soaking the tablecloth down to the wood.

The pounding came again, louder and more persistent.

Squealing, Dicey spun toward the sound, her fingers twisting the dishcloth in her hand.

Mariah folded her napkin and stood. "It's all right, Dicey. I'll go."

Wiping his mouth, Mr. McRae half rose from his chair. "Is there a problem?"

She shook her head. "Not at all."

"Are you sure?" He straightened, watching her. "Would you like for me to go with you?"

"Of course not." The lie raised a knot in her throat. Swallowing hard, Mariah hurried from the room and down the hall. She'd answered the bell to lodgers countless times in her life. Why did it suddenly seem so frightening?

At the entry, she turned the lock and gripped the knob. Holding her breath, she opened the door.

Four strange men stood on her porch, two of them supporting the weight of an old man. Rusty blotches stained his shirt, and dried blood darkened the tuft of white hair on his head, stiffening the wiry strands.

Mariah's breath quickened. "What happened?"

A tall gentleman standing behind the others took off his hat. "We're not sure, ma'am. We found him huddled on the road blubbering and talking out of his head. He's been whacked plenty hard on the noggin."

She stepped aside. "Bring him in, please."

They bundled him over the threshold and followed her to the guest room across the hall from the parlor. Mariah pulled back the quilt and stood wringing her hands while they laid him against the pillows.

She glanced at the two who had carried him. "Stay with him, if you don't mind. I'll be right back." To the others, she nodded toward the hall. "You must be tired and hungry. Won't you join us for supper?"

The big man smiled kindly and shook his head. "A tempting offer, ma'am, but we need to be on our way."

"Very well," Mariah said. "Wait inside the parlor, and I'll pack you something to take with you." Excusing herself, she scurried down the hall, sliding on the plank floor as she turned the corner. "Come quick, Miss Vee. I need your help."

"Heavens," Miss Vee said, clutching her chest. "What is it? You're as pale as a haint."

"Good Samaritans have come bearing an injured man. They've asked for our help."

Mr. McRae yanked his napkin from around his neck. "Do you know them?"

She shook her head. "Strangers traveling the Trace. I've never seen them before."

He seemed edgy. "It might be a trick."

"I'm certain it's not. They found the old man alongside the road a few miles from here. He's hurt badly. A nasty blow to the head."

Mr. McRae's eyes rounded. "An old man?"

She nodded. "Quite elderly, I believe. He's white-haired and toothless as a babe."

Miss Vee shoved back her chair. "I'll find clean cloths for bandages. Mariah, go heat some water. Dicey, take the wagon and find a doctor."

Dicey worried the hem of her apron. "Ride clear to Canton by myself?"

"Of course not. We need him now, not sometime tomorrow. Fetch Tobias Jones."

"That ol' Injun healer?"

"Yes."

"No'm, Miss Vee! All his chantin' and dancin' make me feel all-overish. I'm sorely 'fraid of Tobias Jones."

Miss Vee caught her arm and urged her forward. "Be more scared of me. Now get on with you, and no dawdling."

"I'll put the water on then pack provisions for those nice men in the parlor," Mariah said. "They're exhausted and damp from the rain, but they want to press on."

She followed Miss Vee out, pausing under the arched doorway to glance curiously at Mr. McRae. Judging by his sagging jaw and sickly pallor, the stomach bloat they'd warned him of had hit him full force.

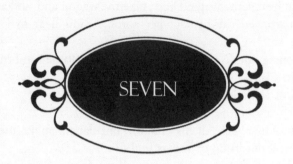

SEVEN

Fear nailed Tiller to the chair.

The flurry of clicking heels and swishing skirts finally swept from the room, plunging him in silence. Dread climbed up his throat and swirled over his head like rushing water. He struggled to draw a breath.

The helplessness was the same he felt while lurking in the shadows of the Trace without the protection of his gang. The heavy cloak of misdeeds weighed him down and sin crouched on his shoulders. He was tired of running but too scared of what would happen if he stopped.

Miss Bell ducked her head around the corner. "Come quick. We need you."

Stunned, Tiller's head shot up, but she had gone.

Panic gripped his gut. How could he traipse down the hall, stroll into the room, and say, "How do," to the man he'd helped put there? Yet how could he refuse?

At best, he'd brand Tiller a coward in front of the women—unless he'd figured out Tiller's part in the robbery. Either possibility meant trouble.

Before he could cipher what to do, Miss Bell rushed past and hurried into the kitchen, quickly returning with a basin of water. She paused to stare. "Are you just going to sit there?"

For as long as it takes, he thought. Nevertheless, his traitorous legs straightened, bringing him upright. Gritting his teeth, he followed her to his doom.

Movement inside the parlor caught his eye, and he glanced inside.

Four scruffy men, as jittery as fleas on a hairless dog, hovered near the fire. One at a time their hollow, weary eyes rose to his.

Satisfied he didn't know them, Tiller nodded and stepped across the hall to the guest room. Lingering outside the door, he watched the women tend to the huddled lump on the bed.

Miss Bell placed the pan of hot water on the bedside table. Miss Vee dipped a cloth, wrung it out, and bent over her patient. Tiller winced when she returned it to the water dark with blood.

Glancing up, Miss Bell caught his eye. "Come in, Mr. McRae," she said in a soft voice. "It's all right. You won't disturb him. I'm afraid he's delirious. Poor man doesn't even know we're here."

Tiller's knees sank with relief. Awed by a streak of luck or grace he didn't deserve, he eased into the room. "How can I help?"

"I've brought down one of my father's old nightshirts." She blushed ruby red and stared a hole in the floor. "Once we get his wound bandaged, we're going to need you to undress him."

"I'll help," Miss Vee announced. "After raising nine brothers and a husband, he can't have much I haven't seen before." She dunked the gory rag and squeezed it out again. "Mariah, go assist those pitiful souls in the parlor. Tiller and I will take care of this one."

Gathering her skirts, Miss Bell dashed for the door.

"Bring fresh water when you finish with them," Miss Vee called. "We'll need it clean to sponge him off."

Miss Bell returned and lifted the soiled container. "I'll do it now, so you can get him settled."

By the time she got back, Tiller had the old man shucked down to his long underwear.

Rosy-cheeked again, she stopped outside the door.

He hurried over, and their eyes met over the steaming basin.

"I want to thank you, Mr. McRae."

"Tiller."

She swallowed delicately. "Tiller. It's very kind of you to help. I realize you don't have to."

"It's my pleasure, ma'am."

She smiled stiffly and lowered her eyes. "I suppose you may call me Mariah. . .if you'd like."

He studied her sweeping lashes. "I'd like it very much."

Miss Vee bellowed for the pan.

They jumped apart, sloshing water over Mariah's hands.

Grinning, Tiller took the basin and hurried to set it beside the bed. When he looked toward the threshold again, she was gone.

He worked beside Miss Vee for the next half hour, ministering to their patient. They washed him head to toe, wrestled him into the long white nightshirt, and redressed his seeping wound.

Caring for him soothed Tiller's aching conscience a little, but the gray, lifeless face against the pillow seared his guilty heart.

Miss Vee pressed her palm to the ashen forehead then straightened with a tight smile. "No fever. That's a blessing, but we sure need the doctor. I can't imagine what's keeping Dicey with Tobias." She rested her hands on her hips. "Where did Mariah run off to?"

Miss Vee wasn't the only one who missed Mariah's company. She ducked in once to say she'd aided the strangers and sent them on their way, but hadn't returned since.

Pointing to the corner, Miss Vee patted his back. "Pull up that chair and sit with him whilst I go scout things out."

She left the room, and Tiller hauled the chair close to the bed—just not too close. Sitting stiff as a plank, he gripped his knees and studied the injured man's face.

His bushy brows bunched in sleep, and his toothless mouth gaped as if to cry out, but no sound came. Tiller wondered if he suffered much pain.

It squeezed his chest to watch, so he turned his attention to the shuttered window. Between the slats, the moon shone from a puddle on the ground, and no raindrops stirred the bright reflection. The storm had passed.

Mariah's pleasing face tugged at his thoughts. In all his rambling years, he'd seen a passel of pretty gals—fetching saloon girls, shopkeepers' daughters, and the painted ladies down on Silver Street in Natchez, crooking their red-tipped fingers from the shadows as he passed.

Mariah was beautiful in a different way, from inky black hair piled on her head to hot coffee glances from under sleepy lashes. She seemed wild in the way of a broken stallion, subdued but never tamed.

"Where am I, boy?"

The shock jerked Tiller to his feet.

Bleary eyes studied him from the bed. "Are you folks caring for me?"

Feigning a sudden itch, Tiller's hand shot up to cover his face. His other hand groped for his head, but without his hat, he couldn't hide his auburn hair. "Y–yes, sir. We are."

The old fellow nodded then winced and probed his bandages with shaky fingers. "I'm hurt bad?"

Tiller set the chair out of his way and backed up several steps. "Not sure yet. We're waiting for the doc."

The man drifted in and out, mumbling garbled words.

Anxious to know whether he was making sense or talking out of his head, Tiller walked to the bed and leaned over.

The wrinkled eyelids shot open, jolting Tiller's heart. The stranger pointed a bony finger, his watery gaze locked on Tiller's face.

Dread pitched his stomach. Now would come the anger. The accusation. A fast run to the door and a frantic ride out.

"Thank ye for helping me, son. I'm much obliged." Spent, his hand fell to the mattress, and his head lolled to the side, out like a candle in a draft.

Relief spreading warmth through his limbs, Tiller slumped in the chair. The old man didn't remember him. Not this time. Would that change when his head cleared?

Tiller should run, no doubt about it. Roll up his pack, roust his horse, and get far away as fast as he could ride. So why couldn't he bring himself to move?

Did he want to be caught? With his secret in the open, the threat of discovery wouldn't loom like a guillotine blade.

He scrubbed his face with his hands then laced his trembling fingers behind his head. What kind of game was he playing, gambling with his life?

A need he didn't understand held him within the comforting walls of Bell's Inn. Something greater than common sense, stronger than fear. He glanced at his pale face in the dressing table mirror. *Something, Tiller boy, or someone?*

Either way, he wasn't ready to saddle up and hit the long, lonely road outside. Until the injured traveler sat up in bed and called him out, Tiller had no plans to leave.

Mariah sprawled across her bed and sobbed. The sweet-faced old gentleman lying wounded downstairs stirred painful memories of her father writhing in pain for weeks.

She sent for Dr. Moony against Father's wishes when a terrible cough began to wrack his thinning frame. Doc slipped from the room after the examination, peered into Mariah's soul, and shook his head. He told her to allow Father his pipe. It wouldn't matter.

Helpless, she stood by and watched as the burly man who raised her disappeared.

Clenching her fist, she gave her pillow a vicious whack. His death was a waste! The cruel disease an unwelcome guest stealing him pound by shocking pound, breath by gasping breath.

Mariah barely had time to accept his illness before he was gone. She wasn't ready to lose him.

Startled, she sat up in bed, surprised she hadn't thought of it sooner. Before long, Doc would ride out from Canton to check on Father's condition. Dr. Moony would never believe the story she'd told Miss Vee.

Gripping her face, Mariah lay back in bed to figure a way out of her latest predicament. Except she couldn't think straight with her heart and mind overflowing with memories.

No matter, she'd work out something before the doctor came nosing around. Whatever the cost, she'd find a way to keep Father's death a secret for as long as possible.

"Tobias is here," Miss Vee called through her door.

Wiping her eyes, Mariah sat up and scooted off the bed. She opened the door, surprised to find Miss Vee still there.

Her penciled brows arched. "I'm getting a little concerned about you, honey. It's not like you to hole up in your room."

Evidently, her efforts to hide her heartache were still lacking. "I'm fine. Just a little tired tonight, I suppose."

Miss Vee frowned. "You said the same thing earlier." She reached to cup Mariah's cheek. "No fever. Still, you must be coming down with something. I could pack for a trip to Natchez in the bags under your eyes." She peered closer. "Sugar, have you been crying?"

Ducking her head, Mariah eased from her grasp. "We'd best get downstairs. If we don't watch him, Tobias will bust up the headboard for kindling and build a ceremonial fire at the foot of the bed."

Miss Vee caught her hand as she passed. "A girl needs her mama, and I know how much you miss yours." Her smile brimmed with compassion. "If there's anything you need to talk about, I'm a good listener."

Guilt an elephant on her chest, Mariah squeezed her fingers. "I'm grateful."

"Grateful for what? I love you like you're my own." Longing softened Miss Vee's features, subtracting years from her eager face. "I know your father might never want me, considering he's so partial to slender women." She sighed. "After all, your mother was as thin as a twelve-year-old boy, and I've been plump all my life." She blushed slightly. "I'm a silly old woman. I shouldn't be saying such things to you."

Mariah squirmed inside but patted her hand. "It's all right."

"No, it's not, but what I'm trying to say is this—if John Coffee ever did take a shine to me, if we were to actually get married, I'd be honored to call you my daughter." She ducked her head and drew in her shoulders. "That is, if you didn't mind."

Bile rose in Mariah's throat. She swallowed and forced an answer. "You know I wouldn't mind."

"Really?" Miss Vee lit up, and a brilliant smile replaced the uncertain set of her lips. "Well, that means so much. God chose not to bless me with a child of my own, but I've always wanted a daughter. Of course, I'd never be able to take Minti's place." She sighed so hard she shuddered. "Not for either of you." Her haunted gaze swept the room in a wide arc from floor to ceiling. "I still feel her presence in this place. In every board, every nail, the very air we breathe."

"The inn was such a large part of who Mother was."

She nodded, her voice barely a whisper. "And she'll always be part of the inn."

"Miss Vee? Miss Bell? Anybody?"

With a shared look of surprise, they hurried from the room and rushed to the head of the stairs.

Tiller stared up from the bottom step. A spate of freckles Mariah hadn't noticed before stood out on his whitewashed face. "I think you ladies might want to come down here."

Mariah took the stairs two at a time. Respectability be hanged. Tobias Jones was in her house.

Behind her, Miss Vee moaned. "What is it, son?"

Tiller shook his head. "I can't rightly say. I've never seen anything like it before."

It was all Mariah needed to hear. Clutching her skirts, she sprinted for the sickroom.

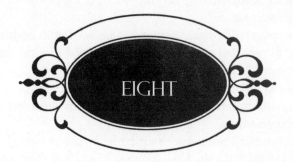

EIGHT

Mariah spun out of the parlor and across the hall, lurching to a stop outside the guest room. She stared at the scene before her, dumbstruck.

Their patient, as bare as the day his mother bore him except for a sheet draped over his middle, sprawled on the floor in front of a blazing hearth. His skinny arms were stretched out to the sides. His pasty legs and knobby knees were on display.

The Choctaw healer knelt at his side with puckered lips pressed to his forehead like a child drawing juice from a lemon.

Too shocked to look away, Mariah found her voice. "Stop it this instant."

Ignoring her, Tobias lifted his mouth and spat in his cupped palm, then gracefully rose and shook an unseen substance off his hand into the fire. A bright red mark appeared on the old man's brow.

Mariah had heard of the Indian practice of dry cupping, but she'd never witnessed the procedure. Most felt it a silly superstition, with no real power to heal. After seeing it in action, she tended to agree.

"We brought you here to care for his injury. To clean it and apply healing herbs." She waved her hand over the scene. "Not for all this nonsense."

"Sucking near the wound draws out the poison."

"So will a poultice of cotton-tree root."

Tobias's glare held scorn. "Old way better."

Mariah cautiously approached the poor soul stretched out on the floor. Moisture beaded his top lip and pooled in the hollow of his chest. "Why is he sweating so?"

"China root tea. To cleanse from *isht abeka*." Tobias nodded firmly. "Infection," he repeated as if she hadn't understood him the first time.

She frowned. "How'd you get it down him?"

He crossed his arms, his scowl deepening.

She'd questioned his skill, insulting him. Her shoulders drooped. "All right. Never mind."

Movement from the corner startled her. Tobias's sons, Justin and Christopher, stood in the shadows, trying in vain to hide their amusement.

Recalling what Miss Vee said about her black-ringed eyes, Mariah lowered her head and touched her burning face with her fingertips.

Tiller pushed past and stood over the man on the floor. "What's he done to Mr. Gooch?"

Mariah's head came around. "You know him?"

Tiller blanched like beans in hot water. "Just his name."

"But, how?"

"He, um. . .came to for a minute. Thanked me for taking care of him. Before he passed out again, he said his name. Otis, I think it was." He nodded and backed toward the corner. "Otis Gooch."

Miss Vee swept inside and took command. "Whatever his name, with him sweating like this, we should cover him. He'll catch a draft." She motioned to the younger men. "Help me get him back in bed."

Grinning and casting furtive glances in Mariah's direction, Chris and Justin took Mr. Gooch's arms. Tiller hoisted his legs. They carried him with ease and gently placed him against the pillows.

Miss Vee hustled to his side with a dry towel to wipe his face. "He'll stink now. After all the care we took to get him washed."

Tobias stood his ground in front of the fireplace, mumbling under his breath. As always, despite his irritation, he watched Miss Vee closely from under veiled lids.

Mariah propped her fisted hands at her waist. "Are you quite finished?"

He grunted. "All done. He'll be better now."

She shot him a doubtful look. "What do I owe you?"

"Corn bread."

She tilted her head. "Did you say corn bread?"

He nodded. "Whole pan. Butter, too. Big tub."

Miss Vee paused from tucking the quilt under Mr. Gooch's chin. "See, Tiller. I told you this girl was known for her cooking."

Mariah sighed. "I don't have any corn bread prepared, and it's too late to start. Can you come for it tomorrow?"

Tobias quirked his mouth then gave her a solemn nod. "By noon. No later. My boys will fetch it."

"I'll have it ready."

The Jones men filed past her out of the room. Chris winked as he passed, and Justin smiled and touched her arm, both so handsome up close her toes curled.

Cursing her twisted fate, she groaned inside, wishing with all her might that they weren't Choctaw.

Tiller's brows lifted. Tilting his head, he took another look to be certain of what he'd seen.

Mariah stood in a trance, ogling the cumbersome broad backs and prissy long hair of the departing braves. She watched them go, the dreamy look turning to pouted lips and an angry scowl.

Tiller cleared his throat. "Mariah?"

Her shoulders twitched and she spun. "Yes? I'm sorry."

He smirked. "Forgive me for interrupting your musings."

A crimson blush swept up from her collar. "Not at all. I was just—"

His eyes held hers until she lowered her lashes. He couldn't contain his knowing smile.

"Is there anything else before I turn in?"

Her gaze flickered up then dove to her feet. "Thank you, no. Miss Vee and I plan to take turns sitting with Mr. Gooch. You've done more than enough, and it's very late. I'm sure you had a tiresome day on the road."

He offered a small bow. "I'll say good night then."

"Just a minute, please," Miss Vee called in a hushed tone. Hurrying over, she ushered them into the hall. "Actually, I need to talk to you both. Now seems as good a time as any."

"Our guest said he's tired," Mariah protested. "Can't this wait until morning?"

Miss Vee cocked her head at Tiller. "Are you too bushed for a little chat? I have a business proposition." By the eager glow on her face, she had something big to say.

He grinned. "I suppose I can fend off sleep, now that you've piqued my interest."

"That's what I thought." Ignoring Mariah's furrowed scowl, she pointed at the parlor. "Take a seat inside. I'll fetch us some tea."

Tiller raised his hand. "None for me, ma'am. Keeps me awake."

"Don't worry"—she waved him off—"I'll brew a pot of chamomile."

They crossed the hall, and Tiller stepped aside to allow Mariah into the room. She hadn't met his eyes since he'd embarrassed her, and he couldn't help but wonder what thoughts swirled in her head while she stared at the two young men with such admiration.

The possibilities churned his gut and lit a small fire of jealousy in his heart. Surely, she wasn't interested in those two showy braves.

Don't be a fool. You have no right.

He'd just met her, after all, though it seemed he knew her well. He felt a kinship with Mariah. An easy bond greater than simple attraction. Greater and more enticing by far.

She settled into a chair across the low table and folded her hands in her lap.

Tiller studied her, taking advantage of the fact that she refused to look up.

In her frenzied rush to deal with the Indian healer, a few locks of hair had escaped from the topknot on her head. Long and bountifully black, the wispy strands gleamed in the firelight coming from the hearth. Her eyes were the color of chestnuts. This he recalled from memory since only her sleepy lids were visible. Dark brows with a delicate arch set off her sweeping lashes. His meddling appraisal moved to her full lips, and his pulse surged.

Mariah's hand fluttered to her mouth, waking him from his daze. She'd caught him at the very thing he'd mocked her for doing.

Clearing his throat, he shifted his attention to the hearth.

"I apologize for Miss Vee," she said lightly. "She gets worked up at times."

He glanced at her. "I don't mind. She seems to have a good heart."

Mariah tucked in one of her loose strands. "It's very astute of you to notice." She angled her head. "Considering you've known her for such a short while."

For the first time, Tiller took note of the slight crook in her nose. An imperfection, some might say, but it took nothing from her beauty. No more than the pleasing slant to her eyes.

He blinked as the realization hit. The boy he met on the road had said, "Mastah John and his Injun daughter run the finest stand on the Natchez Trace." Little wonder the Choctaw brothers would appeal to her. The elegant mistress of Bell's Inn was an Indian, too.

Did it matter? He'd have to think on it awhile.

"Mr. McRae?" Mariah said softly. "Have I lost you?"

He covered his wayward thoughts with a wide grin. "What happened to calling me Tiller?"

She gave him a shy smile. "Your name bears getting used to. It's very unusual."

"Just think of tilling the ground, and you won't forget. That's why folks started to call me Tiller in the first place. I suppose I'm good with the soil."

Mariah leaned closer. "So it's not your given name?"

He shook his head. "Reddick's on my birth papers, but I doubt I'd remember to answer to it. No one's called me Reddick in years."

She thoughtfully mouthed the name. "I think I like it. Reddick has a nice ring." Her chin came up. "Though Tiller's nice, too."

"I agree." Miss Vee swept into the room on the tail end of their conversation, placing a tray filled with teacups and little cakes on the table. "Tiller's very nice indeed. Why would there be any question?"

Mariah shot him a grin. "Never mind, dear. Let me help you with the tea."

Miss Vee handed Mariah a delicate cup, which she passed on to Tiller. Once she'd served them, they settled down to watch each other over the steaming rims of their drinks.

Tiller's first sip coated his top lip with creamy foam, the warm liquid so pleasant he hated to swallow. He held up his cup. "What did you say this concoction was?"

Miss Vee beamed. "Chamomile. I doctor it to my own peculiar taste. I hope you like it."

He chuckled. "You could say so. What makes it so good?"

Miss Vee set her saucer on the table. "Oh, I'm glad you like it. I brew it like everyone else then add a dollop of beaten cream and a teaspoon of honey. Sometimes I scrape in a little cinnamon, but I didn't this time."

Tiller shook his head. "I like it fine the way it is."

"Tastes positively cozy, doesn't it? It'll help you sleep, too."

"Is that a fact?"

Mariah sat forward. "Speaking of sleep, it's well past everyone's bedtime, so if you will, kindly get on with it."

Swiping foam off her lip with the back of her hand, Miss Vee nodded. "You're right. I'll come to the point." She shifted toward Tiller. "Were you serious when you said you were in no hurry to leave?"

He glanced at Mariah. "Well yes, but—"

"Good, because we're in no rush to see you go."

Mariah's cheeks colored. "Dear lady, what are you suggesting?"

Miss Vee seemed not to hear. "Like I told you before, Mariah's in need of a strong, trustworthy man."

Mariah's pretty face paled and she gulped air.

Still ignoring her, Miss Vee tilted her head at Tiller. "At supper you said there's no family to speak of, correct? No wife and passel of kids tucked away, waiting for you to come home?"

"Miss Vee!"

The lady finally glanced over her shoulder. "Keep your garter fastened, honey. It's not what you think."

Tiller came to the rescue. "Listen, I'm not sure what this is about, but I can only stay until my pockets dry up." He raised his hands and shrugged. "And the truth is I'm not carrying that much cash."

Miss Vee clapped her hands. "Perfect. My idea may be the solution to both your problems."

Standing so fast her teacup sloshed, Mariah scowled at Miss Vee. "I don't know where you're going with this nonsense, but I've heard quite enough." She set her saucer on the table. "If you'll excuse me, I'm going to bed."

Miss Vee caught her wrist. "Hear me out." Her pleading gaze seemed to hold Mariah tighter than her restraining hand.

Mariah sniffed. "With the way you started, I don't think I want to hear the rest."

Wringing her hands, Miss Vee colored. "Oh fiddle! That's because I'm not saying it right. Sit down and let me start over."

Easing into the chair, Mariah picked up her cup. "Very well, but make it quick." She narrowed her eyes. "And choose your words carefully."

Miss Vee grimaced. "Yes, of course. I'll try." She raised her chin. "I've been mulling over the facts in my head, honey. About the inn being so neglected."

Mariah colored and shot her a warning scowl. "A few things may need a hammer and a coat of paint, but—"

"You said it yourself, the walls are collapsing on our heads." She followed Mariah's pointed look at Tiller. "No need in posturing. I doubt the state of this place has escaped his notice."

Mariah huffed her frustration and fell against the back of her chair. "What's your point to all this?"

The older woman's face lit up. "I'm proposing that Tiller stay on and make the repairs in exchange for room and board—with a few buttered rolls thrown into the bargain." She winked. "If you think her yeast bread is good, wait till you taste her pies."

Her eyes darting between them, Mariah scooted to the edge of her seat. "Oh my, you really should've run your plan by me first. You see, I already have the repairs worked out."

Miss Vee crossed her arms. "Let me guess. You intend on tackling them yourself, don't you?"

Mariah opened her mouth to speak, but Miss Vee's hand shot up. "Young lady, you have more than enough to say grace over. Dash your pride and accept Tiller's help." Her bottom lip trembled. "For pity's sake, accept my help. I feel responsible for you in your father's absence."

Pulling a handkerchief from her waistband, she wiped her eyes. "I'm suggesting this idea for John's sake as much as yours. He'll still be recuperating when he comes home. I won't have him climbing ladders and toting lumber." She shook her finger in Mariah's face. "One thing's certain, he'd roll over and die before he'd allow you to do it."

Mariah's cup shattered in a spray of milky-white tea and shards of porcelain. Flinching, she dropped the jagged remnants at her feet.

Miss Vee struggled to stand. "Oh, honey! I'm so sorry. It must've cracked when I poured in the hot water. Are you hurt?"

Tiller snatched a folded towel from the tray. Skirting the table, he inspected Mariah's hands and found a cut, small but deep enough to bleed. He wrapped the cloth around her wound while Miss Vee shook the broken pieces from her frock and blotted creamy splatter from her chin.

"I'm all right," Mariah said quietly. "It's nothing. Please don't fuss."

"We're going to make sure, if you don't mind." Miss Vee peered at her face. "I pray no glass flew inside your eyes. Do they sting when you blink?"

Mariah shook her head. "Really, I'm fine." She swiped at her wet skirt. "Though I would like to get upstairs and change."

"Of course, dear." Miss Vee slid her arm around Mariah's waist. "Come, I'll help you."

"What about Mr. Gooch?" Mariah asked.

"Don't fret," Miss Vee said, urging her forward. "I'll take first watch."

Concerned, Tiller followed them to the landing.

At the foot of the stairs, Miss Vee paused. "We'll all sleep better if we get this thing settled." Biting her bottom lip, she raised her brows. "Will you do it, Tiller? Will you stay on at Bell's Inn and help us?"

He studied Mariah's face, but it offered no hint to her thoughts. "If I were to agree, would it be all right with you?"

Her sigh, sweet with the smell of honey, stirred the air between them. "I can't think of a good enough reason to say no."

Tiller smiled. "Tell you what. . .I'll chew on it overnight and let you know my decision in the morning."

Winking, Miss Vee pointed at the tray on the table. "While you ponder, chew on one of Mariah's iced cakes. If you decide to hang around, there will be plenty more to follow."

Once they'd gone, Tiller bit into the confection, rolling the buttery goodness over his tongue. Delicious. Only sweetness didn't set right in a mouth filled with questions. The proud mistress of Bell's Inn, hard to figure from the start, just became a delightful riddle.

Mariah may have Miss Vee fooled, but not Tiller. Hot water had nothing to do with the broken cup. Some word or deed clenched the girl's fingers so fiercely she'd crushed it to bits.

Was it Miss Vee's reminder of Mariah's responsibilities? The rebuke about her pride? Perhaps the mention of her father, wherever the absent man might be.

Snatching one more cake, Tiller munched on it as he made his way to his room. He intended to replay every second of the evening in his mind until he figured out what thistle had so sorely pricked Miss Mariah's winsome hide.

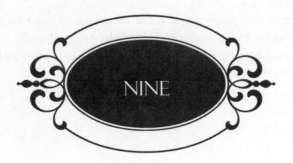

NINE

The sun began a slow crawl up the far horizon as Joe reached the end of his rutted lane. By nightfall, it would slide down the backside of the sky and sleep closer to Myrtle than he would.

He had a long ride ahead to reach Mississippi, and the same distance to come back. In between loomed the time it would take to convince John Coffee to release Mariah.

Joe halted his pony and shifted in the saddle to stare behind him. His ancestors left their Mississippi homeland in tears, but the place Joe had carved out of the vast Indian Territory was *apookta*. His happy place. Long, lonely days stretched ahead before he could return.

Gray smoke swirled from the crooked stovepipe, reminding him of the pleasant morning spent with his wife. Myrtle had slipped out of bed early or else hadn't turned back the covers at all, since she'd managed to wash and pack all of his clothes, load his rucksack, and prepare a breakfast fit for three men.

In light of the fact Joe was leaving, and considering the news she'd served alongside his eggs and fried bread, she probably hadn't slept a wink all night. Tears had brightened her eyes in the firelight—tears of joy or fear, he couldn't tell—before she lowered her chin to her chest and whispered the words he'd waited twenty years to hear.

Myrtle would bear him a son, for surely a male child wrestled for life beneath her bosom. He'd been too patient, too hopeful for the babe to be anything else. They'd call him George after George Hudson, the first principal chief under the new Choctaw constitution. Joe would teach him to hunt and fish, to honor his mother, and to sit tall at tribal council.

Myrtle said the miracle came to her in November, near the time of the white man's Thanksgiving. For the first time in Joe's life, there would be cause to celebrate the season.

He couldn't help but wonder why fate waited until all hope had dimmed. Why the gift had come at a time when he wouldn't be home to share its unfolding.

In the distance, Myrtle stepped out of the front door with a dishpan in her hand, hustled to the edge of the porch, and let the water fly in a silvery arc that caught the morning light.

Watching her dart inside, Joe sighed with contentment, a smile lifting the corners of his mouth. His wife had carried the child and the secret close to her heart for nearly six months, which meant the boy would come by the dawn of the Mulberry Moon.

Sudden pain squeezed his chest and worry tickled the back of his mind. Myrtle was spritely for her age but hardly a girl. Fretting drove her to bustle about, looking for work to fill her hands and occupy her troubled mind. She'd toil hard, sleep few hours, and eat too little until he returned. He imagined her lumbering about the cabin, hauling water, chopping wood, bent over the washboard, her body swollen with his child.

The picture set his teeth on edge. John would not stand in his way this time. Mariah would be a comfort to her aunt in her condition and a great help with the baby. With his niece settled in his home, his obligation to his sister fulfilled at last, Joe could relax and enjoy his new son.

Ghostlike, Myrtle appeared again, drifting across the porch with one hand on her stomach, the other splayed over her heart. She stared toward the southern pasture, her back to him. Joe knew she wept even before she leaned into the rail and gripped her face.

He clenched his jaw and fought the urge to turn the dun pony and race to her side, take her in his arms, and soothe her fears. With a leaden heart, he forced his eyes to the front and tapped the horse's flank with his heels.

Home wouldn't be apookta for Myrtle until Joe returned, but his spirit couldn't rest until he settled his business with John Coffee. The sooner he began the journey, the better for all concerned.

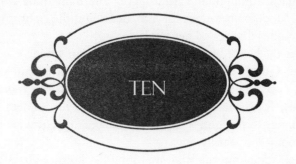

TEN

To the honorable Dr. T. Moony
Canton, Mississippi

Dear Dr. Moony,
*   This letter serves to inform you of my father's recent demise.*
As you predicted, his condition worsened day by day until, on the
evening before last, shortly before the midnight hour, he lost his
feeble hold on this life and passed into blessed rest. I want to thank
you for your kind administrations in our hour of need.
*   Respectfully,*
*   Miss Mariah Minti Bell*

P.S. The enclosed should cancel the balance of my debt.

Mariah laid down her pen, the tightness in her chest beginning to ease. She would seal the letter and hire Rainy to deliver it first thing this morning. The money tucked inside should satisfy her debt in full and cancel her prior arrangement to make payments for Father's care. Once she'd paid her bill, Dr. Moony would have no reason to return to the inn. They had no friends or relatives in Canton, no close connections in town, so the good doctor wouldn't likely mention the death of John

Coffee Bell to anyone there.

Her shoulders tensed as Mr. Gooch's pain-wracked face drifted into her mind. She and Miss Vee had taken turns sitting with their battered guest throughout a fitful night. The right thing would be to bring Dr. Moony out to care for him, but doing the right thing would roll the boulder that sealed her tomb.

Unlike the blessed Savior, there'd be no resurrection.

If Mr. Gooch took a turn for the worse, she'd have no choice. For now, everyone seemed perfectly content with the Indian healer. Thankfully, Tobias accepted goods in trade for his services since she had no money to pay him—she patted the bulging envelope addressed to Dr. Moony—especially now.

Mariah stared out the window, biting her bottom lip. Which need would get the meager few dollars she had left? The help's salaries or stocking the pantry? Feeding Sheki or repairing the loose boards and chipped railing?

Jutting her chin, she counted out the few dollars she owed Miss Vee, Dicey, and Rainy and set them aside. Those dear ones wouldn't suffer lack because of her deception. She'd find some way to cover the other needs.

A knock on the door brought her hand up to hide the letter. "Yes?"

Miss Vee peered in. "Are you awake?" She stepped inside, her brow etched with concern. "You're usually downstairs brewing coffee by now."

Crumpling the letter, Mariah hid it in the folds of her skirt. "Gracious, I know. I'm dawdling worse than Dicey this morning. A lingering touch of spring fever, I suppose."

"We're two days into June, Mariah. The time for spring fever is past." Mariah shot her a pointed look, and she held up her hand. "All right. I won't hover." At the door, she paused and smiled. "But hurry along, will you? We have to fill Tiller's stomach in case he's decided to accept your proposition. He'll need strength to tackle all those repairs."

My proposition? Hardly. Miss Vee and Tiller had worked out the terms of the arrangement across the top of her unwilling head. "I'll feed him, though I have doubts about filling his stomach. Go on down. I'll be right along."

Laughing, Miss Vee pulled the door closed behind her.

Mariah glanced up and frowned at her anxious face in the mirror.

With Miss Vee's reminder, the web of deceit tightened. If Tiller accepted the job, he would need building material. Lumber, shingles, and nails weren't free.

The thought of her redheaded guest quirked her mouth to the side. Tiller had wriggled under her skin on several different occasions. So far, this day fared no better. How dare the insufferable man ride into her life and provoke such angst?

First, he'd positively leered at her in front of the Jones brothers, implying with his crooked grin that he'd read her private thoughts. Last night he'd tracked her up the stairs with a knowing gaze that peered right into her soul.

She cringed. Tiller couldn't possibly know why she broke the cup, but she had been admiring Christopher's flashing eyes and Justin's dazzling smile, so he wasn't far off the mark on that score. Even so, a gentleman wouldn't blatantly accuse her. Blast his foul manners!

How dare Miss Vee ask him to stay on against Mariah's wishes? Could she bear having Tiller McRae and his bloated self-assurance underfoot every minute of the day? With a man like him around, a woman's secrets weren't safe.

A shudder took her, and she slanted her eyes from the mirror. One secret he mustn't guess. She determined to bear the weight of it with more care, no matter how heavy it lay on her shoulders.

Tiller fastened the last button on his shirt then plopped on the bed to pull on his boots. The familiar rattle of a woman in the kitchen drifted down the hallway, along with the unmistakable smell of brewed coffee.

Whatever breakfast came of the clanging pots and pans would be welcome, but Tiller needed the coffee. He had flipped like a gambler's nickel half the night, twisting the quilt around his legs and dragging his sheets from the bed.

Once he admitted he wasn't ready to leave Bell's Inn whatever the risk, the decision to accept Miss Vee's offer came easy. After that, so did sleep, what little he got before the sun peeked through the blinds.

He pulled the snaggletoothed comb from his pocket and smoothed back his hair, grateful the bright orange color of his youth had mellowed some to match his beard. Fingering the two days' growth on his chin, he decided shaving could wait one more day.

Feeling refreshed but a little reckless about the decision he'd made, he ducked out the door and made for the kitchen. He didn't feel foolish about staying on to help two women in need, more for the reasons he couldn't make himself leave.

For one, he felt at home in the aging, broken-down inn in a way he hadn't since the day he left Uncle Silas's house. When he turned the corner, his second reason stood barefoot at the stove stirring gravy in a cast-iron skillet.

"Where's Dicey?" Mariah asked without turning around.

"She's late," Miss Vee fired over her shoulder. "As usual." She spun again, staring at Mariah's feet. "Where are your shoes? These old boards are bound to be cold."

Miss Vee noticed Tiller lurking on the threshold and smiled. "Well, good morning. Take a seat. You'd best be hungry. We're stirring up a feast."

Mariah stiffened, tucking in her chin. She didn't offer an explanation about her shoes or a greeting for Tiller.

Winking at Miss Vee, he pulled out a chair. "I could do serious damage to a feast, but let's start with a mug of hot coffee." He cleared his throat to dislodge the lump. "Um. . .morning, Mariah."

She glanced over her shoulder. "Good morning."

From the glimpse at her swollen eyelids, she hadn't rested so well herself. Or she'd been crying. After the way she smashed her teacup to bits, his bet was on the tears. The thought stirred his heart to pity and stoked his curiosity to a flame.

Miss Vee swung around from the counter and set a heaped-up plate in front of him. He shot her a grateful smile before she returned to buttering biscuits. "How's Mr. Gooch this morning?" she called to Mariah.

The sound of the old man's name lodged so tight in Tiller's craw, he choked on his first bite of food.

Miss Vee laughed and pounded his back. "Gracious, son. Did that griddle cake take the wrong chute?"

Hacking furiously, he nodded.

Mariah picked that moment to come to the table, casting alarmed glances at his burning face and streaming tears.

Recovering somewhat, Tiller blew his nose on the napkin by his plate.

"Let me just get you a new one of these," Miss Vee offered, pinching the corner of the cloth and tossing it in a basket behind her.

Mariah set two more plates on the table. "Do you mind if we join you?"

Unable to answer, he waved for her to sit.

She pulled out a chair and tucked into her food, thoughtfully giving him time to recover.

Miss Vee took her place opposite Mariah. "So Mr. Gooch is all right this morning?"

Unfolding her napkin, Mariah dabbed at the corners of her mouth. "Actually, our patient seems much improved. He awoke twice during the night, asking questions and thanking us again for helping him." She smiled across the table. "I believe he did the same with you, right, Miss Vee?"

She beamed. "He sure did. The old fellow seems a kindly sort." A sudden frown creased her brow. "Not the type to deserve a whack on the head, that's for sure. Such a shame that evil men roam the earth taking advantage of innocent souls like him."

The buttery bite of pancake melting on Tiller's tongue swelled to cotton. He swallowed carefully and pushed aside his plate.

Mariah's startled gaze jumped to his food. "Is something wrong?"

He tried to smile. "Not at all. It was delicious."

"But you've hardly—"

He pushed back his chair and slapped his legs. "I've made my decision, ladies. I'm ready to get to work on your repairs. If you'll direct me to the proper tools, I'll get started."

Miss Vee leaned across the table. "You mean you'll stay on and help?"

Tiller pasted on his finley tuned grin and saluted. "For as long as you can stand me."

She whooped and clasped her hands. "Mariah, isn't that the best news?"

Mariah's brows gathered. "Yes, wonderful." She pointed at Tiller's full plate. "He hasn't eaten his breakfast. How can he work on an empty stomach?"

"I'll grab something later. I'm pretty anxious to get started." Standing, he clutched a fistful of bacon in one hand, his coffee cup in the other. "I'll just take this with me, if you don't mind."

The kitchen door flew open, yanking Tiller's heart to his throat. He leaped back so fast he sloshed his coffee in splatters around him.

The girl, Dicey, stood panting on the threshold. "It's Rainy's fault, Miss Mariah, his and my daddy's. Rainy's always late, and Daddy's bullheaded."

Miss Vee crossed her arms and scooted her chair around. "Good *afternoon*, Dicey. Do go on with your latest excuse. This one has the makings of an imaginative tale."

"No'm, Miss Vee. This ain't no kind of tale. Daddy say I cain't walk myself to work no mo'—not with some ramblin' fool going about busting folks in the head. So Rainy say he gon' walk me out here, and I say, 'How nice, Rainy!' Then he say, 'For a penny of your wages every day.'" Her fists balled at her sides and she scowled. "I don't hold with paying that shiftless boy nothin', but Daddy say it's the only way I'll be keepin' my job." Dicey pinched her mouth, breathing through her nose in short blasts. "Only Rainy jus' now showed up to fetch me." She cast a sinister glare over her shoulder. "Those big feet mired up in molasses."

In the distance, a tall boy ambled away, both hands shoved deep in his pockets. With a second look, Tiller recognized him as the young man who first directed him to the inn.

Mariah stood in a rush. "Rainy's out there?" She raised her skirt past her bare ankles and whirled around the table. "I have an errand for him."

Pouting her lips, Dicey stepped aside. "He headed home lickety-click. Runnin' away from my scolding, I s'pose. I lit into him all the way here." Her angry scowl became a simper. "You can see it ain't my fault I'm late, Miss Mariah. Now cain't you?"

Without pausing to answer, Mariah hurried past her calling Rainy's name.

Miss Vee jumped up and crossed to the door. "For pity's sake, Mariah Bell. You're barefoot!" She flapped her dishcloth so hard it popped. "The bottom of that girl's feet must be tanned hide."

Tiller pressed in behind Miss Vee as Mariah caught up with the boy and handed him what looked like a thick letter. "I reckon a person with natural leather soles wouldn't see the necessity for shoes."

She snorted. "Not exactly proper, is she?"

Tiller suppressed a grin. *Proper? Maybe not, but decidedly intriguing.*

Miss Vee stared after Mariah with a puzzled frown. "What do you suppose that's all about?"

"I was about to ask you the same," he said.

She shrugged. "We don't have time to find out, do we? Dicey has a kitchen to clear, and I have a box of tools with your name on it." She wiggled her fingers. "Come along, I'll show you where they're kept."

Tiller followed her down the back steps, so intent on watching Mariah he nearly ran into a stump.

With a knowing smile, Miss Vee took his arm and steered him clear.

The early summer day promised to be a mild one, considering the dew still wetting the ground and the faint chill in the morning air. He glanced around, admiring the well-kept grounds. "Who keeps up the yard?"

She snapped off a low-hanging magnolia blossom and held it to her nose. "Young Rainy. The boy loves working outside. He has a gift."

Tiller thought back to Rainy grinning from atop the rise. *"Jus' look for the best tended grounds in Madison County."* Chuckling, he shook his head.

"Rainy keeps the vegetable garden, too."

"You have a garden?"

Miss Vee smiled over her shoulder. "Just the best in the county. We turn out a fine, healthy crop every year, and it's a special blessing. Without a good harvest, we couldn't keep the customers fed." She veered toward the corner of the yard. "Follow me, and I'll show you."

She led Tiller to a nice-sized patch with rows of green beans climbing sticks and big heads of lettuce sprawling around the outer edges. Young melons, tomato plants, peas, and squash would soon be bursting for harvest.

Reminded of himself at Rainy's age, and of his own skill in working the soil, Tiller swallowed a sudden knot crowding his throat. He longed to linger in the inviting garden, to drop to one knee and bury his fingers in rich, black dirt. It had been too long since he'd soiled his hands in worthwhile pursuits instead of deception and crime. "The boy does a fine job."

Miss Vee nodded. "He sure does. With Rainy's knack for growing things and Mariah's gift for cooking, they make a tasty combination." Laughing, she tugged on Tiller's sleeve. "You've tricked me into dawdling long enough. Let's get to those chores."

Instead of heading for the crooked little lean-to, Miss Vee led him to the barn. Lifting the bar from across the heavy doors, she yanked them open with a grunt. "Mariah keeps her thingamajigs in here to protect them from the dampness of the shed. The girl is more particular with these old wrenches and hammers than most men are with their wives." She winked. "Count yourself among the privileged few she allows to touch them."

Miss Vee crossed the shadowy barn and ducked into a small storeroom in the corner. From inside a built-in cabinet with squeaky doors, she pulled a wooden box with shiny tools of every sort nestled beneath the curved handles like eggs in a basket.

Tiller glanced at Miss Vee. "These are Mariah's?"

She held them up for a closer look. "Every oiled and polished piece."

He cleared his throat. "I thought they'd belong to her pa."

A grin lit Miss Vee's face. "Not hardly. Mariah's the handy one. At least when she has the time." Her eyes warmed. "For all his talents, John Coffee's not so good when it comes to repairs." Her bosom shook with laughter. "Chores either, for that matter."

By her smitten look, Mr. Bell's failings didn't bother Miss Vee one bit.

"If you don't mind my asking, ma'am. . .where is Mariah's pa?"

She motioned with her head for him to take the toolbox. He obliged, and she closed the cabinet with a squeal of hinges. Pausing for several long seconds, she studied him, the love-struck shine faded to worry. "Poor John is sick, I'm afraid. Gravely ill, the last I heard. Some ailment afflicting his lungs."

"Well, I'm sorry to hear it," Tiller said. "Will he"—he cleared his throat—"recover soon?"

Her apple cheeks swelled with glee. "Yes, he will," she said, stressing each word. "The doctor sent him away to get better. 'Healed once and for all,' to quote Mariah." She sobered. "It burdens my heart that he's gone who-knows-where, depending on who-knows-who to care for him, but he'll be home soon, just as feisty as always." Her thoughts busy elsewhere, she stared mindlessly at Tiller's chin. "Then all the folks who love him can get on with living again."

Tiller gave her a knowing smile. "Yes, ma'am. I expect you will."

Oblivious, she drew up her shoulders and returned to the present. "Here you go again, distracting me to get out of doing your work." She jabbed him in the chest with her finger. "Well, it won't work, mister. Come with me." She ducked out of the storeroom and led him across the barn. "I figure you'll start from the top and work your way down, which means the roof comes first."

"Yes, ma'am."

"If you look in the shed, you'll find enough shingles to get you started. For the rest, I'm going to ask your help with a minor duplicity."

Tiller angled his head. "Ma'am?"

"A little harmless deceit for a good cause."

He shoved the door open. "What are you up to?"

She gave him a playful wink. "Starting tomorrow, you'll have the supplies you need. If Mariah asks, you say you stumbled across them in the shed or behind the barn." She grinned. "As in fact you will, once I give Rainy the funds to run into Canton. I just need a list from you and your promise to keep my secret."

Tiller shoved back his hat. "Lumber and nails are expensive."

She shrugged. "What else do I have to spend money on?"

He ducked his head to catch her eye. "It's very generous."

"Oh, pooh." Miss Vee waved him off. "After all, I live here, too." She hooked her arm through his. "Let me show you where to find the ladder. Then I'd best go see about Mr. Gooch. We've left him untended far too long."

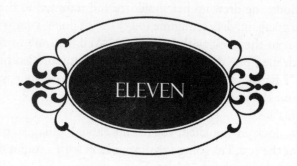

ELEVEN

Scuffletown, North Carolina

Hooper McRae tightened his fingers on the reins and eased the wagon to the right, dodging a gaping muddy rut straddling the middle of the road. Warmth stole over his heart, despite his aching shoulders and stiff hands. Soggy lanes and swampland were the first signs of nearing home.

Glancing at his sleeping wife curled on the seat beside him, he grinned and nudged her awake.

She moaned and stirred then squinted up with a drowsy smile, her pretty face dappled by the sunrise peeking over the horizon. "Hello, handsome stranger."

Hooper smoothed her red hair. "How do you sleep all bunched in a knot?"

Dawsey scratched her nose with the back of her hand. "It's not easy, I can tell you that much. In fact, I'm not really sleeping. . .just dozing a little." Her groggy voice faded. "Merely resting my eyes."

Leaning closer, Hooper's grin widened. "Were you planning to *doze* clear to Scuffletown?"

She yawned. "Don't be silly. I intend to keep you company along the way."

"I appreciate the effort, honey, but you're too late. We're here."

Her startled eyes flashed open. Bolting upright, she stared around her. "We're in Scuffletown? Hooper, that's impossible." She spun to gaze at him. "You drove all night?"

He laughed around the yawn he'd caught from her. "I didn't go to. The wheels kept turning while the road unfurled in front of me. Next thing I knew, we were pulling into Lumberton. No sense stopping twelve miles short of home."

Dawsey scooted closer on the seat and gripped his hand. "You're no longer a Scuffletown resident, Mr. McRae. Hope Mills is where you hang your hat now and has been for more than ten years."

He shook his head. "Sorry, dumplin'. If I live in Hope Mills fifty more years, this bogged-down swamp will still be my home."

She giggled and stretched. "Oh Hooper, I can't believe we're here. I can hardly wait to see Dilsey and the twins."

He held up a warning finger. "Ellie, not Dilsey. If you insist on calling her that name, you'll only make her mad."

She shot him a pout. "I do wish we could've brought our daughters to see your parents."

Hooper shook his head. "We made the right decision, Dawsey." He held up his fingers to count off the reasons they'd discussed. "It's a long trip, and we don't know when we'll see Hope Mills again. The girls are in school. All their friends are there. They're better off staying with Aunt Lavinia this time.

"Besides"—he winked—"a few days with their Aunt Ellie and your prissy daughters would be done up in britches, toting rifles, and tracking hogs through the swamp."

Dawsey's laughter echoed off the passing trees. "You're right, they would. I've always said it's a blessing Dilsey had sons."

Hooper raised his brows. "Two sets of twin boys born less than a year apart? Is that a blessing or double trouble? Those four scamps run their mother aground."

"And provide endless joy for your pa," she added, laughing harder. Sobering, she squeezed his hand. "I wish my father had lived to see the last two born."

"So do I." He patted her hand. "I really miss the old man."

Dawsey tilted her head. "Do you ever wonder what might've happened if the Wilkeses and McRaes hadn't found each other? I'd never have known I had a sister." She pointed between them. "Or that we share a sister, as madly improper as it sounds unless you know the story. And—the most amazing part of all—that you and I would fall in love and get married, forever blending our families."

He laughed. "Take a breath before you grow faint."

She fanned her flushed face. "I'm sorry, but after all these years, I'm still awed by the way God worked out the details."

Hooper smiled. "If you think about it, our families were blended from the day Pa brought our Ellie home."

Dawsey wrinkled her forehead. "You mean the day he kidnapped *our* Dilsey Elaine to raise as his own." She seemed to stare into the past. "I never thought I could forgive your father, but as it happens, Silas McRae is an irresistibly charming man."

Familiar tightness stung Hooper's throat. "I'll always admire the Colonel for forgiving Pa. It meant so much to him."

Glancing at his brimming eyes, Dawsey fished for her hankie and wiped tears from her cheeks. "I was awfully proud of Father. Showing mercy to the McRaes didn't come easy for a man like him."

They rode in silence until Dawsey nudged his shoulder. "If you think about it, God used Tiller to bring us all together. If I hadn't taken him under my wing, and if you hadn't come to Fayetteville on a mission to return him to Scuffletown, we never would've known such joy."

Hooper chuckled. "You're right. One skinny, carrot-topped boy set the whole thing in motion. Only Tiller ran away before he saw how well things turned out."

She inhaled sharply. "And we never got to thank him."

Hooper draped his arm around her and tugged her close. "Don't despair, Dawsey. Our visit home could change all that." He squeezed her shoulders. "And speaking of home, look. . .we're here."

Spirits soaring, Hooper turned the wagon down the lane to his old homestead. Peering to see in the early morning light, he could just make out the cabin in the distance. As they drew closer, a dim light shone from the open doorway, and milling shapes were gathering on the porch.

"They've heard us coming." He swallowed the lump in his throat. "Won't they be surprised to see it's us?"

A fact Hooper would soon make clear if he had to call out their names. Despite the few years of relative peace throughout the swamp, there would be half a dozen guns trained on the rig.

Dawsey shifted her weight impatiently. "I still say you should've wired ahead."

He shook his head. "The old man knows I'd never leave our farm this time of year. He'd have worried fit to bust until we arrived." He blew a long breath through his nostrils. "I wish we were here on a pleasure trip instead of this distasteful business."

"We'll get the unpleasantness out of the way first," Dawsey said, patting his hand. "Then we can enjoy ourselves with the family." She peeked up at him. "What do you think Silas will say when he hears the shocking news we're bringing?"

Hooper's stomach lurched. "He'll start all over again blaming himself that Tiller ran off." He tightened his jaw. "I don't relish causing him hurt, but I have to tell him, Dawsey. I have no choice."

She squeezed his fingers. "Of course you don't." Her eyes sparkling, Dawsey pointed at a slim figure standing on the porch. "Oh, Hooper! I think that's Dilsey." She leaned to squint. "Yes, Dilsey's here, and so are Wyatt and the boys."

He shot her a pained glance. "Do you plan to call her that the whole time we're here? If so, tell me now while there's still time to turn around. I'm not in the mood for Ellie's temper."

Her darting eyes trained on the cabin, Dawsey dragged her attention back to him. "Don't be silly. I'm the only person Dilsey tolerates on that score, but she allows me the one small indulgence." She gave him a look from under her lashes. "It's her real name, after all."

"Try to convince Ellie. . .only wait till I'm out of the house."

Smiling, Dawsey pointed with her chin. "Speaking of the house, I don't believe it's changed one whit."

Hooper gazed toward the ramshackle cabin. Smoke poured from the skinny stovepipe on the sagging roof. Firewood stacked high on the rickety front porch nearly covered the dirt-smeared windows. Shimmering puddles in the waterlogged yard mirrored the surrounding trees.

"You're right." He beamed at Dawsey. "Not a whit."

A high-pitched scream followed by a dancing, bobbing ruckus meant the family had identified the wagon.

As Hooper pulled to a stop a few yards from the beaming hoard on the porch, Dawsey leaned to whisper. "Don't say anything right away. It'll spoil their fun."

He lifted one brow. "What happened to getting the unpleasantness out of the way?" Climbing down, he winced from the stiffness and turned to help her to the ground.

She puckered her face at him, but anything else she thought to say got swallowed up in Pa's welcoming shouts and Mama's sloppy kisses.

Dawsey flew into Ellie's waiting arms, both women laughing and crying at once.

Pa squeezed between them and yanked Dawsey into his burly arms. "Little Dawsey. You're a delight for these old eyes. How's my boy treating you?"

"Hooper still pampers me like a bride, Silas."

"Well, he'd better," Pa shouted. "Else I'll twist his ears."

He spun. "Hooper, blast your hide! You don't come home near as often as you should."

Hooper winked at Dawsey. "See? Pa knows where home is."

With tears streaking her rosy cheeks, Ellie gave a war whoop and slung herself at Hooper.

He lifted and twirled her around, then set her on the ground, his arm crooked around her neck. "Have you given Wyatt plenty of trouble, little sister?"

She gave a solemn nod. "Every day."

Hooper gripped Wyatt's offered hand. "It's been awhile."

Wyatt's fingers tightened. "It sure has."

Ellie's four boys shoved closer, the elder twins waiting their turns with silly grins. When the grown-ups gave them room, they bolted for Dawsey and Hooper, clinging until Wyatt plucked them off.

One of the younger twins gaped at Dawsey, his brow furrowed under the cowlick in his hair. Squeezing between his parents, he tugged on her skirt. "Hey, you look like our ma."

His identical brother curled his lip. "She ain't nothing like our ma. She's too prissy and girlie."

Ellie gripped their necks, ignoring their howls. "This prissy lady is your Aunt Dawsey, sprouts. Go on and give her a hug."

Dawsey knelt in front of them. "Don't you remember me, boys? You've seen me many times before, though I'll admit it's been awhile."

Never one to let the point of a matter ramble in the dark, Papa ushered them toward the steps. "Let's move this shindig inside, family, so they can tell us why they've come." He clamped his meaty hand on Hooper's shoulder, a tiny frown gathering on his brow. "I get the feeling there's far more to this visit than a long overdue howdy."

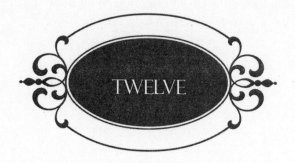

TWELVE

Mariah knelt in the cold, wet patch of grass covering her father's grave, the ground beneath her lumpy from unsettled clods of dirt.

With no windbreak on the rise, the morning breeze flapped her scarf against her face. The whistling wind in the overhead branches sang a haunting song, an endless tale of loss and broken hearts.

Contrary to the rest of God's creation, trees slipped into bright green coats to brave the sweltering heat only to shed their clothes and dance naked through the winter, waving their bare arms and groaning in protest. The foolish practice made as little sense as the mess Mariah had made of her life.

"Aki, tell me what to do. I'm lost without you." She sniffled and wiped the back of her hand under her nose. "I'm hurting Miss Vee, though I never meant to, and I know her sorrow would not please you."

Mariah had watched over the past months as her father had warmed toward the spunky, determined redhead. He'd begun to watch Miss Vee fondly as she went about her chores, a secret smile on his lips and a growing tenderness in the lines of his face.

How could Mariah tell her? *Father did care, dear lady. He'd come to admire you greatly, only now I'm afraid he's quite dead.*

She leaned over and gripped her face. "Miss Vee will be so angry when she finds out I've deceived her. Robbed her of the chance to grieve."

Mariah's head came up and snapped around to the other grave as if Mother had stepped across and caught her by the chin.

Promise, daughter. You must promise. Mother had pleaded until Mariah swore an oath to keep the land. Then she'd closed her eyes and slipped away, leaving her only child with a pledge she didn't know how to keep.

Mariah buried her fingers in the thick Mississippi grass, the land her mother's people had owned for decades under article fourteen of the Treaty of Dancing Rabbit Creek. Since then, her tribe had suffered indignities at the hands of greedy settlers. Hoping to drive the Choctaw off their land, these men had taunted them, burned their homes, torn down fences, and driven out their cattle.

They succeeded with Mariah's Uncle Joe and many others of her family. Father's name had protected her mother. Mother loved Bell's Inn and loved Father all the more for securing it for her. Running the inn made her feel like a great lady, not a mongrel only fit for the reservation.

A proud member of the Pearl River Clan of the Choctaw, Onnat Minti Bell loved the land even more. As a child, she raced along the same sandy bank as Mariah. Ran barefoot through the same backyard. Visited her mother's grave on the same grassy knoll.

Mariah cast a sheepish glance behind her. On the high bluff where she knelt lay the bones of generations of her ancestors, their unspoken hope a pressing burden.

Spinning, she scowled at Mother's tombstone. "It was Father's promise to make, yet you asked it of me?" She brought her fists down on her legs. "Why charge it to me? It's too heavy."

Oh Aki, why indeed?

Mariah knew the answer, one she'd never speak aloud. Her lighthearted father took one day at a time and lived as carefree as possible. He left responsible matters for Mother to tend, and when she died, the burden fell to Mariah. If Father had sworn to protect the land for Mariah and her children, he'd have died a failure. Mariah was her mother's only chance.

Gabriel Taber's jowly face and slack mouth flashed in her mind. He wasn't a God-fearing man, a fact that grieved her. No matter. She'd have to stop putting him off. The time had come to put her plan into motion.

With a shuddering sigh, Mariah pushed to her feet. Shading her eyes, she watched the Pearl River meander past on its way to places she'd never been. She wondered what it would be like to sail off the bank into the rippling brown water and go along for the ride. She'd cross her arms behind her head and float belly-up along the mud banks and sandy shores, the groves and cypress swamps, on past Jackson and down to the open seas—the inn and her promise be hanged.

Instead, she did what she'd always done. Girding herself under the oppressive weight of duty, she hoisted her lie and the promise to her shoulders and trudged to the tree where Sheki waited, his neck stretched so far toward a tasty bush his reins were taut enough to strum.

"Leave it, beast." Mariah pulled him around to a stump and mounted him bareback. "If you had your way, there'd be nothing green left in Madison County except for buttonbush, and then only because they're poison." She smiled to herself. Lucky thing they were bitter, or the gluttonous pony would wind up on his back, belly bloated, and stiff legs aimed for the sky.

Tangling her fingers in Sheki's mane, she whispered in his ear. He lifted his head and broke into a trot. Tensing her legs, Mariah tightened her hold on the little paint's neck.

"Kil-ia!"

Sheki's nostrils flared and his muscles gathered beneath her. He bolted, and Mariah curled close to his body.

Cold air blasted her face. She gulped and ducked her head. The wind tore at her scarf, the knot working loose from under her chin. The flimsy cloth trailed behind her until a sudden gust wrenched it away. She didn't dare turn loose to catch it.

They thundered past the birch grove and roared into the yard, scattering chickens and raising dust. Mariah slid to the ground bubbling over with a jumble of laughter and tears—until a flash of color caught the corner of her eye. Peeking over Sheki's back, she cringed and ducked her head.

Miss Vee and Tiller stood gaping at her from just inside the barn.

The ladder slid to the ground with a clatter, but Tiller hardly noticed. In all his years, he'd never seen a more fetching sight.

Mariah's dark eyes flashed and her chest heaved. Waist-length hair, tangled by the wind, puffed like shiny black tumbleweed around her delicate seashell ears. The deep flush of high spirits tinted her mouth and cheeks a glorious rosy hue. The genteel daughter of the innkeeper had become a wild and beautiful creature.

Defiantly meeting his stare, Mariah gathered her hair over one shoulder and lifted her chin. "I see you're finally starting to work."

Startled from his trance by her voice, he realized his lips had parted. He clamped them shut and nodded. "Miss Vee showed me where you keep the tools."

As if sprung into action by the sound of his voice, Miss Vee bustled toward Mariah. "Gracious, child. What have you been tromping through?"

Leaving the ladder, Tiller followed, stealing a peek at Mariah's feet. Clumps of mud clung to them in thick gobs, and red clay oozed between her toes. At least four inches of her hem was soaking wet.

"I—went for a walk," Mariah stammered. "Along the river."

Miss Vee's forehead crinkled. "Last we saw, you were talking to Rainy."

"Yes, I finished with him and decided to take Sheki out for a while."

"At this time of day?"

"I had a sudden impulse. It's such a nice, cool morning."

"Before your chores?" The older woman pressed, ignoring her explanation. "What were you thinking?"

Mariah's delicate brows lowered. "I was thinking to take a ride. Why are you questioning me?"

"Because it's not like you. With your father away, you have added responsibilities."

Mariah's fiery gaze flashed hotter. "I'll thank you to mind your business. I'll run this inn as I see fit."

Miss Vee's temper ignited to meet hers. "I don't understand your behavior, young lady. Something is quite off kilter." She scowled. "Just look at you, straddling a horse in a dress, showing off your knees to half of Mississippi. You have mud up to your ankles and grass stains covering the front of your skirt." She bent to dust off Mariah's garment. "Have you been crawling on the ground?"

With a sharp inhalation, Mariah yanked the fabric out of her reach.

"Certainly not."

Straightening, Miss Vee's chest heaved. "Mariah Bell, if your father was here, why he'd—"

Mariah glared. "Well, he's not! And try to remember you're not my mother."

Miss Vee drew back, flushed as bright as her hair. Shock and pain darkened her green eyes. "I hardly recognize you." Clutching her blotchy face, she whirled for the back door.

Snatching up her pony's leads, Mariah stomped inside the barn.

Captive, Tiller followed.

At the stall, she flung the door open and slapped the animal hard on the rump. "Hurry up, you worthless fat horse."

The pony startled then hustled through the gate like a chastened child.

Mariah slung the door closed, fastened it, then spun around—stopping with a muted cry at the sight of Tiller. "What are you doing in here?" She narrowed her eyes. "Why are you following me? Don't you have work to do?"

As surprised to be standing behind her as Mariah was to find him there, Tiller couldn't answer the first question. The second seemed a whole lot like the first, so he let it pass and went for the third. "I reckon I have plenty to do." He held up the hammer still clutched in one hand. "At the moment, I'm supposed to be up on your roof, but I wanted to make sure you're all right."

"Why wouldn't I be?" Her scowl would blister paint.

He shrugged. "I get the feeling you women don't usually go at each other like that." He nodded at the pony. "Or you and the horse."

Mariah's gaze dropped to the ground, and her pretty mouth puckered. Tears brimmed perilously close to spilling, and she chewed her bottom lip so hard Tiller winced.

He took a step closer. "Mariah?"

With a moan, she lunged to open the stall door and fling her arms around the horse's neck. "Oh, Sheki. I'm so sorry. Did I hurt you?"

Obviously deciding to forgive, the handsome animal stood still while Mariah pressed her forehead against the side of his face.

"Miss Vee's right. I don't recognize myself either."

Tiller took off his hat. "Is there. . .anything I can do?"

Mariah shook her head against the pony. "There's nothing anyone can do." She peeked at him. "Though I'd appreciate your pardon for our behavior. I'm ashamed we aired our grievance in front of a guest."

Tiller grinned and wiggled the hammer. "I don't qualify as a guest anymore. I'm officially part of this operation."

Mariah lowered her lashes, a faint smile softening her lips. "So it's all right to rail like shrews as long as we confine it to the staff?" She straightened, staring toward the house. "I suppose I'd best go mend things with Miss Vee, or she'll mourn herself sick. I do regret saying those things to her. She's been good to me since my mother died."

Tightening the grip on his hat brim, Tiller ducked his head. "I'm real sorry."

"Thank you." She smiled. "It's been two years, but I miss her every day." Mariah left the stall and brushed past him to lean against the rail. "Miss Vee's been the closest thing to a mother ever since. I can't believe I spoke so harshly to her."

Tiller nodded. "I suspected you two were more like family than anything else. I know she can't take your ma's place, but she sure does fret like one."

Mariah studied his face. "What about you? Is it true you don't have a family? A wife or mother somewhere who worries about you?"

"A wife?" He drew back. "Hardly. No one will have me." The familiar ache filled his chest. "As for my ma"—he quirked his mouth—"she'd run me off with a broom if I stepped one foot on her porch."

Mariah laughed. "I doubt that."

Grinning, he gaped at her. "Well don't. It's a fact." He sobered and shook his head. "I have family up in North Carolina that used to care about me a little. My uncle Silas and aunt Odell plus a few rowdy cousins and a handful of friends." He sighed. "But I haven't seen them in a good long while."

Mariah tilted her head. "How long?"

"Oh, about ten years now."

"Gracious. Why?"

Tiller offered a shaky laugh. "That's a long story, and I won't bore you with it."

Her steady gaze said he hadn't fooled her. "Tell me about them."

He tucked his chin. "Really?"

She nodded.

Crossing his arms, Tiller leaned against the stall in deep thought. "My folks are Lumber River Indians from a place called Scuffletown." He shrugged. "Come to think of it, I suppose I am, too. At least a part of me."

"You're Indian?" The fact seemed to please her. "With that crop of red hair?"

Tiller grinned. "That's the other part, I suppose." He feigned an accent. "The Irish."

With an air of fascination, she scooted closer. "Keep going."

"You're sure you want to hear all this?"

"Positive."

Her earnest answer stirred his heart. "I suppose Uncle Silas sticks out in my memory the most." Warmth he'd not felt in a while made him smile. "The old man could spin a yarn from here to China. Far-fetched tales about warriors, giants, and magic lanterns." He laughed. "I was nearly sixteen. Old enough to know better, but he had me believing most of the things he said."

Mariah giggled. "What about your aunt Odell?"

Tiller stared at the ceiling. "Ah yes, Aunt Odie. She worked magic with a frying pan the way Uncle Silas did with his stories."

He shot her a sidelong glance. "If I remember right, her cooking was almost as tasty as yours." He winked. "Not quite, but close."

She bumped him with her shoulder. "And what of the cousins?"

Tiller called out their names, ticking them off with his fingers. "There was Hooper. His brother, Duncan. Their little sister, Ellie." He grinned. "And Miss Dawsey Wilkes, who was Ellie's twin sister, but no kin to the rest."

She frowned. "That makes no sense at all."

"You're right, it doesn't, but I'll try to explain. You see, Ellie was raised by my aunt and uncle instead of her real parents, so the girls never knew they had a sister until they ran into each other by accident."

Mariah angled her head. "Are you making this up?"

Laughter bubbled up from Tiller's belly, the first genuine glee he'd felt in a while. "That story's a doozey and would take all day to tell." He waved his hand. "Don't get me started."

Mariah joined in the laughter. "It sounds fascinating. You'll have to make time one day to fill me in."

The warmth of her arm pressed against his. Sobering, he turned his head toward her, wondering how she wound up so close. "I sure will, if you want me to."

"I want you to." Her big brown eyes, inches away, lured him.

His breath grew shallow, and he couldn't draw air. The floor seemed to tilt, and his ears buzzed like they were stuffed with honeybees. He longed to stroke her cheek with the back of his hand, and his fingers twitched with the urge to touch her bottom lip. "Mariah, I—"

Behind them, the pony snorted and pawed the ground, jolting Tiller's heart. Blushing, he leaped to his feet. "Look at me dawdling again. I suppose I'd best get going. I've got a roof to mend."

Mariah glanced up with a shy smile. "By all means. Now that you're part of this operation, you'll have to toe the line. I can't have an idler on my payroll."

With ease that came of much practice, Tiller slid into his cocky role as smoothly as slipping on his boots. "Well, if you'll excuse me, ma'am..." He tossed his hat on his head, bowed, and turned to go.

"Tiller?"

He pivoted on one heel. "Yes, boss?"

"You should go up to North Carolina. Pay your folks a visit. Sounds like you're long overdue."

Tiller worked to keep his roguish grin in place, but his traitor mouth trembled. Drawing in his bottom lip, he scraped it hard with his teeth. "Nah, it's too late. After all this time, they don't remember my name."

THIRTEEN

Tiller's mama is dead?"

Hooper tensed. "I'm sorry to say it's true, Pa." For a moment, he wished they'd heeded Dawsey's inclination to wait a bit before they sprang the news, but with Pa sniffing around, the story was bound to come out.

Despite the dismal report, Hooper rejoiced at being home. Inside the tiny cabin, the folks he loved most in the world huddled in a tight circle around Papa's rocking chair. The cheery fireplace crackled, stoked by Ma to ward off the morning chill. The smell of breakfast hung so thick in the air, he could almost taste crispy bacon and golden, flaky biscuits. The only thing missing from the familiar scene was his younger brother, Duncan, who married a Lumber River girl and moved across the swamp.

Papa gripped the arms of his rocker. "So my poor brother's widow passed on?"

"Yes, sir. Aunt Effie's neighbors found her five days ago. We had to bury her right away." He glanced at the twins playing a board game around the table and lowered his voice. "She'd been gone a day or so when they found her. She died all alone, though I think she might've preferred it that way."

His eyes red-rimmed and moist, Pa sat forward in his rocker. "Effie perished more than a week ago, and I'm just now finding out?"

Hooper swallowed against the tightness in his throat. He hadn't shared the worst yet. "There were. . .complications, Pa. This is the quickest we could come."

"You couldn't send a wire?"

Hooper and Dawsey exchanged glances.

Before Hooper could answer, Pa lost interest in the question. "Poor old soul." He reached over his shoulder for Ma's hand. "Effie never had much of a life, did she, Odie?"

Mama shook her head. "She did without things most folks take for granted. Her plight grew even worse after Sol died, God rest him."

Papa's jaw tightened. "If he's resting, I don't see how. I'm ashamed to speak ill of the dead, but the truth is my brother didn't provide well for his family. He left Effie and Tiller penniless, living off the kindness of strangers and begging for crumbs of bread. It's no wonder Effie sent Tiller to live with us. She didn't want the poor lad to starve."

With a quick look at Dawsey for courage, Hooper waded in. "You've got it all wrong, Pa. The only one starving Tiller was Aunt Effie. She lived poor all right, but she didn't have to."

Papa frowned. "Don't talk foolish. No sane person would live Effie's life if they had a choice."

Ma nodded in agreement. "Papa's right. What are you saying, son?"

Hooper stared at their puzzled faces. "I'm saying Aunt Effie wasn't sane. Tiller's plight grew worse when his pa died, because Uncle Sol wasn't there to stand between the boy and his mother's greed."

The high color faded from Pa's wrinkled cheeks. "Come again?"

"I'm saying Aunt Effie was a miserly old woman who never spent a nickel she didn't pinch. She died richer than Ma's apple potpie."

Mama gasped, and Pa swung his chair around and stared.

"It's true," Hooper said. "The bed Aunt Effie died on was stuffed to bursting with money." They gasped, and he nodded. "A treasure in greenbacks and gold coin."

Ellie touched Hooper's arm. "How is that possible? Tiller was a bag of bones when he came here to live."

Hooper patted his sister's hand. "I remember. He couldn't keep his trousers on without a tight pair of suspenders."

A purple vein stood out on Papa's neck. "Effie's been squirreling away money since my brother died?"

Hooper snorted. "A far sight longer, considering her bulging nest egg. The old skinflint tucked nearly every dollar Uncle Sol earned in her cotton tick mattress. Besides being tight with her family's purse strings, she inherited a sizable fortune from her parents when they died. I doubt she spent a dime of it."

Papa stared around the circle with bulging eyes. "Which means. . ."

"Tiller's a wealthy man," Mama finished, her brows lifted to her hairline. "And he don't even know it."

Hooper nodded. "I've deposited the money in a Fayetteville bank in Tiller's name. It's sitting there waiting for him." His fists clenched. "When I think how Aunt Effie starved that boy, made him go without, I get mad all over again."

Lowering his face to his hands, Papa groaned. "All these years I've judged my brother a shiftless no-account, begrudging his wife and son the necessities of life. When all the time, his sin was not having the backbone to stand up to Effie."

"In fairness to Uncle Sol," Hooper said, recalling his own daunting encounters with the fearsome woman, "she was a mighty hard person to stand up to."

Papa began to cry quietly, the only evidence his quivering shoulders.

Mama glanced at Hooper, and he stepped behind the chair and wrapped his arms around his papa's neck. "Don't weep, sir. I feel mighty bad to be bringing you this news. I know how you've grieved for that boy."

"And shouldn't I grieve? It's my fault he ran off. At the first spell of trouble between us, I threatened to send him back to Fayetteville, straight into Effie's stingy arms."

He gazed up at Hooper with tears wetting his cheeks. "Son, it all makes sense now. No wonder the boy ran away. In his shoes, I'd be done with the lot of us, too."

Pa wiped his face with his sleeve. "I wish he was standing here now, so I could tell him he'll never have to go without again."

Ellie squeezed in behind him and kissed the top of his head. "You tried to find him, Papa. We all did."

He raised tortured eyes. "But we quit looking. We never should've stopped until that boy was home again."

Wyatt slid his arm around Ellie's waist. "Sir, my family searched for Nathan right alongside you. It's tough to find someone who doesn't want to be found."

Ma patted Wyatt's back. "Forgive us, dear. We get so caught up in mourning Tiller, we forget your brother's missing, too."

Wyatt shot her a wry glance. "You're being kind, Miss Odie. We all know Nathan's not missing. He ran away and hauled your nephew with him." He sighed. "Tiller was just a boy. Nathan was old enough to know better." He gripped the arm of Papa's chair. "Mr. Silas, if anybody's at fault, it's my little brother."

Pa wagged his grizzled head. "I suppose the days for blame is past, son. Ten years have come and gone since those two left the swamp. God forgive us, what did we do with the time?"

Ellie knelt at his side. "We built homes and bore children, pitched in to help Scuffletown recover from the war. It's been a busy time for us all, but things are quieter now." She glanced around the room. "Why can't we start our search again?"

Hooper gave her a tender smile. "Actually, that's why we're here. I aim to do just that. And this time I'm going to look until I find them."

Ellie's face lit up, and she shot to her feet. "I'll go."

Leaning to see around her, Hooper widened his eyes at Wyatt. "What do you say, old man? I'd like for you and Ellie both to come."

A tiny frown rippled Wyatt's forehead. "But, sugar. . .what about our boys?"

Hooper nodded at his wife. "That's one reason Dawsey's here. She's willing to stay behind and care for the twins."

Wyatt flashed Dawsey a grimace then pushed back his hair with both hands. "I don't know, Hoop. We could be gone for weeks. Dawsey doesn't realize what she's signing on for."

Ma pushed into the circle, worrying a tattered dishrag. "I'll help out, Wyatt. I'll go over to your place every day to untie her and put out the fires."

Dawsey's wide eyes swung to the boys. All four wore angelic smiles.

Hooper absently patted her shoulder, his attention turning to Ellie. "It's a long time to be away from your boys, little sis. I wouldn't ask if you didn't track a man better than a hound dog."

Pa shook his head. "There's nothing left to track. The trail is long cold."

"Maybe not." Hooper squatted in front of the rocker. "Aunt Effie's

99

neighbor spoke of a local fellow who went to see Effie a few months before she died. This man had just returned from a trip to Mississippi. He swore he saw Tiller strolling along the boardwalk in a town by the name of Canton."

Pa's eyes lit up. "You don't say?"

"Aunt Effie called him a fool among other names. She said he had to be drunk or seeing things because Tiller was dead and gone. That got him mad, so he's had plenty to say around town. I looked him up and talked to him myself."

"And?" Pa asked.

"I believe him. I think the man he saw was Tiller."

"Why do you set such stock in a stranger's opinion?"

"Because"—Hooper's gaze jumped to each of them in turn—"when the stranger called Tiller's name, he spun around to look and then ducked down an alley."

Excitement surged in the room like the tension before a storm.

"And Nathan?" Wyatt asked, his tone hopeful.

"Sorry, buddy. Tiller appeared to be alone, but if he's in Canton, Mississippi, you can bet Nathan's close by."

The corners of Papa's eyes crinkled the way they did when he was thinking. "I know where Canton is. About twenty. . .thirty days' ride on a good horse."

"Thirty days," Ma said. "That's a long time."

Hooper nodded. "Yes, it is. That's why we're taking the train. We'll book passage to Jackson then hire some horses. If we have to, we'll ride every inch of the state until we find a good lead."

Wyatt worried his bottom lip, his brow creased in thought. "Suppose Nathan and Tiller don't want to be found, Hoop? Did you consider that possibility? We're not looking for boys this time around. They're grown men and likely to be settled somewhere. Raising families."

Pa slapped the arm of his chair. "No sir, I don't believe that for a minute. Those two have been up to no good. Only shame will keep a man away from home and family this long." He sighed. "Still. . .we can't let that stop us."

He shifted his gaze to the glowing hearth. "Tiller may not want to be found—that wouldn't surprise me—but if the boy ever decides to come home, it'll start by learning he's welcome."

FOURTEEN

Mariah stuck her muddy foot under the spout and worked the pump's squeaky handle. Ice-cold water shot out in a burst, splashing her bare ankles. She squealed and jumped back then forced her toes under the flow, wiggling to wash the thick, dried clay from between them.

Next she washed the basket of lettuce she'd cut from the garden. She told herself she might as well pick a few heads while she was dressed for grubbing in the dirt. In truth, she was stalling while she found the right words to apologize to Miss Vee.

Shading her eyes, she scanned the rooftop until she found Tiller kneeling next to the side gable. As hard as she tried, she couldn't stop watching him.

He had rolled up his sleeves and unbuttoned his shirt since leaving the barn, probably once he climbed onto the sun-baked shingles. A dark circle of sweat moistened his back, and his shirttails flapped in the breeze.

She admired the pleasing way his chest appeared chiseled and his tanned skin glistened in the sun. Even more, she liked how he'd laughed like a small boy in the barn and then gazed at her so boldly. In his own way, Tiller McRae was more fetching than the sons of Tobias Jones.

Stop it, Mariah! Embarrassed, she tugged her attention back to washing her feet.

She may as well get such thoughts right out of her head. No matter how striking she found him, she needed a weak-willed nahullo. One she could lead by the nose and persuade to do her will. Swaggering, self-assured Tiller simply wouldn't do.

By his own admission, he lived the life of an aimless drifter with no family ties. Not exactly the sort of man to trust with the reins to Bell's Inn. Or with her heart.

Balancing on one foot at a time, she dried them on her dress. Giving the handle one last crank, she leaned to the spigot for a drink and saw Tiller from the corner of her eye, watching from the roof. By his appreciative stare and the way his hammer slowed, Tiller found her just as much the distraction. Mariah hid her smile and pretended not to notice.

Straightening, she started across the yard, glancing up in time to see Tiller miss the nail and hit his thumb. With a howl of pain, he shook the battered appendage then stuffed it in his mouth.

She covered her mouth to suppress a giggle and scurried across the yard to the back porch. Ducking through the door into the kitchen, she paused at the mirror to gape at her dirt-streaked chin and messy hair, mortified that she'd sat with Tiller in the barn acting the grand lady when she looked like a windblown wretch.

She needed to change her soggy, mud-splattered dress, but first she'd find Miss Vee and beg forgiveness.

"Mornin' again."

Mariah spun, clutching her bodice, and glared at Dicey grinning from the pantry. "Dicey Turner! Must you creep around all the time?"

Dicey tilted her head. "Since when is fetching the lard creepin'? Folks in this house mighty jumpy." Her startled gaze leaped to Mariah's tangled locks and filthy dress. Pointing as if Mariah might not be aware of her bedraggled state, she gasped. "Look here what the cat dragged in. What done happen to you?"

"Never mind. Just get on with the piecrusts then start kneading the bread. It'll be lunchtime soon."

Still staring, Dicey heaved the lard bucket to the counter. "Yes'm, but I hope you plan to wash up and change 'fore you start messin' about this kitchen."

Mariah smiled. "I'm going upstairs to clean up, but I'll come right back in to help." She started for the hall then turned. "When you're done with the dough, run out to the smokehouse and get a ham. If I'm not back in time, trim the fat for a pot of beans and put the rest in the oven. While you're there, bring in a link of venison sausage." Remembering Tiller, she glanced toward the roof. "Best make it three."

"Miss Mariah, you sure?" Dicey blinked her confusion. "It ain't like we got us a full house. Who gon' eat all that?"

Mariah sidestepped to the mirror again to wind a coil of hair at the base of her neck. "They'll come. I'm praying hard for guests."

"You praying for miracles."

"We need one," Mariah said over her shoulder. "The coffers are on their last breath. In the meantime, we have meat in store and a man on the roof working up a healthy appetite."

Dicey rolled her eyes. "Ain't nothin' healthy 'bout the way he eat. For a tall, skinny man, he got a reckless hunger."

Mariah's fingers stilled on her hair. "You really think he's too thin? I don't find him the least bit skinny."

Dicey cocked her head to the side and grinned. "Uh, huh. It's like that, is it? Jus' how does you find him?"

Tugging her eyes from the mirror and the slow flush crawling up her neck, Mariah turned. "Miss Vee's been reading to you from those trashy dime novels again. Now, where did she get off to?"

"She tending that old man. He finally decide to wake up."

"He did? Oh, Dicey, why didn't you say so?"

Dicey cocked her hip. "I jus' did."

Mariah hurried down the hallway to what she'd come to think of as the sickroom. Pausing at the door, she cautiously peered inside.

Miss Vee had a chair pulled up to the bed, her back and shoulders rounded as she leaned to feed her patient spoonfuls of what appeared to be oatmeal.

Otis Gooch sat up in bed, dutifully opening his mouth. He gummed the cereal with pursed lips, smacking disgracefully.

"Last bite," Miss Vee said then wiped his mouth as if he were a child. Standing, she placed the bowl on the nightstand.

Mariah slipped up from behind and caught her hand, stretching to whisper in her ear. "Forgive me?"

Miss Vee's rigid body relaxed. Her fingers twined with Mariah's and squeezed. "Look, honey. Our patient's on the mend."

Mr. Gooch lay propped against two pillows, a weak but contented smile on his face. "If my head didn't hurt so fierce, I'd swear the Almighty sent two ministering angels to escort me home." He chuckled. "But I reckon I'm still earthbound. If'n I was in heaven, you wouldn't be covered in muck, little missy." The man peered closer. "Though I'm thinking this one might be one of your angels, Lord, muddy or not. She sure looks like one."

Mariah smiled down at him. "No angel here, sir. Just a flesh and blood woman, uncommonly prone to frailties and faults." She glanced over her shoulder. "Just ask my dear friend."

Mr. Gooch winked. "Honey, you'll do just fine."

He held out his trembling hand and Mariah took it, settling in Miss Vee's vacated chair. The bony fingers felt fragile in her grip, and the wrinkled, paper-thin skin softer than silk to the touch.

"I can't tell you how grateful I am," he said. "You folks are like the Good Samaritan come to life right out of the scriptures."

Mariah shook her head. "Not at all. We're just the innkeepers. The real Samaritans were the men who brought you here and left without telling us their names. They saved your life."

He frowned and tilted his head. "One of them a red-haired fella? I seem to remember someone..."

Mariah patted his hand. "You must mean Mr. McRae. He's a guest here." She glanced at Miss Vee. "At least he was until we hired him on. He works for us now, so you'll be seeing him again."

"Well, that's good because I—" He grimaced, and his wobbly hand rose to his temple. "I want to thank him, too."

Miss Vee touched Mariah's shoulder. "Come along, sugar. We're tiring him."

Standing, Mariah stepped aside to let Miss Vee move closer to the bed. She pulled the extra pillow from behind Otis's head, easing him down. "You rest up, now. I'll brew a cup of feverfew tea for that headache."

Wincing, he shaded his eyes against the light. "I don't want you ladies fretting about the cost of my keep. I can pay you for your trouble. You can count on that." Struggling to sit up again, he waved his skinny arm. "I have money. Lots of it. My whole life savings is"—he strained forward, craning his neck to search the room—"s–somewhere."

His bleary gaze focused on a point across the room, and he lifted one bent finger. "There he is. That's the man I was talking about."

Miss Vee and Mariah turned toward the door, but no one was there. They gave each other knowing looks.

"Well, I'll be." The poor man seemed confused. "The fella' disappeared. Just like that." He blinked at Mariah. "Why's he all wet?"

Squeezing past Miss Vee, she gripped his shoulders and urged him against the bed. "Just rest, Mr. Gooch."

Grinning, he waved her off. "I ain't never been mister nobody, honey. Call me Otis."

Moaning, he relaxed as if suddenly spent, and then his eyelids flew open again. "Say, did I ever thank you nice girls for helping me?"

"I'll fetch that tea," Miss Vee said, backing away. She motioned for Mariah to follow and hurried from the room. In the hallway, she pulled Mariah toward the kitchen, whispering in a low voice. "I swear, that old man is a caution. Do you reckon he was already crazy, or can a bump on the head bring on insanity?"

Mariah bit back a smile. "Shame on you, Viola Ashmore. How can you speak so harshly about such a kindhearted old gentleman? I don't think Mr. Gooch is crazy." She shrugged. "A bit peculiar perhaps."

"A bit?" Miss Vee clutched her arm. "One minute he's talking to God like He's perched at the foot of the bed, the next he sees Jesus peeking around the corner."

"Is that really so bad? We should all be having more talks with God."

"Maybe so, but he's seeing things that aren't there and forgetting the rest."

Mariah glanced behind them and shushed her. "Mr. Gooch has a nasty bump on the head. I'm sure he'll be fine in a few days." She frowned. "I'm more concerned about the other thing he said."

"What other thing?"

"Didn't you see? He was searching for his money." Mariah pressed her fists to her temples and groaned. "Evidently, his attackers robbed him of all he had." Hot tears stung her eyes. "The poor old soul. He said it was his life savings."

Miss Vee shook her head. "It's a pitiful shame, that's what it is."

They reached the entrance to the kitchen, and Mariah followed her inside. Tiller glanced up from the table where he sat draining a tumbler of lemonade.

Dicey stood over him, ready to pour another glass as soon as he finished. "It must be blazing hot on that roof," she said, fanning him with a dishcloth. "This poor man be drenched in sweat."

Tiller had stumbled into Otis Gooch's room, looked fate in the eye, then tucked tail and ran.

The old man had recognized him. Pointed him out. Instead of numbering his days at Bell's Inn, Tiller could count his stay in minutes, maybe seconds, depending on what Otis told Mariah.

His hand shook as he raised his glass for another long swig of the tart drink. Looking everywhere but straight at them, he waited for the ruckus sure to come.

Climbing off the roof after he made the repairs for Mariah felt good. For the first time in years, he'd used his hands for something useful. Leaving meant she'd be back in the same rough patch where he'd found her, burdened with a broken-down inn. And he'd be back on the Trace, running from what he'd become.

Funny how the work he wasn't sure he should take on suddenly seemed like the most important job in the world.

"Miss Mariah, why you still sashaying around in them filthy clothes?"

Tiller stole a peek out of the corner of his eye. Dicey was right. Mariah wore the same dirty dress, the mud splatter dried to light patches and her hem a stiff gray circle around her feet.

He might've smiled if his situation weren't so dire. He'd never seen a woman so opposed to wearing shoes.

"I'm going up now to change, but lest I forget"—she tapped his shoulder—"Mr. Gooch would like to see you when he wakes up."

Tiller's heart sped up and his mind raced. So, that's how much time he had, as long as it took an old man to take a nap.

Odd how Mariah didn't sound angry. Maybe she handled things differently than most.

He scratched his head, trying to think. Could it be that Gooch didn't tell them what he knew, so he could run Tiller off himself?

Miss Vee chuckled, the sound grating on his taut nerves. "He wants to thank you, Tiller." She shook her head. "Again."

His puzzled frown bounced between them. "For what?"

The women laughed.

"He thanks us over and over for helping him," Mariah said. "Each time he wakes up, he repeats himself again. Poor soul can't remember a thing."

The mirth disappeared from Miss Vee's face. "I'm telling you, Mariah, he's worse off than we thought, and that whack on the head could be the cause." She pointed toward Otis's room. "The old codger has lost his memory right along with his good sense."

Tiller raised his head. "Mr. Gooch can't remember?"

Ignoring him, Miss Vee took a sugar spoon from the counter to scratch up under her mound of red curls. "You reckon we should fetch Doc Moony after all?"

Mariah's body tensed and her hands fisted. If she'd been drinking from a cup, the inn would be short another piece of china. "Oh, I don't think that's necessary. Not just yet. Let's give him a chance to heal. He's bound to be as good as new in a day or so."

With a strained laugh, she clutched the skirt of her dress and stared at the smear of grass stains. "For heaven's sake, I need to get out of this silly thing."

"Been telling her that all mornin' long," Dicey pointed out.

As Mariah rushed up the winding stairs, Tiller wondered why she'd picked that particular moment to listen.

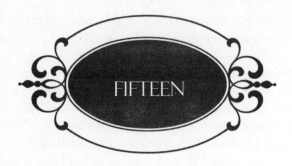

FIFTEEN

Mariah stripped off her dress then splashed her mud-freckled legs and sweaty face with cold water. Going downstairs to heat more would take too much time from her mission.

After washing off, she fumbled with the strings of a clean petticoat and barely laced her corset. Pulling on her stockings and a clean frock, she hurried out the door.

Five paces from the stairs she remembered her blasted shoes and ran back to slip them on. Taking the steps by twos, she raced across the parlor, not slowing until she reached the door to Otis Gooch's room.

In the light of Miss Vee's fears, she had to see him again to reassure herself that he was all right. If not, did she have the courage to call Dr. Moony?

Outside the door she spun, pressing her back to the wall. *Mother, what have you done to me?*

"Who—who's out there?"

There was nothing wrong with his hearing.

Mariah drew a deep breath and pasted on a smile. "Only me, sir," she trilled, edging into the room. She approached the bed, her trembling hands behind her back, praying Miss Vee was wrong. "Am I disturbing you?"

Otis seemed groggy, the effects of the feverfew tea. "Not at all."

He struggled to sit up, but Mariah hustled to his side and touched his shoulder. "Please don't rouse yourself. I won't stay long."

He smiled. "Stay as long as you like, missy. I'm grateful for the company." With a shaky finger, he pointed to the bowl and pitcher on the dressing table. "You wouldn't mind wetting a rag, so's I could wash my face?"

Mariah hopped up. "Of course not." Dipping a cloth in the steaming bowl, she wrung it out and handed it to him.

Otis buried his face in it and moaned. Concerned, she bent over him, but he emerged with a toothless grin. "There. Don't that feel better? I was getting a mite crusty." When he finished washing, including his neck and ears, he returned the rag with a contented sigh.

Relieved to see him acting so spry, Mariah sat back in the chair and crossed her arms.

Watching her, Otis leaned back and crossed his, too. "Whatever you're itching to say, you might as well get it said."

She launched forward, resting her hands on her knees. "How are you, Mr. Gooch? I mean, how do you really feel?"

His brows knitted. "Well, my headache seems lessened today." He reached for his bandage. "Still hurts to push on my wound, but I expect that's normal."

"Do you believe you're on the mend?"

Otis shrugged. "I ain't no doctor, little lady, so I'm not smart enough to say." He motioned her closer. "But I had me a talk with God, and He reminded me I'm in good shape either way." He pursed his lips and winked.

Mariah tilted her head. "It's interesting that you should mention a doctor because I was wondering—"

"If you're asking if I'm about to breathe my last, the answer is no. I'm too miserable to die." He gazed around the room. "And too hungry. Got any more of that oatmeal?"

The burden lifting from around her heart, she reached for his hand and gave it a squeeze. "We can do a whole lot better than oatmeal, if you think you're up to it."

He rubbed his stomach. "I'm up to it, all right."

"How does a bowl of beans and a link of venison sausage sound?"

He sat up straighter and rubbed his hands together. "With a square of buttered corn bread?"

She preened. "The best in Mississippi, or so I've been told."

His eyes lit up, the twinkle so bright it chased Mariah's fears to the shadows. "Fetch me them vittles," Otis said. "See if I don't make quick work of them."

Laughing, she patted his hand. "Give us a while to get it ready, and we'll give you a chance to prove yourself."

Plain tired of running.

Tiller braced his hands on each side of the washstand and leaned to stare at his ashen face in the mirror. The green striped walls of the cozy room, more like home than any place he'd slept in years, closed in around him, urging him to make a decision.

If Otis Gooch planned to accuse him, he'd just as soon have it done. Waiting for the gallows floor to drop from beneath him had his stomach twisted in knots. The old man had asked to see him, and it seemed like the perfect time.

"March down to that room," Tiller ordered his reflection. "Take a front row seat, and give Otis a good long look to be certain."

If the old man sat up and pointed the finger, Tiller had two options worked out in his mind. He could apologize. Lay his hand on the Bible Mr. Gooch set such stock in and swear he'd mended his ways. He'd confess that meeting him on the road had triggered a change of heart. He'd throw himself on Gooch's mercy and promise to repay every cent if only he'd keep his mouth shut to Mariah. If that didn't work, he'd deny the charge and swear the man's injury had addled his mind.

Tiller stilled as the second idea turned to soot and sifted away, leaving him nowhere to hide. What was happening to him? How could he consider confronting his doom? He must've fried his own brain on that blasted hot roof.

"Like I told you before," he said to his image, "I'm plain tired of running."

He dried his face so hard his whiskers chafed, threw the towel in the laundry bin, and smoothed back his hair. A haircut and shave were in order. He'd ask one of the women first thing in the morning. . .if he was still around.

With the slow easy pace of a man who'd made peace with his fate,

Tiller strolled down the hall to the last room on the left and peered inside. Clutching the doorpost, he drew back and stiffened to bolt.

"This is my lucky day," Mr. Gooch crowed. "Two visitors at once. Come in here, boy. Don't be shy."

Too late to escape, Tiller gritted his teeth and shifted back into sight. "How do, sir."

Mariah peered over her shoulder. "You'll be happy to hear Otis is much better today."

Sweating like Judas on judgment day, Tiller's courage waned. "I'll come back later. I don't want to barge in."

Otis waved his scrawny arm. "You ain't barging into nothing, and that lintel don't need you to hold it up. Get over here."

The urge to duck his head tugged at Tiller's chin. *No sir. No more hiding.* He raised it high instead and strode to the foot of the bed.

The closer he came, the wider Mr. Gooch's welcoming smile.

Tiller tried to smile in return, but his lips felt like wood. "How are you feeling, sir?"

"A sight better than yesterday, thank ye. I was just telling the little missy here that I'm feeling mighty hungry." He quirked his brows. "That's a good sign, ain't it?"

Mariah's merry laugh eased the tightness from Tiller's shoulders. "You're making up for lost time, I suppose."

Mr. Gooch nodded. "I don't remember the last thing I ate until those few paltry spoons of oatmeal."

Mariah squeezed his knobby hand. "Poor man." Her tone hardened. "Heaven knows how long those ruffians left you lying there helpless."

Tiller's stomach flipped, squashing his resolve. His shuffling feet itched to race for the door.

"I've been pondering that myself," Mr. Gooch murmured, scratching his balding head. "Do you suppose the men who brought me here could be the same gang who ambushed me to start with?" He bobbed his head. "You know, riding for help once their consciences started throbbing?"

Mariah spun with a little gasp. "Do you suppose Otis could be right, Tiller? Did we entertain the very devils who beat and robbed him?" Her pretty brow creased. "By the grace of God we didn't wind up sharing his fate." Realizing what she'd said, her hand rushed to her mouth. "Oh, Otis..."

All the starch seemed to drain from his wasted body. His shoulders slumped against the headboard, his watery gaze fixed on the ceiling while he stared down the awful news. "They got my money?" He flinched. "My horse and wagon, too?"

Her fingers pressed to her lips, Mariah nodded. "You had nothing when they brought you here. I'm so sorry."

Staring overhead, he gnawed the inside of his cheek. "Well, sure they took it. I'm a fool to think otherwise." He touched his head. "That's why they gave me this knot." He cut his eyes to Mariah. "Don't feel bad, little missy. I'd have figured it out for myself once my head cleared."

Regret twisted his features. "It took me the better part of my days to save that stash. All gone in a wink."

Shame torched Tiller's gut. Swallowing an apology along with rising bile, he decided on the spot to pay Otis back every dollar, however long it took.

Mariah scooted closer and caught Mr. Gooch's trembling hand. "I don't want you worrying about all this right now. Rest assured that you have a place here as long as you need one. If you decide to go home when you're able, we'll make sure you get there."

Otis shook his head. "I've been a traveling merchant for years. That rig was my home."

Tears spilled onto his gaunt cheeks. "I'll never understand how greed and pure raw meanness can drive one man to hurt another for gain." His swimming gaze sought Tiller's. "Then I run across a kindhearted saint like you, and my hope is restored." He smiled through his tears. "Young fella', I know you washed me, dressed me, sat by my sickbed, and I want to thank you."

Tiller's hand shot up. "You don't need to thank me." He quickly checked the bitterness in his voice and tried again. "Anybody would've done the same."

Mr. Gooch wagged his head. "Not with the care I sensed in your hands." He lifted his chin. "You're truly sorry about what happened to me, aren't you? I felt it in your touch."

Startled by the need to bawl, Tiller blinked and shoved his fists in his pockets.

"That's all right, boy," Mr. Gooch said. "I didn't mean to embarrass you. Just mighty grateful is all."

He pulled free of Mariah's grip and patted her hand. "I'd like to be alone for a spell if you youngsters don't mind. I need to ask God for strength to forgive before a root of bitterness springs up to defile my soul." He paused. "Fair warning from the book of Hebrews if anyone cares to look it up."

Mariah stood. "We'll leave you now. I'll come back soon with your lunch."

Tiller couldn't wait to get out the door. He didn't have the guts to look at Mariah, but he felt her watching him. Head down, he stepped aside at the threshold so she could go first.

"By the way," Mr. Gooch called in a frantic voice. "Did I ever thank you nice folks for helping me?"

Stopping so fast she skidded, Mariah cast a worried glance at Tiller. "Oh my," she whispered hoarsely then turned to Mr. Gooch with a weak smile. "Y–yes, sir. You sure did."

Otis released his breath on a ragged sigh and lay back in the bed. "Good. That's real good to hear."

Mariah's shoulders drooped as low as Tiller's as he followed her from the room.

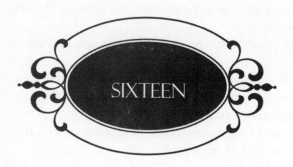

SIXTEEN

Tiller drove a nail into the final board of the new porch and stood up to survey his work. For a man more suited to working the soil than plying a hammer, he had to admit the even rows of cedar planks looked smart. Lifting his hat to wipe his brow, he glanced at his helper. "What do you think, Rainy?"

"Yes, suh." The boy grinned and bobbed his head. "Ain't nothin' wrong with this porch. We make a fine team, don't we, Mista' Tilla'?"

"You certainly do," a voice said from inside the back door. Mariah stepped out with a tray in her hand and tiptoed across the porch like a cat on coals.

Tiller chuckled. "It's all right to walk on it, Mariah."

She beamed. "I can't help it. It's too pretty."

Shrugging, Tiller laid aside the hammer. "I never thought of a porch as pretty, but I suppose this one will do. It'll look a lot nicer once we add the steps and get the rails up."

Mariah handed the tray to Rainy. "I can hardly wait to see it finished. What a wonderful surprise to find all this beautiful lumber behind the barn. Why, it's practically brand new."

Tiller glanced at the boy.

He smiled and ducked his head.

"I've brought you two your lunch," Mariah said. "You deserve a

114

special treat after all your hard work."

Tiller reached for a mug of cold lemonade and held it up. "I don't know if I deserve it, but I sure am grateful." He took a long swig then held out his hand to help Mariah down, brushing away sawdust to clear a place for her to sit. "Those sandwiches look mighty nice, too."

Rainy nodded. "Mista' Tilla' took the words right out of my mouth."

Tiller lifted one corner of the thinly sliced bread. "Corned beef?"

"Spread with fresh dressing I made myself." Mariah handed one to each of them and took one for herself.

Tiller took a hearty bite then winked at her. "Good."

She ducked her head and smiled. "Thank you."

They settled along the edge of the porch, eating together in silence. Tiller stole glances at Mariah, wondering how it was possible he'd known her for such a short while. It took him years to build a fortress around his heart. She'd scaled the walls in six short days.

He'd tried to fight his tender feelings, but the time for turning back was past. He was utterly besotted with her.

"Missy Bell, my sunflower patch be coming up nice," Rainy said. "They poppin' out now, so they'll have nice-sized heads before long."

"Budding already?"

"Yes'm." He gave her a timid smile. "I thank you for letting me plant 'em this year."

"I thought it was a fine idea." She wiped the corner of her mouth on a napkin. "I'd love to see them."

Rainy shoved the last quarter of his sandwich inside his bulging cheek and hopped to his feet, swiping crumbs from his baggy trousers. "I can show you right now."

Tiller laughed. "Rein it in, son. The lady's not done eating." He understood the boy's eagerness. He remembered the joy he once felt from growing a nice head of lettuce or a pretty rose.

Wrapping her sandwich in a napkin, Mariah stood. "I can finish while we walk." She motioned to Tiller. "Come go with us."

They crossed the backyard and took the little stone path to the garden gate. Rainy led them inside, past the tomato stakes and raised beds to the neat row of sunflower plants in the corner. A dozen flowers, each with new buds, stretched proudly toward the sky.

Mariah sighed. "They're going to be beautiful, Rainy."

He seemed to grow taller. "Much obliged, ma'am. Only I don't mind what they look like. I'm in it for the seeds."

Squeezing his shoulder, she laughed. "I sort of look forward to those myself." She gently stroked one of the small green and yellow knots. "Isn't it wonderful how they all face the same direction?"

Tiller took a second look. "How about that? I never once noticed."

"It's a mystery," Mariah said. "From the time the flowers form, they follow the sun across the sky, all in step like tiny dancers."

Evidently as ignorant of the facts as Tiller, Rainy leaned closer to stare. "Well, I'll be switched. They sho' is."

"Each morning they wake up facing east," Mariah said. "By evening, they're watching while the sun sets in the west. Then overnight their little heads swivel around again to greet the sunrise."

Rainy looked duly impressed. "Do tell?"

She nodded. "Once the flowers reach full bloom, they bow to the eastern sky until they die. My father told me they're watching for Christ's return." Sadness darkened her eyes. "He said the sunflower is our example to follow Jesus throughout our lives then go to our graves awaiting his return."

Silence stole over the garden.

Rainy glanced at the distant, haunted stare on Mariah's face and promptly squatted to pull weeds.

Tiller fought the urge to reach for her. Confused by her sudden gloominess, he cleared his throat. "Your father sounds like a fine man. I hope I'll get to meet him someday."

Her baffling sadness turned to great, swimming tears. Brushing them off her cheeks, she spun away.

"Mariah?" He touched her shoulder. "Did I say something wrong?"

"No." She sniffed and shook her head. "It's just a lovely memory, that's all. I suppose I'm missing him."

Shading his eyes, Rainy peered up from the ground. "I didn't go to make you sad, ma'am."

She held out her arms. "Oh Rainy, come here." He came, flushed and shuffling his feet, and she wrapped him in a tight hug. "You didn't do one thing wrong. In fact, it's a compliment to your skill." She held him at arm's length. "Your flowers are pretty enough to make a lady cry."

He flashed a pleased grinned. "Yes'm, Missy Bell. Thank you kindly, ma'am."

She released him and started back up the row. "You've outdone yourself with the rest of the garden, too. It's simply wonderful this year."

"That's on account of it ain't just me," Rainy said, falling in behind her. "Mista' Tilla' been out here, too. Most every day."

Mariah stopped short and turned. "You've been helping in the garden?"

Tiller released a shaky laugh. "Yes, but I take no credit. All the praise goes to Rainy."

"Ain't so, ma'am. Mista' Tilla' got sap for blood. This old patch rise up and clap when it see him coming."

Beginning to squirm under her bold stare, Tiller's cheeks warmed.

"I don't understand," Mariah said. "With all you've accomplished lately, how have you found the time?"

"It only takes a minute here and there."

Concern tightened her mouth. "You really don't have to take on the gardening, as well. It's too much."

He shrugged. "I do it because I like it. Of course, if you mind. . ."

"Mind?" A happy smile lit her face. "Of course not. As long as you two are happy with the arrangement."

"Don't bother me none," Rainy said, winking at Tiller. "We make a fine team."

The back door slammed, turning all their heads at once. Dicey walked to the edge of the porch, the back of one hand resting on her hip and the other shading her eyes. She scanned the yard in a slow arc, stopping when she faced the garden. "There you is, Rainy Boswell," she bellowed.

"She lookin' for me?" Rainy asked in a shrill voice. "Curse my no-account luck. I cain't get away from that burdensome woman."

Tiller chuckled. "What have you done now?"

"It ain't what I done. It's what she want. I wish I'd never struck no bargain to walk her home. She a heap more than a penny's worth of trouble."

Dicey sailed to the earth and bore down on them, her calico dress and white apron flapping in the breeze. She blew past the gate and chugged toward them in a rolling gait. "My daddy gon' be fit to bust, waitin' all day for his lunch. Where you been hidin'?"

"You know where I been. . .helping Mista' Tilla' with the porch."

She ground to a stop and cocked her hip. "I don't see no porch out here. If you growing one, I want me a peek at it." She snatched his sleeve. "Now come on." At the gate, she paused. "You done a fine job building that new porch, Mista' Tilla'. A mighty-fine job."

Tiller ducked to hide his smile. "Thank you, Dicey."

"You welcome."

Their bickering voices echoed across the yard until they slipped past the tree line and disappeared.

Mariah's lilting laugh eased Tiller's heart. "If Rainy was a bit older, they'd make a nice couple."

He laughed with her. "What are you saying? Those two would kill each other before the 'I do's' were said."

"Oh, I don't know." She grew thoughtful. "My mother was spirited, too. Not in the same way as Dicey, but at times she led my father a merry chase."

Tiller followed Mariah outside the gate to a wrought iron bench under a tall maple.

She sat and motioned for him to join her. "My parents were happy though." Her mouth softened and the corners quirked. "They loved each other very much, but I suppose they had to with all they fought to be together."

Tiller slid closer. "What do you mean?"

"Their union was frowned upon by both her tribesmen and my father's people. In fact, his grandparents in England got wind of the marriage and disinherited him."

"That hardly seems fair."

She shook her head. "It wasn't. These days, people are slightly more accepting. Back then, it was very hard."

Tiller couldn't stop watching Mariah worry the folds of her dress nestled in her lap. He itched to reach for her fingers, to cradle her hand and see if it felt as soft and warm as he imagined. "I'm glad folks are more agreeable now," he murmured.

"You are?"

Pulling his gaze from her hands, he squirmed on the seat. "Well, sure. Like I said, it's not fair to treat people so harshly. A person can't help who they love."

She straightened proudly. "It doesn't bother you that my mother was Choctaw?"

"Not a whit."

Tucking her chin, she tilted her head closer and lowered her voice to just above a whisper. "I'm pleased you feel that way, Tiller. I'm glad you're fair-minded and kind and not prejudiced against other cultures."

He swayed to meet her. She smelled of sawdust and tea leaves, green garden shoots, and the wind in her hair. "Mariah. . ." His hand inched toward hers. "Would you mind if I—"

A series of whistles split the air, like the call of a nearby bird.

Mariah leaped to her feet as if she'd been fired on, whirling to stare at the woods behind them.

Laughing, Tiller stood and steadied her shoulders. "Relax. It's just a silly mockingbird."

Still watching the verge, she shook her head.

Two men strode from the woods, one as tall as an oak, the other sturdy and broad.

Mariah stiffened beneath his hands.

Tiller took a second look and saw they were the sons of the Indian healer.

They strutted across the clearing with the sun on their faces, as proud as buck deer and confidence in every step. Two worthy specimens. The pride of the Choctaw.

Fisting his hands, Tiller clenched his teeth and exhaled his frustration.

Mariah watched the brothers come with mixed emotions. Though always happy to see them, their pleasing manner and striking looks affected her good sense.

She usually found herself staring at one or the other, hanging on their words, and laughing too loud at their jokes. Whatever power they had over her behavior, she felt uncomfortable to have Tiller in the mix—especially since he'd caught her at it once before.

"Halito!" Christopher called as they drew near.

"Halito!" Mariah shouted.

Justin's handsome face broke into a grin. *"Chim-achukma."*

"I am well. *Chishnato?"*

"Can't complain."

"What brings you? To barter for more corn bread?"

Chris laughed. "Our father sent us to ask about the old man."

"His name is Otis Gooch," Mariah said. "And thankfully he improves more each day." She frowned. "Though I wish Tobias had come himself. There is the matter of his forgetting things. His memory seems a little shaky."

Justin, in training to be the tribe's next healer, tilted his head. "He's well on in years, Mariah. I doubt it has much to do with his injury, but I'll mention it to Father."

Chris placed his arm around Mariah. "How are you, Lotus Flower? Looking lovely, I must say." He leaned to peer at her feet. "I see you're wearing your shoes today."

Mariah's cheeks warmed. She'd grown up alongside the brothers and their familiar behavior, but Tiller had no way of knowing Chris meant no harm. She lowered her shoulder and let his arm slide away. "Do you remember Tiller McRae?"

"I believe so." Justin stretched out his hand. "You're staying at the inn, aren't you?"

"Yes." Tiller shook both their hands. "But not as a guest. Mariah put me on the payroll."

She nodded eagerly. "Tiller's making our repairs, and doing a wonderful job. Wait until you see the new porch."

Chris pointed over their shoulders. "Right here at the back door? Well, let's go see."

"It's not finished," Tiller said. "It lacks steps and a rail."

Mariah glanced at him. He seemed less than eager to show off his work.

She smiled at the brothers. "I'd ask if you're hungry, but it's a pointless question."

"Well. . ." Justin rubbed his stomach. "It's a mighty long walk from our place to yours."

Mariah laughed. "Follow me, and I'll make you a corned beef sandwich. While you're here, I'll introduce you to Mr. Gooch. He's a very nice man."

"Sure," Chris said. "But will he remember meeting us?"

Mariah punched his arm. "Oh, stop."

Tiller lagged behind on the walk to the house, so Mariah wound up flanked by the burly brothers, sparring and vying for her attention as they always did. Sensing Tiller watching their backs, she didn't enjoy the flattery as much as usual.

She showed off the porch, careful to brag on Tiller's workmanship.

Chris and Justin ran their hands over the wood then climbed up and tested the strength of the braces with little hops. They seemed fittingly impressed by Tiller's skill.

As Tiller helped her onto the porch, he leaned close to her ear. "No one ever taught those two how to button their shirts?"

She pushed down the laughter bubbling inside. Self-assured Tiller McRae was jealous!

"Be thankful they're wearing shirts," she whispered back then led the procession to the kitchen.

Tiller pulled down a glass from the shelf. "I'll just grab another serving of lemonade then get back to work."

Mariah shot him a little frown. "Can't it wait? We'd love to have you join us, and I know you have room for more corned beef."

"Nah," he said, pouring from the pitcher. "I'd like to finish that porch before nightfall."

"Are you sure?"

His mouth a grim line, he tipped his hat and backed out the door.

Watching the brothers devour the rest of the beef, Mariah mulled over Tiller's downright unfriendly behavior. She'd never seen him less than charming, though she'd learned to spot when it wasn't genuine.

Her first guess, that he resented her relationship with the boys, was the only explanation she could conjure. The thought made her smile.

Chris slapped the table in front of her with his broad hand, the sudden noise nearly firing her out of her corset. "What's so funny, Lotus?"

Leaping, she gripped her pounding heart. "Christopher! You mustn't do that."

Justin shot Chris a wicked grin. "That wasn't a funny smile, brother. More of a cunning smile. Tell us, Flower. What evil thoughts were you thinking?"

Heat flashed up her neck. "Oh, stop. You two are scandalous." She stood and faced the counter with a whirl of her skirts. "Besides, a woman never tells, Justin. I should think you'd know that by now."

She poured three glasses of lemonade while regaining control. By the snickering and shoving behind her, the boys seemed certain her smile had something to do with them. Wouldn't they be surprised to know it didn't this time?

Busying her hands at the counter, Mariah pondered her distressing predicament. Three special men within the sound of her voice—thoughtful Justin, with his strong arms, broad chest, and beautiful brown eyes that pierced her soul; uncommonly handsome Chris, confident and daring, lighthearted and funny with a winsome smile; and Tiller—

Her breath caught remembering the yearning in his light green eyes, his boyish face so close she counted blond whiskers mingling with the dark red beard on his chin.

All pleasing suitors, all interested, yet she wasn't free to choose any one of them.

Tiller's irresistible allure frightened her the most. She needed a man she could count on to stay and protect the inn, one she could bend to her will. His need to float high and free like a dandelion seed clashed with her sense of family and strong ties to the land.

Even if Mariah could ground him long enough to marry her, she had no hope of holding him down. At the first strong wind, he'd lift to the sky and drift away again.

She took a deep breath and forced a bright smile before turning to serve the drinks. Her head should be busy with more pressing matters than fending off the wrong beaus. Like feed for the livestock and food for the guests she fervently prayed would arrive. Providing the necessities for her household, for that matter.

Not to mention persuading Gabriel Tabor to marry her before her dreadful secret blew up in her face.

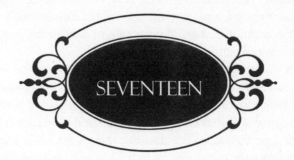

SEVENTEEN

Six noisy men crowded around the breakfast table, never knowing God had used them to answer Mariah's prayers.

They'd checked in the night before, cash in advance, and she quickly sent Rainy to buy eggs, shortening, and a rack of bacon. The merchant had only scraps of sowbelly left, but the box of ends and pieces would have to do. So far, she'd heard no complaints. They were eating too fast to notice.

She set the platter of biscuits on the table, hoping there'd be enough to go around. Glancing at the meager bowl of scrambled eggs, made without cream or butter, she winced. Father's boast that a room at Bell's Inn came with the finest breakfast in the state echoed in her mind, flooding her with shame. The inn's reputation centered on her cooking skills. Whatever the cost, she had to find a way to get the supplies she needed.

It was an unjust cycle. With the last hog slaughtered and the cows sold, she needed money to buy most of her provisions. How could she fulfill her father's promise if there weren't enough lodgers to fill the coffers, especially now that she'd emptied her savings to ward off Dr. Moony?

Mariah grew weary with barely scraping by. Breakfast was the hardest meal to come up with, and the situation got worse every day.

Rainy's garden helped with lunch and supper, but the smokehouse was nearly empty. Miss Vee and Dicey had started to watch her with anxious eyes.

Even worse, Tiller had noticed the lack. He took skimpy portions at every meal, covering his plate when she offered him seconds, insisting he couldn't hold another bite. Yet she caught him in the garden after supper, peeling and eating cucumbers.

Mariah chastened herself again for not riding out to see Gabe. She'd have to stop putting it off. Nothing would change until she did.

"Little lady, you got any more of these larruping good biscuits?"

She dropped a dishcloth on the three she'd saved for Tiller and turned with a pretty smile. "Mr. Lenard, it does my heart good to see such hearty appetites, but you've eaten the last one available, I'm afraid."

Scooping a spoonful of eggs onto his plate, she added a few extra pieces of bacon. "See if this won't fill up your last hollow spot."

Mr. Lenard grinned as if she'd offered him treasure, his bushy mustache fanning. "Much obliged, miss." He took two bites of the eggs and glanced up. "Any chance there might be more biscuits tomorrow morning? If so, I'd be willing to stay one more night."

Mariah's heart soared. "If you gentlemen are here in the morning, I'll make you a double batch." She patted his back. "Along with butter and homemade peach jelly."

"You've got a bargain," he said, his eyes lighting up. "Put us down for one more night."

His companions, their faces buried in their plates, mumbled agreement around mouthfuls of food.

Near tears at the unexpected blessing, Mariah busied herself at the sink. Maybe her cooking was the key to saving Bell's Inn after all.

Once she got her guests fed and out the door to Father's favorite fishing hole, she crossed to the larder and took her last three eggs out of a wicker basket for Tiller. Pouring in the few drops of cream she had left in the house, she beat them good and poured them over bacon fat in the skillet.

By the time she had them nicely set, Tiller breezed through the back door.

She met him with an eager smile. "Good morning. It's about time you showed up. Hurry and wash your hands. Your breakfast is getting cold."

Tiller hooked his thumb behind him. "Already washed up at the pump." He gazed around the empty kitchen. "Where is everyone?"

She quirked her brows. "Dicey's late again. I'm sure she'll turn up eventually. Miss Vee's upstairs cleaning. Our guests are down by the Pearl, yanking catfish for supper."

Happier to see him than she ought to be, her heart felt as light as the wind. She laughed. "With the stampede through here this morning, you almost lost your share."

Concern tightened his face. "If someone else is hungry, I can wait till lunchtime."

Mariah bit her lip, wishing she'd picked her words more carefully. "As hard as you work, mister? No one in this house deserves a hearty breakfast more than you."

In the time Tiller had been at Bell's Inn, he'd transformed the place. No more loose rails. No squeaky boards, upstairs or down. Chipped paint was gone and a new coat applied. Gray, crooked posts had turned to shiny, whitewashed columns. With every day that passed, he brought the inn nearer its former glory.

"In fact"—she nodded for him to sit and handed him his plate with a grin—"you're the only one who got cream in his eggs."

His green eyes flashed with alarm. "You're out of cream, aren't you?"

Heat rising to her cheeks, Mariah lowered her lashes. "That's not your concern." Trying hard not to cry, she twisted her mouth to the side and nibbled the inside of her cheek.

Tiller stood and gripped her shoulders. "It might be true that it's none of my business, but don't tell me what to be concerned about." He lifted her chin. "Or who."

Mariah met his eyes. "I'm no stranger to lack, but we always pull through." She wriggled free and brought his biscuits, placing them on his plate. "It's always a little tight through winter and spring. Once the roads dry up, I won't have a single empty room to let."

Not easily put off, Tiller caught her wrist and gently turned her around. "I believed you when you said I'm part of this operation now. To be honest, Mariah, it feels grand to be part of something good." He lowered his head to make her look at him. "So, if there's anything I can do to ease that frown from your pretty brow; say the word, and I'll bust a gut trying."

His tender words spread warmth through her heart. "Oh, Tiller. That's the nicest thing to say." Despite her resolve, she leaned into him. Nestled close to his chest, she felt safe, comforted.

The nearer she pressed, the tighter Tiller's arms drew her. His fingers touched the base of her neck and slid to her chin, pulling her face up to his. His searching eyes consumed her, and the warmth of his quick breath fell on her lips.

Mariah slid from his arms, keenly aware of a sudden emptiness. "I can't do this."

Worry creased his brow. "I didn't mean to. . . I wasn't—"

She spun away. "I can't be with you."

On her heels, he followed her to the counter. "Why not? You like me—I know you do."

She stepped away and crossed her arms. "It's not enough."

"It's a start." He ducked low to see her face. "I'm not asking to marry you, Mariah. I just want to court you a little. Find out if we're suited for each other."

She tightened her lips and turned her head to the side.

Tiller teased the top of her hand with his finger. "Do you want me to wait and ask your pa? Is that it? Because I don't mind waiting."

Frowning, she jerked away. "You're wrong for me, Tiller McRae."

Anger flashed on his face. "Why do you think so?"

"Because you're a dandelion," she spat.

"A what?" His voice came out shrill. "Woman, you're not making any sense."

Her fury rose to meet his. "You live like the wind, with no ties to anything. The roots you shun have me bound to this place heart and soul."

Understanding softened his eyes. "Mariah, there's more to me than an aimless drifter. If you'd take the time to get to know me—"

Tears washed over her cheeks in an unexpected flood. "That's just it. I'm out of time." Darting past him, she bolted for the door.

Tiller watched Mariah go with sickening dread. Every step she took pounded deeper regret into his wounded soul. He'd felt the same empty sorrow while fleeing Scuffletown, a sense of sudden, irreplaceable loss.

What had she meant by "out of time"? It could only mean she planned to send him packing now that he'd finished most of the repairs.

Tiller slapped the counter so hard his palm stung. He'd miss the hard work. The garden. The little room he'd made his own. Teasing talks with Miss Vee and Dicey. Long walks along the Pearl with Mariah.

Without her, he'd miss the childlike pleasure of a new porch. Bible lessons from a nodding sunflower. Bare feet and muddy toes.

In a rush of certainty, Tiller knew he couldn't leave her. He belonged with Mariah as surely as they both belonged at the inn. He had to find a way to make her believe it.

Reaching the back door in purposeful strides, he yanked it open.

Mariah stood on the top step, watching a big man climb down from his wagon.

Tiller tensed, his eyes jumping to the hammer he'd laid outside the door.

Mariah didn't seem threatened, though she drew back her shoulders and stiffened her spine. "Morning, Gabe. Did you read my thoughts?"

The man's bulging stomach reached the steps before him, his large, drooping mouth seconds later. Hauling the rest of him closer, he hitched up his pants and tilted his head to the side. "I ain't read nothing, Miss Mariah." His bushy brows drew to a frown. "You know I can't read."

She laughed as if he'd said something funny. "Oh, Gabe. I just meant that I was thinking about you, and here you are."

"You was?" He drew in his fat bottom lip, no small feat, and slurped, catching a string of drool before it escaped down his chin.

"I was indeed."

"Well, I'll be." A leer replaced his befuddled stare. He didn't have enough sense to hide his lurid thoughts. "I've been thinking about you, too."

The garden gate squealed on rusty hinges, and Mariah's head swiveled toward it.

Miss Vee puttered along the path with a basket of vegetables, headed for the house. Raising her head, she missed a step then came to a full stop, staring at Mariah and her guest.

With a quick glance at Tiller, Mariah took the steps to the ground and linked her arm with Gabe's. "Walk with me."

"Sure thing." His heavy gaze fixed on Mariah like she'd asked him to supper and she was the bill of fare. "Where to?"

Tugging his bulk into motion, she ignored his question and hurried him along beside her. "I've been meaning to ride out and check on you and Mr. Tabor. How is your father's health these days?"

They strolled past Gabe's rig, their voices still carrying but not their words.

Miss Vee reached the porch, stopping with one hand on the rail to stare after them. "My eyes tell me Mariah just left with Gabe Tabor hanging off her arm like a bloated tick. My common sense can't believe it."

Tiller blew out a breath. "Your common sense lost the bet."

"What's she doing hugged up to the likes of him?"

Leaning for the hammer, Tiller wiped it clean with the tail of his shirt. "I was wondering the same. Who is he?"

Miss Vee pursed her lips like she wanted to spit. "Little vermin owns the neighboring farm. At least he will when his ailing pa dies. More's the pity. Won't be long before Gabe runs that place underground."

Tiller took the basket from her hand. "Why's that?"

"He's simpleminded. Lacks the sense to keep his boots strapped. His daddy does all but wipe his nose for him." She shook her head. "Gabe makes it hard to feel sorry for him though. He's full to the brim with mischief."

Tiller stiffened and stared toward the river just as their bobbing heads disappeared down the sloping bank. "Should I go after her?"

"Mariah can take care of herself. She knows how to handle Gabe." Miss Vee frowned over her shoulder as if battling second thoughts. "But if she's not back soon, you and that hammer might want to take a stroll." Patting Tiller's shoulder, she pulled his gaze from the Pearl. "Have our fishermen returned?"

"No ma'am. Not yet."

She grinned. "I hope that means catfish for supper. I think I can scratch up enough meal for a nice creel of fish. Enough for a batch of corn fritters, too, if we're lucky."

"That sounds pretty good on an empty stomach."

Her green eyes widened. "Mariah didn't fix your breakfast?"

"She did." He glanced toward the river. "I got a little distracted from my plate."

With a sympathetic smile, she tugged on his sleeve. "Let's go see if it's fit for warming. After you eat a bite, you can help me give Otis a bath. It's been a week since his last one. The poor man's ripe as a split fig."

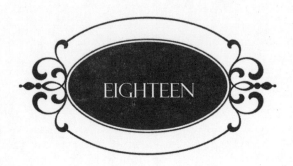

EIGHTEEN

Still wary around Otis Gooch, Tiller followed Miss Vee inside his room with a sloshing pan of water. Each time Tiller saw him, he wondered if that would be the day Otis remembered.

He slept drawn up on his side with his face to the wall, his scrawny behind jutting halfway off the bed. They drew near, and Tiller decided Miss Vee was mistaken. Otis had passed ripe days ago. Warmed by the fire they kept stoked for the thin-skinned old man, the air sagged with the smell of rotted armpits.

Miss Vee made a face.

Tiller grimaced and shook his head.

She nudged the side of the mattress with her knee. "Come forth, Lazarus. It's time for your bath."

Otis rolled toward them, his toothless mouth a gaping maw. Drawing in a wheezing breath, the tail end of a snore, he coughed and mumbled.

When his body relaxed into sleep again, Miss Vee banged the bed harder. "Come on, now. Time to wake up."

One eye opened a slit; then the other followed suit. "Mornin', good lady."

"Morning is said and done. It's nearly lunchtime."

He frowned and scooted up on his pillow. "Did I miss breakfast?"

She shook her head. "You ate hearty and enjoyed every bite. Don't you remember?"

He didn't answer, but doubt swam in his eyes.

Tiller scooted past her to set the water on the table. "Are you ready to get clean?"

His wrinkled face lit up. "Howdy, Tator."

"It's Tiller, sir."

He held up his crooked finger. "I was close. I knew it had to do with growing things. How are ye, son?"

Tiller grinned. "I can't complain."

Otis scratched his wiry head. "I sure could, but complaining don't do any good." He motioned with his fingers. "Come close and I'll tell you a secret, boy."

Trying not to breathe through his nose, Tiller leaned in. "Yes, sir?"

Otis squinted at him. "Did you say your name was Tiller?"

Biting back a smile, he nodded.

"Well, Tiller, I learned some time ago that a grateful heart will take you miles farther than grumbling." He nodded firmly. "I'll tell you something else, too. This old heart has plenty to be grateful for."

Tiller stared in disbelief. The man was penniless and sleeping in a borrowed bed. He was dressed in another man's nightshirt with his head bashed in and strangers tending his needs. As far as Tiller could see, he didn't have one thing going his way. What could he possibly have to be thankful for?

"Let's get on with the washing," Miss Vee said, throwing another log on the fire.

While Otis chattered endlessly, Tiller got him shucked and scrubbed down the best he could. Discreetly holding her nose, Miss Vee traded him a clean union suit for the soiled nightshirt.

Holding the one-piece garment in front of Otis, Tiller opened and closed the button-flap drop seat in back, as if demonstrating the ease of use. He glanced toward Miss Vee, who was warming her hands by the fire, and they shared a quiet chuckle before Tiller helped him to slip it on his frail body.

Otis beamed. "I reckon nightshirts are more in fashion, but there's nothing like a union suit for keeping a body warm." He stretched to see around Tiller and called to Miss Vee. "All done, dear lady. You can turn around."

She crossed to them and lifted the pan of dirty water. "Will you be needing anything else?"

"Not a thing. I'm much obliged for the clean clothes." He cut grateful eyes up to Tiller. "And the bath."

Tiller smiled down at him. "It's nothing. No trouble at all."

He reached to take the dirty water from Miss Vee, but Otis caught his arm. "The Lord wants you to know He don't see all you've done for me as nothing, and He's in charge of settling accounts. He said to tell you so."

Tiller's head began to roar. The gnarled fingers circling his wrist shot sparks to his flesh like cotton socks on a wintery morn. Unable to move a muscle, he stilled, watching Otis.

"When you do the will of God from your heart, you're doing service to the Lord, not to men. And God will reward each of us for the good we do." Otis nodded and released him. "It's true. The Good Book says so."

Warmth flooded Tiller's body, and weakness shook his knees. He reached for the tub Miss Vee held out, fearing he might not have the strength to carry it.

She seemed unaware of his distress, but the old man's kind eyes followed him across the room.

Miss Vee paused at the door. "I'll be back in a while with your lunch. We'll make it something so special you're not likely to forget."

Otis smiled, but he still watched Tiller. "You come back in here after lunch, boy. We'll continue our little chat."

With a hesitant half nod, Tiller followed Miss Vee into the hall.

"What was that?" he asked breathlessly once he'd put some distance between himself and the room.

She lifted her brows. "What was what?"

He pointed. "You didn't hear? Didn't feel. . ."

"All I could manage to do in there was smell." She chuckled. "We'll have to do better by him from now on, or we'll miss that reward he keeps crowing about." Turning the corner into the kitchen, she laughed aloud. "I'm just glad it's God who's keeping score and passing out prizes. Left to Otis, he wouldn't remember long enough."

Dazed, Tiller jumped when Mariah opened the back door.

Ashamed that he hadn't thought of her well-being once they got busy with Otis's bath, he breathed a relieved sigh that she'd returned safely.

She stepped over the threshold, a basket overflowing with bright red berries on her hip. "Look what we found. A big patch of wild strawberries. Aren't they nice?"

Miss Vee grunted. "I saw that deplorable Gabe Tabor. What did he want?"

Mariah dunked her basket in a pan of fresh, cold water, drew it out and shook it, then rested it on the counter. "Did you know the fields in the South were once covered by these? Like a great red blanket spread out for miles. Mother told me about seeing them as a child. She called it a glorious sight." She gathered a double handful and dropped them into a bowl. Bending under the counter, she rummaged in the cutlery jar and withdrew a paring knife.

"What were you thinking to go off alone with that man?" Miss Vee persisted. "What was he doing here?"

Mariah ducked her head. "If you must know, he asked me to go on a picnic."

Miss Vee's mouth fell open. "For heaven's sake. I hope you told him what bank of the Pearl to jump off."

Mariah turned the color of the glistening fruit in her hand. "I told him I'd love to go." She began to cut thick slices into a bowl on the counter. "In fact, I'm making a pie for the occasion."

Rendered speechless, Tiller stared. He could almost accept the Choctaw brothers as rivals. Any fool could guess what a woman might see in them. But the gangly, potbellied dullard with a lustful glint in his eye? Impossible.

Evidently, Miss Vee shared his thoughts. "Mariah Bell. Please tell me you jest."

Mariah frowned. "Oh, stop. He's not so bad. His father's an unreasonable old toad, but Gabe can be quite nice when he wants to be."

Miss Vee hissed through her teeth. "Gabe Tabor couldn't be nice tied up and knocked unconscious. That son of a toad is twice as warty as his father. At least the elder Tabor has some semblance of morals."

Mariah wiped her hands on her apron. "For pity's sake. It's just a picnic. Besides"—she shot an angry glance at Tiller—"I won't discuss my personal life in front of the hired help."

He winced and started for the door. "I'll just get on back to work."

Miss Vee clutched his sleeve as he passed. "No, you won't. We all know you care about this thick-headed girl as much as I do." She glared at Mariah. "Tiller stays. I want him here with me to help talk sense into you."

Mariah whirled to the sink. "There's nothing more to talk about."

Miss Vee gripped her arms from behind. "Honey, can't you see how much you've changed? Overnight you've become a stranger. The sensible girl I know wouldn't let that horrible man stand in her shadow, much less court her." She gave her a little shake. "Tell me what happened. What crawled under your skin? You can tell an old friend." She glanced back at Tiller. "And a new one who seems mighty concerned about you right now."

Mariah stood in silence.

Miss Vee tried to turn her around.

Drawing in her shoulders, she shrank farther away. "I simply refuse to talk about this."

Going red in the face, Miss Vee gave Mariah's back a determined nod. "Very well. Your father will be home soon. We'll see what he has to say about Gabe as a fitting suitor." Grit in her fiery glare, she pursed her lips at Tiller. "Mark my words. John Coffee will set this mess to rights in a Mississippi minute."

Avoiding the back door, Mariah hurried around to the front of the house and slipped inside on tiptoes.

She'd heard Tiller hammering in the barn as she passed. Her six sunburned guests sprawled on benches near the garden, resting their full stomachs after lunch and swapping fish stories. Dicey's high-pitched chatter drifting from the kitchen told her Miss Vee must be with her, the two of them clearing the dishes.

The only one left was Otis. She'd slip by him then sail to her room and scour the hand Gabe Tabor held, scrub the cheek his wet lips kissed. On second thought, she'd strip and scrub from head to toe, since there wasn't an inch of her his roaming eyes and leering grin hadn't bared.

Mariah crossed her arms protectively and shuddered. Easing past

Otis's room, she lifted her skirts and prepared to dash for the parlor stairs.

"Whoa, missy. Could I trouble you for a minute?"

Groaning inside, she froze. She considered pretending she hadn't heard, but her conscience wouldn't allow it. Taking three steps back, she peered into the room. "Yes, sir? Do you need something?"

He motioned her inside. "Just a spare second, if you have it."

She wavered, every nerve in her body screaming for the comfort of her room.

Otis smiled and motioned again. "Just a smidgen of your time. I won't keep you long."

Pushing aside her distress, she approached the bed with a weak smile. "All right, I'm here. Now what can I get for you?"

"Nothing for me." He flashed his gaping grin. "This here's about you, little missy."

Mariah frowned and cocked her head. "Me?"

Sobering, he nodded and gripped her hand.

The room dimmed, despite the sudden flame that roared up in the hearth. She tried to glance toward the fire, but Otis's somber gaze held her.

"The burden you carry ain't your load to bear. I'm supposed to tell you so."

A rushing sound filled her ears. "W–what?"

His kind eyes glowed with compassion. "Like a tender shoot pushing to the surface, truth always seeks the light." He shook his head. "You can't keep the secret you guard so close, honey. It's bound to come out."

She fought to look away from him but couldn't. Stumbling backward, her grasping hands searched for the bedpost to hold her up. "What makes you think I have a secret?"

With a knowing smile, Otis pointed up in the air. "'Blessed be the name of God for ever and ever: for wisdom and might are his. . . . He revealeth the deep and secret things: he knoweth what is in the darkness, and the light dwelleth with him.'"

Following his finger, Mariah gaped at the low ceiling. Tingly hairs rose on her neck and the backs of her arms, and her heartbeat pounded in her ears. "That's impossible. How could you know anything about me?"

Otis shrugged. "I don't. Not really. God don't always provide me with the details." He gave her a wink and a warm smile. "Just enough to pass on the message. . .and to pray." He held out a trembling hand. "Can I pray for you, little missy?"

Afraid to take her eyes off him, Mariah backed to the door. When her groping fingers closed around the frame, she launched her body into the hall and streaked for the parlor. Taking the stairs by sets of two, she hurled herself into her room and bolted the door.

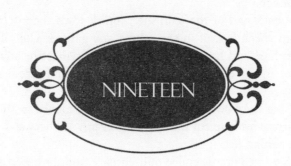

NINETEEN

Rowdy laughter and a curious commotion drew Mariah to her bedroom window for a peek.

The men had carted the dining room table outside under the big oak and spread it with a tattered white tablecloth. Like a colony of ants, they paraded single file between the table and the house, bringing chairs, napkins, and sloshing pitchers of drinks. The last item to arrive appeared to be a brightly colored relish tray, sectioned by green pickles and olives, purple beets, and quarters of sliced red onion.

Mr. Lenard, the lodger she'd promised a double batch of biscuits in the morning, settled a fiddle to this chin and raised his bow. Music filled the air, and Dicey, on her way from the house with a platter of sliced bread, broke into a little jig. Smiling, she danced across the yard to the table and delivered her tray.

Mariah leaned to search the yard for Tiller. She found him standing over the fire pit, tossing catfish fillets into a kettle of roiling fat.

Miss Vee appeared, trailing Dicey, and guilt struck Mariah's heart. She'd claimed to be ill when Miss Vee poked her head in asking why she hadn't started supper. Knowing how the woman worried, Mariah felt downright cruel to add to her fears. With a full house, Miss Vee worked half the day cleaning and washing linens. Now she bore the added burden of Mariah's kitchen duties, and the strain showed in her slumped shoulders and halting steps.

With a determined sigh, Mariah closed the curtain and hurried from her room. She could face anything as long as she didn't have to see Otis Gooch.

At the back end of the hall, she slipped down the kitchen stairs. Stopping to check herself in the mirror, she gasped. The pillows had mussed her hair, and her eyes were red from crying. She straightened her topknot the best she could, but only time would ease her swollen eyelids.

Snatching the bowl of peeled potatoes, she moved to the counter for her sharpest knife to cut them into slices just as Dicey and Miss Vee breezed in behind her.

Dicey's excited prattle ended midsentence, and she gaped at Mariah with startled eyes.

Mariah laughed. "Don't fret. I'm not sick in the body. It's my mind that's vexed, and that's not contagious."

There were many things Miss Vee might have said at that point, but she thankfully declined. "I'll finish cutting those, Mariah. Take this batter out to Tiller, if you will. You look like you could use the fresh air."

Mariah wasn't eager to face Tiller, but she didn't know how to refuse gracefully. Her unbearably trying day had taken another foul turn. Wiping her hands on a cloth, she slid it under the bowl to catch any spills and pressed open the door with her shoulder. Her teeth gritted, she stepped out to the lively strains of Mr. Lenard's fiddle and his friends singing "Turkey in the Straw" at the top of their voices.

"Met Mr. Catfish comin' downstream.
Says Mr. Catfish, 'What does you mean?'
Caught Mr. Catfish by the snout,
And turned Mr. Catfish wrong side out.
Turkey in the straw, turkey in the hay,
Roll 'em up and twist 'em up a high tuckahaw
And twist 'em up a tune called Turkey in the Straw."

A gentle breeze lifted her hair as she crossed the porch. With the early summer sun resting on the treetops and a wide patch of shade under the oak, it was a perfect evening to take a meal outside in the yard.

The aroma of golden fried fish reached her before she reached Tiller, and a deep, hungry growl rumbled her stomach. During her lunchtime picnic, Gabe's determined advances kept her too busy to eat a bite of her lovely sandwich or taste a nibble of her strawberry pie.

"Any room in the pot for these fritters?" she called.

Tiller glanced up from the iron kettle, the thoughtful frown on his handsome face warming to a delighted smile.

Mariah's heart stirred. The man seemed achingly glad to see her—unexpected after the way she'd treated him.

"Miss Vee said you were feeling poorly. I was just weighing the consequences of sneaking upstairs to check on you."

She handed him the batter. "You mean the threat of catching my illness?"

He grinned. "The threat of a skillet upside my head if Dicey caught me skulking near your room."

Tilting her head, she laughed into his merry eyes, but the familiarity of the moment sobered them.

Mariah lowered her lashes. "It's kind of you to be concerned about me. Especially after I. . .well, you know."

He plopped a dollop of batter into the hot fat, jumping back when it sizzled and splattered. "After you set me on my swaggering ear. . .and rightfully so?"

She searched his face for the cocky manner he used to cover his feelings. There wasn't a trace.

"I mistook your kindness and offer of friendship for something else." His features softened, and he smiled. "I apologize. It won't happen again."

She longed to cover her ears, to stretch out her hand and cover his mouth. Instead, she touched his arm. "Oh, Tiller."

The fiddler reached the end of his song and swiveled in his chair. "Smells mighty good, young fella'. Got any samples of that fish yet?"

"I'd even taste a bite of fritter," another man called. "Whatever you've got, bring it over."

Laughing, Tiller hefted the heaping tray of catfish. "I'll go tame them down with this batch. You'd better hurry Miss Vee along with the rest of the meal. I'm not sure how long I can hold them off." He stepped toward the table then spun on his heel. "Mariah, Miss Vee may have the right to frown on the man who courts you. I reckon I don't, only. . ." He chewed his bottom lip then released it. "Please be careful, won't you?"

Squirming, she couldn't hold his gaze.

"If you ever need to talk, I make a pretty good listener," he said then turned to go.

Mariah clutched his arm. "If you don't mind my saying, you seem different."

He laughed softly. "I'm not surprised. I feel different. I had a long talk with Otis after lunch. I can't explain it, but the old man knows things about me no one is supposed to know."

Her heart surged. "He does?"

Tiller nodded thoughtfully then blushed. "He said not to worry about the way I feel about you. Said he couldn't tell me the outcome, but he promised everything would turn out right in the end." He gave her a slow smile. "Once he finished praying, I believed it, too."

Mariah watched him go, holding the platter high over his head and whistling "Turkey in the Straw." Spinning, she tripped over the exposed roots of the oak then stumbled for the house.

First Otis, who seemed to hear directly from God, had read her secret thoughts. Then Tiller, without a whiff of deceit or false charm, had wormed his way deeper into her heart. Now the two seemed in cahoots on some scheme concerning her.

Like it or not, the time had come to persuade Gabriel Tabor to propose.

Tiller stole a peek over his shoulder and smiled. Mariah lurched toward the house, her mind clearly on something besides walking. He felt a little underhanded because he hadn't told her everything. A gambler kept a few cards close to his chest.

Waving the platter under their noses, he centered the fried fish on the table in front of the men. "Here you go, boys. This ought to hold you until we get the potatoes done."

Returning to the cooking fire, Tiller dropped a few more spoonfuls of batter into the steaming fat. They bobbed and danced before settling to the bottom in a ring of bubbles. In the same way, his insides had bobbed and danced before settling in to hear the rest of what Otis had to say.

After Tiller shared his fears about the black-hearted Mr. Tabor's intentions, Otis sat straight up in bed and promised with glowing eyes that God would deliver her out of the rascal's clutches. Then he winked and patted Tiller's hand, promising to pray every day that Mariah would one day be his.

As Tiller told Mariah, Otis knew things. His messages were cloudy but seemed miraculous for a man who couldn't remember a name past five minutes. His peculiar insight into people's hearts convinced Tiller that the gift, talent, or whatever a man might call it, came from a higher source.

Tiller might not be cozy with the Almighty, but he believed. As a frightened boy in Fayetteville, dodging broomsticks and scratching for crusts of bread, he'd felt God's sheltering arms many times. Living with a half-crazy mama will get a boy searching for something to believe in.

Rescue came when his ma sent him to Scuffletown to live with Uncle Silas. When Tiller heard he'd be leaving her house, he sensed the hand of God reaching down to pluck him from a terrible fate.

Yet with the rash self-centeredness of a foolish boy, he'd managed to spoil everything. He fell in with a group of unruly youths in Scuffletown and barreled headlong into his own destruction.

The women's voices pulled his head up from the bobbing fritters and his thoughts from the dreadful past. He shuddered as his mama's shrill taunts faded to 1871 where they belonged.

"Here are the potatoes," Miss Vee said, handing over a large bowl brimming with thin slices.

Tiller took up the crisp fritters then dropped the potatoes by double handfuls into the iron pot. "It won't take these long to fry." He nodded toward the men hunched over the platter of fish. "And even less time to eat them." He chuckled. "It might be a good idea to cut the pies. You'll be dishing them up before long."

Dicey swung around to a smaller table where they'd lined up rows of Mariah's fresh-baked desserts under a low, shady bough of the oak.

Miss Vee gathered a stack of small plates. "Wait, Dicey. I'll help."

Mariah seemed wary and fretful. Keeping her distance, she watched him from under her lashes.

He'd said too much. Turned her skittish.

Laying aside his tongs, Tiller turned with a smile, but the reassuring words he planned to say turned bitter in his mouth.

Over her shoulder, Tobias Jones and his nuisance sons strolled toward them with wide grins.

Mariah spun to follow Tiller's gaze, and her shoulders stiffened.

Tobias reached them first. He took off his battered slouch hat and nodded. "Halito, Mariah. Thank you for inviting us to supper."

A tiny frown gave her away. Mariah had no idea she'd extended an invitation. "You're always welcome, Tobias." She accepted the hand he offered. "All of you."

Miss Vee scurried over. "My, my. Ain't this a nice surprise?" A surprise to everyone but her.

Chris slipped up beside Mariah and gently touched her back. "Hello, Flower." His warm eyes and affectionate tone were as familiar as a kiss.

Tiller glared, but basking in Mariah's answering smile kept the brash boy too busy to notice.

Miss Vee turned a bright smile on Tobias. "I hope you're hungry."

Beaming, he nodded eagerly.

Wringing a napkin into a knot, Mariah's anxious gaze flitted between her newest guests and the six boarders.

Tiller guessed what had her jumpy. The meal kept the men too busy to cast more than a few curious glances, but if Tobias and his boys pulled a chair alongside them, it could become a problem.

Tipping his chin, Tiller grinned. "Not much room over there, and it looks like they'll be busy for a spell. Why don't we move the kitchen table out to the porch?"

Mariah gripped his arm and whispered her thanks as she passed. "Dicey, you and Rainy drag out the table. Miss Vee, fetch a clean cloth and help with the chairs, please. I'll see if our fishermen can spare a few pieces of their catch."

Grinning, Tiller handed her a plate and a pair of tongs. "Careful. You may wind up with a few less fingers."

She winked. "Not if I trade them for a slice of my strawberry pie."

With her bright smile and coy glances, it didn't take her long to charm a heaping plate of food right out from under the beguiled men.

Passing Tiller without a backward glance, she handed the plate to Dicey and took Chris's and Justin's arms. "I can't decide which of you I'd rather sit by, so let's set a place for me in between you, shall we?"

Watching her go, Tiller's temper flared as hot as the bubbling grease.

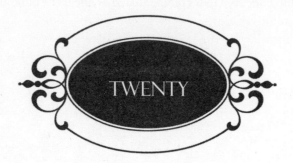

TWENTY

Mariah sat at her dressing table dragging a brush through her hair, her riotous thoughts sure to cost her a night's sleep.

She scowled at her reflection, seeing Miss Vee's self-satisfied smile. The meddling woman knew exactly what she was doing when she invited the Jones boys to supper. She figured if Tiller wasn't enough to distract her away from Gabe, then Chris or Justin might.

Grumbling to herself, Mariah focused her anger on the real conniving female in the room. How could she have played those simpering games—shamelessly flirting with the boys in front of Tiller just to test his reaction? It wasn't like her to toy with men's affections. Such behavior was indecent, especially since she planned the shortest engagement ever with another man entirely.

She slammed the brush down hard on the vanity. Why should she feel guilty for engaging in the harmless fun considered normal courting behavior by most Southern girls?

Yet wasn't that her problem? A Pearl River Indian fighting to save her ancestral land was far from a normal girl.

Besides, Tiller was guilty of toying with her affections, too. Whatever nonsense had gone on between him and Otis, Tiller wasn't the marrying kind. He had plainly stated the fact down in the kitchen. *"I'm not asking you to marry me, Mariah. I just want to court you a little."*

Blast his slippery hide. She needed a sight more than a "little" courting, and she needed it now. In her weakened state, her yearning heart betrayed her. If only Tiller intended to stick around, if he'd make his intentions clear, she could lay aside her fears.

She could lay aside most anything for him.

The admission pained her stomach. Gripping her middle, she rested her flushed cheek on the tabletop, weary from battling her muddled emotions.

"Mariah? Are you all right?"

She raised her head. If she didn't answer, perhaps Miss Vee would go away and leave her in peace.

The door creaked open, and Miss Vee's wide eyes peeked around the edge. "I heard a ruckus. Is something wrong in here?"

Mariah sighed and spun toward her. "Nothing's wrong. Come on in."

Miss Vee entered wearing her faded dressing gown, a tasseled nightcap, and a worried frown. "What on earth was that banging? I could've sworn it came from in here."

Mariah slid her brush into the top drawer. "You can see for yourself that I'm fine." She managed a grudging smile. "Go back to bed. You must be worn to a frazzle."

"Who, me?" She blinked. "I'm no worse off than the rest of you. We all worked hard today."

"On the contrary." Mariah lifted one brow. "You took on the added weight of managing my personal life."

Miss Vee's shoulders slumped. "So you caught me." Shuffling to the bed, she plopped down with a grimace. "I'm not very skilled at trickery, am I?"

"At least have the grace to seem contrite."

She leaned to squeeze Mariah's knee. "I don't mean to meddle, honey. Please understand, I feel responsible for you in your father's absence." Her eyes widened. "What would John say if he came home to find his daughter rubbing cozy shoulders with the likes of Gabriel Tabor?"

"I think Father would find my interest perfectly reasonable. After all, Gabe stands to inherit his father's plantation one day."

Startled, Mariah realized it hadn't stung to speak of her father's homecoming. Did it mean she'd grown callous in her deceit? Or had she pretended so long she'd started to believe it herself?

Disgust flickered in Miss Vee's eyes. "That's what this is about? With a man like Tiller McRae pining after you, you'd sell yourself for a patch of Mississippi dirt?" She shook her head. "Minti Bell's daughter or not, I wouldn't have believed it in a hundred years." Standing, she gazed at Mariah in disbelief. "It's possible that what I said earlier is true. I don't suppose I've ever really known you."

Tiller glanced at the ceiling then back at Otis.

Otis stared overhead, his brows raised so high he looked owlish. "That's a lot of throwing things and slamming doors, even for a couple of women."

Tiller scooted to the edge of his chair. "Should I go see what's going on up there?"

Otis grinned. "I wouldn't. You might get your ears handed to you."

They listened together as a set of stomping feet reached the end of the hallway. After a last wall-rattling slam that shook the oil fixture above their heads, silence fell over the house.

The old man blew out a breath. "See what I mean?"

Tiller couldn't help but chuckle. "For two people whose hearts seem so close-knit, Mariah and Miss Vee go at each other with shocking regularity."

Otis nodded. "Just means they've passed up friends and turned into family." His smile dimming, he shivered suddenly and tugged his blanket up around his shoulders.

Tiller helped him tuck the covers around his thin frame then patted his bundled arm. "Sit tight. I'll throw on another log."

They were into the second week in June, but the weather hadn't bothered to check the calendar. The days were mild enough that the meager daytime heat didn't carry into evening, so at night Miss Vee had Rainy bank fires in all the hearths. Otis's burned all the time.

Before long, the extra wood ignited to a roaring blaze. They sat quietly in the close little room, so warm and cozy Tiller felt drowsy.

The glowing fire wasn't the only thing that set his heart at ease. Sitting beside the strange little man beneath the quilt soothed Tiller without a word ever passing between them. When they did share long talks, especially when Otis spoke his God-words, Tiller's heart soared to receive them.

The only blight on their peculiar friendship was the dreadful truth. Tiller's part in the terrible thing that happened to Otis was a leaden weight around his shoulders.

He sat forward and patted Otis's arm. "Are you sure there's nothing else I can get for you tonight?"

Otis shook with laughter. "Not since the last time you asked. Or the time before." He cocked his head. "You ain't gettin' befuddled same as me, are you?"

Tiller longed to confess his sins and purge his sore conscience, but a streak of yellow held him back. He forced a grin. "I'm just trying to make sure you're comfortable."

Otis sat up in bed. "You know, boy. . .there is one thing I sure would like, if it's not too much trouble."

Eager to please, Tiller leaned closer. "Anything at all. Just name your poison."

The rheumy old eyes darted past the foot of the bed. "I've been locked inside these four walls for quite a spell. I'd sure like to see what's outside that door."

Warmth flooded Tiller's heart. "You know what that means, don't you?"

Childlike, Otis glanced up and shook his head.

"It shows you're getting better."

"Sure enough? Well, how about that?"

Tiller slipped one arm around his shoulders and helped him sit up. Otis swung his feet to the floor and scooted to the edge of the bed.

"Take it slow, now," Tiller warned. "Are you ready?"

He nodded. "A little shaky, but I think I can make it. . .as long as you don't turn me loose."

"There's not a chance of that happening. Let's go."

With a grunt, Otis pushed to his feet. He'd grown so thin and frail, holding him took no more effort than steadying a child.

Tiller guided him across the room and through the door. He paused in the hallway to study Otis's face. "How are we doing?"

Otis grinned. "Not sure about you, but I'd take kindly to a seat in that nice parlor yonder."

They passed under the archway and made it to the settee in mincing steps. Tiller changed his mind at the last minute and steered him to a set of overstuffed chairs pulled close to the crackling hearth. "How's this?"

"Fine, son. Just fine."

Otis reached for the padded arm, and Tiller eased him down. "Can I get you anything?" He wished he knew how to make Miss Vee's foamy white tea. "A cup of coffee or a slice of pie?"

His movements a bit wobbly, Otis leaned to pat the opposite chair. "I just need you to sit right here beside me."

Tiller slid dutifully into the seat.

With a contented sigh, Otis nestled into the soft, tufted fabric. He sat quietly for so long, his mouth ajar, he appeared to have fallen asleep.

The heat from the blazing flames toasted Tiller's arms and face. Before long, his own eyelids grew heavy, and he drifted in a pleasing fog. Resting against the pillowed headrest, he thought to doze awhile himself.

"She needs you, boy."

Tiller startled awake at the voice. He spun his head toward Otis, certain he'd dreamed the grim words.

Firelight danced in Otis's eyes. "Mariah's in a frightful mess." He shook his head, the weight of sadness sagging his cheeks.

Terrified, Tiller's breath stilled while he waited for Otis's God-words about the woman he loved.

"The Lord didn't tell me." The old man pointed up the stairs. "I got this from the little missy herself."

Swallowing hard, Tiller nodded. "She told you something?"

"Not in words." Otis leaned to prop his chin, his thoughtful gaze fixed on the floor. "We were having a little talk. I gave her a message from God about some secret she's keeping, and well. . .it hit her hard." He glanced at Tiller. "Poor girl jumped like she'd stepped on a darning needle. Nearly shook her right out of her skin."

"A secret?" His interest piqued, Tiller scooted to the edge of his chair. "What did you tell her exactly?" He blinked. "If you're free to say."

Otis thoughtfully scratched his cheek. "That's the trouble, son. I don't know if I'm free to say or not. I can't remember what I said."

Frustrated, Tiller pressed him. "Try harder, Otis. It could be important."

A pained look crossed his face. "It's no good. I've strained my thinker since it happened. Nothing comes to me. Not a whiff."

Tiller patted his trembling hand. "Easy. Don't rile yourself. We'll find another way to help her."

Otis pulled his hand free to squeeze Tiller's fingers. "I know you'll bust a gut trying, son. Because there's nothing but good in you."

The flames grew unbearably hot, and the room closed in on Tiller. He ducked his head. "Please don't call me that, sir. I'm a long way from good."

Otis smiled. "Ain't we all when you get right down to it? The Good Book says, 'For all have sinned, and come short of the glory of God.' We're all sinners, boy. You've done no worse things than me."

Tiller swallowed hard, but the painful knot refused to budge. He slid out of Otis's grasp. "I reckon that's not so. I'm afraid I've done far worse. In fact, there's something you need to know about me, and it's time I told you the truth. Otis, I—"

Footsteps over their heads stemmed his words. Angry at the interruption, he scowled up at the stairwell.

Mariah stood a few steps off the top landing, her hand clutching the neck of a white dressing gown and her flowing hair draping her shoulders like a lustrous black cape. She was a vision straight from a man's dreams.

Her expression was the only flaw, and the most striking thing about her. Sheer panic had frozen her features and paled her beautiful face.

Gaping at Otis as if she'd stumbled onto a ghoul, she spun on her heels. "I'm sorry. I didn't mean to interrupt."

Otis stirred and reached his hand toward her. "Little missy, don't go."

Leaping from his chair, Tiller started after her. Before he reached the bottom stair, she was gone in a whirl of white lace.

"There, you see?" Otis said, wonder in his voice.

Stunned, Tiller stared over his shoulder. "For pity's sake. She was scared stiff."

Otis pointed a shaky finger. "That's the same look she had when I gave her the message from God."

TWENTY-ONE

The road home had changed. Not because of overgrown trails or washed-out bridges—things a man might expect. Joe felt the difference in his spirit, a restless sense of going in the wrong direction.

On other trips to Mississippi, the past lured him. Each step closer to the land of his ancestors stoked an eager fire within. This time the miles drained him as he rode away from the cabin he shared with his wife.

The full moon overhead lit his way. After the first long day, Joe had traveled at night when most of the world rested. At first light, he sought hidden places to sleep before the roads filled with travelers. This way, he fell asleep knowing he would see trouble before it spotted him.

He followed a winding, scum-coated creek for miles until the water ran fast and clear again. Reining the horse beside a mayhaw thicket, he eased his aching body from the saddle and lay on his belly for a drink from the rushing stream.

After tending the animal's needs, he built a fire to heat a tin of beans. With his bones warmed and belly full, he spread his bedroll in a clutch of trees as fiery orange rays from *hvshi* peeked over the tall grass on the horizon, setting it aflame.

Overhead, a spiraling cyclone of buzzards rose and fell over a distant carcass. The birds reminded him of an ancient tale, the day the animals held a powwow to decide who would steal fire for their tribe.

Brave buzzard volunteered to fly to the people of the east and return with fire, which he did without delay. Swooping close to the flames, he hid a burning ember in the long, beautiful feathers on his head. For his trouble, he got a bald, blistered skull to wear for the rest of his days.

Smiling at the old legend, Joe yawned and smacked lazily, the pleasing taste of beans lingering on his tongue. He closed his eyes, wondering if his skirmish with John Coffee would earn him the same fate as the poor buzzard. In previous battles, they'd parted company with the stench of burning feathers in the air. He doubted this time would be different.

Joe loved Mariah, felt a pressing weight of duty to see her marry well. He couldn't deny that the promise of three fine horses and a passel of land sweetened the deal.

With his niece wed to the chief's son, Joe would move into a choice position within the tribe. With little George coming, it was a fine place to be. These things he wouldn't bother telling John. The man seemed blind to their traditions.

For all his trying ways, John's love for Mariah was great. John's devotion to his daughter was Joe's biggest hindrance, but this time he wouldn't leave Mississippi without her.

He drew the musty blanket over his eyes to shut out the rising sun. Just a few more days to reach the Mississippi crossing. Less than a week and he'd arrive at his destination. He still had plenty of time to work out a plan to steal John Coffee's fire. For now, his biggest need was rest.

Hooper dashed the dregs from his coffee cup into the fire and kicked dirt over the ashes. They'd slept too long, but after days of hard riding, they were a sore and sorry lot—with a lot more ground left to cover.

Wyatt approached, a bleary-eyed version of himself. "I've packed the horses, and Ellie's scouting the trail. You about ready to go?"

Hooper groaned. "Not in the least. What happened to us, Wyatt? Our gang used to ride the swamp for days, short on sleep and provisions with muddy water lapping our stirrups and a posse on our tails." He reached to rub the small of his back. "I don't remember once feeling this stiff."

Wyatt grinned. "Good thing you mended your ways, old man." He tightened the neck of his flask and slung it over one shoulder. "Hoop, that was ten years ago. We're not that band of raiders anymore."

"Still, it don't make a lick of sense," Hooper said. "I work as hard as any man running my farm."

"Not the same. It's not easy sleeping on a train for days or riding the overgrown trails around Jackson. These saddles bore in deep after so many miles."

Hooper lowered his voice. "Don't let on to Ellie, but I miss my feather bed."

Wyatt burst into laughter. "Ellie's hero? Missing his comforts? You can bet I won't tell her that."

Ellie ducked out of the trees behind them. "Tell me what?"

Wyatt spun. "Take my word, honey. You're better off not knowing."

Hooper nudged him. "Why doesn't my sister look any worse for wear? She woke me up at dawn, scurrying around camp like a youngster on an outing."

Wyatt slipped his arm around Ellie's waist. "This stuff is in her blood." He gave her a little shake. "Besides, running after our boys keeps her able-bodied. I doubt those sweet cherubs of yours give much of a chase."

Ellie grinned. "Things will change when they're courting age, Hoop. You'll stay fit chasing suitors from your door."

He frowned. "No lop-eared boy will come closer than shotgun range. Not a second time, at least."

Wyatt slapped him on the back. "Best keep a good stock of shells around the house. As pretty as your two gals are, half the boys in Hope Mills will be plucking buckshot from their behinds."

Hooper hefted his pack and nodded toward the sun. "Let's get going. We should've been on the road two hours by now."

Ellie pulled away from Wyatt to straighten Hooper's collar, an obvious excuse to search his eyes. "Do you think we'll have any luck this time?"

Hooper ran his hand along the back of her head. "We have a good lead. If Tiller's alive, we're bound to stumble onto more information." He squeezed her shoulder. "Don't fret, Ellie. We'll search Mississippi until we find him."

TWENTY-TWO

The blustery weather seemed the right setting for the storm brewing within the walls of Bell's Inn. Since Tiller opened his eyes, the house had echoed with deafening silence. The kind wrought by the mutual cold shoulders of quarreling women.

If not for their angry steps on the stairs and their scornful snorts as they passed in the hall outside his room, Tiller would swear no females lived in the house—until a ruckus commenced in the kitchen.

His stomach growled, but with the alarming clatter of dishes and the banging of pots and pans, he didn't dare venture out to fill it. He worried about the poor men who'd paid to spend another breakfast with Mariah and Miss Vee. He doubted Mariah's biscuits were worth blundering into that skirmish.

Another glance past the curtains at the swirling cloud bank drew his concerns to a more pressing matter—whether or not they'd wind up running for cover. He didn't relish spending the morning huddled in the cellar with Mariah and Miss Vee. Considering the whole house didn't seem big enough for their spat, he'd sooner take his chances with a twister.

Lightning flashed outside his window, filling the yard with brilliant light. The peal of thunder that followed and the way it shook the house made the cellar seem like a good idea after all.

Braving the tempest in the kitchen was unavoidable. He had to warn the women.

Tiller snatched his hat from the hook on the wall, reliving for a moment how he'd swiped it right off Nathan's head. Pushing aside the prickly memory, he swept out the door and down the hall.

At the kitchen door, he took a deep breath and boldly stepped inside. Gloom hung from the rafters like cemetery fog. Just as he feared, the poor lodgers hunkered over their plates picking at their food in silence, their wary eyes skittering between Miss Vee and Mariah.

Formidable, stiff-shouldered Miss Vee scoured a cast iron skillet so hard she'd soon wear through the bottom. Scowling, straight-backed Mariah scrubbed the silver off her utensils, tossing them on the counter with a loud, careless clatter. Dicey lurked inside the dim pantry, staring out with frightened eyes.

Mr. Lenard, the wretched fellow who'd requested more biscuits, nibbled on the corner of one, frowning like a man forced to eat sawdust. Bickering women could sure ruin a man's day.

Noticing Tiller on the threshold, his face lit up as if he'd spotted a lifeline. "Look, boys. Here's our fish fryer. How are you this morning, son?"

Tiller nodded. "I'm fine, sir. At least for now." He lifted the curtain from the back door to peer out. The oak tree seemed to reach for him, pleading with wildly waving limbs for a rest he couldn't give. It wouldn't do for a tree that size to be split by lightning or hurled by the wind. If the big oak fell on the house, there'd be nothing left to repair. "Hasn't anyone noticed it's blowing up a powerful gale?"

All three women glanced his way.

"There's been a little thunder and wind," Miss Vee said. "I just figured it for another rainstorm."

Tiller's somber gaze moved from her to Mariah. "If we're lucky, rain is all we'll get."

Mariah opened the wooden blind over the sink with her thumb. "It's that bad?"

Dicey crowded beside her to peek out. "Mercy sakes, them pines swaying right for us."

"It's not the pine I'm worried about," Tiller said. "If the wind kicks up a notch, that oak will be joining us for breakfast."

Dicey tried to smile, but her chin wobbled. "Mista' Tilla', you funnin' us."

"I wish I was." He met Mariah's frightened stare. "Is the root cellar fit for company?"

She looked dazed. A white ring of fear lined her mouth. "I honestly don't know. I haven't been down there in so long." Drying her hands on her apron, she tugged the strings and laid it aside. "What will we need?"

Tiller shrugged "Water, I suppose. A lantern or two." He opened the door, and the wind rushed in, wildly billowing curtains, tablecloths, and the ladies' skirts.

"Shut it, Mista' Tilla', please!" Dicey screamed, stooping to the floor and covering her head.

Ignoring her shrill cries, Tiller held Mariah's gaze. "I'll go down and check things out. Wait here unless I call you."

She nodded.

"Hold up, son." Mr. Lenard wiped his mouth and stood. "I'll go with you."

Miss Vee stood on tiptoe to pull down a candle and a box of long matches. "Take these. You'll need them."

Mr. Lenard fisted them and scurried out the door on Tiller's heels.

Tiller had spotted the cellar doors from the roof when he made his repairs. Clutching his hat, he ran to that side of the house. With his free hand, he latched onto the handle and motioned for Mr. Lenard to take the other side. They pulled together, and dirt sifted like flour into the dark hole in the ground.

Tiller went first, feeling his way down the slanted ladder. Before ducking inside, he paused for another quick look at the storm. The sky held a greenish cast, and the peaks of the tall, dark clouds were churning.

Mr. Lenard stood above him staring at the fearsome sight, his clothes flapping around his large frame. He glanced at Tiller with an ominous shake of his head.

Tiller descended into the darkness, batting away spider webs and crumbling dirt dauber mounds from the rungs. At the bottom, he moved aside for Mr. Lenard, who sprang to the ground and turned his back on the drafty opening to light the candle. Shielding the flame with his palm, he held it aloft.

Evidently, the cellar had gone unused for some time. Tiller supposed the women preferred the comfort and convenience of their roomy indoor pantry. Looking around, he couldn't say he blamed them.

The musty smell of damp earth rose with every footfall, mixed with the pungent odor of spoiled onions and rotted potatoes. A long abandoned termite nest took up one corner, explaining the crumbling boards he had replaced throughout the house.

A raised platform along one wall stood off the dirt floor about two feet, stacked with crates and assorted old canning jars filled with blackened food. Mr. Lenard bent over the shelf and dripped wax to set the candle. "Over here, son. Help me clear this ledge. If the boards are sound, it'll make a good place for the women to sit."

Together, they filled the crates with the ruined preserves and other assorted rubbish and set them in the opposite corner.

Tiller dusted his hands. "With a couple of quilts for padding, this should do fine."

Smiling, Mr. Lenard opened his mouth to answer, but a strong gust doused the candle, plunging the corner into darkness.

They made their way to the dim square of light atop the ladder and climbed outside to a shower of hail.

"This is bad," Tiller shouted. "We'd best hurry." He bailed for the house with Mr. Lenard on his tail.

Halfway to the porch, a muffled roar hauled them to a stop. Tiller stared in disbelief as the boiling black clouds pitched a monster to the ground. The twister seemed a hundred acres wide. He couldn't tell how close, but it surged toward them, a black devil on a ruthless path.

"Let's go!" he cried, but Mr. Lenard had already run ahead.

A line of anxious faces awaited them inside the kitchen. With the memory of what he'd just seen spurring him on, Tiller wasted no time. "Dicey, fetch all the quilts you can carry. One of these men will help you. Miss Vee, take the others and open as many windows as you can.

Mariah, bring lanterns, oil, and plenty of matches. Now hurry!"

Covering her ears, Dicey backed into Miss Vee, her wild gaze darting from face to face. "What's that noise I hear? What's out there?"

Miss Vee gripped her arm and thrust her forward. "Doomsday. Unless you want it to get you, you'll do like you're told."

With a high-pitched squeal, Dicey shot out the door and skidded toward the guest rooms.

Frightened people scattered in every direction, leaving Tiller and Mr. Lenard alone in the kitchen. "How can I help?" he asked.

Tiller tugged his sleeve. "Come with me."

They raced down the hall to Otis's room. Curled in his usual position, face to the wall and his rear jutted over the mattress, he slept like a carefree baby.

"Can you believe this?" Tiller asked Mr. Lenard.

They shared a quick smile.

Tiller shook the bed. "Otis, wake up."

Mumbling, he waved them away.

Tiller took his arm and gently pulled him over. "On your feet or carried, Otis? It's your choice. We have to get you to safety."

Startled awake, he blinked up at Tiller. "What's the trouble?"

Bracing his back, Tiller helped him to his feet. "Twister. A big one headed right for us."

Mr. Lenard took his other arm. "There ain't a minute to spare, old-timer. Let's get you underground."

The roar closed on the house, rattling the walls. The churning rumbled like madly rushing water one minute, howled like an angry, squalling beast the next. Mariah's heartbeat thundered.

The wild-eyed parties finished their appointed tasks and met at the back door awaiting orders from Tiller. Motioning over his head, he and Mr. Lenard led the way with Otis's skinny legs dangling between them. Mariah and the others followed, cowering like children.

Halfway to the cellar, overwhelming curiosity drove her to raise her head. Fear like she'd never known brought her to a standstill.

The twister bore down on them, a moving explosion. Wide at the top, engorged, it narrowed to a whirling cloud of debris at its base. In the distance, a herd of panicked deer darted out of its course, leaping and soaring to escape.

The hail had stopped, but rain pelted her like a shower of bullets. The wind shrieked, whipping past her eyes until they stung. A force tugged at her body, her hair, her clothes, as if the nightmarish, spinning top sought to draw her, to feed on her along with everything in its path.

Mariah steeled herself, but the pull was too strong. Terrified, she stumbled forward, longing to cry out for God's protection. To her shame, she didn't feel worthy. When had she stopped praying?

In a rush, Tiller's arms engulfed her from behind. Digging in his heels, he held her while the twister danced just over the Pearl.

Breathless, her gaze darted to him. "It stopped moving?" The wind ripped the words from her mouth, and she didn't think he heard.

His throat rose and fell. "I think so," he shouted in her ear.

"Is that possible?"

Tiller laughed. "It must be. It's happening right in front of us." He tugged on her arm. "It won't last. Let's go."

Bowing into the wind, she let him drag her to the cellar. Clinging to his comforting arm, she swung her legs over the top of the ladder.

Tiller stood over her, his hair whipping, his shirttail beating wildly. Reaching past her, he handed the oil and lanterns down to Mr. Lenard.

As Mariah's head cleared the opening, Tiller lowered the door.

Startled, her hand shot out to stop him. "What are you doing?" she shrieked. "Come inside."

"I'll be back."

"No! Where are you going?"

He jabbed his thumb over his shoulder. "The horses. I have to turn them out."

Sheki! How could she have forgotten him?

In the moment where she almost forbade him to save her horse, her feelings for Tiller became clear. She lowered her lashes, certain her love for him shone from her eyes.

Tiller glanced over his shoulder, the set of his jaw grim. "Get inside," he yelled. "It's on the move again." He shouted something else before he ran, but building pressure in Mariah's ears muffled his voice.

Mr. Lenard climbed up beside her to help close the doors. Her muscles strained from the effort, and still the handle jerked up repeatedly, nearly pulling her arms from the sockets.

One of the other men tugged her down and took her place. Between the two, they managed to force them shut, blotting out the meager light and some of the noise.

Miss Vee met her at the bottom rung. "Honey, please forgive me. I can't die at odds with you." Her voice shook with fear. "If we survive this, I promise never to meddle again."

Mariah forced a wobbly smile for Miss Vee's sake and leaned into her, so frightened for Tiller she couldn't speak.

A lantern flashed to life in the corner. Then another, casting long flickering shadows on the floor. Miss Vee wrapped a quilt around Mariah's wet, shivering body and led her to a nest of blankets spread over a low storage shelf.

Crawling across on her knees, Mariah pressed her back to the wall, her gaze fixed on the overhead doors. She covered her ears to drown out the hideous moaning wind and prayed. For Tiller, Sheki, and the lives of those around her.

To plead for the safety of the inn entered her mind, but the words never formed in her heart. If the tornado ripped Bell's Inn from the face of the earth, the promise would go up with it, along with the burden she carried. Good riddance to all, as long as it spared those she loved.

Dicey yelped and hid her face when the doors sailed open.

Mariah's spirit soared to meet Tiller on the stairs.

This time it took all the men to shut out the storm. Then Tiller beat a path to her side. Clearing the platform on one knee, he pulled her close as if he knew she needed his strength.

She'd been wrong about her dandelion seed. The first strong wind hadn't whisked him away. Instead, it blew him straight into her arms.

The cellar groaned and rattled as the house danced over their heads. A deafening crack brought shrill screams from Miss Vee and Dicey. Mariah clung tighter to Tiller's chest.

The twister sucked one of the doors free and spun it away. With a wrenching squeal of metal, the second spun crazily on one hinge before it shot straight up in the air. The tempest raged overhead, a leering black wolf belching threats down a rabbit hole.

Sheltered in Tiller's arms, Mariah gazed in terrible awe as the world spun past in a dizzying blur.

TWENTY-THREE

Faster than it came, the twister was gone. The danger had passed, but Tiller couldn't turn loose of Mariah. His jaw ached from clenching, and his muscles bunched in knots.

But for the groan of settling boards and a quiet sniff from Dicey, eerie silence filled the cellar. The square patch of sky overhead was deathly still.

No one seemed able to move—until Dicey began to wail.

Miss Vee patted her back. "Now's not the time to cry. It's over. We made it."

Tears wet Dicey's rounded cheeks. "I ain't bawlin' for me." Her frantic gaze darted over their faces. "I'm worryin' 'bout my daddy."

Understanding dawned in Miss Vee's eyes. "Don't fret, honey. I'm sure he'll be fine."

"But it's headed our way, and we ain't got no root cellar." Wriggling to the edge of the platform, she struggled to her feet and started for the ladder. "I gots to run home and see."

"Wait," Tiller called. "It could be dangerous."

She stilled and turned, wringing her hands. "What you mean by dangerous?"

He ducked his chin at the opening. "There's no telling what we'll find up there. Let the menfolk go first. We'll have a look around, and then I'll walk you home to check on your pa."

She retraced her steps and settled obediently on the rim of the shelf.

Realizing he still held Mariah, Tiller glanced down. "Are you all right?"

Her face tilted up, trust shining from her eyes. "I think so."

A smile twitched his lips. "Let me know when you're sure."

She ducked her head and nodded. "I'm sure."

He gave her a little squeeze then released her to let her sit up. Gazing around in the flickering light, his eyes lit on Otis. "How are you faring, sir?"

Otis chuckled and pulled the quilt tighter around his shoulders. "Missing my bed and my hearth. And this empty belly's asking for lunch."

Dicey spun to gape at him. "How you gon' eat after all this?"

Otis beamed. "Hand me a drumstick, and I'll show you."

Miss Vee snorted. "Let's pray there's still a kitchen left to fry a drumstick."

Tiller heaved himself off the ledge. "Who wants to go up top with me and find out?"

Mr. Lenard and his troop stood one at a time, shaking the dust off their clothes. Two of the older men looked a bit shaky.

Tiller nodded at them. "I'd be obliged if you'd wait here to keep an eye on the women."

He didn't have to ask them twice.

First at the ladder, Tiller climbed, dreading what he might see. The loud crack they'd heard could've been anything, but his money was on the oak. He hoped it hadn't split Bell's Inn down the middle when it fell.

His anxious gaze cleared the opening. Groaning, he couldn't believe the devastation.

A blanket of debris covered the backyard in a patchwork of mismatched rubble. Brightly colored quilts tangled with splintered tree limbs. A feather pillow peeked from under a wagon wheel. Shredded wallpaper and cracked lumber mixed with twisted tablecloths, busted frames, and shards of china dishes. Large sections of walls, ceilings, and broken gables scattered the grounds, along with a ripped-out kitchen sink.

Tiller spun.

Bell's Inn stood untouched behind him, except for two whitewashed planks jutting from the wall. The wood, once part of the garden fence, had impaled the house without breaking, driven in like a hammer drives a nail.

The oak tree, its twisted roots jutting to the sky like gnarled rope, had rolled the dice, and the house won. The barn hadn't been so lucky.

"Is it bad, son?" Mr. Lenard called.

"Well, sure it's bad," Miss Vee said beside him. "Can't you see the man's dumbstruck?" She tugged on Tiller's pants leg. "The house is gone, ain't that right? Everything is gone."

He ducked his head inside. "You don't get off so easy, Miss Vee. You'll still be frying chicken."

Miss Vee cheered and clasped hands with Dicey. Whirling, she drew Mariah into a smothering hug.

Tiller sought Mariah's worried brown eyes. "It's a shocking mess up here, but you still have a roof over your head." He cocked his head. "I can't say the same for Sheki."

"The barn?"

He tried for a comforting smile. "You'll need a handyman for a while longer."

"Do you see Sheki?"

After a quick scan of the property, he shook his head. "No sign of any of the horses, but don't fret. When they calm down, they'll come home." Clearing the top of the ladder, Tiller peered below. "Come on out, but watch your step."

The men came first, followed by Miss Vee, gasping and clutching her chest.

Then Dicey, moaning and sobbing.

Mariah came last, drawing in a quick breath as she reached the top. She tented her hands over her brow and whirled in a circle. "Oh my. It's inconceivable. Where did all of this come from?"

Tiller grimaced. "The storm dumped half of Mississippi in our lap."

Staring across the backyard, Mr. Lenard heaved a sigh. "To think that just last night, I sat over there playing my fiddle and eating fish." He pointed. "Look. The cook pot's still there." He chuckled, wonder in his voice. "Took the tree but left the kettle. Fickle old thing, weren't it?"

"Oh no, Mista' Tilla'." Dicey tugged his sleeve. "Look what else it took."

He turned to follow the direction her finger pointed, and his heart seemed to stop. "By thunder, it's gone. Ripped up down to the soil."

Mariah clutched his arm. "Even the sunflowers. What will I say to poor Rainy?" She lifted dazed eyes. "We'll have nothing to eat. Nothing to feed our guests."

Tiller gripped her taut knuckles. "I'll set all this right, Mariah. You'll see." He swept his arm over the wreckage. "I'll clear the yard, repair the barn, and with Rainy's help, I'll replant the garden." He squeezed her hand. "In a few weeks' time, you'll forget this ever happened."

She tilted her head up, and Tiller cupped her chin. "Bell's Inn will be even better than it was before. I give you my solemn word."

Though Dicey's ramshackle house stood directly in its path, the twister had jogged off course long enough to spare her home and family. She returned to the inn, smiling and singing, to help with the cleanup.

Mariah was grateful for the effort, since every muscle in her body ached and hysterical tears threatened to surface.

The beast had spared the inn but demanded a high price for the favor. The destruction inside looked much the same as the yard. The storm had roared through the windows, turning the rooms upside down.

Tiller assured her the inn hadn't taken the twister's full force. "If it had," he said, "you wouldn't have a mess to clean because you wouldn't have a house."

Mariah tried hard to be grateful.

Even Otis's room on the opposite side suffered damage. The wind sucked his curtains out the window, soaking them through, and rain had wet his mattress.

Otis didn't want to give up his cozy den, so Tiller hauled the bedding from an upstairs room then changed the sheets and blankets himself. He pulled down the wet curtains, hanging a quilt in their place. Once he had a roaring fire going, he dressed Otis in a clean nightshirt and put him to bed.

Mariah took note of how affectionately he cared for Otis, and it warmed her heart.

After he had the old man tended, Tiller appeared at the parlor door. "Here you are," he said from the hallway.

She glanced up. "Did you get Otis settled?"

"I think so." He hurried to help her pull the settee away from the open window. Tossing out leaves and small branches, he pulled down the sash. "Mr. Lenard and his men are cleaning their rooms as best they can. Only one of them took in water. We may have to move that man to a different bed for the night."

She bit her bottom lip. "I thought they were leaving."

"They offered to stay one more night to lend a hand, and I agreed. We can't afford to turn down the help.

"Although"—he winced—"I don't think you can charge them in this case."

Her mind jumped to the near-empty pantry. "No, of course not."

He gathered her hands and squeezed. "Don't worry. We'll manage."

She nodded. "Except I don't have another empty room. Otis has the mattress from the last one."

Tiller bit the corner of his lip. "I know. I'm willing to give up my bed." He nodded at the settee. "I can bunk in here, if you don't mind."

Mariah shook her head. "I won't allow it. That's your room, Tiller. You've earned it with the sweat of your brow." She blew a determined breath. "One of them can sleep out here. Or they can double up. I'm sure they'll understand in the circumstances."

Tiller winked and saluted. "Whatever you say, boss." He took her hand and led her to the sofa. "I know you have plenty to do, but will you sit for a minute? There's something I want to say."

Curious, she perched on the edge of her seat.

Sitting beside her, he ran his hands through his hair. "I know with the repairs almost finished, my time here was nearing an end. I figured any day you'd hand me my bedroll and send me down the Trace."

She pulled in her lips and struggled to keep the truth to herself. Sending Tiller away hadn't entered her mind.

"But now"—he waved his hand to take in the chaos around them— "I think you need me more than you need my empty room."

Mariah started to agree, but his hand shot up.

"Hush, and hear me out." His lively grin reminded her of the Tiller she'd first met.

"When I promised to put this place right, I meant every word." His dancing eyes glowed. "I looked over the wreckage of the barn. It won't take much to rebuild."

She had to stop him. "I can't afford the lumber, Tiller."

As eager as a boy at Christmas, he scooted closer. "You won't need to buy a single board." He pointed behind them. "There's enough wood on your felled oak to build a small town."

Her chin came up. "Gracious, I forgot about the oak."

He nodded. "It's a fine, sturdy tree. A lot of them are hollow in the center, but yours is solid through and through."

"But how will we cut it?"

He patted her shoulder. "Leave the details to me. I have a few friends in Canton."

She stared at her hands, twisting in her lap. "But I can't pay you."

He widened his eyes. "Sure you can. In room and board and the best hot rolls this side of the Mississip'."

Catching his mood, she giggled. "I don't feel so helpless now." She beamed at him. "How can I ever thank you?"

He shrugged, a mischievous glint in his eyes. "Just keep those rolls coming, I guess." He picked up her hand and squeezed. "And let me help Rainy replant the garden. I can't think of anything I'd rather do."

For a man who boasted of wanderlust, he was certainly in no hurry to leave. In fact, he seemed to care about Bell's Inn as much as Mariah did. She tightened her fingers around his. "I think it's a wonderful idea."

He released her and stood. "It's all settled then. I'll let you get back to work. Miss Vee asked me to help sweep up in the kitchen."

As he strode away, Mariah couldn't help glancing at his boots. The carefree drifter once claimed to hit the road before roots sprouted from his feet to pin him down. Grinning, she sensed the presence of little green shoots between his toes.

Tendrils of hope broke the surface of her despair. Like Rainy's sunflowers chasing the sun, they yearned after Tiller as he loped out the door.

TWENTY-FOUR

Mariah stepped out on the porch and searched the sundrenched yard for Tiller. In the six days since the storm, he'd wrought miracles. The green grass gleamed in the bright daylight, picked up and raked free of every scrap of trash.

Piece by piece, the huge oak had disappeared, hauled off by wagonloads and returning as stacks of lumber. Most of the wood, gleaming in the afternoon light, jutted bare and skeletal over the barn, a sturdy frame awaiting wallboards and shingles.

The furious winds had carted off the two magnolia trees beside the pump, and good riddance. Since the morning when she'd carried Father's body from the house, the sweet-smelling blossoms had reminded her of his death.

The storm had spared the wagon, one of the many miracles for which Mariah was thankful. Sheki, nickering outside her window the morning after the twister, was another.

At first, Mariah thought he'd come home begging for oats, but the shameful horse was bloated from a rampant eating spree and returned in need of a stomach cure. Thankfully, Rainy knew a thing or two about horses and fixed him right up.

Sheki and Tiller's gelding slept in the corral for a few days, but once Tiller raised and braced the walls, they returned to their stalls to oversee the rest of Tiller's handiwork.

Shading her eyes, Mariah spotted Tiller high on the roof of the barn, his sun-toasted back and shoulders gleaming with sweat. She hurried down the steps with his lunch, waving when he raised his head. The warmth of his smile crossed the distance.

She entered the newly set doors, peering up through the unfinished gap. With a grizzly growl, Tiller leaped from behind, howling and spinning her around when she screamed.

Mariah clutched her heart. "You fiend! I almost threw this tray at you."

Laughing, he lifted the corner of the napkin and sniffed. "What a shame that would be."

He lifted his shirt from a hook in the corner and slipped it on. Straddling a hay bale, he patted the one next to him.

She cocked her head. "Is this your way of inviting a lady to lunch?"

Nodding, he held out his hands for the tray. "If a lady will do me the honor."

Mariah smoothed her skirt and sat, watching him eagerly plunder the food. She accepted a spoonful of potato soup and a roll stuffed with a bite of pork roast. It seemed only fair since she'd brought him her share to begin with to make sure he filled his stomach. Besides, it smelled too good to resist.

The small roast was the last of a wild young pig, the rolls from her last cups of flour. After Otis and Miss Vee ate their fill, there wasn't much left in the kitchen. Thank heavens Rainy and Dicey took their midday meals at home with their folks.

Mariah wiped her mouth on the corner of the napkin. "How are things in town? I heard you drive up and wondered why you never came inside the house."

Tiller had left for Canton the day before on more business with the sawmill. He returned in a rush then went straight up on the roof and set to work.

He glanced at the sky through the gaping hole. "Rain clouds chased me most of the way home. I wanted to get the roof finished before Sheki got his ears wet, but I got fooled. It looks like the bad weather took a turn." His ears reddened. "Just because I didn't come say hello doesn't mean I didn't think about you."

Mariah's cheeks warmed and her hand came up to stifle a giggle. Ten minutes in his presence, and she'd turned into a blushing girl.

Tiller's eyes widened. His throat made a choking sound, and he stood so fast he nearly upset the tray. "Curse me for a blasted fool. I can't believe I let this slip my mind."

Steadying his soup bowl, Mariah gaped at his eager face. "Gracious, what are you blathering about?"

"I have something for you." He shoved his hand deep in his pocket and came up with a bulging white hankie tied up with all four corners. Grinning, he held it out to her.

Mariah took the bundle and the weight sagged her arms to her lap. One knot loosened and bright coins spilled out in her hands.

Her head shot up. "What is this?"

His toothy smile lit the barn brighter than the sunbeam pouring through the roof. "Maybe it's been quite a spell since you saw any, darlin', but that's money."

She shoved it toward him. "I can see that much, but it's not my money."

He withdrew his hands, refusing to take it from her. "It's yours, all right. Every dollar."

Her heart pounded. "I'm scared to ask where you got this, Tiller, but it doesn't belong to me. Take it back this instant."

He wrapped his big hands gently around hers and guided them, handkerchief and all, back to her lap. "Our friend, the twister, cleared a path from here to Yazoo city and points north, creating a serious demand for lumber."

Tiller let go and straightened with a hesitant smile. "The oak wasn't the only tree down on your property. With Rainy's help, I've been hauling them to the mill and selling them. I took the last one this trip. Apart from a few dollars to Rainy for his trouble, you're holding the profits." He shoved back his hat and quirked one brow. "I hope you don't mind."

Stunned, Mariah's gaze dropped to her hands. One finger twitched and more coins tumbled across her palms, more money than she'd ever seen in her life. Enough to run the inn for a year, maybe more, if she didn't have a single paying guest. "It's really mine?"

He nodded.

"I don't know what to say." Laughter bubbled up in her throat. "I thought it took you an unreasonable number of trips to haul one tree." She glanced up. "Miss Vee said it seemed like the miracle of the loaves and fishes. God multiplying the oak." Awed, she shook her head. "I suppose in a way He did."

Tiller tucked his chin. "So it's all right?"

"It's more than all right." She shot up with a squeal and threw her arms around his neck. "I'm so grateful I could burst!"

Remembering his shirt was unfastened, she pulled away blushing. "How forward of me. Please forgive me."

His hands fumbled with the top button. "No, it's my fault."

She couldn't contain her joy for long. "Oh, Tiller. We can eat again."

He gave her a crooked smile. "Why do you think I went to all the trouble?"

Leaning across the distance she'd put between them, she stretched to kiss his cheek. "Because you're the dearest man in the whole world."

"What's this?" an angry voice snarled behind them.

They spun, still beaming brightly.

Gabriel Tabor loomed on the threshold.

Mariah stepped away from Tiller. Fisting the money, she dropped it with a jangle into her skirt pocket. "Gabe. What a nice surprise. I didn't expect you today."

His bottom lip hung looser than usual, and fury blazed in his eyes. "I can see you didn't." He pointed a murderous finger at Tiller. "Why's he half naked and pawing at you?"

Mariah had a moment to consider the absurdity of the charge. How preposterous for a man with a dozen untamed hands to accuse decent, respectful Tiller. She drew herself up. "I assure you he did no such thing."

Gabe took three steps closer, his hulking size a tad frightening. "Don't you lie, Mariah Bell. Maybe I ain't real smart, but I ain't stupid."

His bulk shifted to Tiller. "Mister, you trying to steal my girl?"

Tiller held his ground as Gabe approached. "Can a man steal a girl who wants to be taken?"

"Huh?" Gabe balled his fist. "Don't think you can get out of a thrashing by fast talk and riddles."

Easing into a swaggering stance, Tiller clenched his hands at his sides. "I'm saying Mariah's free to choose. If she wants you, I'll step out of your way. But if she wants me, I'm staying right here." He jutted his jaw. "And you'll have to kill me to keep me away from her."

Tiller's brows raised to question marks as his eyes sought hers past Gabe's shoulder. "Mariah?"

The last ounce of resistance slid from around her heart. Tiller McRae had braved starvation, twisters, giant oak trees, collapsed barns, and now the ugly, big fists of Gabe Tabor. He'd more than proved himself worthy of her trust.

With a teasing smile, she lifted her head higher to see over Gabe's broad back. She didn't need words for the message her eyes sent Tiller.

Gabe stiffened and swung around to blink at her. "Well?"

She lifted her chin. "Gabe, I think it's time for you to go."

"What?" He frowned and jabbed himself in the chest. "You're giving me the boot? After you done kissed me and everything?"

Blushing to the roots of her hair, Mariah lowered her lashes. "Your memory fails you, Mr. Tabor. You kissed me, and without an invitation." She glanced at Tiller. "And only on the cheek."

Gabe shuffled toward her. His meaty, meddling hand snaked around her waist and slid to the small of her back, lingering too long to be respectable. "But you liked it, didn't you?"

Tiller blustered and lunged, but Mariah held up her hand. "Say good-bye, Tiller. Gabe was just leaving."

"You really want me to go?" Gabe hooked his thumb over his shoulder. "I could go on and kill him like he said."

Mariah couldn't hold back a grin. "Killing Tiller won't be necessary, but thank you for the offer." She caught his sleeve and led him to the threshold. "Say hello to your father for me, won't you?"

"Well, sure, but I—"

"Watch your step past those loose boards. You might trip and take a nasty fall."

His droopy eyes bugged. "Mariah!"

"Good-bye, Gabe." Reaching for the barn door, she nodded before pulling it closed.

Leaning her head against the rough wood, she tried to still her thudding heart. Where would she find the courage to face Tiller after she'd just declared her love? Turning slowly, she stood across the barn from him, one hand over her mouth.

He slouched with both hands on his hips, giving her a sideways look and a teasing smile.

A dusty beam of light filtered through the open rooftop, the bright ray anointing his red head with fire. The unearthly glow seemed like the warm kiss of God's approval.

Tiller crooked his finger.

Mariah's stomach flipped. She crossed the barn into the sunbeam and the warmth of his embrace.

Sliding his hand up her neck, he tangled his fingers in her hair and pulled her to his chest. "It's high time you came to your senses, woman."

Breathless, she laughed against his shirt. "I'm inclined to agree."

His arms tightened. "I love you, Mariah Bell."

"I love you, Tiller McRae."

"Enough to skip all that silly courtship business and marry me?"

A thrill shot through her. "I don't see why not." She leaned to frown up at him. "You've taken quite a leap from courting me a little to a proposal. What changed?"

He kissed her forehead and snuggled her close again. "I wanted to marry you from the first. I thought if I told you, it might spook you."

Her joy boundless, she tightened her fingers on the front of his shirt and smiled to herself. "And you really plan to stay on here at Bell's Inn? What about your carefree coattails? Those roots you find so binding?"

Tiller chuckled, the sound a rumble in his throat. "You believed the words of a shiftless drifter?"

She laughed aloud. "A point well taken."

He held her, swaying as if rocking a cherished child.

Mariah swayed too, dizzy with loving him.

Abruptly, Tiller stilled, dragging them to a stop. "What about your father? We need his blessing, don't we? He'll want to be here for the wedding, too." He patted her back. "I understand that you'll want to put things off until he returns."

Her heart surged and fluttered in her chest. "Father will be gone a very long time."

A groan escaped his lips. "How long do we have to wait?"

She shook her head. "I don't think we can. It wouldn't be practical."

He brightened. "So we'll be married right away?"

She nodded and rested her head on his shoulder. "The sooner the better."

Mariah braced for another squabble with Miss Vee. The poor woman would never understand, and Mariah couldn't imagine how to convince her. Most likely, the time had come to tell her the truth.

Tiller sighed in her ear. "You're taking a gamble, aren't you? You don't know much about me." His heartbeat thudded against her cheek. "About my past, I mean."

Caught in her own guilty thoughts, hot tears stung her throat. "You don't know everything about me either."

He cradled her head in his hands and raised her face to his. Determination, heart-stirring affection, and a touch of fear swirled in his eyes. "You won't like some of what I've done."

She bunched her brows. "It can't be that bad."

"I'm afraid it is," he said firmly then drew a deep breath. "But I swear to make it up to you." His throat rose and fell. "To everyone."

He looked so grim. What dastardly deeds could sweet-faced Tiller McRae possibly be guilty of? Mariah shuddered and lowered her lashes. Whatever he'd done, she didn't want to know. Not with their love just confessed.

Besides, she wasn't ready to lay her secrets on the table. There'd be plenty of time later for baring their souls. "Don't say anything else, Tiller. We'll discuss it later." She pushed out of his arms and backed away, despising herself for the pain that flashed in his eyes.

Skirting past him, she picked up the tray. "Miss Vee will be wondering where I am."

He caught her arm as she passed and held her, searching her face.

She summoned a weak smile. "Don't fret. Nothing's changed."

Gnawing his bottom lip, he nodded. "Let me walk you to the house then. I'll get cleaned up and go for supplies."

Crossing the yard, he cleared his throat. "Can we tell the others? Miss Vee, Dicey, and Rainy?"

She grinned. "I suppose so."

A delighted smile lit his face. "Miss Vee first. As soon as we reach the house."

She touched his arm. "Don't mention how soon we plan to marry, Tiller. I'll break that news to her myself."

Nearing the porch, she halted, clutching Tiller's sleeve.

A horse lumbered up the rise bearing a lone Indian. The big man slouched in the saddle with a broad, battered hat tugged low over his face.

Mariah strained to see what the dread in her heart had already confirmed. The worst problem imaginable rode toward her on the sun-dappled Trace. She groaned. "Oh, no. It's really him."

Tiller stared with her. "You know that man?"

"He's my uncle, Joe Brashears. But please don't call him Joe. It enrages him. He prefers Nukowa."

"Nu-who?"

"It's pronounced Nook-o-ah. It means 'angry' in our tongue. He took the name when my mother died." She sighed. "It fits him well, I'm afraid."

"I like Joe better."

Ignoring him, she danced with frustration. "I adore my uncle, but I dread his visits. These days, they're never pleasant."

"I suppose not, if he's angry all the time. What made him mad?"

"He wants something, and he can be very stubborn about it."

"What does he want?" Tiller asked, shading his eyes.

She shrugged. "Me."

"You?" He shot her a glance. "What for?"

"To take me back to the Indian Territory."

Tiller's head whipped around. "What? No!"

"He's chosen a husband for me there."

He growled low in his throat. "I can see I'm going to love Uncle Joe."

Mariah pasted a welcome smile on her face. "Hush. He's almost here."

Tiller slung his arm around her shoulders. "Just in time to share our happy news."

"No!" Mariah whispered harshly, shrugging off his arm. She moved a few paces away. "You mustn't breathe a word of our engagement, Tiller. Not a word, do you understand?"

"Why not?"

She narrowed her eyes. "If you do, I'll be on my way to marry the son of a chief, and you'll be left here scratching your head."

He gaped at her. "I can handle Uncle Joe, Mariah."

"Nukowa," she hissed. "And please leave him to me." She frowned. "Maybe you should go on back to the barn."

"No." Scowling, he closed the distance between them. "If it's all the same to you, I'm staying right here."

TWENTY-FIVE

Joe squinted against the afternoon sun. Surely his tired eyes deceived him. The nahullo beside Mariah had drawn her beneath his arm as if he'd bartered for her and won.

His stomach tightened. Who was the red-haired man at his niece's side, his welcoming smile as forced as hers?

Slant-eyed glances fired between the two. The feud of a couple in love. What mischief was afoot in John Coffee's house, right under his nose?

Joe snorted. He'd arrived just in time to help Blazing Hair find the road.

Mariah strode to meet him. Pink tinged her cheeks, but the warmth of her greeting seemed more fitting. "Halito, *amoshi!*"

"Halito, *sabitek.*" He swung his aching body from the saddle. *"Chim achukma?"*

"I'm fine, Uncle. And you?"

"I need water." Joe swiped his hand across his dry mouth. "I have miles of dusty road in my throat."

"Of course you do," Mariah said. "After such a long ride. Come up to the house, and we'll do even better than water."

Joe dragged his pack off the horse. "You have whiskey?"

Mariah's laugh was as false as her smile. "No, and you have no

175

business drinking strong spirits." She handed the reins to the nahullo without a second glance in his direction. "I'm sure Miss Vee has a fresh pitcher of lemonade."

Joe wasn't fooled by the girl's deliberate shun. She could go on treating the tall young man as if he didn't matter, but Joe had spotted a fox in the henhouse. A lanky red fox.

Over his shoulder, Joe watched the man lead the horse to the barn at an angry stride. He smiled. It wouldn't be the last time he walked away mad, if Joe had his way.

He turned his attention to Mariah. "Your father is well?"

She stumbled a bit and lost her footing.

Joe's quick hand caught and steadied her. "Now I see why you have no more whiskey. Have you been sipping firewater this morning?"

She wound her arm through his and continued walking, but her strained smile didn't reach her eyes. "I'm drunk with happiness to see you, I guess."

He patted her hand. "Is something wrong, sabitek?"

Staring at the ground, she bit her bottom lip. "Father's not here, Uncle."

Joe peered at her. "John's in town today?"

"Not in town. He's...gone away."

Joe stopped so fast he pulled her off balance again. "What do you mean 'away'? Where did he go?"

Mariah angled her head so he couldn't see her eyes. "I'm not sure. Not exactly. He left so suddenly." She looked everywhere but at Joe. "He became very ill and had to leave."

"To the white man's hospital?"

"Not a hospital."

"Then where? Don't talk riddles, Mariah. I've come a long way. When will he return?"

She raised her chin. "He'll be gone for a very long time."

Joe narrowed one eye and tried to read her. The girl's tight mouth and sulky eyes were a black-watered pool.

To what lengths would John Coffee go to outwit him? What trick had he put his daughter up to? Mariah wanted to stay in Mississippi—she'd made this no secret—but it wasn't like her to deceive.

Impatient, he stalked ahead of her. "No matter. I can wait. For as long as it takes." His bold words were a lie. He'd left Myrtle to pull corn and work crops, to grow a son for him, alone and frightened. John Coffee had the upper hand before the battle had ever begun. Furious, Joe reached the porch and spun to scowl at her. "Who is the red-haired nahullo?"

The truth flickered in her eyes but skirted her mouth. "Tiller? He's a drifter we hired to make a few repairs. He works for room and board."

Peering past the haze of anger that had him blinded, Joe gazed around the inn's backyard, seeing it for the first time.

A careless giant had strolled through the familiar grounds. He'd plundered the garden, used the fence posts for toothpicks, and ripped up the oak for a parasol.

Joe's wandering gaze stopped at the half-finished barn. "What happened here?"

"A twister." Mariah closed her eyes and shuddered. "It was awful. We hid in the root cellar."

He whistled. "All this damage and the house still stands?"

Mariah nodded. "The inn shook above our heads like a wet dog, but it held together."

Smiling, Joe took in the old house from the eaves to the foundation. "She's faced down worse in her time."

He patted the railing on the new porch. "Nice job." He glanced at Red Hair scaling the barn like a nimble goat. "His doing?"

Mariah nodded. "Tiller made all the improvements to the inn." She slid her fingers along the smooth wood with the pride of a mother caressing her child. "He built this porch in two days."

Joe stuck out his jaw. "I thought you planned to quench my thirst."

She swept past him to the back door. "Right this way, and I'll pour you that lemonade I promised. You must be starving, too."

Grumbling, he followed her through the kitchen door. Tossing his wide-brimmed hat at the rack, he glanced across the hall. An ugly white stain marred the hardwood floor where the dining room had taken in water. The curtain rod hung by a loose nail, and the drapes were missing. More damage from the twister, no doubt. Thankfully, the kitchen, with the broad behind bending over the stove, was just as he remembered. "Woman, you haven't changed a bit."

Viola glanced around then sprang up and slammed the oven door. "Joe Brashears. You old rascal." She scurried toward him, wiping her hands on her skirt.

Joe braced for her smothering hug.

"How are you, Joe?"

He'd given up on her calling him anything else. "It's been awhile."

Viola released him, just barely, her painted lips stretched in a smile. "If you're not the last person I expected to see in my kitchen. . ." She pulled out a chair. "Here, sit down. Let me fix you something to eat."

Mariah hurried for the pitcher. "He's more thirsty than hungry, Miss Vee."

Joe shifted the weight of his pack. "Right now, I'd like to put this down somewhere." He glanced toward the hall. "Is my room empty?"

Mariah paused, the lemonade she poured slowed to a drip. "I'm afraid it's taken." Her eyes flashed a warning at Viola, but it came too late.

"That's Tiller's room now," Viola said. "It has been since he got here. I doubt you could blast him out with a scattergun."

The best plan Joe had heard all day. Scowling, he dropped the heavy pack with a thud. "I always take that room."

Mariah finished filling his glass with shaky hands. "But Uncle," she said with a nervous laugh, "we didn't know you were coming."

"You do now. *Tiller* can move."

"Oh, but it wouldn't be fair, would it? He's all settled, and—"

"I have an idea," Viola interrupted. "We'll move young Tiller upstairs to your father's bedroom, Mariah." She shot the girl a look Joe couldn't read. "You know. . .the one right across the hall from yours."

Handing her wide-eyed uncle his drink, Mariah bit back a smile. "What a wonderful idea, Miss Vee. After all, it's the largest room in the house, and a big man like Tiller McRae needs room to stretch his legs."

Uncle Nukowa cleared his throat. "On second thought, there's no reason for the boy to move his things." He set the glass on the table, grabbed his pack, and started up the kitchen stairs. "If John's room is empty, I'll take it."

Miss Vee winked at Mariah. "Get washed up, Joe. I'll have you something fixed to eat before you can say. . ."

His footsteps faded up the stairs.

"Bamboozled," she whispered.

They fell against each other laughing.

"What's he doing here?" Miss Vee asked.

"Do you need to ask? I'm surprised he's not in war paint."

Miss Vee's hands fisted at her waist. "Joe needn't think he can start badgering John the minute he returns. I won't have it, you hear me? I just won't."

Mariah released a weary breath. "Let's not borrow trouble, dear. 'Sufficient unto the day is the evil thereof.'"

Miss Vee sniffed. "Now you sound like Otis."

"Speaking of Otis, where is he?"

Since the storm, Mariah's terror of the little man had eased. She avoided being alone with him, but otherwise things had returned to normal.

Otis had started to venture out of his room more often, always supported by Tiller's ready arms, but he still had a way to go toward regaining his strength.

"Last I saw, he was napping. He sleeps more than a newborn babe."

"I suppose he's still recovering." Mariah glanced toward the stairs. "I need to explain Otis to my uncle before he trips over him in the parlor in his union suit."

Miss Vee's laugh came out a snort. "Especially since the poor thing can't keep his flap fastened."

They giggled together like naughty children.

Sobering, Miss Vee tied on her apron and opened the pantry. "Now then, what am I going to feed Joe? I've never seen the larder so bare."

Mariah grinned. "It won't be empty for long. Tiller's taking me to town to buy supplies."

Her casual announcement caught Miss Vee's attention. "Granted, you and Tiller are a handsome pair, but I doubt the merchants will trade your looks for goods. How do you plan to pay for these supplies?"

With a saucy wink, Mariah jiggled the pocket of her skirt, letting the coins clink together.

Miss Vee's eyebrows soared. "I know the sound of money when I hear it. Where'd you get those coins?"

"Isn't it wonderful?" Mariah kissed her cheek. "Tiller's been selling trees downed by the storm. He surprised me with a handful of gold."

Miss Vee clasped her hands toward the ceiling. "Hallelujah! Our troubles are over. I knew that boy was a blessing in disguise."

Mariah longed to share the rest of the morning's good news, but with Uncle Nukowa around, she didn't dare trust Miss Vee to keep it quiet.

"I can hardly wait to get to town and fill the pantry." She parted the kitchen blinds, searching the roof of the barn for Tiller. "Where is that man? We need to be on the road. It's getting late."

Miss Vee shooed her with her hands. "Go roust him, honey. The sooner you leave, the quicker you'll get back."

Mariah hurried to the back door. "Prepare a list of all we need. I'll tell Tiller to hitch up Sheki and pull the wagon around."

"Where are we going?"

Her startled gaze jumped to Uncle Nukowa on the stairs. He had washed the gray film of grime from his face and loosened the cords that held his long braids. Gleaming hair draped his shoulders, still as black as when ten-year-old Mariah dogged the heels of her handsome young uncle, learning to hunt, fish, and trap on their Mississippi land. Watching his stern, rigid face, it seemed a long time ago.

"It's just a supply run, sir. We'll be back tonight."

"We?" He reached the bottom landing, his face drawn to a pucker. "Do you mean you and that. . .Tiller?"

She nodded.

He raised a staying hand. "I don't think so. It's a long drive, and you've waited too late to strike out. We'll go tomorrow."

Mariah shifted her weight impatiently. "But Uncle, we're out of supplies. I don't have eggs or meat for breakfast."

He shot her a warning glare. "A matter you should've already tended. It's settled. We go in the morning."

To defend herself would mean revealing more than she intended about the inn's waning business. He didn't need more ammunition in his war to make her leave.

She raised her lashes to peek at him. "We, Uncle?"

"It's been awhile since I've seen Canton." He picked up his empty glass and strolled casually to the waiting pitcher. "Now then, Viola. Where's this fine meal you promised?"

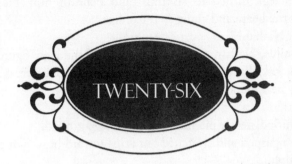

TWENTY-SIX

Tiller pounded the head of the nail until it disappeared inside the splintered wood. Growling, he forced himself to stop before the board split in two.

As long as he could remember, life had been an unlucky hand of poker. Any reasonable man would admit he'd suffered an unjust childhood. The mess he'd made of things since could be pinned squarely on his own shoulders, but not the way he got started in the unsavory way of life.

Just when he'd taken steps to turn the game around, fate had dealt him a marked card in the form of Uncle "I'm angry" Joe. Tiller tightened his grip on the hammer. "Thanks to you, I'm not so happy myself, old boy." He took another hard swipe at the nail and stood—spinning toward the river so fast he nearly tripped over his boots.

A lone rider sat on the far bank of the Pearl, dappled by the shimmering reflection off the water. By the easy forward slump in the saddle, his arms crossed over the horn, the dim outline could very well be Nathan Carter.

Tiller's heartbeat raced in his ears. Shading his eyes, he squinted. If the sun didn't shine so bright on the river, he could see that it wasn't so. As soon as he caught his breath, he'd tear across the field and relieve his scattered mind.

Before he could move a muscle, the specter from his former life straightened in the saddle and fired a snappy salute. Reining his horse, he rode off the backside of the rise and disappeared.

Tiller's legs turned to shifting sand beneath him. He lowered himself to the beam and clung to the braces.

Was it Nathan?

Impossible. Nathan wouldn't ride away. If the hazy figure was his old friend, he'd have found a low crossing and rode across boasting about how he'd found him.

"Tiller?"

He whirled, nearly pitching himself to the ground.

Mariah gasped and stretched her arms toward him. "For goodness' sake, be careful."

He swiped his mouth with his arm. "You shouldn't be sneaking around like that."

She leaned to see out the back window of the barn. "What do you see over there? You're the color of cotton."

"It's nothing. Too much sun on my head, I guess." He scooted across the beam to the ladder and made his way down. "Are you ready to go? It's getting late."

She made a face. "That's what I came to tell you. We have to wait until morning."

"Why?"

"Uncle Nukowa doesn't want me out so late."

Irritation crept up Tiller's spine. "Since when does he make the decisions?"

She took a deep breath. "Since the moment he rode into the yard."

Tiller propped his hands on his hips. "Does he think you sit on a shelf and twiddle your thumbs until he shows up? You've managed just fine without him."

Mariah gripped his arms. "I know it's hard to understand, but please try. In the tradition of my people, my uncle believes I'm his responsibility. Of course, my father never held with the Indian ways. He's never allowed Uncle Nukowa that sort of access."

Tiller set his jaw. "Good for him."

"When Mother died, my uncle assumed I'd be returning with him to the Indian Territory. He became enraged when Father forbade it."

Twirling the soft hair beside her ear, Tiller frowned. "You're not exactly a child anymore. Shouldn't the tug-of-war be over?"

She gave a somber shake of her head. "Not until my wedding day. It's up to my uncle to make sure I marry well."

"I'll be happy to relieve him of that obligation." He leaned to see her face. "And very soon, I hope."

Her gaze shifted to his. "Within our tribe, Tiller. After Mother broke with custom and married an outsider, he'll be extra vigilant to see it doesn't happen to me."

Mariah reached for his hands. "That's why you must promise to keep our engagement a secret." She tightened her grip. "Uncle Nukowa will go to any lengths to make sure we never wed."

The passion in her plea struck sudden fear in Tiller's heart. "What's to keep him from whisking you away from here?"

"He won't. Not against my father's wishes." She shook her head. "My uncle's not here to kidnap me. He's here to settle a feud and win a longstanding war of wills."

Tiller pulled her close. "Suppose your Father comes back and agrees to let you go? Do you hold enough sway to talk him out of it?"

With a weary sigh, Mariah leaned into his chest. "Believe me, that's the last thing we have to fret about."

He caressed her head, the silky feel of her hair making it hard to stay mad—until the unmistakable moan of a hungry stomach sprang them apart.

"Yours or mine?" he asked.

She blushed and shrugged.

"Blast it! You're hungry. Joe should credit me with enough sense to get you to Canton and back so you can eat tonight."

"It's not so different in any culture, is it? Show me an uncle who wouldn't be concerned about his niece traveling the roads at night. Alone with a man, at that."

Tiller blew out a frustrated breath. "This is different. We need food." He pushed back the dread of another long, lonely ride so soon. "If there's no changing his mind, I'll just go by myself."

"I'd rather you didn't." She jingled her bulging pocket and smiled. "I've got my heart set on going into town."

Tiller drew back and laughed. "You're still carrying that money around? Shouldn't it be tucked away in the safe?"

She rattled the coins again. "Would you deprive me of my music? I'm rather enjoying the sound of plenty."

Unable to resist, he drew her into his arms. "All right, maestro. We'll go in the morning. But in the meantime, what will you eat?"

"I think we'll be fine. Miss Vee is a wonder at making something to eat out of scraps. She's inside now turning a basket of wilted potatoes into soup and the leftover meal into fritters."

"And in the morning?"

"We found an old tin of flour in the back of the pantry. I'll make flapjacks and cover them in honey so we won't miss the butter. And I still have a few pieces left from the box of bacon." She gripped his hand. "We'll make do, Tiller. Then we'll leave first thing after breakfast."

He rubbed his forehead. "I wish I'd brought some things back with me from Canton."

She cocked her head. "Why didn't you?"

"It wasn't my money to spend." He cupped her chin. "I want you to always be able to trust me, Mariah. No matter what you may hear in the future, just know you can trust me."

A tiny frown appeared between her brows, but she smiled. "I do trust you, Tiller. Someday you'll know just how much."

He smoothed the soft skin of her chin with his thumb. "Then there's the other reason I didn't bring home supplies. . ."

"Yes?"

He gave her his best roguish grin. "The thought never entered my mind."

She shoved him away. "Oh, you!"

Laughing, he gathered her close. "The more I think about it, the more I like the idea of waiting for daylight." He winked. "That way I can stare at your pretty profile all the way into Canton."

She lowered her lashes. "I hope you find as much pleasure in staring at my uncle."

Tiller's brow shot up. "Joe's coming?"

"I'm afraid so."

He groaned. "Can't you talk him out of it?"

"I dare not try, or he'll be suspicious."

"If it's a chaperone he's worried about, we'll take Miss Vee. Or Rainy."

Mariah patted his chest. "I'm sorry, Tiller. He's coming along, and that's the end of it. My uncle's a very stubborn man. Once he gets an idea in his head, you can't drive it out with your hammer."

Tiller glanced at the tool in question, hefting its weight. "It wouldn't take a forceful blow. Just enough for an afternoon nap."

"Tiller McRae!"

He grinned. "You know I'm teasing, but the idea is tempting." He softened his eyes. "There are things I'd planned to say to you, but the matter won't bear your uncle's prying ears."

Blushing, she nodded. "I'll admit I looked forward to those hours alone with you to talk about our future."

" 'Our future.' That has a nice ring to it." He gave her a lazy smile. "Hours alone with you sounds even better."

Planting her fingers against his chest, she pushed away. "I'd best get back, or he'll come looking for me."

Tiller walked with her to the barn door. "I'll do like you say, honey. I'll keep our secret as long as it takes." He dropped a soft kiss on her ear then lingered to whisper. "I only hope it won't be a lengthy wait."

Watching her go, he recalled Otis's God-words promising that things would turn out good in the end. Maybe his ill-fated life had taken a lucky turn at last. If he had to be patient for a spell, Mariah was worth the wait.

A shadow crossed the floor, and Tiller spun.

Just the wind dipping a branch past the window.

He shook himself and released a shuddering breath. It wasn't the time for seeing ghosts. He had his hands full enough with the old warhorse setting up camp inside Bell's Inn.

TWENTY-SEVEN

Tiller tugged the reins and eased Sheki around a miry hole in the Trace, leftover from the relentless summer rains. As long as he avoided the low places, the going was easy. His frequent trips into Canton had reestablished portions of the road, pushing back the heavy overgrowth threatening to reclaim the old trail.

He headed west as soon as he could and followed the trail into town. As Mariah predicted, Uncle Joe's stern profile, nowhere near as pleasing as hers, glowered beside Tiller on the front seat of the rig.

Mariah made small talk, pointing out the wild herbs and strawberries and commenting on the greening of the hillsides, helped along by the recent downpours.

Joe answered in grunts, meeting Tiller's few comments with a raised brow and harsh stare. Even when the old coyote nodded off, his head bobbing to his chest, he slept with one ear open, raising his head to glare when Tiller spoke quietly to Mariah.

The miles and hours dragged. Tiller sagged with relief when the tall white spires of Canton's Grace Episcopal Church came into view over the treetops. He decided to speak his mind whether Uncle Joe liked it or not. "I'll drop the two of you in the square then take the wagon to have the wheels looked at. The way they're squealing, the rear axle needs greasing."

"Will you be joining us soon?"

The hopeful lilt in Mariah's voice spun Uncle Joe around so fast it's a wonder his neck didn't squeal.

She ducked her head. "I just meant that it's very close to lunchtime. I thought we might sit for a meal before we start shopping."

Tiller turned aside to hide his grin. If Mariah wasn't careful, she'd give up her own secret. He leaped to the ground and handed her down before Uncle Joe had a chance, raising both brows and winking when Joe turned his head. She rewarded him with a blush and a shy smile.

Tiller tipped his hat. "I'll drop off the rig then meet you in front of the courthouse. There's a café next door that serves fork-tender roast and fairly respectable rolls." He winked. "Though not as good as yours."

Joe swept around the back of the wagon. "We don't have time for such dawdling, Mariah. There are many supplies to buy, and it's a long way home. We'll find some hardtack and jerky."

Mariah's bright smile slid away. "Oh, Uncle, please. I'm starving. Our breakfast didn't have enough substance to stick." She tucked her dainty chin. "It would be such a treat to have someone else do the cooking for a change."

Joe's resolve wilted under the spell of Mariah's big eyes. He gazed toward the courthouse. "Where is this place you speak of?"

Grinning, Tiller ducked his head. They had something in common after all. He pointed out the narrow building with the checkered curtains in the windows. "Go on over. I won't be long."

"Maybe they have coffee fit for a man to drink," Joe mumbled as Mariah took his arm. "The slush John Coffee has Viola trained to make tastes like swamp water."

Shaking his head, Tiller climbed aboard the wagon and turned Sheki toward the smithy. He couldn't get shed of the horse and rig fast enough. After giving instructions concerning both, he hustled up the boardwalk, eager to belly up to the table. Even the strong coffee Joe mentioned sounded good.

Tiller couldn't remember the last time he'd eaten his fill. His shirts were baggy, his ribs stuck out, and his trousers drooped down past his waist. "The lean times are over," he told himself, loping toward the café. The checkered curtains were just ahead, and his darlin' waited inside with a pocketful of money. One thing was certain—he wouldn't leave Canton hungry.

The waitress frowned at the empty basket. "Dreadful sorry, folks." She picked it up. "I thought I just filled this with rolls."

Mariah laughed. "Oh, you did. My friend here enjoyed them very much. Bring us another basket if you don't mind."

Tiller's cheeks were too full to speak, but he nodded his agreement. Uncle Nukowa shot him a contemptuous scowl. "Just like the greedy white man, always taking more than he needs."

Mariah seethed. He spoke in their language, but she answered in English. "Yes, he has quite an appetite, doesn't he? It's the hunger of a hardworking man." She let the fire in her eyes say the rest.

Her uncle's hand swept over the stack of empty dishes and the slice of apple pie in front of Tiller's plate. "Who pays for all this?"

Mariah wished he'd stuck with Choctaw. Her patience at an end, she decided the time had come to set her uncle straight. "My understanding with Tiller is between us. Please don't insult him again or dishonor me by questioning our arrangement."

He shrugged. "I was just asking."

Tiller calmly pulled the pie plate toward him and poured a dollop of cream over the top. "It's all right, Mariah. Your uncle's looking out for your interests." Leaning over the table with a bold stare, he raised his chin. "Sir, if there's ever a day when I don't earn my keep around Bell's Inn, I hope you'll invite me to leave." He nodded. "Are we understood?"

Before her uncle could respond, Tiller continued. "I'm not in the habit of allowing a woman to fight my battles, but since Mariah has opened the can, let me stir the worms." He laid down his fork. "On the subject of battles, I'm not sure why you've declared war against me. Since you hardly know me, I don't feel you have just cause."

Uncle Nukowa watched Tiller with guarded eyes.

"That said, if I've done anything to rile you, it wasn't deliberate, and I apologize." Turning on the full force of his charm, Tiller offered his hand. "So I say we shake and start over."

Nibbling at her pie, Mariah held her breath.

The sullen wall Uncle Nukowa had erected crumbled twitch by twitch on his proud face, toppling with a grudging smile. "I suppose we could do that," he said, reaching across the bread basket.

Before their palms met, a light touch at Mariah's elbow spun her around.

"I thought it was you, dear." The tall, gaunt man behind her smiled warmly. "It's good to see you, Mariah."

Blackness swirled. Mariah gulped for air to clear the murky fog. Her chest thundered and her tongue forged to the roof of her mouth. She tried to bolt from her chair and flee, but her limbs wouldn't budge.

"How have you been holding up?" Dr. Moony asked, his eyes a sea of compassion.

She made a strangled sound, followed by a guttural moan, worsened by the bite of spiced apple hung in her throat. Frantic, she silently pleaded with Tiller across the table.

Staring back helplessly, his freckles stood on tiptoe.

TWENTY-EIGHT

Mariah was choking. Or having some sort of a spell.

Tiller's gaze jumped to the tall man at her side. Somehow, it was this geezer's fault.

He half rose from his chair. "Mariah?"

She struggled to swallow as if something had her by the throat and then sucked in a breath of air. "D–Dr. Moony," she finally managed, blinking up at the stranger. "How nice to see you." Pulling her napkin from her lap, she dabbed the corners of her mouth, the starched cloth no whiter than her face.

Relief settled Tiller against his chair.

"I planned to ride out and check on you," the man was saying. "Then I got your letter." He patted her shoulder. "I was sorry to hear that John Coffee was gone."

Mariah shot to her feet, loudly clearing her throat. "Doctor. . ." She pointed at the door. "May we continue this conversation outside?"

He held up his finger. "In a moment." With a warm smile, he nodded at Joe. "I'm happy to see you've come to stay with your niece. I hated to think of her all alone out there."

The pallor of Mariah's cheeks rose to a fiery mottled red. "Please, sir?"

"The onset of John's illness was sudden," the doctor continued. "Of course, his leaving us so quickly was no surprise."

"Didn't surprise me, either." Joe swung his chair around and casually crossed his legs. "It's just like my brother-in-law to run off and leave his responsibilities on someone else's shoulders."

Flustered, the doctor stared. "Forgive me, Joe, but it's not like the poor man had a choice. John was quite ill, you know."

Joe folded his arms over his chest. "Just so he returns stronger than when he left. I have a few things to say to him."

The doctor's throat bobbed a few times before he nodded. "Of, course. You mean when he"—he twirled his finger in the air and rolled his eyes—*"returns."* He gave a nervous laugh. "I must say, you people have the quaintest customs."

Mariah hooked her arm in his and urged him toward the door. "If you don't mind, I have something of a delicate nature to discuss. In private."

Nearly pulling the lanky man off balance, Mariah hauled him over the threshold.

Tiller's puzzled gaze met Joe's across the table. "What do you suppose that was about?"

Joe shrugged. "The mind of a woman is a deep river. I try not to fish there."

Nodding thoughtfully, Tiller cut the rest of his pie in half and slid a portion onto Joe's empty plate. "That was Mr. Bell's doctor?"

Joe pulled the offering in front of him and took a bite. "Yes. For many years."

Tiller nodded. "Do you know what sickness he has?"

Joe shook his head. "I suppose I should've asked."

His motives a mite selfish, Tiller posed a thought. "To hear him and Mariah talk, Mr. Bell could be gone a long. . .*long* time."

"You're right." Joe craned his neck to stare at the door, the concern Tiller had hoped to rouse creasing his forehead. "Maybe I should go ask him."

"So you see, doctor," Mariah said, "among my people the subject of death is forbidden, so the less said about the departed, the better. Once we've completed the mourning ritual, we're not allowed to utter their names again."

Dr. Moony took both her hands and squeezed. "I'm a blundering old fool, dear. I'll be more careful next time."

She tightened her fingers. "It's my fault. I should've said something before now. And I'm very grateful for all you've done."

He flashed a warm smile. "I'm happy to see you're all right. I watched you suffer right along with your father."

A cleansing rest flooded Mariah's soul, and grateful tears welled. She felt comforted to speak openly of her father's death, especially with someone who understood the depths of her pain. She tugged a hankie from her waistband and wiped her eyes. "Thank you, sir."

Despite how good it felt to grieve, to linger would be folly. She pointed over her shoulder. "I'd best get back inside. They'll be wondering where I am."

"Yes, and I have patients to see." He leaned to kiss her cheek. "You know how to reach me and the missus. If you need anything, don't hesitate to call on us." Mariah clung to his hand as he backed away smiling. "Anything at all, you hear?"

She nodded, letting his fingers slip from her grasp. "I won't forget." A throbbing ache in her chest, she watched him stroll to the corner and disappear. With a shuddering sigh, she returned to the café and met Uncle Nukowa on the doorstep.

He pushed past her and peered up and down the boardwalk, his bushy brows drawn to peaks. "Where's the doctor?"

"Gone," Mariah said, clutching his sleeve to draw him inside. "He had patients to tend."

Avoiding Tiller's curious stare, she approached the waitress to pay the bill. Once she'd counted out enough coins, she tucked the leather pouch away. "Miss, where is your. . .?"

The girl pointed. "Through there and out the back to your left."

Nodding her thanks, Mariah headed down the long hallway, forcing herself not to run. At the end of the longest walk of her life, she yanked open the door of the cramped little building. Slumping against the roughhewn wall, she allowed the bitter tears to fall.

Joe had a newfound respect for Tiller McRae. The boy stood in the wagon bed shifting boxes of canned foods and shoving crates of dry goods aside to make room, attacking the job with the same strength of character he'd shown while defending himself in the café.

Tiller had a strong back and willing hands when it came to hard work, qualities Joe prided himself on. Unfortunately, the brash buck couldn't hide his desire for Mariah.

The two thought him a witless fool. A blind man could see their lingering looks, the quick twining of their fingers when she handed up her bundles, his thumb stroking the back of her hand each time they passed.

Clearly, Mariah loved him. Despite Tiller's charm, or maybe because of it, Joe hadn't decided if he loved her, too.

Maybe greed clouded Tiller's vision. The chance to own Bell's Inn and acres of Mississippi farmland would tempt a man even with an ugly woman thrown into the bargain. Mariah, her father's only heir, was as lovely as a spotted fawn.

Hadn't Joe suspected the same of John Coffee? But his sister had closed her love-struck ears and married the spineless man despite Joe's warning.

Mariah handed the last bundle to Tiller, her eyes twin stars of admiration. Leaning to take it from her hands, he winked.

Joe ground his heel in the dirt and gritted his teeth. Whatever it took to prevent it, Mariah wouldn't make the same mistake as her mother.

Tiller kicked the end of a box, wedging it between a crate and the side of the wagon. "There now. Maybe we can close the tailgate." He jumped to the ground, tilting his head at Mariah. "You must be finished shopping since you've emptied all the stores."

She glanced up from checking things off her list. "I suppose that's all we need. Can you think of anything we may have forgotten?"

He raised the gate and shoved home the latch. "I don't see how. There's at least one of everything in town back here."

Her cheeks colored. "Oh, you."

Already they sparred like husband and wife. Angry with himself for making peace with Tiller, Joe tugged down his hat to hide his glowering face. "Are we ready to go? It's a long way home."

"Yes, Uncle." With a flourish, she scratched off the last item on her list. "We're ready."

They climbed aboard, Mariah giggling the way she had as a child when Joe held her down and tickled her. "I can't wait to see Miss Vee's face. It's been a while since our cupboard was full."

Tiller shifted around to look at her. "With all these different foods, I can't wait to taste whatever you two come up with."

Joe couldn't help frowning at him. The bottomless man couldn't be hungry.

"I promise you fine meals for your patience, Tiller," Mariah said gleefully. "And baked goods in abundance. Have you ever seen so much flour and sugar and butter?"

Grinning, Tiller glanced over his shoulder. "I'll get the meat straight into the smokehouse. Those salted hams and racks of bacon should last a good while."

"Yes, and I bought extra meal. In case we catch more fish."

"More fish sounds good. With Rainy's help, I'll make sure that happens." His smile widened. "Which reminds me. . .the garden is coming along fine. In no time, we'll have plenty of fresh vegetables again."

"That's enough," Joe growled, sweeping off his hat and slapping his leg with the brim. "What's going on here?"

Two sets of stunned eyes blinked at him.

"What do you mean, Uncle?"

He spun around. "The two of you talk like you've been starving. Why is the pantry and smokehouse so empty?"

Squirming like a guilty child, her gaze jumped to Tiller.

Joe lifted his hand. "I don't want my answer from him. You tell me, Mariah. Why has John Coffee allowed my only niece to go hungry while the rest of her tribe prospers?"

TWENTY-NINE

It took the better part of the ride home to smooth Uncle Nukowa's ruffled feathers. Mariah explained that in the aftermath of the storm, and with the usual decline in travelers during the winter months, the coffers had dwindled. Now, thanks to Tiller's fine head for business, she had enough money to last a good long while.

She didn't dare mention the cost of father's illness. Weary of half-truths and careful omission of details, she neglected to explain how she'd emptied her safe into Dr. Moony's pockets to avoid the very confrontation she'd just faced.

Uncle Nukowa vented his frustration on Tiller by hinting the money would last longer without the price of his appetite.

Mariah jumped to Tiller's defense. "That's highly unfair, Uncle. While it's true that he enjoys his food, I've watched this poor man go without until every last member of the household was fed."

Her uncle cut his eyes to Tiller. "Is that true?"

"Maybe." He shrugged. "I reckon it is."

Uncle Nukowa sat against the side rail, watching Tiller as if he didn't quite know what to make of him. "Then I owe you an apology."

Tiller slapped her uncle's knee. "I wouldn't fret, Joe."

Mariah cringed, but Uncle Nukowa didn't bat an eye.

With the extra weight of the load on poor Sheki, the journey back took longer. Dusk had settled over the land as they turned off the Canton road onto the Trace. So close to home, Tiller didn't bother with the lantern. Mariah supposed they were all relieved, especially the horse, when the warm glow of lights from the inn appeared between the trees.

They pulled into the backyard, and Miss Vee met them on the porch with a lamp. "Hallelujah! I've never been so happy to see three faces in my life. Excuse me, Sheki—make that four." She grinned. "I can hear Otis smiling from here. The poor man's hollow as a gourd."

She ran down the steps and peered over the side of the wagon, running eager hands over the boxes. "How did you sneak up on me, Tiller? I've been straining to hear those squeaky wheels for hours."

"Had her greased, Miss Vee," he said.

"So you tricked me, you rascal." Her dimpled cheeks were shadows in the dim light. "Never mind. You're here now. Let's get this load in the house and go to cooking."

Guilt fell heavy on Mariah's shoulders. While they'd frolicked and feasted in town, poor Miss Vee and Otis suffered hunger. She scurried down. "We'll unload, Miss Vee. Go warm up the stove."

"I've had a fire in the oven for hours. The burning wood was starting to smell tasty."

Mariah passed a ham over her shoulder. "Take this inside. Get it sliced and put it on to fry. I'll be in to make skillet bread as soon as I can."

Tiller unhooked the latch and lowered the tailgate. "Go ahead, Mariah. Me and Uncle Joe can handle things out here."

Cringing, she waited for her uncle's flash of anger at Tiller's familiar tone. Instead, he eased his body stiffly to the ground and took the first heavy crate from Tiller's hands. "Don't worry," he said, huffing up the steps to the back door. "I remember where everything goes."

Miss Vee took a box and followed him inside.

Flashing Tiller a grateful smile, Mariah held out her hands. "I may as well take one on my way."

He reached for her, drawing her into his arms with a quick intake of air. Checking over her shoulder first, he lifted her to her tiptoes and kissed her soundly. Not the bare brush of lips against her cheek, but a crushing, dizzying kiss that robbed her of her senses.

Setting her on her feet, he handed her a box of canned goods and gave her a gentle shove toward the house. Glancing back, she found him grinning smugly. "What was the meaning of that, Tiller McRae?"

He lifted one shoulder. "Just collecting my due."

"Your due?"

He hefted one of the heavier crates, nodding at her to get moving. "The price of keeping your secret against my will. The penalty for making me wait when I'd marry you tomorrow."

She hurried onto the porch then turned. "Was it sufficient payment? I like my debts paid in full."

"Oh no, ma'am." One foot on the bottom step, he raised a teasing brow. "Consider it the first of many installments."

She jutted her chin. "It's hardly chivalrous to make a lady weak in the knees and then hand her a load to bear."

Amusement danced in his eyes. He opened his mouth to speak, but the squeal of the back door stifled his answer.

Uncle Nukowa bustled past. "Viola's watching for you, niece. She's anxious for you to finish the bread so she'll have something to wrap around her fried ham."

Fatigue seeped into Tiller's bones, and sweat dampened his shirt. Unable to pass another kitchen chair without resting his throbbing feet, he sank into the next one he came to. He'd lost count of the trips it took from the wagon to the pantry and then the smokehouse, but they finally found the bottom of the rig.

The well-stocked larder filled him with a happiness he hadn't felt in years—and not for the reason Uncle Joe might think. Tiller savored the knowledge that his idea to sell off the downed trees had filled Mariah's little safe with money. A good stash of coins promising ample food and a measure of security that lifted a burden from her shoulders for a good long while.

It felt good to take care of Mariah. Right somehow. He planned to spend the rest of his days looking after her.

Watching her bustle near the stove, flipping crisp golden circles of skillet bread, Tiller couldn't stop thinking about their kiss. He'd meant no disrespect. In fact, he'd set out to give her a teasing peck on the cheek. At the last second, her lips had drawn him like cool water on a summer day. He'd held his breath and taken the plunge, drowning in her sweetness.

As if she felt him watching, she looked over her shoulder and smiled. "You look tired."

He leaned forward and gripped his knees. "I suppose I am, but we're all exhausted. Especially poor old Sheki." He forced himself to stand. "I'll go get him tended for the night."

Mariah caught his arm as he passed. "No, I'll go. I haven't just unloaded a month's worth of supplies." She handed her spatula to Miss Vee and untied her apron. "Finish the bread, please. I'll be back in time to set the table."

Pausing at the door, she winked at Tiller. "You might want to follow my uncle's lead and freshen up before supper."

Aware of how he smelled after toting all the boxes, he stumbled toward her with his arms outstretched. "All right, but hug me first."

She squealed and darted outside while Miss Vee shook with laughter.

Tiller passed his room by and ducked in on Otis. "How are you this evening, sir?"

Otis waved merrily then rubbed his stomach. "Ready for grub." His eyes widened. "Is supper about ready?"

Tiller grinned. "It won't be much longer. Can I do anything for you before I clean up?"

Otis sank against his pillow. "Keep a close watch over little missy," he said. "Something's weighing on my spirit where she's concerned. Been praying for her all day."

Thinking of Mariah's cantankerous uncle and his determination to take her out of Mississippi, Tiller nodded. "Keep praying, sir. I think I know what it's about."

A dazed look in his eyes, Otis shook his head. "This ain't about her secret. I'm sure it's something else."

Leaning against the doorjamb, Tiller stared at Otis as the truth sank in. He knew Mariah's secret. In fact, he *was* her secret—the truth she couldn't tell her uncle Joe. How did God and Otis see a thing coming before it happened?

"You listening to me, boy?" Otis seemed upset. "You watch her close, you hear?"

Dazed, Tiller nodded. "I will, sir. I promise." He entered the room and eased Otis down on the bed. "Just rest until we bring your supper." He pointed behind him. "I have to go get cleaned up now."

Stopping on the threshold, he turned to look back, worry gnawing the back of his mind.

Otis shook his skinny finger. "Watch her."

Tiller fretted the whole time he washed up and changed his clothes. Was the old boy trying to tell him their secret was bound to come out? Was he warning Tiller that her uncle was about to steal her away?

Otis knew things, after all. God-things too wonderful for Tiller's mind to grasp.

The whole thing reminded him of the lie he'd told Otis that first day on the trail. His made-up story of a wife named Lucinda and her brutish brothers, who came in the night to snatch her from his arms.

It seemed a hundred years ago he'd spun the fanciful tale. Could it be coming to life in the form of Uncle Joe taking Mariah out of Tiller's arms, catching him in his own deceitful web?

He left his room determined to be more cautious, to guard Mariah's secret with more care.

Miss Vee had already set the dining room table then graced it with heaping platters of ham, fried eggs, and skillet bread. Lifting a hefty plateful, she placed it on a tray with a cup of coffee. "Sit down, Tiller. I'll take this to Otis and come right back to serve you."

Uncle Joe, lounging at the head of the table, stabbed a piece of bread with his fork and started eating.

Tiller pulled out a chair beside him. "Mariah's not back yet?"

Joe raised his head, his bulging jaw working. "From where? I thought she was in her room."

Tiller poured them both a cup of coffee. "She's tending Sheki."

Adding a cube of sugar to his cup, Joe stirred and took a long sip. "Counting my nag and your gelding, there are only three horses out there. She could've tended a stable-full by now."

Tiller shrugged. "You know how she is about Sheki. She's likely brushing his teeth and reading him a bedtime story."

Uncle Joe spewed a bit of coffee then swallowed and laughed with Tiller, wiping his mouth with his sleeve.

Miss Vee hurried into the room rubbing her hands together. "Now then, where were we?" She settled in her place and forked a pile of ham before passing the silver charger. "I'm not sure what's keeping Mariah, but I say we go ahead without her. If she was as hungry as I am, she'd be here by now."

Tiller took a slice of meat then handed the platter to Joe. "Share the bread, will you, Miss Vee. I can smell it from here."

Miss Vee balanced the butter dish on the tray of fried rounds and stretched the whole thing toward him. "Anything else before I get busy?"

"Tiller!" Otis swept around the corner panting hard. "You ain't watching."

Miss Vee's shoulders jerked, and she dropped the tray, scattering bread like savory place mats over the table. The careening butter dish upset the coffee urn, spilling rich, dark liquid in a puddle that soaked the bread.

Tiller leaped to his feet.

Still in his nightshirt, Otis clung to the doorpost, his mouth sagging and his eyes glazed with panic.

The hair on Tiller's arms tingled. "Something's wrong?"

Otis nodded frantically.

Tiller hurled himself past Otis and out the door.

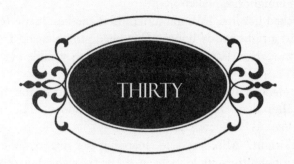

THIRTY

Two steps inside the barn, and Tiller knew. His stomach a quivering jumble of mush, he whirled to face Joe and Miss Vee. "She's gone."

Miss Vee smoothed her hair with a shaky hand. "What do you mean 'gone'? She's somewhere on the grounds. Maybe down by the river. The girl does that sometimes." She started for the door. "I'll just walk out here and call her."

Joe caught her arm. "She won't answer, Viola. Tiller's right. Mariah's gone."

She stamped her foot. "Now blast it, how do you know?"

He pointed at Sheki, still wearing the unbuckled harness and nuzzling Tiller's hand for oats. "She brought him to the barn, but that's as far as she got."

Miss Vee spun to face Tiller. "I don't understand. Mariah wouldn't just walk away."

He shot her a pointed look. "She didn't."

Pale and trembling, Joe lurched to a nearby post and clung to it. "Any ideas, son? We need to know where to start looking."

A high-pitched ringing shrilled in Tiller's ears. He rubbed his forehead. "Give me a minute to think."

Joe glanced between them. "Did John Coffee have any enemies?"

Besides you? Tiller shook his head, panic climbing his throat. "She never mentioned anyone."

"A drifter?" Joe persisted. He gripped Miss Vee's shoulders. "Think, Viola. Who might have taken her?"

She licked her lips. "We get all kinds at the inn. Just a few weeks ago, we had a right rowdy bunch. They made trouble, and I ran them off." Her wide eyes flashed with fear. "Maybe they came back to take revenge."

Tiller glanced at Joe. "There was another band of rough-looking strangers after that." He pointed toward the house. "The men who brought Otis."

"That's right," Miss Vee said, snapping her fingers. "We realized once they'd gone they could've been the very ones who robbed poor Otis and left him for dead."

Remembering his ruthless gang, the real culprits, Tiller shuddered and cast her a doubtful look. "I never held with that idea. Believe me, the animals that hurt Otis wouldn't have turned right around and helped him." A picture came to mind of the strange man on the far bank snapping a jaunty salute. "Let's face it, folks. This is still the Natchez Trace. The Devil's Backbone. There's never been anything but greed and mischief along this road." Tiller swept past them to saddle his horse. "Are you going with me Joe? We've got to hurry."

Spinning, Joe grabbed his tack and carried it inside the other stall.

Miss Vee paced and wrung her hands until they led the horses out. "Where will you go?" Her voice shook. "You don't know where to look."

Tiller swung onto the gelding and gathered the reins. "Pray, Miss Vee. Pray that God will give me a taste of what He gives Otis before it's too late."

She clutched his leg and handed him her lamp. "I'll pray. And I'll ask Otis, as well. I promise."

He lifted his chin at Sheki. "Take care of him for Mariah, would you?"

Tears in her eyes, she nodded.

Side by side, Tiller and Joe barreled from the barn in a flurry of hooves and dust. By lantern light, they combed every trail and stand of brush in a ten-mile sweep around the inn, searching until Tiller's eyes burned from the strain.

Joe dismounted twice. Once to study a clutch of broken twigs near the house and now to crouch and stare at the print of a boot heel in a low spot off the road. "No Indian has her. This man is a clumsy fool."

Tiller squatted beside him with the lamp. "I suppose there isn't one clumsy Indian in Mississippi?"

Joe shrugged. "Among the Chickasaw, maybe."

Tiller watched to see if he was joking. He didn't smile. "If he's such a fool, why don't we know which way to ride next?"

Joe stood, his hands on his hips. "Because it's dark and we're tired." He lifted one shoulder. "Because I'm not the Choctaw I used to be." He sounded close to tears.

Glancing up from the dim circle of light, Tiller sighed. "I'm no Choctaw, but I think I know which way to ride." He stood and pointed toward the horses. "We've got to get these animals to the barn before they drop from under us." Holding up the lamp, he shook it. "Besides, we're almost out of oil." Passing Joe, he gripped his sagging shoulder. "Maybe you should take them home and get some rest. If you know where I can find oil and a fresh horse—"

Joe shoved his hand away. "A woman needs rest. I won't stop until I find Mariah." He sniffed. "We ride back together. You can take Sheki. I'll find myself another horse."

Tiller gazed at him with new respect. "All right then."

A bobbing lantern swept toward them in the pitch darkness as they reined off the Trace into the yard. Miss Vee ran toward them shouting Tiller's name, her shrill voice echoing off the trees.

His heart dared to hope. He laid his heels into the gelding's side and galloped to meet her. "Did she come back?"

Panting, she held her side and gasped for breath. "No. But I know who took her."

Tiller leaped to the ground and gripped her shoulders. "Who?"

"I've been thinking for hours, and it came to me just now. I was about to saddle Sheki and go after her myself."

Joe reached them, jumping to the ground. "You know something, Viola?"

Losing patience, Tiller shook her. "Where is she, Miss Vee?"

Her eyes glowed like an angry cat's. "I don't know why we didn't think of it sooner. Gabriel Tabor's got her."

Shock fired through Tiller. Loose-lipped, potbellied Gabe who couldn't keep his hands or his dirty thoughts to himself?

Joe pushed between them. "Julian Tabor's son? Why would Gabe take Mariah?"

"To get revenge." Miss Vee started to cry. "To ruin her if he can. Mariah's all he's ever wanted, and she spurned him."

Gathering his reins, Tiller smoothed his horse's neck. "Hang on for just a while longer, can you boy?" He slid his boot into the stirrup and threw his leg over then reached for Miss Vee's lantern. "How do I get there?"

"I know the way," Joe said, pulling his horse around. "We'll go as the crow flies. Follow me." He swung into the saddle, shouted a command in Choctaw, and thundered toward the Pearl.

They picked their way over the nearest crossing. At the Tabor's fence line, Tiller kicked an opening in the leaning pickets. "What if we're wrong, Joe?" he asked, guiding the horses through.

Joe glanced up. "We'll owe this man a new fence."

Mounting up, they skirted a pecan grove then sailed over rows of young cotton in a field that seemed to stretch on forever, until the shadowy outline of a stately plantation house rose in the distance. Despite the late hour, lights burned in most of the tall windows.

Joe glanced at him. "Something's stirring, that's for sure."

Tiller nodded grimly. "It's about to get a whole lot worse."

They rode up to the porch and slid to the ground. Tiller strode up the steps with Joe at his heels. Together they pounded with their fists, showing no regard for the hands on the clock and no mercy for the rattling door frame.

A shouting voice ordered them to keep their trousers on, and then the door jerked open. "What's the meaning of this infernal hullabaloo?"

Could the scowling little sprout be Julian Tabor? Tiller had braced for big Gabe or a slightly older version, so the tiny, stoop-shouldered gentleman caught him off guard. Thin and frail, a high wind would carry him off without the weight of his full, gray beard to hold him down. If the man was Gabe's father, Mrs. Tabor hailed from sturdy stock.

Leaning closer, he squinted. "Joe Brashears, is that you? How dare you beat on my door at this hour?"

"Julian, we're looking for Gabe," Joe said through clenched teeth.

Mr. Tabor stood up straighter. "Well, that makes two of us."

Joe narrowed his eyes. "What do you mean?"

"I mean my boy's not here."

Tiller edged closer and peered over his shoulder into the house. "You need to let us in, mister. We're bound to find him."

His hollow eyes flinched, fixing Tiller with a murderous gaze. "I told you my son ain't home. You hard of hearing?"

Joe cleared his throat. "Gabe took Mariah, Julian. He ran off with her."

Interest flickered on his face. "Ran off? You mean to get hitched?"

Tiller shook his head. "No hearts and flowers, sir. He slipped inside the barn and carried her out against her will."

The old man winced. "That's the craziest talk I ever heard. Gabe wouldn't hurt Mariah." His tongue flicked out to wet his bottom lip. "You boys have the wrong man."

Joe glanced at Tiller and heaved a sigh. "I guess it's time to ride for the sheriff in Canton. A posse will ferret him out."

Mr. Tabor's hands shot up. "Now Joe, there's no call to bring in the law. We sweep our own doorsteps out here."

Joe clenched his fists and leaned threateningly. "Then start sweeping."

Backing away from the door, Mr. Tabor motioned them in.

The moment Tiller crossed the threshold, his anxious gaze flitted over the high-ceilinged entry and the fancy parlor off the hall, searching for any sign of Mariah.

"You're wasting your time looking, boy. She hasn't been here." He swallowed hard. "And neither has Gabe." Sadness dulled his eyes. "He's been missing all night, and I'm worried sick. It ain't like him not to come home."

Tiller nodded at Joe over Mr. Tabor's head. "Do you have any idea where he might've taken her?"

The old man's hand shot up. "I never said he did." Breathing hard, he leaned one hand on his hip, kneading his shaggy brows with two fingers of the other. "Let's say for argument's sake that Gabe's your culprit. My boy wouldn't pluck a hair from Mariah's head. He's quite fond of her."

A knot rose in Tiller's throat. "A little too fond of her, isn't he, Mr.

Tabor? Surely you're not blind to your own son's heart."

"The boy's right," Joe said. "There's more than one way to harm a decent woman."

Mr. Tabor glanced away.

Joe shifted in front of his face. "You know something, don't you, Julian? I can see it in your eyes." Clutching his arms, Joe gave him a shake. "Come on, man! This is Mariah at stake. The same little girl who groomed your horses, played in your cornfield, brought soup to your sickbed."

Mr. Tabor groaned and spun toward the parlor. "Come this way."

They followed him inside the well-appointed room, every nerve in Tiller's body yearning for the chase. "We don't have much time, sir."

He stopped in front of the mantelpiece. "This won't take long." Rummaging in an ornately carved box, he turned with a folded paper in his hands. "This is the map to a little cabin I own up near Cypress Swamp."

Tiller lifted his brows at Joe.

"Ten miles from here," he said.

Mr. Tabor leaned against the mantel and crossed his arms over the paper. "If I know my son, Gabe's headed one of two places." He cleared his throat. "If he plans to do right by Mariah, they're bound for Canton and a justice of the peace." He paused. "But if his mind's gone twisted, he's taking her to this cabin."

Tiller watched his weathered face. "Make the call, Mr. Tabor."

Gripping the back of a chair for support, the man seemed to age ten years. His chin slumped to his chest, and he held out the map. "Please don't hurt him, Joe."

Joe's fingers lingered on his hand. "I'll do my best to prevent it."

Mr. Tabor's agony over his son echoed Tiller's dread for Mariah. He touched his sleeve. "Thank you, sir."

One glance at Joe and they bolted for the door.

Mr. Tabor's voice stopped them at the threshold. "Keep a sharp eye. Gabe's bound to be armed, and he won't give her up without a fight."

Outside on the steps, Joe caught Tiller's sleeve. "It's time to bring in some help."

"From where?"

"The same place we'll find fresh horses. Follow me."

Riding hard, Tiller chased him across the river again. Instead of turning left toward the inn, Joe angled right and rode along the sandy bank for about two miles. Cutting into the woods, they rode another half mile before wending past chicken coops and pigsties then up to a rickety back porch.

Joe gave a sharp whistle, holding the lantern close to his face.

A light came on in the house, and a squinting Tobias Jones appeared at the door. "Halito, Joe Brashears! A long time has passed since we've seen you."

"We need your help," Joe said simply. He dismounted and ambled to join Tobias on the porch. In the flickering glow, they continued their conversation in the language they shared.

Tiller caught Mariah's name, and then Gabe's name paired with a foul curse. Sometime during Joe's rant, Christopher and Justin tumbled outside pulling on trousers and shirts. They crowded behind their pa with menacing dark scowls.

Without a word, Tobias lifted his arm. Chris vaulted the rail to his left and disappeared into the shadowy pine. Justin squeezed between them and tore across the junk-cluttered yard to the barn.

Tiller waited while Joe and Tobias plotted quietly in the haunting rhythm of the Choctaw. He didn't understand the words, but their stern, serene faces gave him confidence in the plan.

Justin reappeared, leading two paint ponies from the barn. Tiller pulled the saddle from the gelding and threw it on the closest horse while Justin fixed Joe's saddle to the other. Before Tiller had tightened the cinch, Chris marched out of the woods by torchlight with a cluster of Indian braves.

At least thirty men converged like an army set for battle. Concern tightened some of the faces, anger twisted others, reminding Tiller that these were Mariah's people.

A chill shot along his spine. Would Joe be able to honor his promise to let no harm come to Gabriel Tabor?

THIRTY-ONE

A ballet of tiny green fireflies danced between Mariah and the quaint little cabin. Clusters of glowing mushrooms, their snow-white tops bathed in moonlight, dotted the rustic yard. In the distance, a low-lying mist hung over the swamp, weaving in and out between fat cypress trunks. Her ears rang with the deep-throated croak of bullfrogs and the frenzied shrill of crickets.

In other circumstances, the scene would be a magical dream. Astride a horse, wedged against Gabe's big belly with her wrists bound and his foul breath in her ear, it was a ghastly nightmare.

Gabe climbed out of the saddle and lifted her down beside him.

Shuddering, she shrank away from his beefy hands. "Touch me like that again, and I'll kill you quicker than a dry horse sniffs out water."

Gabe braced his hands on his knees and laughed like a fiend. "I can't help it, Mariah. You're like a sickness to me. A fever in my blood. I cotton to you like a child to a sweet."

She raised her chin. "You're hardly a child, Gabe, except in your mind. You should be ashamed of yourself. Bringing me here against my will is the meanest, mangiest thing you've ever done."

Fury flashed in his eyes. "Hush, gal. Don't talk to me about mean after the hateful thing you done." He shoved her shoulder. "Get on up to the cabin."

She held her ground. "Untie me first. I can't see a thing." She softened her voice. "You don't want me to trip and hurt myself, do you?"

He turned her, fumbled with the ropes, then stilled. "Wait a minute. You'll run."

Mariah crossed her fingers. "I won't. I promise." *Not until the first chance I get.*

Mumbling, Gabe seemed to mull it over then spun her around. "I won't do it. But don't worry, I've got you." Linking his arm through hers, he herded her for the door. She stumbled a few times on the way, but his grip was a cruel vise that held her upright.

Their booted feet thundered on the loose boards of the porch, the echo bouncing off the sagging overhang and resounding in her head. Gabe released her while he fumbled for the knob then shoved the door open in front of them. Before he pushed her over the threshold, he groped along a shelf on the inside wall and pulled down a lantern. Striking a long match, he lit the wick then nudged her in the back with his elbow.

The charm of the cabin ended past the front wall. The moldy odor of dampness reached her first, followed by the stench of unwashed chamber pots and dirty laundry. Mariah turned her face to her shoulder and gagged.

When she recovered enough to speak, she turned watery eyes to Gabe. "Please untie me. I can't stand being bound another second."

Watching her, Gabe fumbled for a long brass key hidden over the door frame. Hanging the lamp from a hook, he inserted the key in the door and turned the lock. Hurrying across the room, he lit another lantern in the center of a small round dining table.

More light was both a blessing and a curse. The dimness made the musty cabin gloomy, but the light revealed the filth and diminished her hope of escape. The tiny cabin had a single door with a window to one side. Watermarked curtains over the sink offered hope of another exit. The rest of the walls were solid cypress logs, set together like interlocking fists to hold her inside.

"Now then. I suppose I could unknot your rope." He gave her a long, searching look. "As long as you promise to behave."

Mariah nodded fiercely. "I promise."

"If you go she-cat on me, I'll tie you up again, only tighter. You won't get loose no matter how much you squawk." He shook his finger in her face. "I swear on my ma's grave."

She lowered her lashes. "I'll behave myself." *As long as you do the same.*

The bulging knot in his throat rose and fell. "First, let me tell you how it's got to be." His hands moved to rest on his broad hips. "I'll hunt up some food in that pantry yonder"—he jutted his chin toward a door in the corner—"whilst you clean up a little in the kitchen. There ain't been no female around here in a spell, so it lacks a woman's touch."

Mariah glanced over her shoulder at the appalling mess. "Yes, I can do that." Anything to keep his mind off her.

"I'll build a cozy fire, and you can make us a nice little supper." He ducked his head, the shy gesture almost human. "I heard how good you cook."

She forced a smile. "I'll do my best."

His tongue darted out to lick his bottom lip. "You set the table real nice, and we'll eat together like a happy married couple."

Her stomach jerked. "Th–that sounds nice."

"Once our bellies are full and the fire burns down to embers, we'll be ready for a little nap." His head made a slow, deliberate turn toward the small rumpled cot in the corner. "How's all that sound?"

Straining against her bonds, Mariah swallowed a scream. She longed to rail at him. Pummel the lurid grin from his drooling mouth. Show him the difference between a she-cat and a she-devil.

Instead, she forced her muscles to relax, her breathing to ease. Pushing Gabe to action would be a huge mistake. She would stay calm and bide her time. Mariah had two important things on her side—her mind and body were quicker than the dimwitted oaf who held her captive.

Gabe slipped around behind her. The rope tightened at first then released in a rush of warmth spreading to her tingling fingertips. She almost cried in relief.

Rubbing her hands to restore them to life, she moved a few steps closer to the stove and held them up. "See? Isn't this better? Now I can get this old kitchen ready for our meal."

He toddled after her. "Can I help?"

She waved him toward the pantry. "Go scout our provisions. I'll be fine."

He glanced toward the exit then back at her.

Mariah tilted her head. "It's locked. Remember?"

Innocent as a lamb, she lifted a broom from the corner and started to sweep, the meager bristles stirring a cloud of ancient dust around her feet. "I'll need a bucket of fresh water once I'm done here."

He raised one finger. "Don't you worry, darlin'. I'll fetch one as soon as I find our grub."

Pausing with his hand gripping the pantry door, he gazed at her with sad, droopy eyes. "You ain't mad at me, are you?"

The trussed-up she-devil surged. "Do you mean because you kidnapped me and brought me here against my will to play house in the middle of the night?"

He nodded dumbly.

Mariah tightened her grip on the broom, entertaining thoughts of beating him with it. "You'll understand if I'm just a little out of sorts? I'm sure I'll get over it in time."

His mouth pouted like a sulky boy's. "Well, don't stay mad too long, you hear?"

The second his bulk ducked inside, Mariah lunged for the kitchen window.

Locked.

Feeling around the casing with trembling fingers, she found the latch and tried it. The sliding metal squealed.

She froze, checking over her shoulder.

Another push and the lock gave, but she didn't dare try to crack the window. The rush of fresh air would give her away.

Fumbling under the curtain, her hand slid across the glass from corner to corner. The opening was small, but when the time was right, she'd find a way to squeeze through.

Dusting rusty grime on her skirt, she resumed her sweeping just as Gabe stumbled out with a crate in his hands.

"Here." Still pouting, he slid the box across the table. "You ought to be able to whip up something with all that."

Mariah put the broom aside to rummage in the box. One part of her mind devised a possible meal from the ingredients. The sensible part reminded her to take her time.

Hours had passed since she stood at the stove frying skillet bread for Tiller's supper. She should be snug in her feather bed, freshly bathed with a full stomach. Instead, she had a greasy kitchen to clean and a full meal to prepare.

No matter. If it took until daybreak to get it done, even better. The longer she stretched out Gabe's cozy meal, the longer she could scramble to escape what came next.

With the tin of beef, cubes of pocket soup, onions, carrots, and potatoes, Mariah would stir up a slow-simmering stew. With the Indian meal, she'd make johnnycakes. Better yet, hasty pudding—just not too hasty.

She'd flood the cabin with smells Gabe would find more enticing than her and fill his barrel belly so full he'd grow sluggish and drowsy in front of the fire. If her plan failed? She had the broom handle and enough white-hot rage to put him to sleep with it.

Either way, Gabe would wake up to find her gone.

Riding the moonlit Trace alongside a somber band of braves, Tiller imagined himself part of a raiding war party. The men, some with paint smeared across their high cheekbones, sat their saddles with the grace born of an ancient treaty with their ponies.

Watching how they rallied to the common call for help, Tiller had gained a new respect for the beleaguered Indians. He glanced around at the silent tribe of warriors, each man lost in his own grim thoughts. By the determination etched in their faces, they would find Mariah. The only question—would they find her in time?

With the new evidence of Gabe Tabor's twisted mind-set, his passionless offer to kill Tiller at Mariah's bidding took a dark and ominous turn. Even if the man wasn't capable of taking her life, his lingering hands and slant-eyed glances left no doubt of the ugly offense he'd be more than willing to commit.

Tiller shuddered and struggled to clear his head. Such thoughts would have him gnashing his teeth and braying at the moon. He needed a steady mind when they reached Julian Tabor's cabin. What they found there would determine the need for snarling fangs.

THIRTY-TWO

Gabe reclined in a chair by the hearth, his arms crossed over his head and his legs stretched out in front of him. He had slipped off his boots and made himself at home.

Mariah couldn't tell whether his relaxed state stemmed from her show of submission, his droopy-eyed fatigue, or the warmth of the fire on his feet. Heating up his holey, disgusting socks had done nothing to improve the smell of the cabin, but the revolting man seemed oblivious.

"You sure have this place smelling good," he called over his shoulder.

More than I can say for you, she thought.

"I don't hear those pots rattling much. Does that mean you're almost done?"

Mariah picked up the spoon and stirred, clanging the sides of the pot for effect. "It shouldn't be long now."

She'd actually pulled the hasty pudding off the fire and drizzled honey over it a half hour ago. The stew she'd finished even sooner.

The drowsier Gabe got the better. Then the meal ought to finish him off.

The hasty pudding began to dry out and crack, and Gabe's anxious glances turned to scowls, forcing Mariah to finish setting the table. She hadn't thought she could swallow a bite around the angry lump in her throat, but the stew looked good and the pudding even better.

Ladling a heaping serving into each bowl, she gritted her teeth and clenched her fists. "Supper's ready."

Gabe's head, rolling groggily on his thick neck, snapped up, and he stared through bleary eyes. "Breakfast, you mean. Took you all blessed night to make a pot of vittles."

He stumbled to the table and took a seat. Still grumpy, he pulled the sloshing bowl in front of him and slurped a spoonful of the rich, savory broth. He grew still, and his face lit up. "This ain't bad, woman. Not bad at all."

Hunkering over the dish, he made quick work of two helpings, asking for a third before Mariah had finished her first.

She warmed inside. Her idea to save herself was working as planned. "Be sure and leave room for something sweet." His head slowly rose, a lewd smile on his face, and Mariah wished she'd minded her tongue.

She shot to her feet and leaned over the pudding. "Let me fix you a hearty serving." Scooping out enough for three men, she poured more honey on top and pushed it toward him. "I made it special just for you."

He dug in, eating far too fast. She had to slow him down. "May I ask you something, Gabe?"

He shifted a wad of food to the other cheek. "I reckon so."

"Well"— she rested her hands on the table, twiddling her thumbs— "I'm having a bit of an argument with myself about why you brought me out here."

His fisted hand, the one shoveling food to his mouth, stilled.

"One side of me," she continued, "the part that's known you since we were children, says you could never hurt me. Especially when we're such good friends."

Gabe glanced up, a touch of anger twitching his brow.

Careful, Mariah! "The other part, the girl you crept up on and snatched from the barn, is scared half out of her wits."

Gabe's mood darkened. He leered, enjoying her discomfort. "Which of those little gals you reckon you ought to listen to?"

The fireplace popped, showering sparks up the flue. Mariah had hoped to talk sense into Gabe, shame him into releasing her. Instead, she'd somehow incited him. "Why the first one, of course. The one who reminds me that you're a true Southern gentleman. A faithful friend and neighbor who's going to take me home the minute we're done with our meal."

Shaking his head slowly, Gabe leaned over the table and snatched her wrist, his wicked eyes aglow. "Don't believe a word that one says. She's a bare-faced liar."

Riding the lead with Tobias, Joe suddenly pulled up his horse and swung out of the saddle. He waited for Tiller to join him then pointed through the heavy tangle of trees. "According to Julian's map, the cabin is close by, and I see lights up ahead of those woods. We'll go the rest of the way by foot."

The other men dismounted, crowding around to await their orders.

"Circle the house," Joe said. "Make sure the dog can't escape."

His voice shook with anger that chilled Tiller's spine. At the same time, it spoke to his own seething rage. "What's the plan to get inside?"

Joe shook his head. "No plan to get inside." He led his horse off the road and tied him to a reedy bush.

Tiller stalked after him. "What do you mean?"

Joe fixed his brooding eyes on a point in the distance. "We bring him out to us."

With an overhead wave, he started to run. The tribe sprang after him, thirty swift arrows nocked and shot as one. A few yards out from the cabin, they scattered in all directions, running on quick, silent feet. Bathed in pale moonlight, they merged with the brush and disappeared.

Tiller followed Joe and Tobias, mirroring their stealth as best he could. Without a twitch of a muscle or a whisper of sound to give them away, they closed in on the little house. A lantern's glow in the single window lifted Tiller's heart. The dark scheme he imagined Gabe plotting seemed unsuited to the light.

As if to prove him wrong, Gabe roared inside the house. Mariah screamed, her shrill, frightened cry echoing in Tiller's heart.

He broke past Joe, running for the door.

Tobias caught him, spinning him around as a shower of stones pelted the house.

A rock struck the window, shattering the pane. A storm of rocks rained down on the roof, rolling off with a jarring clatter. The relentless attack continued for several minutes, and the noise inside the cabin would be deafening.

The onslaught finally over, Tiller spun to stare at Joe. He motioned with his hand for Tiller to stay put and ran to crouch behind a water trough. "Gabe Tabor!" he shouted. "Send my niece out that door."

The butt of a rifle busted the remaining glass from the window. "I'll kill her first."

"An eye for an eye, Gabe. If that's what you want."

A long silence, then Gabe called in a wobbly voice, "I don't know what you mean."

"You have Mariah. We have your pa."

Gabe's pasty face appeared in the flickering light. "My pa?"

Movement overhead caught Tiller's eye. Shadowy silhouettes were topping the roof, inching toward the front eaves.

"You touch a hair of her head," Joe warned, "and we'll scatter his brains."

"I don't believe you," Gabe roared.

"Well," Joe said calmly, drawing out the word, "that won't make him any less dead."

The door opened a crack. Gabe stuck out his head and peered around the yard. "Pa?"

He inched a few steps over the threshold. "I don't see him, Joe." His voice trembled with fear. "Why won't he answer?"

"You come out a little further, boy," Tobias cooed. "You'll see him, all right."

Holding a lantern aloft, Gabe stumbled to the edge of the porch. The shadows above him pounced like big cats, taking him down in a huddle of blows and curses.

With no further invitation, Tiller sprang for the house.

THIRTY-THREE

Mariah huddled beneath a sagging shelf, scared to breathe.

When the barrage of gunfire exploded against the house, Gabe had her by the hair, dragging her back inside the cabin.

Despite his vile threats, he'd drifted off at the table after the second serving of pudding, his head resting on folded arms. When his mouth sagged, releasing loud snores and drool that ran down his arm, Mariah made her break. She got halfway out of the window before he awoke with a bellow and lunged.

When the shooting started, breaking the window, he released her, and she'd scrambled inside the dark pantry to hide. She cowered there, her ears tuned to every sound and her thrashing heart in her throat.

A muffled commotion shot ice to her veins. A man screamed, followed by loud, angry voices. Footsteps and a flickering light paused outside the door.

She pressed closer to the wall, cursing herself for setting her own trap.

"Mariah! Where are you?"

Relief flooded her soul. She shot from the corner and threw open the musty larder. "I'm here!"

In one motion, Tiller slid the lantern onto the table and gathered her into his arms. He clung so desperately, she had to wiggle loose to catch her breath. "Please say you're all right."

Crying too hard to answer, she nodded against his chest.

"I heard a scream."

She rubbed the back of her head. "He yanked my hair."

Tiller stiffened, his voice barely above a whisper. "Did he. . .hurt you?"

Mariah pressed her cheek to his and let their tears mingle. "No."

"Thank God." He slid his mouth to kiss the hollow of her chin then gave a ragged sigh. "Thank God."

They sprang apart as the door swung open behind them. Uncle Nukowa stood on the threshold with tears in his eyes. "Sabitek?"

"Amoshi." She ran to him, throwing her arms around his neck. "I was so frightened."

He smoothed her hair then held her at arm's length. "Chim achukma?"

"I'm fine."

"Do you speak the truth? If not, I will gut that swine and feed his entrails to the hogs."

She patted his cheek. "I speak the truth." Frowning, she rubbed the back of her head. "I'm short a few strands of hair. Apart from that, I'm untouched."

Yipping and chanting from the yard drew her uncle's attention. Tobias ducked his head in the door, a grim look on his face. "She all right?"

Uncle Nukowa beamed over his shoulder. "Yes, I believe so."

Tobias shot Mariah a crooked grin. "I'm glad. You ready, Joe?"

Her uncle waved him on. "Go ahead. I'm coming." Ignoring the question in Tiller's anxious eyes, he nodded at Mariah. "Take my niece home, please."

"What's going on, Joe?"

"Take her home." He raised one brow. "Or shall I ask the sons of Tobias?"

Tiller cleared his throat and slid his arm around Mariah's waist. "Are you up to the ride?"

"Of course."

"All right, let's go."

Outside, Justin led his pony to the porch. "She can take my horse, Joe."

Her uncle nodded.

Concern swam in Justin's thoughtful eyes as he helped her into the saddle. Gazing up at her, he smiled sweetly. "I'm glad you're unhurt, Flower."

She gripped his hand. "Thank you." Raising her head, she glanced around the yard.

Gabe sat on the ground in a tight circle of her people, blubbering into his hands. He glanced up and stretched a pleading hand toward her as Tiller led her past. "Tell 'em I'm sorry, Mariah. I wasn't really going to do nothing. I swear it." His voice rose with hysteria. "Don't let these savages hurt me."

Straightening her spine, she lifted a regal chin and raked him with slanted eyes.

At the edge of the yard, Tiller jerked the reins and pulled her to a stop. Behind them, Gabe's sniveling had turned to babbling shrieks.

Off the far corner of the house, a clothesline stretched from a nail to a leaning pole. The men were dragging him to the post where they'd stacked a pile of kindling. Binding his hands behind him, they tied him to the stake and shoved a dirty rag in his mouth. Gabe went on screaming with his eyes.

Tiller gaped at her. "Merciful heavens! They mean to burn him." With a strangled cry, he let go of the horse and ran.

Uncle Nukowa stepped out of the circle with a lit torch in his hand. His fierce glare held a warning for Tiller. "Don't interfere, nahullo. Go find your horse and ride away."

Mariah's stomach tensed as several men closed in on Tiller, ugly scowls on their faces.

Backing away with clenched fists, he pleaded. "Come on, Joe. You can't." His hands raked his hair. "You'll never get away with it. Julian Tabor will hunt you down." He waved his hand. "All of you will hang."

Fearing for his safety, Mariah slid off the pony and ran. Catching his sleeve, she pulled him along behind her to where the horse stood pawing the ground. Climbing into the saddle, she scooted to make room. "Mount up, Tiller. Please."

He stared at the men in horror. "You're going to let them do this?"

"I can't stop them, and neither can you. Let's go."

Swinging up behind her, he urged the paint through the scatter of young cypress and entered the thick pine forest. In the clearing where they'd left Tiller's horse, he couldn't switch saddles fast enough. Spurring his mount, he trotted ahead, pushing the animal too fast along the unfamiliar ground. They rode toward the Trace until the echoing shouts faded, so distant they were hard to pick out from the other night sounds.

With several miles between Mariah and the dreadful cabin, she pulled up the pony and slid to the ground. A few yards ahead, Tiller did the same. They met in a bright patch of moonlight.

He groaned and crushed her to his chest. "I should've stopped them, Mariah. If they killed me for trying."

She clung to him, comforted by the strength of his arms. "I'm so sorry."

He cupped her face with trembling fingers. "For what? It's not your fault."

Mariah caressed his hands, turned one to kiss the hollow of his palm. "For this. Look how you're shaking." She tilted her head to peer up at him. "I wanted to tell you sooner. I just couldn't until we got away from the cabin."

Tiny lines appeared between his brows. "Tell me what?" Sudden alarm rocked his features. "Oh, honey. . ." Pain glazed his eyes, and his body shook beneath her hands. "Gabe did hurt you, didn't he?"

Her heart skipped a beat. "No, Tiller. I wouldn't lie to you, even for a moment."

"Then what haven't you told me?"

She smoothed his face with her fingertips. "That my uncle and his men won't really burn Gabe."

He drew in his bottom lip, gave his head a little shake. "But they did. I saw them."

She smiled. "They made you think you saw them. Just as Gabe will believe it so surely his blood will run cold each time he sees a fire in the hearth. But they won't go through with it."

Relief washed Tiller pale in the meager light. He spun away from her laughing. "Of course. They were punishing him."

She nodded. "And making sure it won't happen again. For the rest of his days, Gabriel Tabor will cross the street if he sees me coming."

Tiller slapped his knee. "It's brilliant." He chuckled. "And effective.

But suppose Gabe tells his pa? Won't the tribe land in trouble with the law?"

She raised her brows. "Believe me, Gabe won't tell."

He spun her around the clearing then reeled her in close. "Remind me to never get crossways with your folks."

Standing on tiptoe, she kissed his cheek.

He grinned. "What was that for?"

"For rescuing me."

"I had a little help." He nodded toward the cabin. "Mariah Bell's avenging angels."

"My people stick together. I'm afraid we've had to." Ducking her head, she covered a yawn. "What time is it? It must be nearly dawn."

Tiller took her wrist and led her to her horse. "Let's get on the road. You're exhausted, and Miss Vee will be frantic."

The long ride home was harder than Mariah expected. She dozed when she could; her head bobbing like a fat bird on a skinny limb. She stirred, her heart surging with relief when the horse's weight shifted to his haunches to climb the rise into the yard.

Drifting off again, she awoke to Miss Vee's soft clucking and Tiller's gentle hands lifting her from the saddle. He carried her up the stairs, nudging the door open with his foot. Miss Vee pulled the covers back, and Tiller laid her on the bed. She lolled against her pillows, her head spinning like a whirligig.

"Our girl will be just fine now that she's home," Miss Vee said, as if trying to convince herself. She lowered her voice. "She is all right, isn't she, Tiller?"

Mariah fumbled for her hand and squeezed. "Tiller saved me," she mumbled, too drowsy to open her eyes.

Miss Vee's sigh came out on a sob. "Heaven be praised," she said, her voice cracking.

Her footsteps crossed to the door and the hinges squealed. "Your work is done, young man. So if you please. . ."

Tiller's gentle touch on her cheek was as soft as a butterfly kiss. "Rest well. I'll see you in the morning."

Smiling into the fog was the last thing Mariah remembered.

THIRTY-FOUR

Tiller closed the garden gate behind him and strolled to the pump. He felt good enough to whistle, but his mouth was too dry. Working the handle, he waited for the spit and gurgle then plunged his hands under the clear, cold water, washing away the dirt from his late summer plot.

He hadn't seen Mariah all morning. Miss Vee had her safely tucked in bed, resting after her ordeal with Gabe.

The situation might've gone really bad. Suppose Gabe had carted Mariah off to Canton and forced her into marriage? Even worse, he might've succeeded in his cruel plan to take advantage of her. Considering the possibilities soured Tiller's stomach all over again and gave him second thoughts about burning Gabe at the stake.

What thoughts swirled in old Gabe's head that bright, cheery morning? Tiller doubted they centered on Mariah. More likely, he pondered the blessing of uncharred flesh.

Chuckling, he pumped more icy water into a cup and took a long drink. According to the sun, perched high over the house like a joyful smile, it would soon be lunchtime. Mariah would surely be awake by now. He hung the cup on the pump and started for the back porch, pausing when he saw the Jones brothers lounging around the new steps.

Joe sat in Miss Vee's rocking chair, staring toward the barn, his deep bass rumble carrying over the yard. "I'll hear your terms, of course," he was saying to Chris. "Your brother's, too."

He sat forward in the chair. "Perhaps you might consider combining your offers."

The boys shared a glance.

"How would that work?" Justin asked. "Mariah can't marry us both."

Feeling a chill down his back, Tiller held his ground and listened.

Joe laughed. "You'll work it out between you. Compete for her. The one who wins the prize will vow to repay his brother's share."

Chris sneered. "Even if I lost, which I won't, I wouldn't help this cur take my girl."

Justin shoved him with his shoulder. "Mind your tongue. Mariah's my girl."

They sprang off the porch, all long hair and sputter, flexing their muscles and jutting their chests. They took turns shoving each other backward, but neither boy swung a punch. As it should be between brothers, the true urge to fight seemed to be missing.

Joe cackled, obviously entertained by their mock sparring.

Justin rushed Chris. Chris spun to shake him off, and they both tumbled over the steps and sprawled in the dirt.

Joe raised his hand to end the skirmish. "I don't mean compete for her now." He dismissed them with a wave. "Take this match home and present your case before the elders. You won't settle things here in my yard."

Still glaring, they nodded toward Joe then trotted across the yard and disappeared down the sandy slope.

Joe sat back in the rocker, still chuckling.

Harnessing his rage, Tiller swung around the hedge to the porch and sat on the top step. "Afternoon, sir."

Scratching his chin, Joe nodded. "How's your patch of ground coming along?"

Tiller glanced toward the garden. "Mariah will soon have vegetables on her table again."

Joe blew out a breath. "She won't be here to eat them."

Tiller watched him quietly. Lowering his head, he focused on scraping a line of dirt from under his thumbnail. "You're a peculiar man, Joe."

Joe grunted. "You're not the first to say so."

"Is it a game for you?" He nodded toward the path. "Dangling false hope before their eyes? And before mine with your friendship?"

One bushy brow twitched, but Joe held his somber expression. "Neither boy loves my niece. They only think they do. By the end of the challenge I've given them, they'll know the truth in their own hearts."

"And if they don't?" Tiller glared. "Will you sell Mariah to one of them or wait for a higher bid? What was the offer back home?" He sneered. "Pretty high, I'll wager. Since it brought you all the way to Mississippi to fetch her."

Joe gripped the arms of the rocker. "Be careful."

Tiller stood clenching his fists. "I love her, Joe. She loves me, too, and I think you know it." He shifted his weight. "I'm not Gabe Tabor. You can't scare me out of her life."

Joe stood and shoved past him down the steps. "Stay away from her, nahullo. I won't tell you again."

"If you want me away from Mariah," Tiller shouted at his retreating back, "have the guts to light the kindling. That's the only way you'll ever be rid of me."

Groaning, Mariah sat up groping her head. She rubbed the spot where Gabe had yanked, expecting to find it bald. Despite the covering of hair, the skin her fingers probed sorely ached.

She frowned at her reflection across the room. Looking down, she found what the mirror had reported was true. She'd slept fully clothed and in her stockings with her hair pinned up on her head. If it didn't feel so scandalous, it'd be comical.

Mariah grinned. She certainly looked funny with her rumpled clothes, sleep-creased face, and wildly tangled hair. Not unlike a discarded rag doll—played with by dirty hands then tossed aside.

Her bright smile vanished. Gabe had meant to do that very thing. If Tiller and her uncle hadn't come in time, she'd find no humor in the day.

She shuddered at the memory of Gabe's foul touch. How different from Tiller's soft caress on her cheek.

A knock on the door fired her heartbeat to life. Frantic, she stood, ready to hide. Tiller couldn't see her in such an unkempt state.

"Mariah?" Only Miss Vee.

Relieved, she swiped wisps of hair off her forehead. "Yes, come in."

The door opened a crack. Miss Vee peeked in and smiled. "She's decent, Tiller. Go on in." Swinging the door wide, she stepped aside.

In one leap, Mariah landed on the bed and pulled the covers over her head.

Tiller's footsteps paused just inside the room then quietly approached. "Mariah? Are you all right?"

Blushing and fuming beneath the quilt, she wondered how Miss Vee would like salt instead of sugar in her next cup of tea. Maybe soap flakes mixed with her powdered milk? "I'm not presentable this morning. Could you come back in just a while?"

"I need to talk to you. It's important."

Miss Vee cleared her throat. "On second thought, a lady's boudoir ain't the proper place for chatting with a gentleman. You go wait in the parlor. I'll get our girl prettified and send her down."

In Tiller's long pause, Mariah felt him beside the bed, staring down at her. "All right, I suppose. But hurry, please. This won't keep."

When the door closed, Mariah shot upright and gaped at Miss Vee. "How could you?"

Red-faced, she hung her head. "I thought he had in mind a sickroom visit, not an important talk visit."

Mariah huffed. "That's ridiculous. I'm not sick."

"No, but you had quite a shock."

Mariah crossed her arms. "No more startling than the one you just gave me."

Miss Vee hurried to pour water in the basin. "Come wash up while I fluff a clean dress. I don't think Tiller's in the mood to wait."

He paced in front of the settee when Mariah reached the bottom step—feeling much better in a proper frock with her hair pinned. Crossing the room in broad strides, he pulled her close.

Mariah peered up at him. "Aren't you going to tell me how nice I look?"

"I thought you looked nice before."

She frowned. "You didn't see me."

"I didn't have to."

"Oh, Tiller. How sweet."

He pushed her to arm's length. "You won't find me sweet for long." His throat worked furiously. "I have a confession."

The dread on his face frightened her. "Go on."

"I told Uncle Joe that I love you."

Her arms slid from his shoulders and dropped to her sides. "Please say you didn't."

"I told him you love me, too, and he can't keep us apart."

She gripped her brow. "No, Tiller."

Cupping her chin, he raised her eyes to his. "I broke my promise, and for that I'm sorry. You have to know I had good reason."

She turned her back. "I hope so, since you've ruined everything."

Tiller squeezed her shoulders then eased her around. "Joe already knew, honey. He's known since the day he arrived. The only person you've been fooling is yourself."

Mariah shook her head. "He would've left soon. I just know it. Now that you've challenged him, he'll die first." She searched his troubled face. "What reason was so important that you broke our trust?"

Tiller's face flashed red. Indignant, he pointed behind him. "I caught him bartering with Tobias's sons, offering your hand in exchange for goods."

"Chris and Justin?" She lowered her head to hide her smile. "They both asked him?"

Tiller angled his head. "You find this funny? They're out there now, trying to gather enough mules and chickens, whatever they think you're worth, to come back and make a trade. Meanwhile, Joe is sitting back, waiting to see who comes with the best offer."

Mariah gathered his hands. "Yes, I know."

"You know." His angry scowl deepened. "Well, you're pretty calm about your own kin selling you off for livestock."

She laughed. "It's not quite like you make it sound. It's our custom, Tiller. . .my uncle's way to make sure I marry well. He'll weigh several offers, but the value of goods won't be his main concern. My position in the tribe, his position, too, will sway his final decision."

"Position? What about your heart?" Tiller stalked away from her. "It's nonsense, Mariah. You talk like you're just a. . .a. . ."

"A squaw?"

He spun to face her. "I didn't mean that."

"What did you mean?" Pulling free of him, Mariah bit her lip, trying to think.

Tiller cocked his head, his eyes fearful. "Where does all this leave us?"

"After you betrayed me to my uncle?" She hung her head. "I don't know."

He touched her hair, his voice thick with emotion. "Please don't say that."

She turned her face aside.

"You could stand up to him," he said quietly. "Tell him what you want."

Mariah shook her head. "Have you forgotten how fast the tribe came to his aid? One crook of my uncle's finger, and we'd both be headed out of Mississippi. . .in opposite directions." She sighed. "Besides, I won't openly defy him. It would shame my mother's memory."

"Then how can we ever marry?"

She took a deep breath. "If I can get him to leave without me, he'll go on with his life and forget. It's happened before."

Tiller snorted. "Good luck with that. Uncle Joe seems to be settling in for good."

Her temper flared. "Don't mention anything else to him, Tiller McRae. Maybe I can repair the damage." She shook her finger in his face. "Don't speak of our love to anyone in this household, do you understand? Not even to me."

He held up his hands. "I promise."

Mariah jabbed his chest. "Keep your word this time."

Gathering her skirt, she flounced out the door.

THIRTY-FIVE

Six days had passed since Tiller spilled Mariah's secret to Joe. She worked so hard to convince her uncle they weren't really in love, Tiller had started to wonder himself.

Even when they were alone, in the hallway or passing in the yard, she shrank from his touch and pulled away if he tried to whisper in her ear.

She seemed to be a different woman, and it scared him, made him long for her with a passion he'd never known. He hoped her coldness was borne of determination to trick Joe and not a picture of her true feelings.

Pushing aside his worrisome thoughts, Tiller lowered Otis into the cane-bottomed chair on the front porch and tucked a blue knitted shawl beneath his chin. The view toward the river in back was nicer, but it took so much out of Otis to walk the long hallway, he had little energy left to take pleasure in his time outside.

He settled against the cushion and gazed around the yard with a satisfied smile. "Yes sir. Just what the doctor ordered."

Tiller pulled the matching chair around and lowered his lanky body, enjoying the cool breeze on his face. His gaze wandered the grassy yard from Rainy's climbing roses to Mariah's herb garden set off by a border of white stones. Bright green ivy sprawled across the latticed arbor, stretching from the road to the house. Seated beneath its shade and tucked into the shadows of the portico, it wasn't long before he wished he'd brought out an extra shawl. "You warm enough, Otis?"

He nodded. "It's a mite cool for this late in June, ain't it?"

Tiller rubbed his arms. "I suppose we'd best enjoy it while we can. We'll be fuming about the heat come August."

"What sort of weather you reckon Scuffletown is having, son?"

Tiller had shared everything he could remember about his Carolina home and the family he'd left behind. The old man loved the stories and seemed willing to listen for hours.

Time spent with Otis was the most relaxing Tiller had ever spent and the most distressing. The peace in Otis's eyes stirred an emptiness long denied and a yearning Tiller couldn't shake. He longed to purge the guilt that clawed his mind during long, sleepless nights, but he'd found some rest in a recent decision.

It would be selfish to clear his conscience at the little man's expense. Otis needed him, at least for now. When he regained his strength, Tiller would lay the ugly facts on the table and plead for pardon. Whether Otis forgave him or not, Tiller would beg him to stay on at the inn and allow them to care for him.

Mariah would have to agree, but he couldn't discuss this or anything else of importance with her until Joe left Mississippi. Of course, there was still the matter of coming clean with her.

Tiller groaned inside. He'd made such a mess of his life. How would he ever set things right?

Feeling Otis watching, he eased back and unclenched his fists.

Otis continued to stare. "Got something to tell me, boy?"

Squirming, he shook his head.

"Well. . .maybe I got something to tell you."

Tiller spun to the edge of his chair, hoping Otis would bring up the subject of Mariah. He needed assurance that Joe would leave, that things with Mariah would return to normal. He wouldn't tell Otis their secret, but he sure hoped God would.

Otis swiveled to face him. "I sense you're ripe for turning your life over to God, and I reckon it's time you stop putting it off."

The simple words dashed Tiller's hopes and made him uneasy. "I don't have enough church in my background to know exactly what you mean, but I have an idea." He stole a quick glance. "You're talking about baring my sins." He tried to smile. "A thing like that could take awhile."

Otis waved his hand. "There's no need to air your trespasses one by one. God's already acquainted with each of them since they nailed Jesus to the cross." He patted Tiller's hand. "A whispered plea for mercy will cover it."

The ache inside Tiller's heart swelled to bursting. "That don't sound fair to God. Besides, there are a few things I need to set right first."

Otis lifted his chin. "You reckon there's anything in your life He can't handle?"

Tiller glanced away from his searching gaze. "There are deeds I've done that are too dark to bring to Him. I need to mop up behind me before I'll be fit to talk to God."

Setting his lips in a firm line, Otis shook his head. "That's hitching the horse on backwards, boy." He gripped Tiller's wrist. "You think I was lily-white when God found me?"

His words swirled Tiller away to the day Nathan accused him of trying to protect his lily-white conscience. Blinded by the glare of God's righteousness, the notion seemed absurd. He lowered his head to his hands. "My life's been broke for so long, I don't know how to fix it."

A warm, trembling hand touched his shoulder. "You can't."

Embarrassed by his swimming eyes, Tiller shot Otis a troubled frown. "Then what's the use?"

"That's what I'm trying to tell you, boy. None of us have the power to make things right again." His face glowing, he pointed to the sky. "But He can."

The emptiness inside Tiller couldn't be denied a second longer. Guilt weighed him to his knees. "Please, Otis. Tell me what I need to do."

Gnarled fingers rested on Tiller's head. "You just made a good start, son. Repeat this prayer after me, and I'll lead you on home."

Otis's gentle voice overhead, thick with unshed tears, washed over Tiller in waves like warm molasses, the graceful ebb and flow pulling out the years of lonely heartbreak, rushing in with tides of peace.

When they finished praying, Otis hugged him. "You'll never regret this decision."

Patting his bony back, Tiller withdrew and smiled. "I don't see how

I could." He chuckled, deep and free, unlike any laugh he'd had before. "I feel different."

"Because you are." Otis gave a satisfied nod. "That just proves it took."

They beamed at each other like carefree boys trading secrets.

Otis tugged on his arm. "Get up from there before the cold seeps into your bones."

Tiller returned to his chair, wiping tears on his sleeve. "I don't know how I'll ever thank you."

"Don't talk foolish. After all you've done for me?"

"This doesn't come close to anything I've done, and you know it." Tiller stared in the distance. "I suppose I'll always think of you as a father of sorts." He lifted one brow. "I hope you don't mind."

"Mind?" Tears tracked his ruddy cheeks, but he grinned. "I'm honored to know you feel that way." He winked. "But I'm more like a grandfather, don't you think? On account of I'm older than thunder."

Tiller patted his knee. "You're not so old."

Otis snorted. "You must need a pair of spectacles." Scooting to the end of his seat, he held out his arm for Tiller to grasp. "Take me inside before I rust."

Hauling Otis to his feet, Tiller took one last look around. Whether from the haze of recent tears or the freedom of a burden lifted, the front yard blazed with brilliant color. The grass was greener. The roses redder. Patches of sky peered through the ivy-covered trellis, as clear and blue as a newborn's eyes.

"One more thing," Otis said before Tiller opened the door. "You'll need a Bible so you can study on the scriptures." He scratched his head. "I'd give you mine, but it was in my pack when those mangy scoundrels stole it."

Tiller's heart sank, but not with the sickening thud of before. He felt certain God had removed the terrible deed from his account, but if it took the rest of his days, he'd make it up to Otis. "Don't worry," Tiller said. "Next time I'm in town, I'll get us both new ones." He guided Otis inside the house.

Men's voices and heavy-booted footsteps sounded from the dining room, along with the smell of serious cooking.

Otis stared down the hall. "Sounds like Mariah has a passel of new guests. I didn't see them come in off the road, did you?"

Tiller frowned and shook his head. "I suppose they came downriver. I'd best get you settled and go lend the women a hand."

Plopping on the side of his bed, Otis grinned. "We stayed outside longer than I thought if it's already lunchtime." He lifted his finger. "But I ain't complaining."

Patting his stomach, Tiller smiled. "That makes two of us."

When he reached the door, Otis called his name. "Tiller, little missy's better acquainted with God than you were before this morning, only she's lost her way." Lying back on his fresh-plumped pillows, his eyes twinkled. "But don't you worry. He'll reel her in before long."

The details were sketchy, but it was the reassurance Tiller needed. After the morning's encounter with God, it was enough.

He saluted and Otis returned it.

"I'll go see if I can hurry those vittles."

Otis raised his thumb. "Now you're talking."

Smiling, Tiller strolled toward the back of the house whistling a merry tune. He didn't see how life could get much better. Following the lively voices of men enjoying good food and better company, he turned the corner into the dining room—and rocked back on his heels.

The mocking eyes of Nathan Carter, Sonny Thompson, and Hade Betts lifted to greet him, mischief in their depths.

Nailed to the spot, Tiller stared, his blissful joy paled to hopeless loss.

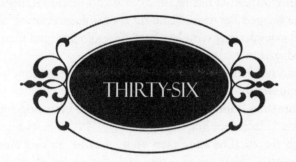

THIRTY-SIX

The sudden stillness in the room brought Mariah's head up from the bowl of mashed potatoes in her hand.

A whitewashed version of Tiller slumped in the doorway, his bottom jaw unhinged.

"Tiller?"

His wide eyes darted to her.

"Won't you greet our guests?"

The youngest of the three men stood quickly and offered his hand. "How-do, sir. I'm Nathan Carter." His friendly smile lit up a handsome face. With his swarthy complexion and dark hair, he looked to be Indian, though not from a local tribe. "Did she say your name's Tiller?"

Tiller nodded dumbly.

The other two beamed up at them. Nathan introduced them by turn. "That skinny, ugly soul to your left is Sonny Thompson."

Sonny's smile revealed a gap in his front teeth. "Nice to know you, Tiller."

"And the old man to my right is Hade Betts."

Mr. Betts stretched his arm past Nathan. "I can't tell you how pleased."

Prying himself from the wall that seemed to hold him up, Tiller allowed Mr. Betts to shake his limp hand, but he didn't seem to put much effort into it. Wiping his palm on his pants leg, Tiller lifted his vacant stare to Mariah. "I'll just"—he hooked his thumb—"go on out and take care of their horses."

Mariah frowned. What had him in such a state? "Rainy's tending them." She bugged her eyes. "Like he always does. Are you all right?" She shared a quick smile with Mr. Betts. "I apologize for Tiller. He's not himself today."

"We can see that, Miss Bell." He winked at Tiller. "Your boy seems a little tongue-tied."

"He sure does," Sonny said, his dancing gaze bouncing from Tiller to Mr. Betts. "He always like this?"

Mariah tensed. The rude men seemed to be making fun of him. None too gently, she plopped a spoonful of potatoes on Sonny's plate and picked up the carving knife. "Care for more beef, Mr. Thompson?"

Swallowing his simpering grin, he sat back in his chair and shook his head.

Glancing up, Mariah found Tiller gone. His behavior, so unlike him, churned her stomach. The way she'd treated him for the past week, his sullen mood had to be her fault.

"Enjoy your meal, gentlemen," she said, untying her apron. "Miss Viola will be in soon with your dessert."

"Where'd Tiller fly off to?" Miss Vee asked, meeting her at the doorway.

Mariah handed her the apron. "Have Dicey bring in the apple pie, Miss Vee. I'll be right back."

"You're leaving me, too?"

Out the door so fast it slammed behind her, Mariah scurried across the yard.

Tiller paced the barn. Sheki, hoping for a treat, followed with his head each time Tiller passed the stall.

Rainy glanced up from brushing down Hade's bay. "Mista' Tilla', you're bound to hit water soon in that ditch you're digging. You got something peckin' at you?"

The barn door squealed open.

Tiller's breath caught at the sight of Mariah. What did she know? How much had the blackguards told her?

"I thought I'd find you here." She pulled the door shut and hurried toward him.

He lifted his chin at Rainy.

Glancing at the boy, she slowed her steps. "Rainy, leave that for now, please. I need to have a private word with Mr. Tiller."

Shoving his hands in his pockets, Rainy pushed the stall open with one shoulder, hiding his grin with the other. He ducked out the door whistling the tune his little brother had sung the first time Tiller laid eyes on them. A lively song about a coming gospel train rumbling through the land.

Tiller's heart squeezed. Something was rumbling toward him all right, and it wasn't the gospel train. Weak in the knees, he felt powerless to stop it.

Mariah's chin shot up. "What happened to you in there?"

She didn't know. Not yet, at least. He shrugged and leaned against Sheki's stall. "I don't like the look of that bunch around the table."

She frowned. "I'll admit they're rude and uncouth, but we've seen worse, I assure you."

Tiller longed to grab her shoulders and shake her, tell her she'd never seen the likes of Hade Betts. He wanted her to promise to watch her back every second the men were in the house. Since he could do no such thing, he vowed to watch her every second himself. Until he found out the purpose of Hade's deceitful game, he'd guard his own back fairly close, too. "Did they pay up front?"

"Of course."

"How many days?"

"Two, but Mr. Betts said they might stay longer." She caught his arm. "What's this about? I've never seen you this way."

"Don't trust them, Mariah. I've got a bad feeling."

She smiled. "Now you sound like Otis. They're just guests, Tiller. In a few days they'll be moving on."

He drew a deep breath. "Let's hope it's a short visit."

Mariah took a step closer. "Are you sure that's what's bothering you? I sense you're angry with me." She reached to finger a button on his shirt. "I've only acted the way I have because I had to. But you should know—"

Tiller brushed her hand away and stepped back.

Pain glazed her eyes until Joe's voice growled behind her. "Mariah, come inside. The guests are fed; now it's time to feed me."

"Coming, Uncle." She whirled away, slipping past Joe at the door. He glared a warning at Tiller.

Smiling brightly, Tiller raised his chin and winked. "Save me some mashed potatoes, Uncle Joe."

His craggy face stiff with rage, Joe spun on his heel and followed Mariah.

Sheki bobbed his head, and Tiller laughed and patted his neck. "You liked that, didn't you, boy? I really put the old man in his place." The thing was he shouldn't have. Mariah wouldn't approve, especially after Joe had just caught them together.

Tiller's desperate sense of swimming upstream had returned. Now with Hade and Nathan showing up. . .

He smoothed his hand along the horse's soft muzzle. "Ah, Sheki. I can't just give up and run. She's too important."

"Well, well."

Tiller's head swiveled to watch Nathan saunter toward him.

"You're slipping, Tiller boy. With that pretty little thing in the house, you're out here snuggled up to a horse?"

Tiller nodded toward the river. "That was you the other day, wasn't it? Across the Pearl."

Nathan grinned and snapped a salute. "That hair of yours stuck out like a red flag atop this roof."

Dread knotting his stomach, Tiller leaned against the stall while Hade and Sonny strolled up behind Nathan.

Sonny ran up and slapped his arm, a huge grin on his face. "I knew we'd find you! Mississippi ain't big enough to hide you from us."

Tiller scowled. "Keep your voice down."

Hade watched him with admiration shining in his eyes. "This is some arrangement you fell into. What's your angle?"

"There's no angle. Just taking some time away."

Hade sneered. "Come on, now. This is old Hade you're talking to. If you want to keep the profits to yourself, go ahead, but at least fill us in."

Nathan spat in the straw at his feet. "I think it's the girl."

"Whooee!" Sonny cried. "She sure is a looker."

"Nah." A lewd smile curled Hade's lips. "Tiller has his pick of the gals. There's something else he's after."

Forcing himself to relax, Tiller crossed his ankles. "More to the point, what are you boys after? What's the reason for pretending you don't know me?"

With a rowdy laugh, Hade slapped him on the back. "Just having a little fun with you. Besides, we're not here to throw a polecat at your picnic." He tightened his arm around Tiller's neck. "We were starting to miss having you around is all."

Sonny sniffed and hauled up his pants. "Hadn't been the same in camp without you and your stories. I suppose you've missed us, too. Ain't that right, Tiller?"

"After all," Hade continued, "I've been like a daddy to you." He reached for Nathan, pulling him into a clumsy three-way hug. "And old Nate has been like your elder brother." He gave them both hearty pats on the back. "I reckon we've been the closest thing you've ever had to a family."

No doubt about it. Hade was up to something.

It didn't take long to flush it out. "I don't mean to sound impatient"— he bumped heads with Tiller—"but how long will it take you to fleece this lamb and come home to our loving arms?"

A rock in the pit of his stomach, Tiller laughed softly and casually drew away. "What if I said I may not be coming back?"

Hade's gleeful eyes hardened to glassy stones. "Well, that won't do, will it?" His fatherly grip became a vise around Tiller's neck. "Not by a jugful. I've lost a lot of revenue since you left, McRae." His rattled exhalation, reeking of roast beef and raw onion, warmed Tiller's cheek. "An unfortunate turn I'm willing to forgive if you'll stop all this foolishness and come back to the camp."

Struggling to stay calm, Tiller steadied his voice. "How have I cost you money?"

Hade gave a breathy laugh. "Look around at these ugly mugs. Would you stop on the road to have a friendly chat with one of us?"

Tiller tightened his jaw. "I'd start shooting and ask questions later."

Loosening his hold, Hade chuckled. "Then you see my problem." He gripped Tiller's chin and shook it. "This pretty-boy face is worth a gold mine."

Nathan, quiet until now, moved closer to the stall. Smoothing Sheki's mane, he cleared his throat. "Look, Hade. . .if Tiller wants out, there's really no way to make him stay. He'll just hang up the fiddle again, first chance he gets." He glanced over his shoulder. "Besides, it ain't smart to place all our bets on one man." He grinned at Tiller. "Little brother here won't always be good-looking."

Hade frowned. "So, I should just let our meal ticket walk out?" He shook his head. "No sir."

Nate drew himself up and strutted a few paces. "I've been doing some pondering. I think it's time we found us a new game. The word's out on the Trace. Folks are leery. Trigger-happy."

He turned. "If we're going to risk getting filled with lead, it's time we thought bigger." His eyes glowed. "Richer."

Hade joined him near Sheki. "Keep talking."

"Boss, I'm thinking banks. . .trains. Real jobs yielding big money."

Sonny's eyes bugged. "Like the James brothers?"

Nathan pointed. "Exactly like the James brothers."

Tiller frowned. "May I remind you that Jesse was shot dead two months ago?"

Greedily rubbing his chin, Hade ignored him. "I think this merits more discussion. How about we grab a cup of coffee and meet around the fire in the parlor to draw up some plans."

Sonny rubbed his stomach. "I'm hankering for another piece of that fine apple pie."

Nathan nodded at the door. "You two go on but save me a slice. I'll be right along."

Tiller drew a deep cleansing breath as Hade and Sonny left the barn. His heart filled with warmth for Nathan, and he shot him a grateful smile. "Thanks, Nate."

Nathan waved him off. "Nothing to it."

"Why'd you step out like that for me?"

Nate glanced up, his eyes shimmering in the dim light. "I suppose I'm trying to make amends for how I've messed up your life." He offered a wry laugh. "Including telling Hade where I found you."

"Then why did you?"

Nathan crossed to where Tiller stood and chucked him on the chin. "I looked for you because I missed you. I wanted you riding with us again. You're the only family I have left."

"And now you've changed your mind?"

"You changed it for me. When I saw you, saw the way that pretty gal looks at you, I knew you were happy."

They shared a long look; then Tiller grinned and swatted his arm. "I'll miss you, pardner."

"Not for long. I'll be stopping by."

Tiller frowned. "Unless you find yourself chained to Hade and Sonny on a Mississippi prison farm. Or worse, wind up like Jesse James."

He gripped Nathan's arm. "Stay here, Nate. Mariah won't mind, and we could use the extra hands."

Nathan gazed around the barn. "Trade my carefree life on the road for this?" He shook his head. "Tilling soil and pitching hay won't cut it for me, I'm afraid."

Staring at his feet, Tiller nodded. "Be careful, won't you?"

Nathan flicked the brim of Tiller's hat—his until Tiller snatched it from his head the day he left. "Nice headgear. Keep it free of holes, won't you?" At the door, he turned. "I'll try to get those two to leave as soon as possible. Until then, keep a close watch on them."

Tiller nodded. "You can count on it."

THIRTY-SEVEN

Hade, Sonny, and Nathan huddled around the settee hatching dastardly schemes until suppertime. Pretty worked up about their new plans, they gobbled Mariah's soup and corn cakes like pigs on slop and hustled right back to the parlor.

Tiller loathed knowing the gang was sowing the seeds of a crime spree around Mariah's cozy hearth, but if it took them away from the inn, he'd have to live with it for now.

His heart soared at how God had used Nathan to rescue him from Hade's clutches. He longed to do the same for Nate, but one man couldn't force his viewpoint on another. The life Tiller found empty and degrading, Nate's reckless nature seemed to feed on. Tiller would chose pitching hay over robbing banks any day.

Seated at the kitchen table playing a game of Dr. Busby with Mariah and Miss Vee, he tried not to focus on the excited voices floating down the hall. Thankfully, Otis slept like the dead, but he prayed the ruckus wouldn't disturb him. The last thing he needed was Otis awake, itching to socialize with the new guests.

Having Otis's attackers in the same house set Tiller's nerves on edge. He'd carefully avoided mentioning to them who Otis was and kept them away from the old man's room by telling them he was sick. If Hade thought Otis might recognize him, he'd kill him with less remorse than swatting a fly.

Miss Vee leaned across the table, interrupting his grim thoughts. "Mariah, I need the Dairymaid's Lover."

She pulled the card from her hand and slid it across to her. "You're good, Miss Vee."

"Okay. . ." Miss Vee touched her chin. "How about Dr. Busby's Wife?"

Mariah shook her head. "Your luck just ran out."

"Oh, pooh. All right, it's your turn then."

The twinkle in Mariah's brown eyes gave her away—she remembered the last card Tiller had lured from Miss Vee.

Grinning, she held out her hand. "Mr. Ninnycometwitch, if you please."

He passed it to her, along with a little squeeze to her pinkie finger.

Blushing, she tapped his shin with her toe. "I'll just take Spade the Gardener, too."

Miss Vee squealed and bounced in her chair. "Watch her, Tiller. She's trying to win this game." Sobering, she rested her chin on her hands and stared over Tiller's shoulder. "I wish John Coffee was here. He loves to play Dr. Busby."

Sadness dropped like a tasseled shade over Mariah's smile.

Tiller hurried to change the subject. "Where's Joe tonight?"

She scrunched her face. "Won't you ever call him anything but Joe?"

He quirked his mouth. "I have no plans in that direction."

Mariah swatted his arm with her cards. "Why not? You know it frustrates him."

"Well, it shouldn't. What sort of name is 'I'm angry' for a grown man? Suppose I took a name based on how I felt?"

"I see your point." She batted her lashes. " 'I'm hungry' doesn't suit you."

Beaming, he returned her swat. "So where is Mr. Mad?"

"Playing cards and drinking ale with Tobias. He said not to wait up."

Miss Vee snorted. "I doubt they're playing Dr. Busby."

They shared a laugh, cut short by the downstairs clock striking the ten o'clock hour.

Mariah stretched and yawned. "Gracious, I'm tired. It's been a long day. I forgot how hard it is to chase after a houseful of guests."

Miss Vee stood to put the kettle on. "I'll make those noisy yahoos a

241

pot of my chamomile tea. Maybe it'll put them to sleep. Or at least calm them down before they wake Otis."

By the time Mariah won the hand of Dr. Busby, Miss Vee had three cups of tea sweetened and spiced, foaming over on a silver serving tray. She handed it to Tiller with a wink. "I hope this works. Take it in for me, will you?"

The men in the parlor had wound down a bit. Sonny sat in Otis's chair, stretching his legs toward the fire. Hade slumped in the seat beside him, chewing a fat cigar. Nathan had slipped off his boots and reclined on the settee, his stocking feet hanging off the end.

"Well, look here," Hade said. "Tiller, you make a pretty little maid."

Sonny laughed wildly, and the other two grinned.

"I'd curtsy," Tiller said, "but then I might spill your tea."

More rowdy laughter from Sonny.

Nathan made a face. "Tea? Has it got whiskey in it?"

Tiller handed him a cup. "You'll think it did, once it hits your belly. Drink this, and you'll sleep like a man with no conscience."

Nate grinned. "By cracker, I'd better have me a double portion."

Mariah swept in, beautiful by firelight in a red dress cinched tight at the waist. Everything else forgotten, the men's hungry eyes tracked her across the room. "Don't let me disturb you, gentlemen. I won't be a minute. I just need my ledger."

Tiller had no inkling of what she was about to do, or he'd have found a way to stop her. Caught up in her charms himself, he stared like a witless boy while she swung open the door of her safe, revealing the bulging leather bag of gold coins.

Whirling, he watched Hade's slant-eyed desire turn to wide-eyed greed.

Hurrying to Mariah, Tiller slid his arms around her waist and drew her upright, slamming the safe with the toe of his boot.

Guileless, trusting, she stared at him. "Tiller? What in the world?"

"Just lending a hand."

Blushing, glancing at the men, she gave him a scathing look and shook off his hands. "Well, thank you, but I can manage." Snatching a pen from her desk, she tucked the ledger under her arm and nodded around the room. "I'll bid you all a good night. Don't forget, breakfast promptly at six. If you're not seated around the table by then, you stand a fair chance of going without."

Tiller followed her to the foot of the stairs. "Where are you going?"

"To bed, if you must know," she whispered. "What's come over you?"

He glanced toward the safe. Surely she had a key somewhere. "I need to speak to you."

"In the morning, if you don't mind. I'm tired. Now, good night."

The room crackled with strain, waiting for her footsteps to reach the top of the stairs and down the hall. When her bedroom door closed, Tiller spun. Stalking to stand in front of them, he pointed at the safe. "Forget you ever saw that, you hear?"

Hade slouched in his chair, puffing his cigar through a delighted smirk.

Sonny's gaze darted around the room like a child with a secret.

Nathan, defeat sagging his face, sat on the edge of the couch twiddling his thumbs.

"Well, now," Hade said. "Who would've thought a dump like this would pull in that kind of dough?"

Sonny giggled like a girl. "I reckon Tiller knew. Ain't that right, Tiller boy?"

Hade leaned forward to rest his arms on his knees, flicking a long white ash on Mariah's rug. "In light of this new development, I'll have to change my mind about the hardship your mutiny caused the gang." His steely gazed fixed on Tiller. "It's time to pony up. I'd say a sixty-forty split in my favor is more than reasonable."

Tiller's chest heaved. "I don't intend to take any of that money."

"Suit yourself." Glancing from Nate to Sonny, Hade breathed a throaty laugh. "I have no problem with taking it all."

Tiller balled his fists and made a move toward the safe. Nathan leaped up to block him. "Don't be stupid, Tiller," he warned, his voice laden with gloom. "Go to bed. By morning, we'll be out of your hair for good."

Tiller shoved closer to Hade, but Nate held him.

"Better listen to big brother," Hade growled. "That is if you want to see morning." He lifted his chin toward the top of the stairs. "More to the point, if you want your friends to wake up tomorrow."

Tiller backed across the threshold into the hall, his eyes flashing a warning. Storming to his room, he swore under his breath that Hade Betts would steal Mariah's money over his cold, dead corpse.

THIRTY-EIGHT

Mariah's eyes shot open. Raising her head from her pillow, she stared over her shoulder into the pitch darkness of the room, listening.

The house had been silent for hours, her guests all tucked into bed. Now a muffled ruckus drifted to her from downstairs.

She swung her legs over the side and quietly lowered her feet. Easing the door open, she crept down the hall in her nightgown to peer over the banister.

Her heart surged. Harsh whispers quarreled, and tall shadows danced a jerky waltz on the parlor walls.

Passing by her room, she paused long enough to lift her wrap from the hook by the door. Grateful that Tiller had fixed the squeaky boards, she slipped across the hall to Father's room.

His scent overcame her as she entered. Standing dazed, she realized she hadn't been inside the room since the morning she carried out his feeble body. The ache in her chest was crippling, but she lingered with the memories anyway, like the tip of a tongue jabbing a sore tooth.

Tears blinding her, she brushed them away. She had no time to surrender to grief. Opening the drawer bedside Father's bed, she carefully lifted the revolver, the weight a comfort in her hand.

In the hall again, she cocked her ears and heard a thud. Scurrying on tiptoe, she took the back stairwell down to the kitchen, her pounding heart drawn to Tiller. The bottom stair creaked under her weight. Wincing, she made a mental note to have Tiller repair it—if they lived through the night.

Tightening her fingers around the handle, Mariah lifted the gun and skulked to Tiller's door, pressing her face against the cold wood. She whispered his name and strained to hear him answer.

Afraid the intruders would hear if she called out again, she gripped the knob and turned, stepping warily inside another room she hadn't visited lately. Here, too, she breathed the familiar scent of a man she loved. The woody, fresh-air scent of Tiller gave her strength.

The sound of his voice spun her around. Tiller argued fiercely in an ugly tone she'd never heard before, but not inside this room.

Her stomach pitched with fear for his safety. Bolting, she dashed for the parlor, one hand cocking the hammer, her finger tensed on the trigger.

Tiller lunged for the bag of coins in Hade's white-knuckled hand. Hade whirled, and his shoulder collided with Tiller's jaw. Tiller fell to one knee and blackness threatened.

The haze took him under briefly, but a high-pitched, wavering voice tugged him back to consciousness. "Hold it right there. . .and I mean you."

Fearing the "you" Mariah threatened could be him, Tiller froze. The way the barrel shook in her hand, she might've been aiming at any one of them.

Blinking up at her from the floor, he reached out his hand. "Mariah? Honey, be careful with that thing."

Sonny's mouth gaped. "Did you just call her honey?" His shocked expression slid into a grin. "Nathan was right. She's your girl, ain't she, Tiller boy?" He reached to pull Tiller to his feet. "I reckon she's the ripsnortin'est gal you ever romanced."

Mariah's wide-eyed stare packed ice around Tiller's heart. "You know these men?" Her gaze shifted to her drawstring bag in Hade's clenched fist. "These are friends of yours?"

Hade leered. "Not just friends, little lady. We're partners. Tiller here is a member of our gang."

Her aim steadied on Hade. "I don't believe you."

Shame seeped from Tiller's pores. "It's a lie, Mariah." He had to talk fast. She was backing away. "I'm not one of them. Not since I—"

"Hey! What's going on in here?"

The roomful of people spun to the door.

Otis tottered on the threshold in his nightshirt. "I woke up hankering for a slice of apple pie, but I see I'm missing a party." He spotted Tiller across the room and smiled. "I called out for you, son, but you couldn't hear me for all the fun you're having."

His merry eyes lit on Hade, and his smile waned. Leaning forward, he squinted. "Wait a minute, now. I know you, mister." His trembling fingers reached for the wound on his head. "You're the no-good rascal who bashed in my skull."

His foggy gaze slid to Sonny and Nathan. "You fellas were there, too." He nodded at Nathan. "You rode up the rise chasing—"

He pivoted in his socks, his shaky finger aimed at Tiller. "Chasing you! By Job, I remember it all now. You're the varmint who left me alone in the hands of these devils."

Mariah's troubled scowl fixed on Tiller. "You? You're the men who hurt Otis?"

Otis stared vacantly for several seconds before his face softened. "I won't hold it agin' you, Tiller. You were thinking of your little bride." He scratched his chin. "What was her name again?"

Tiller took a step toward him. "No, Otis. . ."

One finger shot up, and Otis flashed his toothless grin. "Lucinda! Sweet Lucinda with the big doe eyes." The smile died on his lips and confusion took its place. "But that can't be, can it? Where is she, son? And what are you doing here with little missy? Couldn't you convince Lucinda's pa that your wife belongs with you?"

Tiller's gaze swung to Mariah.

She stood pale and trembling, the big gun dangling at her side. "Your wife?"

Stumbling across the room, Tiller latched onto her arms. "I can explain all of this."

She tried to shrug his hands away, but he held on tight. "Mariah, please."

"You're hurting me." Her voice was steely-calm, and the fire never left her eyes, but her wince of pain cut him to the core.

Nathan lunged and grabbed his collar. "The jig's up, Tiller boy. Let's go."

Tiller's soul cried out to stay and fight for her. Shame spun him for the door.

Bumping shoulders, they bolted, Hade and Sonny fast on their heels. Like the cowards they were, they tore down the hall and out the back door.

And like ten years before in Scuffletown, Tiller's traitor feet followed Nathan from the only place he really wanted to be.

Dazed and speechless, Mariah stared at the door. Whatever madness had just come to light, one truth broke through her shock. Tiller was leaving, taking her battered heart with him. If he rode away from Bell's Inn, she might never see him again, might never understand what he'd done.

Miss Vee appeared on the stairs, tugging her dressing gown around her bosom, her hennaed hair an orange sunburst atop her head. "What the devil's going on down here?"

His eyes clearer now, Otis toddled to Mariah's side and touched her arm. "You're just gonna let him leave?"

"He's already gone." Her voice sounded hollow in her ears.

Otis shook his head. "They're still saddling the horses. But you'd best hurry."

With an anguished cry, Mariah dashed out of the parlor and raced for the kitchen door. Tiller said there was an explanation. She wanted to hear it, needed him to deny the ugly things she'd just heard.

Clutching the knob, she yanked, rattling the doors on its hinges. Pounding hooves sped past, kicking up dust and uprooted grass. She sprang off the threshold, but strong arms caught her in midair. "Whoa, not so fast."

"Let go, Uncle," she cried. "I have to catch him."

Uncle Nukowa set her down, his narrowed eyes boring into her. "Not just yet. You have some explaining to do."

She struggled against him. "Please! They're getting away."

His fisted hand loomed before her face, his raw knuckles blotting out the darkness of the yard. One by one, his fingers opened. Lit by the flickering kitchen light, Mother's bead necklace slid out in a clicking rush, jerking to a dangling stop from the end of his thumb.

The necklace Mariah last saw when she tucked it under her father's gravestone.

Stunned, she cut her eyes to him.

Watching her reaction, he nodded slowly then nudged her toward the door. "Go back inside, Mariah. It's time you start telling the truth."

Tiller rode hard behind Nathan, the rush of wind in his face a harsh reminder. How many times had he fled with the gang, running from the bullet, beating, or noose they deserved?

The unwanted miles stretched between Tiller and Bell's Inn. With every beat of his heart, he longed for Mariah. The sight of her proud face slack with shock, her eyes brimmed with pain, had broken him. To know he caused it rocked his soul.

His only comfort was the horse galloping beneath him—solid proof that he had every intention of returning. What would Mariah think when she found Sheki gone?

She'd add it to his list of sins and curse him for a soulless devil.

No matter. When he returned with her horse and money, it might be enough to convince her to listen. He'd be praying every second for God to work a miracle in her heart.

How to pry the gold from Hade's greedy fingers?

Tiller still had to work that part out, but he planned to succeed if he had to loosen those fingers by death.

THIRTY-NINE

Uncle Joe caught Mariah's wrist and sat her down hard on a kitchen chair. Standing over her, he swung the jasper pendant strung between the wooden beads like a pendulum past her eyes.

She tried in vain to look away, but they held her mesmerized.

"I found the grave, Mariah."

"Mother's grave?" She licked her lips. "You've always known where she rests."

He slapped the table hard. "Enough! The time for lies is past."

Mariah's heart dove as Miss Vee hurried in, her face as pale as her white collar. "What's going on in this house tonight? First that ruckus in the parlor, now this?" She tugged on his arm. "Come away from her. Joe. You're scaring her to death."

His head swiveled. "That's an interesting choice of words, Viola, when death is what we're dealing with."

Mariah shot him a warning glance. "Please, Uncle." She shook her head. "Not like this."

"Death?" Miss Vee repeated. "I don't understand."

Otis appeared behind Miss Vee, his eyes wide and darting. Uncle Nukowa's gaze bounced between them. "I stopped to pay respects to my sister tonight, and what do you suppose I found?"

They blinked at each other. Otis shrugged.

"A fresh grave in the family plot," Uncle Nukowa said. He glared at Mariah. "A hidden grave, though not hid well enough."

"What?" Miss Vee shuddered and rubbed her arms. "Whose, for heaven's sake? We've had no recent deaths."

Her uncle's gaze seared Mariah to her chair. "You can answer her question, can't you?" He raised his chin toward Miss Vee. "Go on. Tell her who's buried beside your mother on the hill. With a rock for a headstone"—he rattled the string of beads—"and these for a marker."

Miss Vee's hand snaked around to take them. "Your mother's necklace?" Her bewildered stare lifted to Mariah. "You placed your prized possession on a grave?" She shook her head. "But whose?"

Otis wagged his head sadly and patted Miss Vee's arm. She glanced down at him and started to wobble.

Mariah lunged for her. "For heaven's sake, Uncle, get a chair."

They sat her down just before she swooned. The men held her upright while Mariah brought a cold cloth to wipe her face.

"Slap her wrists," Otis said. "I hear that helps to bring 'em around."

In the time it took to revive Miss Vee, the events since Father's death tumbled through Mariah's mind like scenes before a drowning man—every chance to change her mind, every missed opportunity to confess.

She hadn't once paused to admit she'd stopped talking to God along the way. If she had, she would've realized she'd veered far from His will. *Forgive me!* her heart cried.

The rage in Miss Vee's glance and the fury in her uncle's stance told her God's was the only forgiveness she could ever hope to get.

"Why?" Miss Vee's single word held a bitter accusation.

"I wanted to tell you so many times. Can you imagine how difficult it was to keep it from you?"

Tears flowing, Miss Vee shook her head. "I can't imagine a single thing about the terrible deed you've done."

Sinking to one knee, Mariah reached for her hands.

Miss Vee yanked them free and turned away.

Mariah sighed. "At least let me answer your question. I did it because I had no choice. Mother made me swear never to lose our ancestral land. Her burial place."

Uncle Nukowa crossed his arms. "It was a promise you couldn't keep."

Her mouth as dry as cotton, she nodded firmly. "But I could, Uncle. If I married a nahullo like she did."

Otis nodded grimly. "Which explains all the nonsense with that wicked Gabe."

Grateful for one ally, Mariah spun. "Yes. Only Tiller came along and we fell in love. He's already asked me to marry him."

She stood and reached for her uncle's arm, relieved when he didn't pull away. "Don't you see? You became the only thing standing in my way. If you hadn't arrived, I'd be Tiller's wife right now, and Mother's land would be safe."

Stunned, Mariah gripped her forehead to still the spinning room. "What am I saying?" She swallowed hard to ease the pain crowding her throat. "How could Tiller marry me? He already has a wife."

Her uncle's head snapped around. "What?"

She tucked her chin. "He deceived me all along. As it happens, Tiller's married."

Otis tugged at her arm. "Little missy, I've been thinking, and I don't think it's true because—"

"I'll kill him." Uncle Nukowa balled his fists, murderous rage coloring his face. "I'll boil the flesh from his rotted bones."

"Stop!" Miss Vee stood, as if waking from a trance. "John Coffee's gone. That's all that matters now." Clinging to the back of her chair, she lifted her chin. "I loved him from the first day I laid eyes on him." She smiled softly. "At first it seemed John might grow to love me, too." Moaning, she clutched her stomach. "Then Minti came along and cast her spell." Her mouth twisted. "I'm not a bit surprised to learn all this grief leads back to her."

Closing her eyes, she let her head fall back. "Well, they're together now, and so be it. Even from the grave Minti's won. If you listen close, you can hear her laughing."

Uncle Nukowa reached to steady her. "Viola..."

Miss Vee glanced his way. "Forgive me, Joe, for speaking ill of the dead." Gazing around the kitchen, she gave an eerie laugh. "But she's not really gone, is she? This is Onnat Minti Bell's inn. Always has been. Always will. Just like John Coffee was hers, and she'll never turn loose of either one." She staggered to the stairs with Otis clinging to her arm.

Longing to comfort her, Mariah edged closer. "Go up and rest,

Miss Vee. Tomorrow we'll sort all this out."

She raised her brows. "Can you undo your lies?" Her laugh was chilling. "Can you bring John back?" Stiffening her spine, she patted Otis's arm then pulled away. "I'm going to bed. Tomorrow, when I come down these stairs for the final time, I'll have my belongings with me."

She glanced around the room as if Mother flitted there. "This is the last night I'll sleep in her blasted house."

Joe caught Mariah's sleeve before she escaped up the stairs. "Where do you think you're going? We're not done."

She whirled, her eyes spitting fire. "How could you be so cruel?"

Otis backed into the hall. "I'm a mite tuckered, myself. Reckon I'll get back to my room." Reeling away, he disappeared.

Gritting his teeth, Joe pointed at his chest. "Me cruel? Do you muddy the pond to avoid your own reflection?"

She hung her head. "I have a lot to make up to her. But you could've been more considerate in how you broke the news."

He raised one brow. "You had plenty of time to tell her any way you saw fit."

"I told you why I couldn't. You know how Mother was. Surely you of all people can understand."

"You lied to me, girl. To everyone in this house." He shook his head. "Such behavior I'll never understand." He tightened his mouth. "And now I learn the dog who urged you to defy me has a wife?"

She held up her hand. "Believe me, I didn't know. Not until tonight."

Biting off a blistering curse, he glanced toward Tiller's room. "Is he in there? Sleeping under my roof?"

Tears spilled onto Mariah's cheeks. She let them flow unchecked. "He's gone. He rode out with his gang as you came in. After they robbed the safe."

"His gang?" Stunned, Joe gaped at her. "Are you saying *Tiller* robbed us?" He wouldn't admit it, but none of the things he'd heard matched what his heart believed about the boy. Taking her by the arm, he led her to the table. "I think you'd better start from the beginning."

Sinking into a chair, Mariah covered her face with her hands. "I still can't believe it myself. My head is reeling."

Joe patted her trembling shoulder. "Do your best, but I need to know what happened."

When she finished her tale of burglars in the parlor, Otis regaining his memory, her stolen gold, and Tiller making a getaway with his band of thieves, Joe was madder than he'd ever been in his life. He stood and lifted Mariah to her feet. "Go to bed and try not to fret. I'm going to round up some men and go after them."

She touched his arm. "Rest first. You haven't slept all night."

"I dozed awhile at Tobias's house."

"Helped along by a few pints of ale?"

He lowered his eyes.

"It's not enough, amoshi." She squeezed his hands. "It's nearly daylight. Rest until then."

He scowled. "This can't wait."

"At least while I pack food and water for your trip? Besides"—she shrugged—"you've said it many times, nahullos are easy to track."

He twisted his mouth to the side and nodded. "I suppose another hour can't hurt."

"Thank you. I'll feel better knowing you've had some sleep." Mariah turned toward the counter, her shoulders slumped in defeat. "Go on up. I'll call you when everything is ready."

Hurting for her, Joe pulled her around and tugged her to his chest. She buried her face in his shirt and wept. "How can you forgive me?"

He grunted. "Because you're right. I know how your mother was."

Raising her head, she searched his face. "You won't hurt him?" She knitted her brow. "When you find Tiller, you won't harm him, will you?"

The ways of women were a deep river indeed. "I should think you'd want his scalp."

She shook her head. "Maybe someday. Not now."

He swiped the tears from her cheeks with his thumbs. "Go upstairs and wash your face before you ready my pack."

"Yes, Uncle."

He walked her to the bottom step, and she climbed as if her legs were made of stone. Halfway up, he called her name.

"Yes sir?"

"I'm sorry about your father. I know how you loved him."

"Yes, very much." Her voice broke, and her red nose flared.

"And Mariah?"

"Yes sir?"

"I want you to call me Uncle Joe now. The time of my anger has passed."

FORTY

Tiller reined Sheki beside the other horses and slid to the ground. Every inch of him hurt as if they'd dragged him the last grueling miles. He supposed in many ways they had. His head throbbed, his heart ached, and his muscles strained to return to Mariah.

Hade lit the lantern then tossed his pack against the trunk of a river birch tree. Sliding to the ground, he propped his back against the worn leather bag, groaning when his knees cracked. "Sure is soon to be setting up camp. We should at least ride until daylight so they won't spot our fire. There may be a posse behind us, and I'd like to see them before they see us."

"I doubt there's a posse," Nathan said. "It would take too long to round one up. The nearest lawman's in Canton." He kicked a rock toward the Pearl. It landed with a *plunk* and a splash. "Besides, I'm tired of running."

Hade yawned and stretched. "I'm just plain tired. I sure could use some coffee. You boys go see what you can do about it."

Sonny pushed off the ground where he'd sprawled to dig a fire pit. "Yes sir. I'll round up some wood."

Nathan pulled a battered coffeepot from his saddlebag then squatted by the riverbank to fill it.

Tiller sat on a log and slid his knife from the scabbard to dig up a piece of chicory root to roast. Anything to add flavor to Nathan's strong, bitter grounds.

He paused, turning the bone handle over in his hand while memories flooded his mind.

The day he fled Scuffletown, he took the time to grab his Christmas gifts from under the tree. The knife, the only gift he'd kept up with over the years, came from his uncle.

Uncle Silas, a gem of a whittler, spent hours carving fine statues and trinkets, and he'd promised to teach Tiller to do the same. If he'd stayed in North Carolina, he'd be carving something besides chicory root and sassafras and might've carved something better out of life.

Uncle Silas once told him, "The blunders you make as a youth can chase you into old age. Don't make a mess of your life while you're still damp behind the ears."

Anger surged in Tiller's heart, and he squinted toward Nathan. He'd been a child when the older boys led him out of town by his soggy ear. For ten years, he'd stumbled along behind a ruthless gang, feeling lost and out of place—years spent away from his family that he could never get back.

Tiller appreciated what Nathan tried to do for him in the barn, but it wasn't enough. He didn't know if anything ever could be. He felt as if a fog had lifted in his head. Otis, Mariah, and the inn had awakened him from a bad dream, and he wasn't about to roll over and go back to sleep.

Lantern light glinted off the knife in Tiller's hand. His searing gaze jumped to Hade, snoring under the tree with Mariah's coins tucked inside his makeshift pillow.

Planted by impatience, watered by desperation, the idea grew, slipping into Tiller's head the way sap oozed from greening bark. He saw no reason to wait any longer.

Fighting tears, Mariah slung eggshells at the sink. Scrambled eggs, his favorite food, reminded her of Tiller. The cream she poured into the eggs he liked stirred into his coffee. Coffee summoned memories of sipping cups together at the breakfast table. The table brought to mind their Dr. Busby games.

How could she forget Tiller McRae when he'd invaded every corner of her life?

Miserable, Mariah's heart lifted to Miss Vee's room. She longed to race up the stairs and knock on her door, but she'd find no comfort there.

Why hadn't she realized how much she loved Miss Vee? She only prayed she hadn't lost her for good. Life would be unbearable if Miss Vee left the inn. The loss would be like losing a mother all over again.

"Little missy?"

She glanced around.

Otis stood behind her wearing the stiff gray shirt and baggy trousers he wore when they first carried him to her door. He'd slicked back his hair and shined up his boots, as well.

"Otis." She blinked at him. "You're dressed."

He grinned. "Well, not quite, thanks to you and Miss Vee. I can't seem to fasten the top button of my drawers, and I don't even need my suspenders."

She hid a smile behind her hand. "I was about to ask if you were ready for your breakfast."

He patted his bulging stomach. "Well, sure. It may be big, but it's empty this morning."

She nodded at the table. "Have a seat. It's almost ready."

He swung into a chair and glanced around. "Your uncle ain't left yet to go hunt Tiller, has he?"

Mariah glanced up. "How did you know he was going?"

"It don't take much figuring to know a man like Joe will go after those men."

She went back to stirring her eggs. "I'm about to wake him. He's eager to get on the road."

"That makes two of us."

Laying aside her ladle, Mariah turned. "You can't go. You're not strong enough."

The banister creaked, jolting her heart. She prayed to see Miss Vee lumbering down to slip on her apron and help with breakfast as she did every morning, her threats to leave forgotten.

Uncle Joe's heavy footsteps descended instead.

Otis lifted his head. "I'm going with you, Joe."

Her uncle smoothed back his hair and tied it with a leather strap then crossed to the coffeepot. "I don't think you can keep up, Otis. We'll be riding hard."

"I'll keep up. I'm stronger than I look."

Uncle Joe poured his coffee and stirred in a cube of sugar. "Why do you want to go?"

Otis swung around in his chair. "I've been mulling over the day I first ran into Tiller on the Trace. The day they took my money and busted my head." He glanced at Mariah. "When Tiller told me he had a wife, he was outright lying."

She gave her head a little shake. "Why would he lie about a thing like that?"

Otis tapped his nose. "Tiller was the bait, you see. Those ruffians used his boyish face and winsome ways to lure folks. Then they'd swoop in and skin their prey." He nodded. "The story Tiller told me that day he made up on the fly. He meant to sidetrack me, get me feeling sorry for him, and take my mind off the danger." He chuckled. "It worked, too."

Hope surged in Mariah's heart, but her anger squashed it. She slid a plate of food in front of both men and pulled out the opposite chair. "If it's true, it's still a crime. And a terrible thing to do."

Otis leaned across the table and peered into her eyes. "You're right, honey. It don't sound like the man we know, does it?"

Mariah bit her bottom lip and shook her head. "Not at all."

He touched her hand. "Why do you reckon Tiller came here in the first place, snuggling in and making himself at home?"

She'd never once asked herself that question. "I. . .don't know."

"He was running from those men because a life of pure meanery and shecoonery never set right in his heart. Tiller rode away and left me that day for the same reason. He's not the kind of man to take part in what happened next."

"He did have a part in it," Uncle Joe said. "He set you up to be fleeced."

Otis stared at his breakfast. "I'm not excusing him for that. He was guilty as sin." He glanced between them. "But Tiller brought that sin to the cross."

Silence settled over the table.

"It's the truth," Otis said. "Yesterday, he knelt at my feet and sobbed his heart out to God. He got up a brand-new man." He reached for

Mariah's hand. "Little missy, Tiller came here for a fresh start, and now he's had a true change of heart."

"Then why'd he run?" Uncle Joe growled.

Otis scratched his head. "I ain't figured that part out yet. That's why I intend to ride along, Joe. I mean to ask young Tiller myself." He squeezed Mariah's fingers. "There are two things I know for sure. One, Tiller didn't go willingly, and two, he loves you, honey."

Mariah got up and faced the counter, her napkin pressed to her mouth. "Then why didn't he tell me about his past? Why did he keep secrets from me?"

Otis cleared his throat. "I seem to remember another secret." His quiet voice soothed and convicted her at the same time. "Did you share all yours with him?"

Dicey swept through the back door, her high-pitched voice shattering the stillness like busted glass. "Sorry I's late. It ain't my fault. That tomfool Rainy ain't been on time one day in his life." Unaware of the strain in the room, she snatched her apron off the hook and set to washing the dishes.

Mariah wiped her eyes and brought another serving of eggs to Uncle Joe. She held the ladle suspended over his plate when Rainy ducked in the back door.

"Missy Bell?"

She glanced up.

"When Mista' Tilla' be back? We s'posed to build fences this mornin'."

She swallowed hard. "You'd best go on and start without him."

He frowned. "Yes'm."

As he ducked out of sight, a thought niggled at Mariah's mind. "Rainy, wait," she called.

He poked his head in again.

"How did you know Tiller's not here?"

Rainy, pointed. "Well, there's you and Mr. Joe. Mr. Otis and Miss Vee don't get on no horse." He grinned. "*Somebody* ridin' Sheki, so it got to be Mista' Tilla'."

Mariah dropped the ladle with a clatter, and Uncle Joe lurched up from his chair.

It felt like Rainy punched her in the stomach. She had to suck air before she could speak. "Sheki's gone?" It came out a croak.

The boy's eyes rounded. "Y–yes'm. Horse, bridle, and saddle."

Mariah shook her head at Uncle Joe. "He wouldn't take Sheki."

Uncle Joe slammed his fisted napkin to the table. "Well, he did," he roared.

Dicey screamed and dropped a plate with a *crash*.

Rainy made himself scarce.

The trembling in Mariah's chest flamed into rage. Of all the betrayals, this one stung the worst. Tiller knew what Sheki meant to her. His actions stank with bold assumption, the cocky action of a man with no conscience and no capacity for love.

In that moment, her heart closed on him and turned a lock. From here on, any reminders of Tiller McRae would taste of bitter swill.

Otis half stood, his eyes pleading. "Now, little missy. . .don't jump to conclusions."

Her hand shot up. "Don't you dare defend him. If Tiller took Sheki, he can't be who we thought he was." She turned to Uncle Joe. "I don't care about the money. Just find my horse."

He nodded. "I'll saddle up and come back for my provisions."

Otis watched Uncle Joe stalk to the door. "I'm going too, ain't I, Joe?"

Her uncle chewed inside his cheek for a moment then sighed. "Against my better judgment, Mariah, pack enough for two." He wagged a warning finger. "I won't slow my pace for you. If you can't keep up, I'll send you back alone."

Otis gave him a quick nod. "Fair enough."

A knock on the front door pulled them around. Staring at the hallway, Mariah clenched her fists. "Oh please, not today. I have no patience for lodgers."

Dicey set the dish towel filled with broken china aside and scurried past. "You want me to send them away?"

Mariah sighed. With her money stolen, she couldn't afford the luxury of her wishes. "Just answer the door, Dicey. See what they want."

Uncle Joe returned to the table and picked up his coffee. "I'll wait here until we find out who they are."

Exhausted, Mariah sank down at the table to wait. The breakfast she'd labored over had looked so good just moments before. Now its smell turned her stomach.

Dicey appeared wringing her hands. "They say they don't need no room for the night. Jus' a hot meal and coffee, if we please, and to fill their canteens at the pump. They willing to pay."

Mariah shared a look with Uncle Joe.

"I need to get on the road," he said. "I won't leave you alone with a rough bunch of strangers."

"We need the money." Mariah bit her lip. "I can handle them. I've done it before."

"Not without Viola." He nodded at Dicey. "Bring them in so I can have a look at them."

She bustled away, returning quickly with two men and a woman trailing behind her. The beautiful redhead was definitely a woman, though she wore jean pants and a youth's checkered shirt. She strutted into the kitchen ahead of her companions with the quiet confidence of a man.

Dust from the road covered them in a fine layer, and fatigue lined their faces, but the unmistakable light of decency shone from their eyes.

"Morning, ma'am," the striking, dark-eyed man said then nodded at Otis and Uncle Joe.

Uncle Joe shook hands all around. "Mariah, these folks look hungry. See what you can do to fix it."

"Yes sir," she said, turning to the stove.

"We need to clean up before we sit at your nice table," the woman said. "We've got many a long mile clinging to our hides."

"Show them to the pump, Dicey," Mariah said. "Take a towel for each of them when you go."

They returned refreshed and sat at the table, eagerly pouring cups of steaming coffee.

Mariah found the oddly attractive group so pleasant to look at she could hardly keep from staring.

Otis, gaping from one to the other, seemed to suffer the same affliction.

Heaping plates with eggs, bacon, fried potatoes, and buttered biscuits, she passed them around. Grinning, her guests shared a pleased look then tucked into the food.

The handsome man, his cheeks bulging, beamed at Mariah. "Ma'am, this is the best spread we've had in weeks."

His friend nodded. "Not since we pulled out of Scuffletown."

Otis shot to his feet. "I knew it! I know just who you are."

The dark-eyed man sloshed his coffee.

His friend seemed to bite his tongue.

The forkful of food headed for the woman's mouth fell to her plate.

They stilled, as if scared to move, gazing stupidly at Otis.

Uncle Joe scowled. "Man, have you lost your senses?"

Ignoring him, Otis pointed to each of them in turn. "You're Hooper. You're Duncan. And you're Dilsey."

Staring blankly, the woman slowly shook her head. "No sir. I'm Ellie. And this here's my husband, Wyatt. But how—"

"Close enough," Otis crowed.

Mariah gasped. No wonder these folks struck a chord in her heart. Like Otis, she already knew them from her long talks with Tiller. The family he hadn't seen in ten long years sat for breakfast around Mariah's kitchen table.

FORTY-ONE

Mariah held her breath and waited, a pulse pounding in her throat. The man Otis claimed to be Hooper didn't deny it. Waking from his daze, he stood. "Tiller's been here," he announced in a steady voice, his eyes brimming with hope. He glanced at each of them, settling on Mariah. "Is he still?"

She wondered if he saw the same bond to Tiller she sensed in him.

"No sir," Otis said. "You just missed him."

Ellie squealed and sprang up to hug her brother. Turning from the crook of his arm, she swiped at her tears. "Tell us where he is. We'll go right now."

Otis cleared his throat. "Well, ma'am, that part's a little tricky."

"If he's coming back, we'll wait," Hooper said. "No matter how long it takes."

Uncle Joe's mouth tensed to a thin white line. "You'll wait a long time. Tiller's not welcome here."

Ellie spun, her green eyes flashing. "Why is that?"

"Tiller McRae is a thief and a liar," he said. "And a no-account beguiler of women."

The three stared in disbelief.

Uncle Joe jutted his chin. "Not to mention a horse thief."

"Who says?" Ellie demanded, her fists clenched.

Wyatt's arm shot out to hold her. "Let him talk, Ellie. It's been a long time since we've seen Tiller. He's not the young whelp you remember."

"I don't care. Tiller's our kin. He couldn't be all those things." Her voice wavered. "He just couldn't."

"Ask my niece," Uncle Joe said, pointing at Mariah. "The swindler proposed marriage to her when he already has a wife."

Ellie gasped and covered her mouth.

Hooper and Wyatt shot troubled frowns over her head.

"Not only that," Uncle Joe continued, "he robbed our safe last night of every cent we owned. I'm on my way this morning to form a posse and go after him."

Showing strength Mariah didn't think he had, Otis pushed between them. "Now blast it! Hold up a minute, Joe. You're only giving them part of the story. Tiller's family deserves the whole truth."

Ellie's hand slid away from her mouth. "If it's any worse than what we've heard, kindly keep it to yourself."

Hooper gripped his shoulder. "Tell us what you know, old-timer."

Otis pulled out a chair for Ellie then gave Mariah a brisk nod. "Brew up more coffee, little missy. This might take a minute."

Uncle Joe fumed. "I don't have time for stories, Otis. If you want to stay behind and flap your jaws, that's up to you. I need to call out a manhunt."

Mariah gripped his wrist. "Please, Uncle Joe. Otis is right. These folks are Tiller's family. They have a right to hear everything and decide for themselves."

Hooper nodded. "I'd be much obliged if you'd wait, sir. Since we're both looking for the same man, I'd like to ride along."

Uncle Joe looked doubtful. "I don't know if that's a good idea."

"We might be of use," Hooper said. "My sister is quite gifted at tracking."

Looking down his nose, Uncle Joe scoffed. "I have no need of her. I can trail a goose in a southbound flock."

Ellie's brow puckered. "I can track a flea in a sandstorm."

They challenged each other across the room.

Mariah sought his hand and squeezed.

With a whispered curse, Uncle Joe nodded and plopped in his chair.

They settled around the table while Otis talked about the kind-hearted Tiller, the man who hovered over his sickbed, bathing and feeding him with gentle hands when he was too weak to care for himself. He spoke of the Tiller devoted to Mariah, rescuing her from the twister and its aftermath and from crazy Gabe Tabor.

Otis told them how Tiller loved the inn, rebuilding it from roof-top to foundation then doing it all over again after the storm. He mentioned the garden, how Tiller spent long hours coaxing green shoots from the ground, determined that Mariah have fresh vegetables despite the destructive tornado.

In a voice filled with fatherly pride, he told of Tiller chopping up trees for days and hauling them off to sell, so proud of bringing every cent to place in Mariah's lap. He ended with the story of Tiller in tears, kneeling on the porch to lay down his sins and invite Jesus into his life. "If there's one thing a man can't fake, it's a repentant heart."

Ellie crossed her arms on the table and lowered her head to cry, strands of her long hair falling in the butter dish.

Dicey lifted her apron to cover her face and ran sobbing into the pantry.

Ducking his head, Hooper wiped his face with his sleeve.

Even Wyatt, Ellie's husband, had shimmering eyes. "That sounds more like the boy we knew."

"So what happened after all that?" Hooper asked. "And what's this about a wife?"

Otis opened his mouth to answer, but Mariah gripped his shoulder. "No. Let me."

Otis glanced up with a sweet smile. "Go ahead, honey."

Taking a deep breath, she told how Tiller had been riding with a raiding gang of thieves. She made it clear that he took off when the real crimes were committed because his tender conscience drove him to. She said Tiller didn't really have a wife, that sweet Lucinda was a story he made up on the fly to gain Otis's trust.

In a proud voice, she explained how Tiller broke with the gang to seek a fresh start, but they followed him to Bell's Inn. She assured them Tiller took no part in robbing the inn. He'd been in the parlor to protect her money from his former gang, not to steal it.

Mariah said all these things to Tiller's family because she knew without a single doubt they were true.

"Then why did he run?" Joe demanded.

Mariah hung her head. "I'm certain Tiller ran from the doubt in my eyes." Her heart breaking, she glared. "But he didn't run for good. Tiller would never steal my horse, Uncle Joe. Leaving on Sheki proves he has every intention of coming back."

"That's it!" Otis cried, slapping the table. "He's planning to ride back here with your money and make you proud. It lines up with everything else the boy's done since he got here."

Mariah crossed her arms over the sudden ache in her stomach. "That could be dangerous, couldn't it? Those men won't let him get away with all those coins. They'll kill him first."

Uncle Joe raised his chin, staring down his nose at her. "You really believe in this red-haired nahullo?"

She smiled through her tears. "With all my heart."

Standing, he offered his hand to Hooper. "Looks like our manhunt just became a rescue."

Ellie's husband seemed anxious. He stood with Hooper, wiping his trembling hands on his trousers. "This thieving gang," he said in a voice filled with dread, "did you happen to catch their names?"

"Yes." Mariah gave him a thoughtful nod. "The one with cold eyes was Hade Betts. The lanky man with a ready smile was Sonny Thompson."

She turned to Otis. "I can't recall the quiet one's name."

"Nathan somebody," Otis said.

Wyatt turned as pale as the tablecloth. "Carter? Nathan Carter?"

Mariah pointed. "Yes, that's him."

Ellie wrapped her arms around Wyatt's neck, and Hooper gently patted his shoulder.

Compassion squeezed Mariah's heart. "You know him?"

Wyatt gave a somber nod. "He's my brother."

"I'm so sorry."

Hooper hooked his arm around Wyatt. "Don't worry. We'll find them both and bring them home."

Wyatt shook his head. "I'd like to believe you, Hoop. Nathan's pretty headstrong."

"Nonsense," Ellie said. "He's bound to be tired of drifting." She smiled. "We'll tell him he has a passel of nephews back home just dying to meet their Uncle Nate."

Wyatt grinned and squared his shoulders. "That might chase him off for good."

Uncle Joe grunted. "I hate to rush you folks, but it's time to ride." He crossed to the rack and shoved his big hat on his head. "The longer we sit here, the farther away they'll get."

He motioned to Otis. "I'll saddle Tiller's horse for you and meet you outside."

Otis waved his hand. "Aw, go on without me, Joe. I'd just slow you down."

Mariah smiled to herself. Funny how fast Otis lost his zeal to go once the tide of Uncle Joe's anger switched off Tiller.

Swiveling on his chair, Otis gazed up at Hooper. "I have one more question, if you don't mind."

"Not at all, sir," Hooper said.

Otis's eyes crinkled in thought. "Why have you come looking for young Tiller?"

Hooper shot him a warm smile. "We've come to take him home."

Mariah's breath caught. "Home? You mean to North Carolina?"

"That's right." Ellie beamed. "Back to Scuffletown where he belongs."

Otis swung around to her. "Why now, after ten long years?"

Pulling on his leather gloves, Hooper lowered his gaze. "It's not the first time we've searched, I can tell you that, but we finally got a good lead." He grinned. "Looks like it paid off."

Beaming, Otis glanced around at them. "I'm glad to know you care about him. Tiller don't know that, you see."

Ellie clenched her hands and fixed determined eyes on Otis. "He'll know soon enough, sir."

Mariah pushed up from the table. "What if Tiller doesn't want to go back with you?"

Hooper's mood seemed to lighten. "He'll want to." He glanced at Ellie. "Once we tell him what's waiting there for him."

Before Mariah could ask what he meant, Uncle Joe herded them out the door.

She called Dicey out of the pantry, and together they finished tying up bundles of food and filling canteens with water. As they carried them out the back door, the rising sun broke through the trees by the river.

Uncle Joe and the others rode up to the porch, and Dicey helped Mariah load their packs and tie on the full canteens.

Feeling her uncle watching from the saddle, Mariah glanced up at him.

He gently caressed her cheek. "Your mother loved you very much."

A lump rose in her throat. "Yes, she did."

"She loved your father, too."

Unable to speak, Mariah nodded.

Straightening, his thoughtful gaze swept his surroundings in a wide arc, from the Pearl River to the Natchez Trace stretching out of sight in the distance. "I'll help you keep your promise, niece. I'll bring home your Tiller so you can keep your mother's land."

Her grateful tears blurred his dear face. "Thank you, Uncle. I love you with all my heart."

He nodded. "I'll stay for your wedding, but then I must go home."

"Already? There's no rush to leave."

A teasing glint sparked his eyes. "There is if I want to be home for the birth of my son."

A hush fell over the yard. "Aunt Myrtle is with child?"

He grinned. "Yes, at last. With my son, George."

Laughing, she reached up to give him a hug. "I'm so happy for you."

Pulling free, he took up his reins. "Enough of this dawdling. Let me go find your nahullo."

They rode down the slope of the yard and onto the Trace, turning left toward Jackson.

Mariah clung to the porch rail and watched as long as she could spot any sight of them flickering past the trees. Her heart felt somewhat lighter, but an unsettled matter weighed heavy on her mind. She had to face Miss Vee. The sooner the better.

There hadn't been a peep from her all morning, despite her determined threat to pack and leave. Sudden fear struck Mariah's heart. Miss Vee didn't seem the type to harm herself, but—

Whirling for the door, Mariah burst into the kitchen and dashed for the stairs.

"She's over here, little missy."

She froze, her trembling hand clutching the rail.

Otis sat across the table from a bleary-eyed Miss Vee, her face bare of makeup, her hair an unholy mess. Through bloodred eyes, the lids puffed like risen dough, she stared at her hands twisting the tablecloth.

Mariah cautiously approached. "Miss Vee?"

Otis stood. "Here, take my chair. She's ready to talk." He backed toward the door. "I'll just. . ." Then he was gone.

Unsure what to say, Mariah slid into his surrendered seat and laced her fingers in front of her, her knuckles white.

Her chest ached when Miss Vee groped for her hand. "I always knew, Mariah. Deep inside, I knew."

A lump crowded Mariah's throat. "That Father was gone?"

Miss Vee shook her head. "That I wouldn't be allowed to have him— not with how bad I wanted him." She raised her eyes. "I'd have lured your father straight from your mama's arms if he'd given me the chance." She shook her head. "Such a thing should never go unpunished."

"Please don't." Mariah squeezed her hand. "Father's death wasn't to punish you."

Miss Vee shrugged. "I reckon I know that in my head. My heart's not so sure." She lifted tortured eyes. "It was an awful lie you told. A terrible, cruel secret to keep." Her gaze held Mariah captive. "You understand that now, don't you?"

She nodded. "To my shame, I understood all along. That's why I have to beg your forgiveness." She lowered her cheek to Miss Vee's hand. "I knew how much it would hurt when you found out."

Miss Vee sat quietly for a moment then caressed Mariah's bowed head. "Pretty girl, you're all I have left of your father. I couldn't bear to lose you, too."

Mariah sat up and flung her arms around Miss Vee's neck, basking in the warmth of her pardon. Clinging together, they sobbed for the heartbreaking loss they shared.

FORTY-TWO

Sonny's boisterous mood and Nathan's loud rustling never stirred Hade. The man slept like the dead and always had. A dangerous inclination for a criminal, but it would work in Tiller's favor. He'd find a way to distract Sonny, and then he'd pounce on Hade.

Licking his lips, he looked around, trying to get some idea of what to do with the gawky court jester who stayed loyal to a fault to Hade Betts.

"What you up to, Nate?" The clown in question leaned over Nathan's shoulder while he rummaged in his saddlebag.

"Going fishing," Nathan said, holding up the hooks and ball of twine he kept in his pack. If not for Nathan's knack with catching fish, many days on the trail the gang might've gone hungry.

Sonny danced with excitement. "Hey, I want to go."

Nathan shrugged. "Sure. Go dig up a mess of worms. I'll rig the poles."

The tension in Tiller's shoulders eased. *Thanks, Nate.* Without knowing it, he'd just solved Tiller's problem.

Squirming with impatience, Tiller wiped his wet palms on his trousers while Nathan cut and trimmed two limber oak branches and rigged them with the makeshift tackle. Pulling his hat low over his face, he saluted Tiller and lumbered upriver, Sonny bounding behind him like a flop-eared hound.

Now that Tiller's chance had come, he couldn't seem to move. His heart pounded and sweat broke out on his top lip. He swiped it away, his nervous gaze fixed on Hade.

In the years since Nate had coaxed Tiller to join Hade's gang, he'd never trusted the man. Never respected his spiteful tactics. Savage as a meat ax, Hade's unpredictable cruelty was the reason Tiller rode away from every ambush. Still, what he was about to do wouldn't be easy.

He stood, flexed his fingers at his side. Raised his head and sought the heavens for courage. Unsheathed his knife and squatted in front of Hade.

His mouth sagging, one arm flung over his head, Hade snored like the call of a bull moose. The leather pack under his neck forced his head back, exposing his fleshy throat like a formal invitation.

His first try, Tiller shook so hard he had to withdraw, taking deep breaths through his nose to settle his nerves.

Biting his bottom lip, he inched the blade forward again.

"Just. . .back away, Tiller boy." Nathan's hoarse whisper jolted Tiller so close to Hade's jugular, he nearly severed it. A firm grip on Tiller's hand guided the knife away from the man's throat. Dropping to his knees beside them, Nathan cocked his head and raised his brows to question marks.

"What's going on?" Hade mumbled, struggling to sit up.

Nathan pried the knife from Tiller and swept moldy leaves from the base of the tree. "Just digging for worms, Hade," he said, twisting the knife in the exposed dirt.

"Worms?" Hade blinked his bleary eyes then hurled a foul curse. "Don't dig them from under me, you fool." He waved his arm. "Go over yonder and dig the blasted things."

"Sorry, pardner. Go back to sleep," Nathan cooed, rising to his feet.

He pulled Tiller up by his collar and marched him across the camp to the river. Smiling brightly, he waved at Sonny, perched on a rock about fifty yards away, dangling his pole over the water. Hauling Tiller around, Nate punched his arm. "Are you crazy? It's a good thing I forgot my cork."

Tiller frowned. "Where did you learn to be so quiet?"

"I'm a Lumbee, remember? We learned to be quiet or be dead."

He shoved Tiller's shoulder. "What did you think you were doing?

You'd never get away with killing Hade Betts. Besides, with your tender conscience, you couldn't live with yourself."

Tiller lifted his chin. "I wasn't going to kill him."

Nate flung the knife, burying it to the hilt in the ground. "I don't know if you know this, Tiller boy, but if you slit a man's throat, he dies."

Bending to yank the blade free, Tiller wiped it on his trousers and shoved it in the scabbard at his side. "I didn't intend to cut him, but Hade had to wake up believing I would."

"If he believed it, he'd kill you even deader." Nathan pointed at the knife. "Do me a favor and leave that Mississippi toothpick in its sleeve. I know what you're trying to do, but you're going about it all wrong." He patted Tiller's back and strolled ahead. "Just sit tight and leave the scheming to me. Trickery's not your style."

Tiller ran up and caught his arm. "What are you up to?"

Nate winked. "Watch and learn." Pulling free, he nodded toward camp. "Go fetch my corks and bring an extra hook for yourself. We need to land a few catfish and get them frying before the old man wakes up again."

After rounding up Tobias and a few able-bodied men, Joe led the party down the Trace toward Jackson. The plowed soil, churned up by pounding hooves, left no doubt which way the fleeing men had gone. They'd burned a path into the rain-soaked dirt for several miles before slowing to a walk. A few yards later, their tracks faded into higher ground and disappeared.

Before Joe could dismount, the red-haired woman, as small and spry as a boy, slid off her horse and scrambled up the grassy knoll. After a spell, she trudged into view at the top of the rise and pointed behind her. "They came up here then veered off downriver."

Joe caught her horse's reins, and the riders climbed the sloping earth wall that bordered the sunken road, cut out by years of rolling wheels, plodding hooves, and determined shoe leather.

Hooper nudged up the brim of his hat. "They wouldn't go much farther without resting the horses. Not after riding them so hard."

Watching Hooper's calm, determined face, Joe saw a man of power, a leader of men. He sensed in him the same strength he couldn't deny in Tiller McRae.

Joe nodded. "Keep watch for signs of a camp along the bank. They'll be long gone by now, but we'll be able to pick up their trail from there." He twisted in the saddle and repeated the charge in Choctaw.

"Hoop, what if the old man and Joe's niece are wrong about Tiller?" Wyatt asked, his throat working. "From what she said, Nathan's in tight with this gang. We could be walking into a gunfight with our own kin."

Hooper wound his reins around his hand. "Once they know it's us, I doubt they'll take a shot." His jaw shifted. "If they do, we'll get out of Joe's way and let his men settle their hash."

Respect for Hooper surged in Joe's chest. The dark-eyed man's spirit was indeed strong and good. "I make you this promise," Joe said. "My men won't harm Tiller unless he strikes first."

"And Nathan?"

Joe raised his chin. "We'll fire if we're fired on. Not before."

Hooper nudged his horse closer and held out his hand. "Thank you, Joe. I couldn't ask for more."

The skillet sizzled over the fire, and the smell of seared catfish hung in the air. Nathan boiled a hunk of venison jerky in water from his canteen, stewing up a savory broth. Flicking weevils from sheets of hardtack, he busted them up in the broth and left it to thicken.

Tiller peeled and roasted the chicory he'd dug earlier, and Nathan brewed a fresh pot of coffee. For the first time since they'd fled the house, Tiller realized his belly was empty.

Fingering the tin plates Nathan kept in his pack, he leaned to peer into the pan. "Is the grub almost ready?"

"Just about." Grinning, Nathan lifted the biggest fish from the grease. "Hand me your shingle. I know it's hard for you to wait."

Hade sat up moaning and briskly rubbing his face. "I smell food."

Nathan glanced behind him. "Almost ready, boss."

Hade gazed around with a blank look until deep furrows marred his brow. "What time is it, Nathan? Why the devil didn't you wake me?"

"Well, good morning to you, too, sunshine," Nate said. "You woke up in a fine pucker."

"Why are you boys hanging around here? There ain't near enough road stretched between us and that blasted inn." Grunting, he struggled to his feet. "You hear me, Sonny? Get this mess cleared up, and you plug-uglies break camp. It's time to get a move on."

Nate went on stirring the hardtack slop. "Load your plate first, Sonny. We eat before we do anything else."

Sonny stood, his hesitant gaze jumping from Nathan to Hade.

Hade stalked to the fire, nervously working his fingers. "I'm telling you, we need to pull foot. Tiller's spunky little innkeeper will have the law on our tails."

Nathan laughed. "She won't turn in our boy. Didn't you see the way she looked at him? The little lady is well smitten after a taste of Tiller's charm."

"Nate's right," Sonny said, dishing up his grub. "Tiller must've poured it on thick."

Tiller's hands tensed until his plate shook. Forcing himself to relax, he squatted in front of the fire. "Don't worry." He turned steady eyes on Hade. "Mariah won't turn me in."

Hade snorted. "I wouldn't be so sure, pretty boy. You know what they say about a scorned woman."

"'Heaven has no rage, like love to hatred turned, nor hell a fury, like a woman scorned.'"

Their heads swiveled to Sonny.

Fried fish clutched in his dirty hand and grease smearing his cheeks, he blinked. "What? You think I got no culture?"

Hade shook a warning finger at Nate. "Eat up then, but make it quick. If we get set on by the law, I'll row you up salt crick." Filling his tin plate to overflowing, Hade settled against the tree to grumble and eat.

Nathan showed no fear of Hade rowing him up a creek. By the time Hade put away his usual three helpings, his bulging gut would be too heavy to give chase, much less give anyone a beating.

Tiller raised his brows at Nathan. His answering smile meant his scheme, whatever it was, must have been going according to plan.

FORTY-THREE

Mariah walked Miss Vee to her room and tucked her in bed, plumping the crocheted pillows at her back. Sitting in a chair beside her grief-stricken friend, Mariah held her hand while they shared memories of the man who was father to one, cherished love of the other.

At last, Miss Vee slept. Her every shudder, every hitching breath laid the finger of blame on Mariah's aching heart. Unable to bear another minute, she slipped from the room and closed the door.

Downstairs, she had Rainy fetch meat from the smokehouse and gave instructions to Dicey about preparing lunch, though she wondered who would have the stomach to eat. The thought of food put sawdust in her mouth, and she doubted Miss Vee would touch a bite.

And with Tiller gone—

The sound of his name in her head shot pulsing waves of pain to her chest. With Tiller gone, the house would go on feeling empty, the food tasteless, her once cheery table a soulless place.

Losing Father had robbed her of the ties to her past. Losing Tiller would mean the loss of her future, a loss she couldn't bear.

She pushed onto the back porch, his spirit rising from every board and nail. Sitting on the top step, she ran her hands along the smooth cedar rail.

How blind they'd been in their innocence. Blissful, content, falling deeply in love—unaware of disaster approaching from three different directions.

Hooper McRae from the east, coming to cart Tiller home to Scuffletown.

Uncle Joe from the west, intent to carry Mariah away, over his shoulder if need be.

Hade Betts and his gang from out of nowhere, determined to lure Tiller back to their degrading lifestyle.

Angry, she brought her clenched fist down on the porch. "Why couldn't they all just leave us in peace?"

"Life seldom works that way, little missy."

She raised her head. "I'm sorry. I didn't see you there."

Otis ambled to the porch, wiping his hands on his baggy britches. "Just washing up at the pump." He glanced heavenward. "One of God's greatest gifts is water. Did you ever consider what a stinking lot we'd be without it?"

Mariah tucked her chin at the mention of the God she'd sorely neglected. "I thought you were resting. What are you doing outside?"

He pointed over his shoulder. "I thought I'd lend Rainy a hand in the garden."

"Oh?" She angled her head. "I didn't know you liked to work the soil."

"You'll find most men do. There's nothing more healing to the soul than the promise of new life." Otis patted her hand. "It's the reason we're awed by a woman ripe with child." He chuckled. "We can't pull that off, but we can give birth to a fine crop of tomatoes."

Mariah's cheeks warmed, but she couldn't hold back a smile.

He leaned back to study her. "That's better. I don't like to see you fret. It paints lines betwixt them pretty eyebrows."

Mariah sniffed. "Lately I've had my share of things to fret over. But the most pressing burden I'm relieved to have off my chest." She stole a glance at him. "How did you know? That day in your room, I mean."

He crooked one brow. "You mean your secret?"

Lowering her gaze, she nodded.

"Well, I didn't really know, did I? God gave me just enough to get

His message across." He laughed. "If I'd known the particulars, I may have turned you over my knee."

Mariah covered her face with her hands. "I'm so ashamed. I don't suppose I'll ever forgive myself."

With palsied fingers, Otis lifted her chin. "It starts with asking God's forgiveness."

She shook her head. "Oh, I couldn't. I can't even find the words."

"Well, that's different." Otis withdrew his hand. "Sorry, gal. I mistook you for one of His."

Her head whipped around. "But I—I am. At least I was."

"Was?" He quirked his brow. "The Book says, 'I have loved thee with an everlasting love.' "

Mariah braced her forehead with her palms. "Otis, I ache for God's pardon. For everyone's."

"What are you waiting for? God says to fess up then bet on Him to forgive. He goes the extra mile and washes us clean." He nudged her with his shoulder. "Why are you making it harder than He did?"

Tears squeezed between her tight lashes.

Otis pulled her close. "Oh, lamb. Why is it easier to accept mercy from your uncle and Miss Vee when God loves you most of all?"

She wiped her nose. "I don't feel worthy."

"None of us are. Don't you see?" He took her hands and peered into her eyes. "Godly sorrow pleases Him because it leads to repenting. Condemning yourself does just the opposite."

She nodded. "I think I understand."

"Good." He stood and hitched up his pants. "I'll leave you alone so you and God can have a little talk."

Mariah stretched out her hand. "Before you go, I have to ask you something."

"Anything, child."

She searched his gentle eyes. "Will Tiller be all right? Will he come back to us?"

A shadow crossed his face. "I can't see the future, honey. But I can tell you one thing—Tiller left here fully intent on coming home."

At the door, he turned. "While you're talking to God, ask Him to be a stone of stumbling and a rock of offense to those disobedient men for Tiller's sake."

Hade lounged across the fire from Tiller, shoveling hardtack mush in his mouth with a wide spoon. After two helpings, he laid aside his plate and pulled the pan off the fire to wolf down the rest.

Sonny tried to elbow in next to him for a share, but Hade turned aside, growling like a dog on a bone. "This here's fine mush, Nathan," he said with bulging cheeks. "Best you ever made."

"You ought to share, Hade," Sonny whined. "I'm still hungry."

He tossed the empty pan at Sonny's feet. "Here, I'll share the washing up. Take that down to the river and rinse it out before I beat you to a jelly."

Sonny bent to grab the handle. "Aw, Hade. That ain't no way to do."

Cackling, Hade watched him go, the corners of his eyes crinkled with glee. "I hope he don't fall in and drown. It wouldn't be near as much fun around here without old Sonny, would it?"

Dodging Hade's grasping fingers, Nathan slid the last fish on Tiller's plate. Hade leaned over and snatched it before Tiller could take a bite. "Let's don't be greedy, boys."

Leering, he took a deliberate bite then tilted his chin. "So, what do you say, Tiller? Are you ready to ride with us again? We've got big plans, and I think you'd fit in real nice." He swiveled to Nathan. "Don't you think so, Nate?"

Nathan shrugged. "I'm not sure Tiller's cut out for robbing banks."

Hade licked his fingers then wiped them on his britches. "Sure he is." He pointed. "With that guileless face, he could spin one of his yarns while we emptied the safe. They'd be so caught up in his tale, they wouldn't notice until we were long gone." He winked. "How about it, Tiller boy? Can we count on you?"

Tiller slowly set his plate aside. "I don't know, Hade. It's like Nathan said. I wouldn't be good at robbing banks."

Hade's features hardened. "Now you listen up. . . . I've invested years in training you. I don't take kindly to folks running out on me."

Tiller gnawed the side of his lip. "I'm not running out on anybody. It's time to split the sheets, that's all."

Chest heaving, Hade pushed to his feet. "We ain't splitting nothing but the take, you hear?" He loomed over Tiller with his fists clenched. "You owe me, boy."

His fury raging to the surface, Tiller stood, but Nathan stepped between them. "Settle down, boys. There's no call to get riled."

Shoving him aside, Hade advanced on Tiller.

Tiller took a step toward him, his hand on his knife.

The frying pan sailed toward them from the brush, spinning across the dirt and landing at their feet.

Wide-eyed, Hade stared dumbly at the greasy skillet. "What the—" He glanced around. "Where's Sonny?"

A large rock arced from the other side of the camp, landing three feet away and rolling past them. Then another that struck the fire, flipping a burning limb into the air and raising a spiral of glowing embers.

With a shout, Hade spun in a circle as a storm of sticks, stones, and pinecones showered from the sky.

Tiller grinned. A familiar storm.

"It's come-to-judgment-day, pretty boy," Hade roared. "They're on us, and it's your fault."

Down and up so fast Tiller couldn't react, Hade drew back the skillet and swung. With a shout, Nathan leaped, shoving Tiller out of the way. The heavy pan hit the back of Nate's head with a sickening thud. He dropped without a whimper.

The clearing erupted with running feet and loud voices just as Hade pulled the pistol at his side. "You've been both blessing and curse to me, son. I should've cut my losses and let you go."

Tiller braced for a bullet, his soul crying out to God, his heart to Mariah.

Four hundred pounds of mad Indian sailed at Hade, knocking him to the ground. The gun went off, firing harmlessly into the trees.

Uncle Joe strolled up and ground his heel into Hade's hand until he howled and turned loose of the gun. Justin and Christopher scrambled off Hade's winded body, standing over him with clenched fists.

Feeling sick, Tiller knelt over Nathan's prone body. He called his name and heard an anguished echo from behind him in a stranger's voice. Shading his eyes against the sun, he glanced up.

The man gazing down at Nathan, his face white with concern, stirred distant memories of mud and misty swamps. "Who—"

The familiar stranger went down on one knee and touched Nathan's back. "Is he alive?"

Tiller stared, afraid to blink. "Wyatt Carter? It can't be."

Nathan groaned, and Tobias Jones pushed close to see to his wound. Standing on shaky legs, Tiller gaped in disbelief as Nathan's long-lost brother hovered by his side. "Where. . .where'd you come from?"

Against the shouting voices circling Hade and Sonny, a woman's quiet sobs reached Tiller's ears. Heart pounding, he spun. "Mariah?"

A tall man with pitch-colored hair held a slight figure against his chest, her long hair the color of a redbird. Clenched fist pressed to her mouth, she wept as one who mourned.

Dazed, Tiller tilted his chin while scenes from another life rushed through his head.

The two moved toward him, enveloped him, and he knew for sure. "Hooper?" Tears blurred his vision. He blinked to see them better. "Ellie, it's really you?"

Wailing, she wrapped both arms around him and clung with all her might.

Hooper, one hand resting on Ellie's neck, the other gripping Tiller's, gazed at him with streaming eyes. "Thank God we finally found you."

"You've been looking for me?" He didn't realize he was crying, too, until he heard his wavering voice.

Hooper nodded. "For most of the last ten years."

Tiller wiped his eyes on his sleeve. "But why?" he whispered.

Ellie lifted her head and smiled sweetly. "Why do you think, silly boy? We're your family, and we've come to take you home."

FORTY-FOUR

Mariah yanked the pins from her hair, kicked off her shoes, and rolled off her stockings. She longed to climb on Sheki's bare back, bury her fingers in his mane, and soar along the river until the rushing wind eased her fears.

She settled for a barefoot run through the cool grass in the backyard then over the weedy verge to the distant riverbank. Padding across the warm bank, she relished the swishing sand between her toes. Gathering her skirt, she lowered herself to the ground and swung her legs into the cold water.

The loose soil swirled, disturbed by her toes, and silvery minnows shot in every direction. Mariah held very still. Soon the water cleared and the curious minnows returned to peck at her skin for a taste.

The Pearl had always been a refuge from the shunning she endured from both sides of her bloodline. As a child, she spent hours exploring along the banks, listening to the mockingbird's song, and watching eagles soar overhead.

Today her haven withheld its comfort. The water felt too cold on her feet, the sun too hot on her head. The water lapping the hem of her chemise wicked clammy moisture to her skin. Leaning back on her arms, she closed her eyes and let the promise of the Lord's enduring love still the pounding of her heart.

Mother's influence had endowed her with a strong spirit. How else could a girl of her tender age endure what she had? Yet through those trials, she'd learned the depths of her weakness and her desperate need for God.

"Great Father, bring my love safely home."

The words were barely past her lips when a distant, tinny voice called her name.

Mariah's head jerked up. Shading her eyes from the water's glare, she squinted down the meandering ribbon of water. The shimmering outline of approaching riders quickened her pulse. A waving hat and a thatch of orange hair brought her to her feet in a stumbling run.

Tiller spurred Sheki to a gallop and raced to meet her. They reached her fast, and Tiller leaped from the saddle before Sheki came to a full stop.

His arms and shoulders cloaked her, his fingers tangled in her hair. He held her so near she felt a part of him, his racing heartbeat pounding in her ears. Pulling her head back, he kissed her, smoothing damp strands of hair from her face with gentle hands.

Lifting his head, he breathed a shaky laugh. "Does this mean you don't despise me?"

Too overcome to speak, she nodded helplessly.

He frowned and shook his head. "You're letting me off too easy. I lied to you. To all of you."

"You didn't lie. You withheld the truth. I'm guilty of the same."

He furrowed his brow but continued. "It's my fault Otis got hurt."

She lowered her lashes. "I hurt Miss Vee."

"I hid things from you about my past."

"I hid worse things from you."

Tiller held her at arm's length. "Why does my apology sound like yours instead? Maybe you'd better tell me what's going on."

Clinging to his hands for courage, Mariah confessed the ugly story of Mother's deathbed promise. She didn't spare herself any sordid detail, from rolling her poor father's body into an unmarked grave, to tricking simpleminded Gabe, to deeming Tiller an unfit prospect to marry.

She ended with how she'd deliberately deceived poor Miss Vee, robbing her of grieving for her lost love.

Listening quietly, Tiller didn't interrupt, though he blinked a few times in disbelief. Before he could respond, Uncle Joe rode up with his family. Tiller stepped away from her and beamed up at Hooper, Wyatt, and Ellie.

These people, strangers before now, held the power to put such joy on Tiller's face? To bring a peace and rest of soul she'd never seen in his eyes before?

Her heart skipped a beat, and she felt a surge of jealousy. What would Tiller choose? Would he stay with her at the inn or return with them to North Carolina? Might he possibly ask her to go with him, and could she make the heartrending choice?

Hooper shoved back his hat. "When you're done here, we need to wash up and meet around the table. We still have a lot to talk about."

Tiller placed his arm around Mariah's shoulders. "We'll be up in a minute." He raised his face to Uncle Joe. "If that's all right with you, sir."

Uncle Joe smiled and nodded, and the four of them rode toward the barn.

Turning Mariah to face him, Tiller's lively green eyes darted over her face. "Everything we've done will right itself with God's help and time to heal, on one condition."

She drew back. "And that is?"

"If you agree to marry me because you love me, not just to save the inn."

This time Mariah grinned. "You doubt my feelings after that kiss?"

Tiller chuckled and pulled her close. "Maybe we'd best have seconds and find out for sure." Before their lips met, he released her and plunged his hand in his pocket. "First, I have something for you."

He came up with the cloth bag that held her coins and dropped it into her hand. "I never meant to leave you, Mariah. Going with Hade was the only way to get this back."

Mariah touched his cheek. "I had assurance of that truth from a couple of witnesses."

He frowned his confusion, and she laughed. "Otis for one. My heart for another."

Recalling Hade Betts's lifeless eyes, she couldn't help glancing over her shoulder. "What happened out there, Tiller? Won't those men come riding back for you?" She shook the coins. "For this?"

"Not for triple the amount." His eyes glowed with mischief. "In fact, they'll cross the street when they see me coming."

She gasped and covered her mouth. "No they didn't!"

He chuckled. "I've never seen two men so scared."

Her brow rose. "Two men?"

The teasing left his voice. "Nathan Carter's hurt. We brought him as far as Tobias's house. They're treating him there."

She touched his face. "Your family explained about Nathan. Is he hurt badly?"

Tiller caught her hand and pulled it to his lips. "We don't know yet." Pain shone from his eyes. "Nathan jumped between me and Hade, Mariah. He got hurt trying to save me. I don't know what I'll do if he doesn't make it."

Holding hands, they led Sheki to the barn. While Tiller saw to the horse's food and water, Mariah brushed his coat to a glossy sheen with loving hands, stopping often to smooth his neck and nuzzle his silky face.

"Mariah?"

She glanced at Tiller over Sheki's back. "Yes?"

"I know you could tend this old feedbag all night, but I'm so hungry his oats are starting to look tasty."

"All right," she said, focused on Sheki's grooming. "Just one more minute."

Tiller ducked beneath the horse's neck and caught her hand. "If I prance and whinny and let you throw a saddle on my back, will you come inside and feed me?"

Laughing, Mariah hung up the brush and traced the faint sprinkling of freckles across his nose. "Granted, you bear the markings of a fine Indian pony, and you do share Sheki's love for food." She patted his cheek. "We'll forgo the prance and whinny and do without the saddle, but you may carry me if you'd like."

With a growl, he swept her off her feet and whirled her out of the barn. Staring into her eyes, he carried her to the house.

Stopping by the pump to wash up first, they hurried onto the porch. At the threshold, she paused to search his face. There were still many questions, and she'd put them off for as long as she could. Mariah sensed the answers, good or bad, waited beyond her kitchen door.

Tiller turned the knob and led her inside.

The back door opened to the sound of laughter and the smells of home. Never so glad to be in a place in his life, Tiller hung up his hat and ambled into the dining room.

His usual place next to Joe sat empty, as if in welcome. He swung into the chair and smiled at Hooper, Ellie, and Wyatt, shaking his head at the miracle of breaking bread with family.

Mariah and Dicey bustled in to ladle stew. Parading in and out from the kitchen, they passed bowls filled with seasoned green beans, buttered squash, sliced tomatoes, onions, and bread, the bounty from their shopping trip to Canton.

The sights and smells of a meal from Mariah's kitchen tempted a man like few things could. His stomach moaning in protest, Tiller laid aside his napkin and pushed away from the table. "I hope you'll all excuse me; I can't eat a bite until I have a talk with Otis."

"Looking for me, boy?"

Blood surged to Tiller's head as Otis rounded the corner, his dancing eyes searching the room. They landed on Tiller, and he beamed his toothless grin.

Standing, Tiller took a hesitant step, but the joy on the old man's face lured him forward.

Otis reached out first, wrapping him around the waist in a warm embrace.

Staring down at his wiry, white head, Tiller's chest swelled with unshed tears. "You should despise me."

Otis grunted. "Pshaw! How could I despise my best friend?"

Tiller pushed him to arm's length. "You have every right to turn me in to the law, and I'll understand if you do. Either way, I promise to repay every cent they stole if it takes me the rest of my life."

Otis shook his head. "I don't expect it."

Tiller gripped his shoulders. "Consider it done, sir. Can you ever forgive me?"

"I forgave before you asked." Otis winked and offered his hand. "It might've been a sight harder if I hadn't got to know you for the fine lad you are. I thank the Lord I got the chance."

Soaring with the freedom born of pardon, Tiller clasped both hands around Otis's hands and shook so hard he nearly pulled him off his feet. Grinning, Otis pulled free and nudged him aside. "You won't find me so forgiving if you didn't save me a bowl of Dicey's fine stew."

Smiling, Mariah slipped off her apron and took her seat across from Tiller. Otis slid into the chair next to her. Her face red and swollen, Miss Vee slipped quietly into the room, patting Tiller's back before taking her place. His heart went out to her, and he reached across to squeeze her hand.

The meal seemed the best he'd ever tasted. The lively conversation and the presence of people he loved etched a notch in Tiller's soul that promised to rival his memories of Scuffletown.

Shoving in his last forkful of blackberry cobbler, Hooper pushed aside his plate and cleared his throat. "Tiller, can we go somewhere and talk?"

God's peace settled around Tiller with the warmth of a quilt. "Whatever you came to say, go on and say it."

Hooper glanced around. "Are you sure? It's of a personal nature."

Gazing at each familiar face, Tiller nodded. "These folks are my family, too. I don't mind them hearing."

Hooper leaned forward. "I'm afraid the first part of our news is bad." His eyes darkened. "It's about your mama, son."

Ellie reached across to take his hand. "Aunt Effie died, Tiller."

Mariah gasped and came around the table to stand behind him, her soothing fingers on his neck.

The words touched his heart but didn't penetrate. He tried to feel sadness but couldn't feel much of anything but regret. "When?" The single word was all he could muster.

"Weeks ago," Hooper said. "I saw to her burial myself."

So they hadn't come to pack him off to a funeral. "What happened?"

"She had an illness." Hooper seemed to squirm in his chair. "A stomach problem worsened by her. . .inability to eat."

Tiller cringed, the stew a surge of bile in his throat. His mother slowly died of hunger while he ate his fill of good food, most of it bought by stolen money. He understood for the first time the depths to which he'd fallen. "I failed her." Defeat washed over him and he closed his eyes. "I left her to die."

"No." Ellie tightened her grip. "You surely didn't." Her strident voice softened. "She failed you."

His gaze shifted to her. "Ellie, don't."

"Let her talk," Hooper said. "What she said is true. Don't you remember? Your ma sent you away."

Tiller leaned back in his chair. "What choice did she have? I was shiftless and troublesome. Couldn't earn enough for my keep. It was either send me to Uncle Silas or watch me starve, too."

Hooper wasn't listening, just watching and shaking his head. "Your memory is skewed. You worked hard tending other folk's lawns and brought home every cent." His face red, he slapped the table. "You were a skinny, starving child who could never do enough to avoid her strap."

"What is this?" Tiller hated that his voice cracked. Wishing he'd agreed to talk in private, he gaped at them. "Did you come all this way to speak ill of my ma?"

Releasing his breath on a sigh, Hooper folded his hands in front of him. "I'm sorry. I just can't bear to hear you blame yourself."

Determination surged in Ellie's gaze. "There are things you still don't know."

Tiller pulled away from her. "Then tell me, blast it. That's what you came for, isn't it?"

Sympathy oozed from the circle around him. Wyatt patted his back, tears wet Mariah's cheek when she leaned to embrace him, and Miss Vee clutched a napkin to her trembling mouth.

"All right, I'll tell you." Hooper sighed. "But there's no easy way to say it." As if an idea just came to him, he pointed at Otis. "Let's start with him."

Fear nudging his heart, Tiller's gaze flickered to Otis sitting across the table, wiping his eyes on his shirtsleeve. "What's this got to do with him?"

Hooper patted Otis's shoulder. "I heard you swear to honor a debt to this man."

"That's right, but—"

"We're here to say you won't have a problem keeping your promise."

Desperate to understand, Tiller blinked from Hooper to Ellie. Her eyes danced and a smile tugged the corners of her mouth. "You have money, Tiller. That's the good news we came to tell you."

Hooper nodded. "Your ma hoarded every cent she ever got her hands on. She lived poor but died rich. Aunt Effie left you a fortune."

Uncle Joe leaned forward and cleared his throat. "How much?"

"Plenty," Hooper said, glancing at him. "Thousands of dollars deposited in a Fayetteville bank in the name of Tiller McRae."

FORTY-FIVE

A solemn procession worked its way down the Natchez Trace to the southwest corner of Mariah's land, the family burial grounds. Her mind flooded with memories of the night she rode the back way along the Pearl with Father's poor ravaged body. Far better to be in the company of loved ones, with the bright sun in her face, than picking her way alone and afraid by moonlight.

Sheki pulled the rig up the bluff overlooking the bend of the river. Uncle Joe hauled back on the reins and parked near the broad oak next to Mother's grave.

Mariah reached for Miss Vee's hand. "Are you ready?"

Dressed in mourning clothes, she pressed a black hankie to her lips and nodded.

Tiller climbed down and offered them a hand, then joined Uncle Joe at the tailgate to help shoulder the weight of Father's headstone.

JOHN COFFEE BELL, HUSBAND OF ONNAT MINTI BELL, LOVING FATHER OF MARIAH.

His name engraved in the cold stone settled the fact in Mariah's heart more surely than carrying his lifeless body. Father was gone. She wouldn't see him again this side of heaven.

Clinging to Miss Vee and Dicey, Mariah led them to the unmarked patch of ground, his final resting place. Pulling off their hats, Tiller's

Scuffletown family and a few of Father's close friends gathered around them. Rainy, along with his father and little brother, held to the back of the crowd. Tobias, his sons, and the rest of the Pearl River clan stood in hushed silence.

Mariah drew strength from their quiet presence, and a load lifted from her shoulders. At last, those who loved her father could honor him in death, as he deserved.

Pulling shovels from the rig, Uncle Joe and Tiller dug a trench and set the gravestone in place.

Miss Vee knelt and placed a handful of wildflowers next to the marker, her fingers caressing the letters of his name. "Oh, John. How I'll miss you."

Crying softly, Dicey patted her shoulder. "He was a fine man, that Mista' Bell. A real fine man. I'm gon' miss him, too." She sniffled and spun away.

Tiller's comforting warmth slid behind Mariah, his hand on the small of her back. "You all right?"

She shook her head. "Not yet."

Raising her trembling chin, she faced the circle of mourners. "I want to thank you all for coming to say farewell to my father. And while you're here"—she forced herself to look up—"I want to apologize for the terrible thing I've done. I pray you can forgive me." She couldn't make out every word from the mumbling, shuffling group, but she felt the healing balm of their acceptance.

Tiller gripped her hand. "While we have your attention, I'd like to make another announcement."

He raised his brows at Uncle Joe who nodded. Mariah clutched his arm to stop him, but his loving smile eased her heart.

"Mariah Bell has consented to be my wife," he said. "We'll be married right away, before we leave for North Carolina."

The wide eyes of the Pearl River clan swung to Uncle Joe.

He squared his shoulders. "It's a good match," he boomed in a loud voice, forever settling the question.

Nudging elbows and broad smiles followed, especially from Tiller's family. Only Chris and Justin Jones cast dark, brooding scowls at Tiller.

Tiller bowed his head respectfully. "Given the circumstances, we'll have a quiet ceremony with just the family as witnesses. I know you'll understand." His voice grew louder. "But after a respectable amount of time, I promise to throw a rousing good party to celebrate."

Amid a curious mix of warm condolences and sincere congratulations, the mourners filed away to their conveyances and scattered.

Mariah leaned her head against Tiller's chest. "Are you certain the time was right to announce our wedding?"

He shrugged. "Looked like the only chance since tomorrow you'll be my bride."

Tobias, the last to leave, paused to give Miss Vee's shoulder an awkward pat. "Miss Viola, if there's anything I can do to ease your grief, you let me know."

Still kneeling at Father's grave, she reached to squeeze his hand.

"Well, I'll be pickled," Uncle Joe whispered, his eyes twinkling. "Did you see that?"

Mariah shook her head. "See what?"

"Tobias is sweet on Viola."

Mariah shushed him with a finger to her lips. "For pity's sake, keep your voice down. Are you certain?"

He raised one brow. "As sure as I'm standing here. I saw it all over his face."

Watching Tobias shuffle across the yard, his shoulders bowed, Mariah recalled how he always grew flushed and tongue-tied in Miss Vee's presence. Was it possible Tobias had pined for Miss Vee while she carried a torch for Father?

Mariah smiled at the thought. She prayed Miss Vee's heart would quickly mend and she'd finally see poor Tobias. It comforted her to hope her friend wouldn't wind up all alone.

Turning to help Miss Vee off the ground, Mariah patted her puffy, sagging cheek. "Let me take you home."

She nodded. "I'm ready."

Mariah wrapped an arm around her waist. "I'll make you a pot of your special tea."

She smiled weakly. "I'd like that."

At the wagon, Tiller gave Miss Vee a boost up while Mariah climbed in the other side. Wrapping a shawl around her, Mariah pulled it snug while she searched her pale face. "Perhaps it would be best if we postponed the wedding."

Miss Vee's head snapped around. "You'll do no such thing. Why would you even consider it?"

Mariah raised one shoulder. "It doesn't feel quite right. You know. . . so soon after."

Miss Vee's trembling fingers locked on Mariah's chin, and her darting eyes roamed her face. "Haven't you learned anything by watching my plight?" She gave Mariah a gentle shake. "Every second is precious, dear. Don't waste a single breath." She released Mariah and slid on her gloves. "Take us home, Joe Brashears. A pot of chamomile tea is sounding better by the minute."

FORTY-SIX

Mariah pinned the last dark curl atop her head then slid her brush in her vanity drawer. Turning her face to the side, she smiled. If she squinted, the strong chin, straight nose, and almond eyes were her mother, gazing back proudly from the glass.

Today Mariah would fulfill her promise. Under the protection of Tiller's name, no one would try to lay claim to her land. In the freedom of his love and care, she'd be able to run the inn exactly as she saw fit. She gave her image a saucy grin. "As long as my husband approves."

Standing, she appraised her gown of black satin with its applied beading, chenille tassels, and needle lace. In the dress, she would marry the man she loved and still respect her father's memory. It pleased her to honor the two most important men in her life on the same day.

Satisfied with her appearance, she slid on her mother's delicate wedding slippers, set aside for this day, and crossed the hall to her father's room. The familiar smells rushed at her. Instead of allowing grief to take her breath, she inhaled deeply, drawing comfort from his presence in the room. "*Chi hollo li*, Aki," she whispered, the love she swore an ache in her chest. "Very, very much."

The beaded necklace her mother had left her, last seen dangling from Uncle Joe's angry fist, hung from a corner of the mirror. Lifting it with shaky fingers, Mariah slipped it over her head and patted the jasper stone at her chest. "I love you, too, Mother. I wish you and Father were here today. I know you would be happy for me."

There would be many more times in Mariah's life when she'd miss her parents' presence. Birthdays, anniversaries, the births of her children. She squeezed her eyes tight against the tears. A bride shouldn't cry on her wedding day.

"Mariah? Where are you?"

She ducked her head out the door. "In here, Miss Vee."

Standing with her head poked into Mariah's room, she spun and gasped. "There you are. You're a vision, honey. Joe's back with the minister." She laughed. "And Tiller's pacing holes in the parlor rug."

Stepping over the threshold of Father's room, Miss Vee's breath caught. "It's the first time I've been in here. You can still feel his presence, can't you?" Gazing around sadly, she wrapped her arm about Mariah's waist. "I wish he could be here to give you away."

Mariah smiled and leaned her head on Miss Vee's shoulder. "I was just telling him the same thing."

Miss Vee pushed her to arm's length. "We'll lay aside our grief and all regret for now. John Coffee wouldn't have it any other way."

Wiping her eyes, Mariah beamed. "To quote Otis, 'This is the day which the Lord hath made; we will rejoice and be glad in it.'"

"Amen!" Miss Vee grinned. "But I'm pretty sure Otis borrowed that from somewhere."

They stood together for a few more minutes, Mariah gazing at the painful reminders of her parents. Would it always be hard to come inside this room?

As if she'd read her mind, Miss Vee walked to the bed and ran her hand along the quilt. "If you don't mind, I'm going to pack away their belongings while you're gone." She glanced over her shoulder. "And move yours and Tiller's in here." She smiled weakly. "After all, you're the lord and mistress of the inn now."

The idea surprised Mariah, yet in a way pleased her. She felt her parents would approve. "Won't that be hard for you so soon? I can always tend to it when I return."

Miss Vee waved her off. "I can manage. I'll have this room so spruced up you won't recognize it." She glanced up. "And don't fret. I'll take great care with their things."

On the way to the stairs, Mariah caught her arm. "Are you sure you'll be all right until we return from North Carolina?"

Miss Vee swatted the air. "Don't be silly. You'll only be gone for a few weeks, and I can run this inn in my sleep. Besides, I still have Dicey and Rainy, if they don't kill each other first." She made a face. "And if they can ever be on time."

Mariah laughed. "Now you're spinning miracles."

Downstairs, Uncle Joe waited in the parlor with the minister of Grace Church. Immediately after Father's memorial service, Uncle Joe had ridden to Canton to fetch him.

Otis stood beside Tiller and seemed to be holding him up.

Uncle Joe had invited Tobias. Mariah was stunned to see Christopher and Justin standing stiff as posts at his side.

The most pleasant surprise was the dark-haired man chatting with Tiller's family. Spotting Mariah, he broke free of the group and approached her. "You're a lovely bride, Miss Bell."

"Thank you, Nathan." She held out her hand. "I'm so happy to see you're all right."

He rubbed the back of his head. "I'm too hardheaded to let an iron skillet keep me from Tiller's wedding." His gaze fell. "That is, if you don't mind."

"Of course not. Tiller told me how close the two of you are."

He winced, his eyes filled with regret. "I haven't been a very good friend, but I plan to change. Starting with asking your forgiveness."

Mariah drew a cleansing breath and gripped his hand. "It's been a season for seeking mercy. How could I offer you less than I've received?"

He ducked his head. "I don't deserve it, but I'm grateful. Thank you for tolerating my presence at your wedding."

She patted his arm. "I'm happy you're here. Will you be riding to North Carolina with us?"

He grinned. "My brother and Tiller won't have it any other way."

"I'm glad," she said. "We'll have a chance to get acquainted. Now, will you excuse me?"

He nodded and Mariah slipped past.

Christopher lowered his gaze as she approached.

Justin turned his head.

Mariah reached for their hands. "I'm so glad you came."

In a sulk, Justin pursed his lips. "Don't be. Our father made us."

Chris nudged him.

Hiding her smile, Mariah squeezed their fingers. "Please be happy for me, boys. It would mean so much."

Justin glared. "Why would you choose the nahullo over one of us?"

She crossed her fingers behind her back. "Dear Justin, how could I ever decide between you? The problem gave me many sleepless nights. I found the only possible solution in giving both of you up. Don't you see? It was the only way."

The boys shared a startled glance.

"Of course." Chris smoothed her hair. "Poor Lotus Blossom."

Justin puffed his chest. "Still, it's a shame you were forced to settle."

"Mariah?"

She turned at the sound of Tiller's voice, so handsome with his fresh-shaved cheeks and wet-combed hair he took her breath. "Yes?"

"It's time to start." His grin held no trace of the rogue she first met. "If you're still agreeable."

She smiled and wiggled her fingers. "I'll be right along."

Uncle Joe caught her hand as she passed. "I'll be leaving right after the ceremony, niece."

She made a face. "So soon?"

Glowing with happiness for her, he patted her face. "What need has a new bride of a cantankerous old uncle underfoot?"

She leaned into his chest. "Won't you at least wait until morning?"

"No, sabitek. I travel best at night." He wrapped a tendril of hair behind her ear. "Besides, you leave soon for North Carolina with your husband, and I'm long overdue at home."

"Mariah?" Tiller stood behind her, worry crowding his brows. "Have you changed your mind?"

Turning, she latched onto his hand. "After all I've been through to snare the proper husband?"

"Then you'd best get a move on. You know our policy here at Bell's Inn"—he glanced at the parlor clock, about to strike the hour—"if you're not standing before the minister promptly at six, you stand a fair chance of going without."

Tiller awoke to find Mariah staring down at him. Propped on one arm, she'd been watching him sleep by the moonbeam filtering through her bedroom window.

With her dark hair loose and flowing and the soft white fabric of her nightdress draped over one shoulder, she looked like an angel.

Tiller pushed up on his elbows and blinked at her. "Honey? What are you doing?"

She smiled sweetly. "Counting my blessings."

"At this hour?" He squinted. "Can't we count them in the morning?"

Mariah threw back the covers and crawled out of bed. "I'm glad you're awake." She held out her hand. "Get dressed and come with me."

Grinning, he allowed her to pull him to his feet. "Where are we going?" he asked, knowing it didn't matter. He'd follow her anywhere.

She held her finger to her lips. "You'll see."

He slid into his trousers while she slipped behind a screen, emerging in a buckskin dress he'd never seen before. Stunned, he stared at his wildly beautiful wife.

She caught his hand when he reached for his shirt. "You won't need it."

Ducking into the hallway, they tiptoed to the kitchen stairs. At the bottom, she skipped the last step and whispered for him to do the same.

They crept out the back door and across the yard to the barn. Catching their scent, Sheki nickered softly before they ever opened the door. Mariah ran to throw her arms around the paint, nuzzling his neck.

Tiller caught up and hugged her from behind. "Do you think you'll ever love me as much?"

She turned into his embrace. "Maybe. Someday." Laughing, she opened the stall and bridled the horse. Leading him next to the rail, she climbed on his back and motioned for Tiller to join her.

"Without a saddle?"

"You won't need it."

He chuckled. "What else won't I need tonight?" Swinging up behind her, he grimaced. "Hopefully I won't need a doctor."

She giggled. "Just tighten your knees and hold on to me."

They trotted into the moonlit yard and veered toward the Pearl. Sheki seemed to need no direction. They'd taken this ride before.

Down a sandy slope, they leveled out on a long stretch of the riverbank. Reaching behind her, Mariah tightened his arms snugly around her waist. "Are you ready?"

He pressed his cheek to hers. "For what?"

"Hold on," she said then leaned toward Sheki's ear. "Kil-ia!"

The pony bolted. Mariah clung to his mane and Tiller clung to her.

They soared past the shimmering water, the wind rushing in their ears. Emotion swelled in Tiller's chest, and prickly hairs stood up on his neck. His heart broke inside him like a hammer on a clay pot, spilling tears down his cheeks and beauty inside his soul.

Anchored tighter to a person than he'd ever been in his life, Tiller McRae had never felt so free.

FORTY-SEVEN

Every bruised muscle and strained sinew crying for relief, Joe urged the nag down the road that led to his lane and his little house at the end. He'd driven himself hard to cut time from his trip, stopping only when he had to and riding half asleep in the saddle.

He felt as old as the crescent moon overhead. So old that the idea of chasing a feisty young son didn't seem quite as appealing as it had at the start of his journey.

He couldn't help but wonder again why fate had played its trick on him and Myrtle. Though they neared the age for bouncing grandchildren on their knees, their firstborn would soon be nursing at her breast and teething on Joe's thumbs.

A sudden thought threatened to choke him. Suppose little George became the first of many? Would their quiet little cabin swarm with crawling babes? Groaning, he pushed the exhausting thought out of his mind.

As selfish as the desire might be, he longed to reach his wife's nimble, comforting hands so she could soothe him back together. Joe held no manly delusions. Myrtle's courage and strength far surpassed his. She would be glad to see him, but Joe needed her.

He turned down his lane, sighing with pleasure at the sight of lights burning in the windows. She wouldn't be expecting him, but it wouldn't take her long to prepare him something to eat. Myrtle could make an old boot taste like a Sunday roast.

The front door eased open, and she peered out, steadying the barrel of his shotgun.

His heart squeezed at the sight of fear on her face. Still a few yards out, he whistled.

Setting aside the gun, she burst out the door and sailed over the porch, wearing nothing but one of his nightshirts.

Laughing, he lowered his stiff, aching body to the ground.

Myrtle flew at him, all tangled hair and white cotton, the feel of her in his arms welcome and familiar despite his sore muscles.

Familiar except for one thing.

Joe held her away and ran his hand over the bump that stood between them.

Crying, clinging to his neck, she fought to press close again.

"Look at you," he cried, his strength renewed and silly fears forgotten. "You've done a fine job of growing our son."

Laughing through tears, she placed a gentle hand over his. "A son is it? You sound quite sure of yourself." She glanced behind him. "Where is Mariah?"

He sighed. "You'll have to manage without her. Mariah is where she belongs."

Myrtle cocked her brow but didn't speak.

Joe pulled his pack off the horse and slung it over his shoulder. "I'm tired and hungry. Feed me well and let me rest, and I'll tell you the legend of the buzzard that journeyed far from home to steal fire."

She nudged him with her shoulder. "You foolish man, I've heard that story many times."

He pulled her close to kiss her forehead. "But my tale has a happy ending. The buzzard makes it home with all his feathers—and learns the fire was there all along."

Smiling, Myrtle tucked her hand in his and led him toward the house. "I'm glad you're hungry. I made rabbit stew." She reached the porch first and grinned over her shoulder. "The fat old thing is a little tough from all your chasing him, but he still tastes good."

Joe stilled with one foot on the bottom step. "Woman, tell me you didn't."

With a gleeful laugh, she scurried inside.

Pausing, Joe patted the doorpost. The sun would rise to find him under the same roof with Myrtle and George. It felt good to be home.

Tiller strolled out of the Fayetteville haberdashery decked in finery from head to foot. He doffed his bowler hat at Mariah, and she covered her mouth and laughed.

There wasn't a speck of pomp or pretense in his decision to buy new clothes. It started with his desire to buy her something nice. Once he had, he didn't feel properly dressed to walk her down the street.

Neither did he intend to put on airs with their mode of transportation. It wasn't his fault the last conveyance available for hire was a garish, pretentious carriage. "Well, we need a rig," he'd murmured, drumming his fingers on his chin. "I can't have you straddling a horse in that getup."

Looking down at her dress of black taffeta and velvet, she nodded. "Yes, it would be difficult."

"Then we'll do it," he announced. "It might be fun. Lord knows I can afford it," he added with a wink.

Handing her aboard, he started to laugh. "It's a good thing the others decided to wait in the hotel. Can you imagine Ellie riding in this contraption?"

Mariah laughed. "Actually, no. I can't."

He angled his head. "If you don't mind, I'm going to ride past the old house before we go to the cemetery."

She patted his hand. "I think it's a fine idea."

Heads turned as the carriage rolled through the narrow alleys of the poor part of town. Gaunt, hungry faces stared up as they passed, striking a chill in Mariah's heart. Wishing they'd given the fancy clothes and high-flown rig more thought, she tightened her grip on Tiller's arm.

They pulled up to a broken-down shanty, a study in hopeless gloom. The sagging roof had caved in places, allowing the weather to rot the eaves. The outer walls—what was left of them—were a dirty, paint-chipped gray. Weeds had sprouted through and overgrown the walkway from the porch to the street.

Mariah couldn't imagine anyone living inside, and it saddened her to think Tiller once had.

Climbing down, they made their way toward the door. Tiller pulled to a sudden stop and caught her hand. "This is far enough. I don't think I want to go inside."

Concerned, she studied his pale, sickly face. "Of course."

His gaze roaming the dilapidated house, he sighed. "I could've done so much to help her."

"No, Tiller." She squeezed his fingers. "We both know how expensive repairs can be. She wouldn't have let you spend the money."

He bit his lip and nodded.

Glancing around, Mariah saw they'd drawn a crowd of curious people, closing in from all sides. Nervous, she drew closer to Tiller and nudged him with her elbow.

Awaking from his daze, he took off his hat and nodded. "Afternoon, folks."

An older man, short in stature, stepped up and held out his hand. "Reddick McRae. I'd know you anywhere."

Tiller beamed. "Mr. McLean. How are you, sir?"

The little man enveloped Tiller's hand in both of his. "Not as well as you, I see." His remark held no resentment. Instead, he smiled warmly. "I'm happy to see you've done well for yourself."

Mariah held her breath, waiting to see if Tiller would mention where his fortune had lain hidden for years.

He smiled graciously. "It was none of my doing, sir. I fell into a blessing is all."

Mr. McLean laughed. "Just like when you were a boy. Everything you touched turned to a blessing." He pointed. "I still have the finest roses in the neighborhood, thanks to you."

Tiller introduced Mariah as his new bride. Thrilled each time she heard the words, she accepted the round of well wishes.

Mr. McLean scooted closer and nudged Tiller. "My cousin is the one who first spotted you in Canton, son." His brow furrowed. "We tried to tell your ma. She just didn't believe us."

Tiller fingered his hat brim. "I'm real sorry about that, sir."

The man pounded on Tiller's back. "That's all right. I'm just happy to see that other fellow looked you up." He blinked uncertainly. "This is what happened, ain't it? You do know your ma is. . .well, no longer with us?"

"Yes, I heard. And I'm obliged to your cousin. You'll tell him for me, won't you?"

"I sure will, son."

Shading his eyes, Tiller stared down the street. "As a matter of fact, we're on our way to the cemetery now to pay our respects."

Awkward silence fell over the crowd. Backs straightened and feet shuffled. Smiling faces turned to frowns, and some looked away in disgust.

Excusing themselves, Tiller and Mariah climbed aboard the carriage and drove away.

Tiller sat so quietly in thought, Mariah began to worry. Leaning on his arm, she peered into his face. "Will a penny buy some of those weighty thoughts?"

He flashed a weak smile. "You were with me at the bank, Mrs. McRae. You have a sight more than a penny to barter with."

She stretched to kiss his cheek. "Are you all right?"

Tiller sighed. "Just sorting a few things out." He tipped his chin. "Those folks back there want me to be mad at Ma. I reckon paying her respect was the last thing they'd want me to do." His gaze softened. "Most likely, if I hadn't had me that talk with God, I'd feel the same."

She nodded. "We've both had a few lessons in mercy lately."

"That's true, but it's more than mercy I feel. My ma wasn't mean for meanness' sake. She was different when I was younger. Outright kind and gentle. She turned into a stranger after pa died."

The pain in his eyes took Mariah's breath.

"But I think I understand now that it wasn't my fault she treated me bad. After all I've heard, I realize Ma was sick. Sick in body, mind, and spirit." He smiled through his tears. "Knowing that truth, I intend to pay respect to my ma and tell her good-bye. I'm going to lay flowers on her grave then walk away from Fayetteville, free of bad memories once and for all."

Grinning, he wrapped his arm around Mariah's shoulder and sat taller in the seat, shifting the bowler to a jaunty angle. "Free of my past and ready for the future with the woman I love."

FORTY-EIGHT

Tiller's breath caught as they turned their horses toward the lone cabin in the distance. His anxious mind flooded with old memories of his first sight of the tiny house. Looking around that day at the crooked porch, swampy yard, and flooded rain barrel, he'd refused to believe they were at his uncle's house in Scuffletown.

"I'm too tired for teasing," he'd said to Hooper. "What is this place?"

Despite what the outside lacked in charm, once past the front door, that sad, frightened boy knew he'd come home at last. Within those unassuming walls lived good times, great stories, welcoming arms, and love that stretched the seams.

"Home sweet home," Hooper said beside him, speaking Tiller's thoughts aloud.

Frowning, Mariah pointed. "That's the house?"

Tiller smiled. He knew just how she felt. "Don't worry, it's cozy inside," he said, offering the same assurance Hooper had given him that day.

The jumble of thoughts in Tiller's mind was nothing compared to how his insides felt. Though he'd finally accepted that his mama's plight was not his fault, he couldn't say the same for his uncle's pain. He'd rehearsed a dozen times what he'd say to Uncle Silas.

Glancing at Nathan riding tense and tight-lipped beside Wyatt,

Tiller knew he must have been dreading his own reckoning.

Neither of them would be putting it off for long. The door burst open, and a dozen shouting people spilled onto the front porch.

Tiller's eager eyes searched for Uncle Silas. Grayer than Tiller remembered, moving a little slower, he tottered down the steps behind a whole passel of squealing youngsters with Aunt Odell at his side.

"Look at that," Hooper said, smiling from hither to yon. "My girls are here."

Ellie leaned in the saddle and stared. "Blast it, Hooper, I knew it. What has your wife gone and done to my boys?" She sped up and rode ahead, reining her mount in front of two sets of dapper boys standing quietly with folded hands.

Hooper laughed so hard he almost fell out of his saddle.

Grinning, Tiller pointed. "Ellie had twins?"

Wyatt groaned. "Two pair as rowdy as they come." He chuckled. "At least they were when we left."

The prettiest little things Tiller had ever seen scampered, dainty and giggly, toward Hooper's horse. He slid to the ground and swung them up, one at a time, for a kiss on the cheek. "Girls, come meet your cousin, Tiller."

Pausing to draw his smiling wife under his arm, he led his family to where Tiller and Mariah stood holding their reins.

"I'd like you to meet our girls." He placed his hand atop one chestnut head. "This here is Della, named after Ma, and the younger one"—he patted her curly head—"is Olivia. We call her Livvy after Dawsey's aunt."

Tiller bowed and kissed their hands. "I'm happy to meet you, ladies."

Blushing, they ducked behind their mother's skirt.

Beaming into his eyes, the woman reached for his hand. "I can't tell you how happy we are to see you again. I do hope you remember me."

He smiled. "Of course I do. . .Dawsey." Tiller knew Hooper's wife as Miss Wilkes, the young woman he'd worked for in Fayetteville, so it was hard to think of her as anything else.

Ellie caught Dawsey's shoulder from behind. "All right, Dawsey McRae. What have you done to them?"

Dawsey turned and gathered her into a hug. "Sweet Dilsey. I'm so glad you're home."

Ellie pushed away her hands. "There will be none of that until you've explained yourself." She pointed over her shoulder at the docile boys. "I want you to take away these charlatans and bring back my young'uns."

Wyatt squatted in front of his sons, smoothing their slicked-back hair and patting their rosy, scrubbed cheeks. "I don't know, Ellie. I could get used to them like this."

In the hubbub, Tiller learned the elder twins were Silas and Gerry, named for their grandfathers. The younger set were Duncan and Hooper, named for Ellie's brothers—but Hooper, the quiet one with serious green eyes, they called Tiller because of his uncanny knack with the soil.

Quiet throughout the how-dos and welcomes, Uncle Silas nudged through the crowd to stand in front of Tiller. As solemn as a deacon, he quietly took his hand.

The years had been hard on him. His shoulders stooped, and deep creases marred his weathered face, but the bright eyes were the same. Roguish eyes, twinkling with a thousand untold stories.

Tiller pulled Mariah forward. "Uncle Si"—he nodded—"Aunt Odie, I'd like you to meet my wife, Mariah."

His aunt, as pretty as ever despite her age, wrapped them both in a tearful hug. "We missed you, Tiller. I prayed every day for your safe return."

Uncle Silas released Tiller and reached for Mariah's arm. "Let's go inside by the fire, pretty lady."

Mariah smiled and let him lead her away.

On the porch, he stopped and waved his hand. "You children find something to do outside while the grown-ups have a little talk."

His grandchildren scattered for the woods.

Nathan hung back as everyone crowded for the door. Frowning, Wyatt tugged on his sleeve. "It's all right, Nate. Let's go inside."

He shook his head. "I don't think I'm welcome. The old man never glanced my way."

"It doesn't matter," Wyatt said. "You can allow him a little anger. You owe him that much."

Tiller grasped Nathan's shoulder. "I've made up my mind to offer an apology whether he accepts it or throws me out on my ear." He tightened his grip. "It's like Wyatt said. We owe him."

Wyatt pointed toward the house. "If you can't stand up to that little man in there, how will you face our parents?"

Doubt wavering on his face, Nathan glanced toward his horse.

Tiller shook his head. "Don't do it, Nate. If you run now, you'll be alone for the rest of your life."

"Nathan Carter!"

They swiveled toward the house. Uncle Silas meandered across the yard, dodging scattered kindling by the porch and mud holes near the rain barrel.

Unable to read the expression on his uncle's face, Tiller held his breath.

He glanced at Nathan. The poor man's hands shook, and he stared like a cornered animal. Backing up two steps, his body tensed to run.

Uncle Silas reached them, his smile a little shaky, but the hand he extended to Nathan was steady. "It's been awhile, young fella'. In all the ruckus, I didn't get to tell you how glad I am to see you."

Nathan pulled off his hat, wadding it in his trembling fingers. "Mr. McRae, it's good to see you, too."

"You weren't leaving, were you? I know you're in a hurry to see your folks, but I was hoping you'd stay for a cup of coffee at least. We can catch up on old times."

Nate's throat worked up and down. "I don't want to intrude, sir."

"Intrude? It'll be a sorry day when I don't enjoy the company of an old friend."

Tiller and Nathan had grown too tall for Uncle Silas to reach around them, so he rested a hand on each of their arms and led them to the house.

Crossing the threshold felt like stepping back in time. Glancing around, Tiller saw that nothing much had changed. Aunt Odell had spread the kitchen table with food, Uncle Si's rocker faced the crackling hearth, and the mats they used for extra beds were rolled up against the wall. He almost expected to see the one he'd slept on years ago spread for him in the corner.

"If anyone's hungry, there's plenty. Just grab a plate and fill it."

Aunt Odie didn't have to offer a second invitation. The hungry travelers bustled close to the table, laughing and rubbing shoulders.

Uncle Silas caught Tiller's arm and pulled him aside. "I know you're probably starved son, but I reckon we need us a talk first."

Tiller nodded. Best to get the apology over so he could stomach the food.

They watched each other with wary eyes. "I'm sorry," they blurted at the same time.

Tiller drew back with a puzzled frown. "What do you have to be sorry for?"

"I let you down, son. I wanted you to feel welcome here, then I threatened to send you back to your ma the first time you made a mistake." Tears spilled onto his cheeks, tearing at Tiller's heart.

"You don't owe me an apology, sir. I owe you one. I gave you nothing but trouble from the first day I came."

Hooper squeezed in between them. "I say you call it a draw and come to supper."

A squeal from outside sent Wyatt stumbling for the door. "Mercy, it sounds like somebody's getting skint out there."

Hooper and Dawsey shared a grin. "You're not used to the way girls express themselves, Wyatt," she said. "Livvy's just excited, that's all."

"About what, I wonder?" Hooper said, peering over Wyatt's shoulder.

The rest of the children set to squealing, too—Ellie's boys the loudest. She shot Dawsey a look of pure disgust.

Hooper spun with a grin. "I see what has them worked up. Their Uncle Duncan and his family are riding this way."

Wiping his eyes, Uncle Silas beamed at his wife. "The Lord has blessed this day, Odell McRae. All of our children will sleep under one roof tonight."

She clasped her hands. "It's been a long time since that happened."

As was their custom, the family rushed outside to greet the newcomers. Tiller took the chance to pull Mariah aside for a kiss. "What do you think of your new family, Mrs. McRae?"

Wrapping her arms around his neck, she rested her head on his shoulder. "I can see where you get your humor, goodness, and amazing gift for love." She angled her head. "Not to mention your irresistible charm."

He raised her chin with his finger. "You see all that in this rowdy bunch?"

She nodded. "They're wonderful, Tiller."

"I'm glad you think so because there's one more to meet. You'll like Duncan. He has a bigger appetite than me."

"Oh my." She regarded the table with a worried frown. "Will there be enough to feed you both?"

Laughing, Tiller tugged her toward the door. Clinging to each other's waists, they squeezed onto the porch like true McRaes to be part of the welcoming party.

FORTY-NINE

Mariah followed Tiller off the Trace and into the yard, her muscles tired and sore from riding the train. Rainy had met them at the station in Jackson and brought their mounts. Rounding the house, they found Otis, Miss Vee, and Dicey smiling from the porch. It reminded Mariah of huddling in the mists on a different porch with her Scuffletown family.

After hugs and kisses all around, Dicey and Rainy went back to work, and Mariah led the horses to the barn, thrilled with the familiar routine. It felt wonderful to be home.

Later, seated around the kitchen table with their loved ones, she and Tiller shared stories of their journey, including one of Silas's tales that had Otis bouncing and clapping his hands—until Tiller shot out of his chair, wiggling his finger. "I almost forgot, Otis. I have something for you."

Spinning, he hurried to the pack he'd tossed into a corner. Rummaging inside, he came up with a bundle wrapped in newspaper and tied with a string. Handing it to Otis, he straightened with a smile.

Otis blinked up at him. "What's this?"

"Go on, open it."

Otis seemed unsure whether to look at Tiller or the package in his lap. With trembling fingers, he yanked the end of the string. The paper fell away to reveal legal tender in large denominations, stacked on top of a fat leather book. Otis gasped and cut his eyes to Tiller. "This here's my money." He gently ran his thumb along the spine of the book. "And my new Bible."

Tears in his eyes, Tiller nodded. "I got one for myself, too." He glanced up at Mariah and Miss Vee. "One for each of us, in fact."

Otis shook his head. "It's too much currency, son. I never had this much stashed in my life." He peeled off more than half of the wads of cash and handed it up to Tiller. "Take this back."

Tiller wrapped his hands around Otis's and guided the money to his lap. "I won't be taking anything back, sir. Consider it interest on a loan."

Sniffing, Otis wiped his eyes on his sleeve. "It's a blessing you didn't get shanghaied on the trail, carrying this much loot around."

The irony of his words struck the group at once, and laughter rang out.

When the room grew quiet, Miss Vee reached for Mariah's hand. "I don't want to spoil your good mood, honey, but I suppose you have to know." She glanced at Otis. "There wasn't a single boarder the whole time you were gone."

Mariah smiled at Tiller. They'd spent time on the long trip home discussing the future of the inn. "I'm not surprised, Miss Vee."

She blew out a breath. "Well, I am. We always pick up in the summer."

Mariah smoothed a wrinkle in the tablecloth. "The Trace is fading into disuse. I expect there will be less and less traffic in the months ahead."

Miss Vee seemed near tears.

Her own eyes filling, Mariah smiled at them both. "Would it be so bad if Bell's Inn became just a house where people live and raise a family?"

Disbelief narrowed Miss Vee's eyes. "You mean close our doors?"

"We'll accept weary travelers who wander by," Tiller said, "but in the meantime we'll go on like we have."

Otis sat so quietly, Mariah nudged Tiller.

"Is something troubling you, sir?" Tiller asked.

Otis barely glanced up. "Nothing important."

Mariah leaned across the table. "Go on, tell us."

His mouth worked, but nothing came out."

Miss Vee wiped her eyes. "Otis was thinking to ask for a job and stay on here. But now, well. . ." She shrugged.

Tiller couldn't contain his glee. Jumping from his chair, he knelt beside Otis. "I think that's a fine idea, considering I planned to ask you to stay on and help me around the place."

Otis perked up. "You reckon there's enough to keep us both busy?"

Tiller patted his back. "I'll make sure of it." He gave Miss Vee a firm nod. "Both of you have a home here as long as you want."

As if she couldn't take it in, Miss Vee stared at Mariah. "So we'll all just go on living here?" She blinked. "Like a family?"

Tiller smiled. "We are a family, Miss Vee."

She pressed her fingers to her quavering mouth and nodded.

Mariah reached for her hand. "One day, I'd like for Tiller to build me a big house on this spot." She winked at him. "To make room for dozens of little McRaes. For now, I'm quite happy where we are."

Miss Vee pushed up from the table. "That reminds me. You two come see your surprise."

They filed up the kitchen stairs and followed her down the hall. At the door to Father's room, Mariah had to stop and remind herself that it was hers now. Hers and Tiller's.

Miss Vee swept inside then stood back to await their reaction.

Tiller looked stunned then roared with laughter.

Mariah gasped and spun in a circle, trying to see everything at once.

Miss Vee had worked a marvel. The space was a perfect blend of their personalities. Tiller's hat rack stood in the corner beside his washstand. Mariah's vanity with all her favorite trinkets on top had replaced her mother's. Miss Vee had repapered the walls, half with the pattern from Mariah's room, half with Tiller's. Even the bedspread was an expression of their union. She'd cut their quilts in two and sewn the pieces down the middle.

Mariah ran to hug her neck. "It's the most perfect surprise ever. Thank you so much."

Obviously pleased with herself, she beamed proudly. "I put a lot of love in it, honey. I hope you'll be able to feel it."

"We already do, Miss Vee," Tiller said, kissing her cheek.

Otis tugged on her sleeve. "Let's go, Viola, and let these young people rest and enjoy your gift."

"Hmm? Oh yes, of course." Blushing, she backed out the door behind Otis.

Melting into Tiller's arms, Mariah breathed deeply of the new smell in the air. No longer the stench of death, the scent was a pleasing blend of wallpaper paste and new rugs, her rose water and Tiller's hair pomade.

Mariah made a vow on the spot to forget the suffering she'd witnessed inside the room. Instead, she'd cherish her parents' memories and honor them by taking joy in her new life.

She would remember to be grateful for every breath she breathed, and to thank God every day for His mercy.

Johnnycake

Scald 1 pint of milk and put to 3 pints of Indian meal, and half pint of flour—bake before the fire. Or scald with milk two-thirds of the Indian meal, or wet two-thirds with boiling water, add salt, molasses and shortening, work up with cold water pretty stiff and bake as above.

Indian Slapjack (Skillet Bread)

One quart of milk, 1 pint of Indian meal, 4 eggs, 4 spoons of flour, little salt, beat together, baked on gridles [sic], or fry in a dry pan, or baked in a pan which has been rub'd [sic]with suet, lard, or butter.

Amelia Simmons, *American Cookery*
(Hartford, CT: Hudson and Goodwin, 1796)

Hasty Pudding (circa 1833)

Boil water, a quart, three pints, or two quarts, according to the size of your family; sift your meal, stir five or six spoonfuls of it thoroughly into a bowl of water; when the water in the kettle boils, pour into it the contents of the bowl; stir it well, and let it boil up thick; put in salt to suit your own taste, then stand over the kettle, and sprinkle in meal, handful after handful, stirring it very thoroughly all the time and letting it boil between whiles. When it is so thick that you stir it with great difficulty, it is about right. It takes about half an hour's cooking. Eat it with milk or molasses. Either Indian meal or rye meal may be used. If the system is in a restricted state, nothing can be better than rye hasty pudding and West India molasses. This diet would save many a one the horrors of dyspepsia.

Lydia M. Child, *American Frugal Housewife*,
facsimile 12th ed. (Boston: Applewood Books), 65.

CHOCTAW RECIPES:

PASHOFA

1 pound cracked corn, pearl hominy
2 quarts water, add more if needed
1 pound fresh lean pork, meaty backbone
Salt

Wash and clean corn. Bring water to boil and add corn. Cook slowly, stirring often. When corn is about half done, add the fresh pork. Cook until the meat and corn are tender and soft. The mixture should be thick and soupy. Cooking time is about four hours. Add no salt while cooking. Each individual salts to his/her own taste. (If meaty backbone is not available, use fresh chopped pork, small pieces. Pork chops are good to use.)

BANAHA

2 cups cornmeal
1 teaspoon salt
1 teaspoon soda
1½ cups hot water
Corn shucks, boiled 10 minutes

Mix dry ingredients. Add water until mixture is stiff enough to handle easily. Form small oblong balls the size of a tennis ball and wrap in corn shucks. Tie in middle with corn shuck string, or use oblong white rags (8x10 inches) cut from an old sheet. They are much better boiled in shucks. Drop covered balls into a deep pot of boiling water. Cover and cook 40 minutes. Serve.

Article from the Choctaw newspaper *Bishinik*, unknown date.

Marcia Gruver

Marcia is a full-time writer who hails from Southeast Texas. Inordinately enamored by the past, she delights in writing historical fiction. Marcia's deep south-central roots lend a Southern-comfortable style and touch of humor to her writing. Through her books, she hopes to leave behind a legacy of hope and faith to the coming generations.

When she's not plotting stories about God's grace, Marcia spends her time reading, playing video games, or taking long drives through the Texas hill country. She and her husband, Lee, have one daughter and four sons. Collectively, this motley crew has graced them with eleven grandchildren and one great-granddaughter—so far.

OTHER BOOKS BY MARCIA GRUVER

TEXAS FORTUNES SERIES:

Diamond Duo
Chasing Charity
Emmy's Equal

BACKWOODS BRIDES SERIES:

Raider's Heart